THE
DUELING
DUCHESS

Also by Minerva Spencer

Dangerous
Barbarous
Scandalous
Notorious
Outrageous
Infamous
The Boxing Baroness

And read more Minerva Spencer in

The Arrangement

THE
DUELING
DUCHESS

MINERVA SPENCER

KENSINGTON
PUBLISHING CORP.

www.kensingtonbooks.com

For Brantly

Acknowledgments

A *huge* thanks to Brantly and George, both of whom get me through each and every book. A special thanks to Elodie, who helped me write the few lines of "bad French" I have Guy speaking in the story.

I'm also grateful to my writer friends Vanessa Kelly, Jeffe Kennedy, Dianne Freeman, Anna Bradley, and Katie Lane. These ladies are my trusted and favorite coworkers, even though we work alone in our separate offices, scattered around the country. Without fellow authors to gossip and plot and laugh with, this job would be very lonely.

Thanks so much to Pam for being supportive and loving my work.

And last, but never least, thanks again to Alicia for giving me a chance.

Prologue

Paris, 1794

"Manon Cecile Tremblay Blanchet!" Michel Blanchet hissed.

Cecile always knew she was in trouble when her father used her entire name.

"I'm hurrying, Papa," she protested.

"You must hurry *faster!*" he whispered, his grip on Cecile's arm painful as he pulled her along.

Cecile knew better than to complain or argue. It had been months since either she or her father had gone out on the streets of Paris in broad daylight. Not since her father's patron—the Duc de La Fontaine—had left one night to meet a man about smuggling them all out of France but had never come back.

Her father had heard nothing about the duke's fate until yesterday, when he'd received a message from the aged aristocrat himself. It seemed the duke had been arrested and thrown into the infamous La Force Prison.

As much as Cecile loved the duke—he was like a grandfather to her—she wished that her father could have found some other way to see the old man.

And she wished that way didn't involve her going with him.

"He is dying," her father said when she'd asked why they needed to go to the terrifying prison. "He kept us alive all these years, so going to him when he asks to see us is the least we can do. We will be safe; the guards have been paid well to allow both us and the priest to visit. We will be under the protection of God."

Cecile was only fourteen, but even she knew that God had forsaken both the church and its priests—at least in France. Only a few weeks ago she'd read about the slaughter of unarmed priests and nuns by state-sanctioned killers.

But even the minions of the state were no longer safe in France; the beast was eating itself; only last month the loathed and feared Robespierre had himself gone to Madame Guillotine.

Cecile wasn't sure her father was telling the truth; it felt as if all she'd ever known was violence and death. Could there really be a country where it was safe to walk down the street without fearing arrest?

"Watch where you are going!" Her father's angry voice cut into her thoughts.

Cecile glanced up and saw that she had almost walked into three gendarmes while she'd been gathering wool.

"I'm sorry, Papa," she whispered, peering from beneath her lashes to see if her behavior had drawn unwanted attention. But the three men merely continued on their way, laughing raucously and paying no attention to the crowds of people who cringed away from them.

Up ahead La Force Prison loomed like a monster sprouted from the ground itself. If walking down a street in daylight was terrifying, then entering the most infamous prison in France—now that the Bastille was nothing but a tumble of stones—was even more horrific.

"Keep your eyes down, Daughter," her father murmured. "And remember that you cannot speak."

She nodded sharply and schooled her features into a slack expression, twitching her shoulders under the ugly lump her father had attached to her shoulder with sticking plaster. It had been their neighbor, Madame Dubois, who'd taught her father how to apply theatrical face paint and disguises, and the two of them had worked on Cecile until she didn't even recognize herself when she looked in the mirror.

They'd even changed her hair, rubbing so much charcoal dust into her almost black curls that the glossy locks had turned a dry and brittle gray brown.

She looked like an old, hunched-over woman, and when she allowed her jaw to hang open, the teeth that Madame Dubois had blackened made her look witless.

Cecile shuffled beside her father as he went through layer after layer of prison authorities, the dull clink of coins sounding with each transaction. New France might have scoured society of the exploitative presence of the aristocracy and church, but myriad levels of bureaucracy had sprung up like rampant weeds to take their place.

Finally, they made it through to the prison itself.

Just as Cecile was about to follow her father and their escort into one of the narrow, grim corridors that led to the cells, a guard grabbed her arm.

"The old lady stays here."

Cecile felt as if her heart had blocked her throat, allowing only a whimper to escape.

"I paid for her entry, too," her father insisted.

"Not me, you didn't."

Cecile didn't look up, but she could hear the smug leer in his voice.

Her father reached a shaking hand into the pocket of his ragged coat. He had to dig deep before he located a coin. "This is the last of what I have," he said as he handed it over.

The guard grunted, clearly displeased by the small denomination. "What about her?"

"She is simple. I give her no money."

The guard gave a grunt of disgust. "Well, come on—a quarter of an hour is all you have."

Her father grabbed her shoulder and Cecile shuffled beside him.

They walked past several rooms where dozens of prisoners were all shoved together. People called out to them, begging for food, asking them to bear messages, the voices quickly drowning each other out.

They tried to walk faster, to escape the din, but the man escorting them seemed deaf to the agony around him and moved at the pace of a snail.

Cecile had to grit her teeth to keep from screaming; by the time this oaf delivered them to the duke, their quarter of an hour would be over and they would have to turn back again!

Eons seemed to pass before the man stopped and dug around beneath the heavy gray wool coat all the gaolers wore, the clatter of many keys filling the dank silence. He fumbled with the lock for another eternity and then shoved opened the door, the shriek of metal on metal making both Cecile and her father jump.

"Ten minutes," the man growled. "And tell the priest he will have to leave then, as well."

They plunged into the near darkness of the cell, the only light a weak, smoky candle in the corner.

When the door slammed behind them, Cecile felt as if she'd just been sealed into a tomb.

"Michel?" The weak voice came from near the candle.

As her eyes adjusted, she saw that the priest was kneeling in front of the duke, their two figures making one large shape.

"I'm here, er—citizen."

Cecile cringed as her father almost slipped and used the duke's honorific. Although it felt as if they were alone, they'd learned the hard way that even bricks and mortar had ears.

"He doesn't have long," the priest said, pushing to his feet and turning to them.

Although the man wasn't foolish enough to wear the collar of a priest, he carried a plain rosary in one hand. The candlelight illuminated his pinched features, and he frowned when his gaze flickered over Cecile. "I'm not sure how I feel about this. The girl is so young—and there can be no consum—"

Her father cleared his throat, interrupting the man. It was rude and unlike him. What had the priest been about to say? What about her? Why was—

"You know the reasons we are doing this," her father whispered in a heated voice. "You agreed already. And now—after I've spent every sou I have, you are changing your mind? Do you realize—"

The priest raised his hands in a placating gesture. "I will not go back on my word. I just wanted to make sure she is aware of what will happen here today."

Cecile looked from one man to the other, perplexed. "Father? What—"

"Shh." He pulled her past the priest, toward where the duke was lying on a pallet covered by a filthy, ragged blanket. He was so thin and pale she hardly recognized him.

Her father bowed his head and sank clumsily to his knees beside his former patron, pulling Cecile down with him.

"Your Grace," he whispered, and then leaned forward and took the old man's frail hand, kissing the place where his seigneurial ring had sat for so long that there was a permanent indentation in the flesh. "I'm honored that you called upon me in your time of need."

The duke's heavy-lidded gaze was on Cecile, not her father. "Have you told Manon the truth, Michel?"

Cecile wanted to remind all three men that she was right *there*. She also wanted to remind the duke that she went by *Cecile* now, not her hateful first name. But her father would be mortified, so she remained silent.

Michel Tremblay opened his mouth, hesitated, and then turned to Cecile. "The priest is here to marry you to His Grace."

Cecile thought her jaw would come unhinged. She tried to form words, but nothing would come.

A low, raspy chuckle filled the dank chamber. "I cannot blame you for looking so horrified, Manon."

Shame flared in her; she had just insulted a dying man—a man who'd taken care of them like family over the past few years. "I'm sorry, Your Grace. I didn't—"

"Hush, child. I can hardly expect you to be joyous about marrying a corpse." His faded blue gaze flickered to the priest and back. "I'm afraid we have little time. Other than scattered, distant relatives, I am the last of my line, Manon. When I die, everything I have will go to those same jackals who've harried me for years. It is likely my will may be invalidated, but a spouse has rights that cannot be gainsaid, even by the godless rabble who've seized our great country by the throat. This—this *nightmare* will not last forever. And when it is over, you, Manon, will have all that remains to my name."

Her father squeezed Cecile's arm when she could only stare. She would be a duchess?

Perhaps there had been a time—when she was a little girl—when such a thing would have brought joy, but now? Now possessing a title was a death sentence.

"Speak, Cecile," her father whispered, anger pulsing in his voice.

"Of course, I will do it—I will be honored," she amended when her father squeezed her arm so hard, she winced.

The duke's proud face looked so grateful that she felt guilty for a moment. After all, he was doing this to leave *her* wealth.

Their lives were nothing but lies, hiding, and secrets. What did one more secret matter?

Two weeks later

The wind was blowing so hard that the tattered tricolor outside the shack was horizontal.

Cecile had to shout to be heard. "Surely he won't sail in this weather?"

"He will be here," her father yelled back, and then doubled over with another of the coughing fits that had become worse and worse over the past week.

"Papa! This isn't safe—let's go back to the village. We have enough—"

He made a familiar slicing gesture with one hand: *enough!*

Cecile sighed and pulled her ragged black shawl tighter around her. Her father had promised her this was the last time she'd need to wear this horrific disguise. She was tired of looking fifty when she was barely fourteen. She was tired of hiding day and night. She was tired of—

"There!" Her father pointed to where a tiny boat was struggling to get to shore.

Cecile stared. It looked like the flimsy paper boats she used to make when she was a child. "*Mon Dieu!* Surely we cannot go in *that?*"

Either her father didn't hear her or didn't care to reply. Instead, he strode toward the boat, his posture telling her that he was fighting another bout of coughing.

She hurried after him and wrapped an arm around his shoulders, which had narrowed and slumped with terrifying speed. Only a month ago he had been her sturdy, fierce Papa. It was true he'd always been a small man, but he'd been strong. Now he was a shell, becoming hollower with each day that passed.

But *so* stubborn. They should stay here—he should be in bed.

Cecile gritted her teeth when her father tried to go into the water to catch the little craft. "You stay," she shouted. "I'll help him."

He nodded, coughing.

Cecile pulled her skirts between her legs and tucked the hem into the bodice, baring her legs to mid-thigh. It would have been shocking under other conditions, but nobody cared just then.

The boat was even smaller when she got closer. Was her father insane? The two men inside were so big they took up most of the room. Although both would be needed to row because they could not use the tiny sail in this howling storm.

Cecile helped her father in before she climbed in after him, pushing the boat off the pebbled beach. Regardless of the fact she'd pulled up her skirts, she was soaked to the hips and the rest of her wasn't faring much better.

They crouched together in the bow of the boat while the two behemoths pulled the oars.

Her father pressed something into her hand and she looked down to find the small leather purse he habitually carried.

"Papa, what—"

He shoved something else into her hand; it was the oilskin packet that he always kept on his person. It contained his gun designs, a few family documents, and Cecile's wedding lines, along with a copy of the duke's will.

Rather than argue with him—impossible in this weather—Cecile shoved the purse into the pocket in her petticoat, which had three buttons to keep it closed. The packet was too big, so she tucked it into the battered leather satchel that held her change of clothing and a miniature of her mother.

Her father held a similar bag, but his contained the remaining tools of his trade; Michel Charles Tremblay had once been the personal gunmaker to the last king of France, Louis XVI.

Cecile took her father's bag and slung it over her other shoulder. He caught her hand and gave it a weak squeeze. They clung together, her father's body shaking worse and worse as the dark, starless night dragged on. The storm, rather than abating, became worse, the waves that pummeled the boat like something out in the ocean rather than the channel.

She knew the men had never planned to row the full twenty-one miles, no doubt hoping to go by sail when weather permitted. Soon, they were exhausted and took turns rowing while one rested.

As one dismal hour led to the next, she lost track of anything but her own misery—her frozen hands and sodden clothing, the wind howling incessantly.

"We're going back!"

The voice jolted her out of her personal hell, and she glanced up at the two men. She couldn't tell who'd yelled at her, but they both looked half-dead. One of them pointed to lightning off the portside of the boat. Bolt after bolt cleaved the sky, almost as if it were walking in their direction.

The men were frantically rowing as if they could race Mother Nature herself.

Cecile turned to her father. "Papa! We're going back!" she shouted at his bowed head.

But he didn't move.

"Papa?" She grabbed his shoulder and shook him.

His head flopped back and the weight carried him off the bench and onto his back. He stared up at her with wide, sightless eyes.

"Papa!"

Blinding light illuminated the sky, and every hair on her body stood on end. One of the men screamed and lurched to his feet, dropping his oar in the process. The man who'd been next to him was slumped forward, flames leaping from his body.

The boat tipped precariously as the other fisherman stumbled, his weight throwing the small skiff off balance.

Cecile clung to the gunwale as the world turned upside down, taking her with it. The water muffled her screams and one of her arms was caught in the bags she'd crisscrossed over her torso, trapping her beneath the boat.

She choked on a mouthful of water and tugged on her arm. The straps of one of the satchels had somehow bound her hand to an oarlock. Cecile yanked hard, screaming as something in her hand twisted and snapped.

Clutching her hand to her chest she kicked her feet, struggling to reach the surface. But when her head bumped wood, she realized she was trapped beneath the boat, where a pocket of air had formed.

Cecile reached overhead with her uninjured hand and discovered a rope that must be attached to the boat. She clutched the rope and treaded water. It was quiet—eerily so, the only sound water slapping against the wood and her own ragged breathing.

Papa is dead.

The sudden thought was like a knife to her chest. Cecile had not cried for years, not since the *sans culottes* had come and burned down the duke's castle. Although the duke had been in Paris at the time, that had not stopped the rabble from killing servants—people who'd been her friends and family all her life.

And now her father was gone.

Even if she survived this storm, she'd be alone.

We have a cousin in England, Cecile, her father had said more than once. *You can go to him if you are ever in need.*

But her cousin Curtis was just a name; he was a stranger.

She had no one.

The grim weight of her future was heavier than the soaked garments that tugged her down. It would be so easy to just let go—to sink into oblivion and join her father.

But her hand refused to release the rope. And when the air in her shelter became thinner and thinner, instead of letting go, she kicked herself out from beneath the boat and clung to the hull as the storm raged around her.

Hours later, after the driving rain had turned into a gentle patter and the shrieking wind was little more than a brisk breeze, Cecile was still holding on as dawn broke over the horizon, and England.

Part I

The Present

Chapter 1

Whitechapel, London
February 1816
Twenty-two years later

Cecile shot the playing card out of the handsome young man's hand, and he screamed and jumped.

She let out a stream of curse words, both English and French strung together.

"I'm sorry! I'm sorry!" Gerry Wheeler said, squirming beneath her wrath.

Gerry was twenty-three years old and—by far—the most beautiful man Cecile had ever seen. He was also the most cowardly.

Cecile slid her pistol into its custom-tooled holster, took a deep breath, and forced herself to speak slowly and kindly—neither of which were her forte.

"Gerry, I think it is time we part ways."

"Oh, please, please, please, Miss Tremblay! I'll get better—I swear I will."

"It has been two months, Gerry. You scream more now than you did your first day."

He caught his plush lower lip with perfect white teeth. "I don't mean to—I don't know what's wrong with me."

Cecile had to laugh at that. "Nothing is wrong with you, Gerry; most people—at least normal ones—do not care to be shot at."

"But I love working at the Fayre, Miss Tremblay. It's become a home to me."

He wasn't the only one—Farnham's Fantastical Female Fayre was like a home for Cecile, as well.

She sighed and patted him on his broad shoulder—having to reach up quite a way to do so. "I'm sure we have something here you can do. I shall talk with Beryl and Wilfred tomorrow and see what there is."

Beryl and Wilfred were Cecile's managers and they kept the Fayre, with all its different theatrical acts, running smoothly.

"Oh, *thank you*. Miss Tremblay, you won't be sorry, I promise."

She probably would be, but she would deal with that when it happened.

It was Sunday, the only night of the week there was no show at the theater, so there was not much activity backstage.

Cecile liked to practice her routine and work on her ledgers on Sundays because she enjoyed the feeling of having the entire building to herself.

Her building and her business.

Well, that wasn't quite accurate. Although she operated Farnham's Fantastical Female Fayre—the very first all-female circus in England, although now there were several imitators—she didn't actually *own* it outright.

Instead, she was part of a four-person syndicate that included three wealthy investors whom she'd convinced to purchase the Fayre from Marianne Simpson.

Marianne—who was also Cecile's closest friend—had inherited the Fayre from her uncle Barnabas, who'd died last year.

At first, Marianne had tried to just *give* Cecile the business.

"I can no longer operate it, Cecile, and it's not as if I need the money I'd get from selling it."

That was because Marianne had married the extremely wealthy Duke of Staunton.

As much as Cecile had appreciated Marianne's generous gesture, the theater on Newcastle Street and the large house attached to it were worth a great deal of money, and it did not sit right with her to accept such an extravagant gift.

As things stood, she would be paying her three partners until she was old and gray. But then what else did she have to do with her life?

Cecile strode uninterrupted through the quiet theater, heading to the tiny room she'd set up as her business office.

She had added a dressing table and screen to the room so she didn't have to share the already cramped dressing room that all the other female performers used.

Today, since she'd just been practicing, the only thing she had to remove was the holster that held two of her pistols.

If it had been an actual performance, she would have worn heavy face paint and her provocative costume—a gown that had been designed by Barnabas Farnham.

When she'd first started working at the Fayre four years ago, Cecile had loathed the revealing dress, but now that she operated the circus, she could not deny that the way she looked—exotic, sensual, and dangerous—was important when it came to attracting wealthy, privileged men to purchase the expensive tickets to her show.

The first thing she did was clean her pistols—a lesson she'd learned from her father.

While Cecile worked, she considered a subject that had been on her mind a great deal of late: her appearance and how critical it was to her income.

Although she was still beautiful at thirty-six—why deny an obvious truth?—she was well past her prime years. Who knew how much longer she would be able to draw men to watch her?

She needed to hire an apprentice; somebody reasonably handsome to take her place when she was no longer an attraction. Finding a woman or girl who could shoot was only part of her worries. What she needed was somebody with presence and a certain . . . verve.

Shooting was something she could train almost anyone to do, with enough practice.

Cecile had grown up around guns—first those her father produced, and later the ones she herself made—but it had never been her plan to earn her living as a markswoman in a circus.

Unfortunately, the cousin who'd vowed to help establish Cecile as a gunsmith had, instead, stolen her father's designs—designs that Cecile had painstakingly re-created from memory after losing his precious packet of papers in the storm that long-ago night—and then kicked her out of his home.

The guns her cousin Curtis Blanchard—the anglicized version of the Blanchet name—produced were substandard and it infuriated her that they bore the Blanchard name, even if few people connected Blanchard with its more famous French cousin *Blanchet*.

But there was little Cecile could do to stop him, although she took some enjoyment from the fact that his company had gone out of business five years ago.

Cecile frowned at her unproductive thoughts as she finished oiling the second pistol and placed it back in the lacquered box. Thinking about Curtis only made her angry and discontent. She had a different life now; while it wasn't the one that she'd planned for herself, it was still better than she'd hoped for.

She had a successful business and a job that she did well, though she didn't love it.

She even had a friend—something she'd not been able to claim before coming to work for the Fayre—and although Marianne no longer worked with or shared a house with Cecile, they were still as close as sisters.

Now that Marianne was gone from the Fayre, Cecile kept hoping that Josephine Brown—Cecile's mysterious and reserved blade expert, whom everyone called *Blade*—might also become a good friend. But even after the dangerous months they'd spent traveling together in France last year—which just happened to coincide with Napoleon Bonaparte's escape from Elba—Blade was as closed as an oyster when it came to who she was and where she came from.

Blade was one of the most self-sufficient and resilient people she'd ever met, but all Cecile really knew about her was that she worked as a mercenary of sorts, her skills so impressive that at least one European monarch had seen fit to hire her.

As much as she hated to admit it, she might never know Blade very well because it was virtually impossible to engage the woman in a conversation. Lord knows Cecile had plenty of secrets in her past, but she had never met a woman as reserved, mysterious, and private as Josephine Brown.

You are putting off your work, her conscience scolded as she continued to stare blankly at her desk.

Cecile sighed and turned to the ever-present stack of correspondence that was part of owning and operating a business. She worked her way methodically through the bills and letters from prospective theatrical acts.

Not until she'd almost reached the bottom of the pile did she find a copy of yesterday's London *Examiner,* a thrice weekly newspaper.

Cecile had canceled her own subscription to the paper months ago. Indeed, she'd stopped reading newspapers entirely at the beginning of the New Year. One of her employees must have left this for her, thinking to do her a favor.

She glared at it, a familiar craving swirling in her belly.

Once upon a time the London *Examiner* had been her favorite paper for the shameful reason that it had the very best society section of all the newspapers that circulated the country.

For years and years—especially when she had lived in near exile in far-flung Massachusetts—gossip columns had been her guilty pleasure. They were a way to escape a mundane life and read about the wealthy, beautiful, and powerful men and women of the *ton.*

But the pleasure she'd taken in reading about the antics of the rich and glamorous had palled when she'd become acquainted with several of those glittering creatures herself last year during her weeks in France.

Even now, almost a year later and with Marianne married to

one of the aristocrats they had journeyed with, Cecile could hardly believe all that excitement—dodging the armies of Europe, evading ragged militias, and foiling the opportunistic criminals who prospered during times of war—had been real.

And it was especially difficult to believe that she'd been the lover of Gaius Darlington, the man the scandal sheets called the Darling of the *Ton*.

The very same man that Cecile had read about and fantasized about—along with at least half the female population of England—for years.

As affairs went, it had begun perfectly.

They had both agreed from the start that they'd only look to each other for carnal pleasure.

There would be no confidences, no expectations, and no attachments.

Most importantly, they'd agreed that everything would end the moment they returned to England.

It had been easy, if not painless, to accept those limitations.

After all, Cecile was first and foremost a realist. And the reality of the situation was that Cecile was a circus employee, while Guy was a peer of the realm who had responsibilities to both his family and his dukedom. He would never be free to marry Cecile.

That, too, had been perfect because the last thing Cecile wanted was a man who would try to control and direct her actions or treat her like his possession—she'd already had her cousin Curtis show her just how well that sort of arrangement ended for a woman.

Right up to boarding the packet back to Dover, Guy had abided by their agreement.

Then—at the last minute—he had shown his true colors.

Cecile realized her jaw was clenched tight and forced herself to relax.

But even a year later, just thinking of their last morning together was enough to make her blood boil. Like powerful men all over the world, Guy had decided that he wanted to have his piece of pie—and then keep the rest of the pie, too. He'd offered her a carte blanche, wanting to set her up in an establishment somewhere convenient for him and keep her at his beck and call. In short, he'd wanted to make her into his own personal whore.

Meanwhile, Guy would go off and marry a young, nubile, respectable heiress who could rescue his family from penury and fill his nursery with babies.

Cecile was neither young nor respectable. She was a circus sharpshooter rapidly hurtling toward her fortieth year.

As for nubile?

Well, to be honest, she wasn't exactly sure what that word meant, but she suspected it was something sexual. Although she'd spoken English almost exclusively since she was fourteen, she still thought in French whenever the English language—or English people— frustrated her.

Speaking of frustration . . . Why are you thinking of him *again? Throw that newspaper away* immediately *and get back to work!* the tyrant in her head ordered.

She growled and was about to obey when she paused.

Cecile had stopped reading the scandal sheets for months, not wanting to discover something painful about Guy. It was bad enough that the *ton* was atwitter about him finally seeking a wife and settling down.

But now, quite suddenly, she was angry at herself for giving up such a pleasure because of *him*.

"You are a coward who has allowed him to change you," she accused.

Hearing the words out loud made her brave.

Without closing her ledger or lowering her quill, she opened the newspaper with a flick of her wrist, leafing through the sections until she reached the one she wanted.

Less than ten seconds later she was finding it difficult to breathe.

The words seemed to dance and caper in front of her, mocking her.

It had finally happened—what she'd feared and dreaded, the reason she'd stopped reading the damnable papers: the Darling of the *Ton* was betrothed.

Cecile heard a snap and looked down to see she'd broken her favorite quill. *"Merde!"*

That's what came of thinking about Gaius Darlington; precious things got broken.

Why are you surprised? You knew this was going to happen. Why are you behaving like a schoolroom chit with her first infatuation?

Cecile knew all that was true, and she tried to push him from her thoughts—to shove away the pain as well—but she couldn't stop thinking of him or seeing him.

Strangely, the image in her mind's eye wasn't the way he'd looked that last day on the packet from France back to England—desperate, hurt, and angry, as if *she* had been the one who'd betrayed *him*.

No, what Cecile saw, as clearly as the most vivid oil painting, was Guy as he'd looked more than a year ago, the day she met him . . .

Part II

The Past

Chapter 2

London
Late January, 1815
Approximately one year earlier . . .

It was Sunday, Cecile's favorite day of the week. Not only could she have the dressing room to herself and rehearse her routine in peace and quiet—well, except for the sound of her pistols firing—she could also relax afterward and enjoy her guilty pleasure without nosey employees or the Fayre's owner—Barnabas Farnham, who was prone to nagging—bothering her.

After pouring herself a hot cup of black tea and replacing the pot on the tiny stove in the corner of the room, she shoved the mountain of garments, costumes, and other detritus off the settee and onto the floor, making a comfortable space for herself.

She sat, put her feet up on a rickety Windsor chair, and then opened the first of the newspapers she had collected during the week.

It wasn't accurate to say they were complete newspapers, rather, they were select sections : the society sections. Or gossip columns, as those who despised such entertainment often referred to them.

Every week she saved the columns to read and enjoy on her Sunday morning.

She'd begun reading the gossip columns years ago when she'd

first moved to Boston. She'd been so homesick that she had spent a sizeable portion of her measly quarterly allowance purchasing London newspapers.

It didn't matter how dated the newspapers were, the delicious parts—those which dealt with opulent ballrooms, lavish women's gowns, and dashing, daring aristocrats—never grew stale.

As time passed, she became a connoisseur, learning that the various papers offered different tidbits. She'd begun to ask people—her neighbors, coworkers at the millinery shop where she had worked for years, and even her lovers—to save their newspapers for her.

None of them knew that she only wanted a few precious pages.

A secret vice was only pleasurable if it was secret, after all.

Now that she was back in London and earning far more money than she had before, she could indulge her vice without having to beg for castoffs.

But she saved the papers up and read them only one day every week.

She sighed with contentment and opened the first newspaper, *The World Examiner.* She kept them stacked in order of least to most favorite, keeping the best for last, as it were.

What made one paper better than another? Well, some of them specialized in following certain members of the *ton.*

While Cecile adored reading about all the social luminaries who comprised the *haut ton*, she did have her favorites.

The World Examiner was of little interest—only a story about *a L____ L____ G____ who'd fallen into the champagne fountain*—which were all the rage this year and which Cecile would love to see—*at the D____ of M____'s betrothal ball for her daughter.*

Although the articles were written using this clever sort of code, the players' identities were crystal clear to the readers who avidly followed the stories week after week.

L. L. was actually Lady Louisa Garber, a scandalous marquess's daughter in her third Season. Lady Louisa was frequently observed losing part of her apparel or falling off things or into things.

The D of M was the Duchess of Merriton. Everyone knew that her daughter, Lady Ophelia, had just become betrothed to the Earl of Singleton's heir.

That was all stale, uninteresting news.

Cecile had to read through three more papers until she got to a juicy story—one that required a second cup of tea—in the London *Observer*.

This was an *exclusive*—as the newspaper men called them—and was about one of the wickedest and most outrageous men in England, Gaius Darlington, the Marquess of Carlisle, *the Darling of the Ton.*

Cecile gobbled up the story as if it were a sticky mass of Turkish delight.

"It will be no surprise to readers to learn that the M___ of C____ has been up to his tricks again! This time with none other than the lovely and elusive wife of the D____ of L_____, who has, up until now, been as heavily fortified against invaders as Edinburgh Castle. Not only did C_____ breech those defenses, but he was captured in the middle of his . . . assault by none other than the D_____ of L_____ himself!"

Cecile lowered the newspaper, her jaw sagging at what she'd just read and then reread.

The Darling had been caught in flagrante delicto with the breathtakingly lovely Duchess of Leicester? Cecile knew the duchess was lovely because she'd seen more than one illustration of the brand-new peeress in various print shop windows. Not only was she surpassingly beautiful, but she was also twenty-five years younger than her reputedly doting husband.

Oh, the Darling was *so* wicked and shameless!

Was there nothing the outrageous Lord Carlisle would not do?

Not that cuckolding other men was anything new for the Darling. No, hardly a month passed in which he wasn't caught escaping from some woman's boudoir—on one infamous occasion he was seen scaling down a three-story trellis—or engaging in some other scandalous imbroglio that usually involved beautiful women and a less than proper complement of clothing.

But for a husband to actually catch the marquess in the act? No, that was something entirely new.

And deliciously, despicably debauched.

There was no denying that a scandal of this magnitude was likely to be immortalized in Mr. Humphrey's print shop window.

Although there were dozens of print shops in the city that posted satirical cartoons in their windows for the enjoyment of passing pedestrians, Mr. Humphrey's *always* had the latest and the most risqué. The poor man had been hauled off to jail on more than one occasion for the lewd content of some of his illustrations.

Cecile smiled and shuffled the papers back into a neat stack. If this story was already in the paper, there was a good chance the illustration might be in Humphrey's window this very afternoon.

She would read the rest of her papers later. Right now, she would have to change into her new navy walking costume and make her way—

The door to the dressing room swung open, and Marianne—who was scowling rather ferociously—entered the room with two men on her heels.

When Marianne saw Cecile, her scowl turned to surprise. "Oh, I didn't know anyone was in here. We can go—"

Cecile stood. "No, no, I was just leaving." Her gaze flickered over the two men, both tall and dressed like laborers, standing just behind Marianne, and then back to Marianne, whose pale cheeks were flushed, her hazel eyes flashing.

"Is something wrong?" Cecile asked.

"No. Nothing wrong," Marianne said, her cheeks getting even darker.

Did her friend look . . . *guilty*?

Cecile glanced from Marianne back to the men.

There was something familiar about one of the men, whom she saw—upon closer examination—was actually quite startlingly handsome.

Now where had she seen him before? He wasn't dressed like one of the punters who normally came to see the shows, but neither did his worn clothing look quite . . . right.

She shrugged off the thought and turned to look at his companion.

Interesting. He was also attractive.

Exceptionally attractive, actually.

Cecile turned back to the first man again.

He frowned at her.

She blinked and his image seemed to shift slightly.

Cecile's jaw dropped. No wonder he looked familiar! She *had* seen him before, but he'd looked utterly different. The man was none other than the Duke of Staunton—whom society columnists called Lord Flawless and His Grace of Flawless, among other things.

She recognized him because she had seen him in the audience several times over the past few weeks, both at her performances and Marianne's boxing matches.

The Duke of Flawless was known as something of a social reformer, so his presence at the Fayre had made Barnabas nervous. He'd worried Staunton was looking for moral violations that would give the authorities reason to close down the circus.

Cecile thought Barnabas's worries were all bosh. It was her opinion that the duke came to stare at Marianne.

And here he was actually *with* Marianne and looking far, far different.

His distinctive pale blond hair was now a flat brown and he was wearing spectacles, although they did nothing to disguise his striking pale green eyes.

He'd been in expensive evening blacks before, and now he was garbed in the humble attire of a working man.

Not that he really *looked* like a working man when one examined him closely.

Aside from his reform work, Cecile didn't know much about the Duke of Staunton because his behavior was so flawless that he made poor fodder for the society sections.

Indeed, it was ironic that Staunton—a man who was never mentioned in gossip columns—was bosom beaus with a man who was
rarely *not* in one.

The very same man that Cecile had just been reading about
in fact.

Cecile turned slowly to the second man, who was looking right
back at her and smiling.

She knew she was gaping like an unlettered hayseed, but her
brain refused to believe her eyes.

No.

It can't be.

It is impossible.

Cecile knew she looked like a fool with her mouth hanging
open, but she seemed to have lost any power to shut it. Besides, it
was the only way she could draw enough air into her lungs, because
it was as if his very presence sucked all the oxygen from the room.

Good God! It is he!

Yes, it was. The god standing before her was none other than the
Darling of the *Ton*.

He was gorgeous.

And perfect.

Cecile would have known him even if he'd worn a wig and
ballgown. The only reason his paltry disguise had fooled her for
so much as five seconds was because of the sheer improbability of
the Darling himself walking into the Fayre's cluttered dressing
room.

She'd seen dozens and dozens of illustrations of the Darling but
had never seen him in the flesh.

And oh, what flesh.

To say he was six feet of masculine perfection was to criminally
understate the case.

He was perhaps an inch taller than the duke but slightly leaner
than his friend, and everything about him shrieked patrician ele-
gance.

His thick hair was a dark, glossy mop of loose curls. His eyes were the warm golden brown one saw in stained-glass windows in churches.

But there was nothing religious in the look shining out of his exquisite orbs.

Indeed, the Darling was taking Cecile's measure every bit as intimately as she took his, those bedroom eyes lingering on the bodice of her gown with a speculative look that made her heart clatter wildly in her chest.

She'd actually dreamed about him looking at her that way—the sort of dreams one couldn't admit having even to one's best friend. The sorts of dreams that made one's thighs clench just recalling them.

Cecile knew from the stories in the newspapers that he was thirty-two—a few years younger than she—and the faint lines fanning out from the corners of his eyes only made him more gorgeous, as did the grooves in his lean cheeks, which appeared to have been formed by smiling.

Naturally the thrice-blasted man had dimples in both cheeks.

Lord, but he was beautiful and perfect.

He might actually be too perfect. Indeed, he was that rare sort of man who rendered her breathless and giggly—two things she never was—and her body responded to him in a way that was distinctly distracting, heat pooling low in her belly and making her aware of parts of her body that she didn't normally think about.

Cecile wrenched her gaze from the marquess's smirking face and turned back to her friend. Although she felt as if she'd been standing there goggling for a lifetime, it couldn't have been more than a few seconds.

Marianne wore a pleading look and the message in her eyes was clear: Please don't ask any questions.

Cecile raised her eyebrows. Really? She really expected Cecile to say *nothing*?

Marianne mouthed the word *please*.

Cecile inhaled until it felt as if her chest would explode and then jerked a nod while giving Marianne a look that told her how much her friend would now owe her for going along with this charade.

And so instead of grabbing Marianne and shaking some answers from her, she forced a smile and asked in a voice that sounded shockingly normal, "Ah, two new employees?"

Marianne's shoulders sagged slightly and she gestured to the duke. "Yes, this is John Sinclair." She paused, and then added, "He, er, goes by the nickname *Sin*."

Sin? Cecile had to bite her lip to keep from laughing. What delicious irony that one of the most virtuous men in England was calling himself Sin.

"Miss Tremblay," the duke said, inclining his head.

Cecile nodded at him and turned to the marquess, who was wearing a smile that was surely one of God's masterpieces. And the devilish lights dancing in his melting brown eyes said that he knew it, too.

"And this is Guy Darling," Marianne said.

Cecile snorted. Guy Darling? Was that really the best they could come up with?

The marquess bowed. "*Enchanté*, Mademoiselle Tremblay."

She winced at his atrocious French accent.

Well, so much for his perfection. Thank God the man was flawed in some way.

Knowing that he wasn't perfect made her feel a bit less like a yokel and more like herself.

"These must be the new carpenters Barnabas was talking about hiring?" Cecile asked, flashing Marianne a mocking look.

"Er, no. Mr. Sinclair will take Jack's place on our upcoming tour," Marianne said.

Cecile had no words for that announcement; surely she must be dreaming.

"Mr. Sinclair is taking Jack Nelson's place as your trainer when we go on our tour of the Continent," Cecile repeated carefully, not wanting to speak too loudly and wake herself up from this fascinating dream just yet.

"Yes, that is correct," Marianne said.

Cecile nodded as if there was nothing at all out of the ordinary about a duke joining a circus and training a female boxer.

Cecile turned to the other man—the man whose face was too often in her fantasies. "And Mr. . . . Darling?"

"He will drive our caravan, care for the horses, and do other odd jobs."

Cecile looked from man to man, expecting one of them to chuckle and confess that it was all a jest. A strange one, granted, but a jest, nonetheless. After all, aristocratic men often engaged in foolish wagers to alleviate the boredom of their privileged lives.

But nobody laughed.

Instead, Marianne turned to the Duke of Staunton, who scowled back at her.

For the first time since entering the room, Marianne smiled— and not a pleasant one, either.

"You will be delighted to hear that both of them will be, er, volunteering in your and Blade's routines."

Cecile's eyebrows shot up.

She would get to shoot at the Darling?

No. Impossible. It couldn't be true.

And yet judging by the murderous look the Duke of Staunton was giving Marianne, it must be.

How utterly glorious!

Cecile smiled so wide, it hurt her face. "That is fortuitous. I was going to tell Barnabas that I needed to find a new *volunteer*."

Marianne smirked. "Oh dear, is Donald still having trouble?"

"Yes, he needs to find some other job. One of these days he'll jump *before* I shoot and it will be a problem." Cecile smiled at the duke, who looked like a human thundercloud. "I would like to start practicing with you both immediately."

Staunton cut Marianne a look of barely suppressed fury and bit out, "If you want me to *volunteer* to be shot at, then you'll need to ask Miss Simpson if there is any room in my busy schedule."

The marquess lifted an elegant hand, just like a well-behaved schoolboy, and said, "I am available immediately, Miss Tremblay." He still wore that same charming, devastating, wits-obliterating grin.

Cecile had never met a man so eager to be shot at.

"And there is a third man," Marianne added.

Cecile could hardly wait to see whom her enterprising friend would bring in next. The Prince Regent? And what would his job be? Shoveling manure and cleaning the privy?

Indeed, Marianne was proving to be a better thaumaturge than Francine Gordon—the Fayre's official magician—pulling aristocrats, rather than rabbits, out of her hat.

"I'll schedule all three men with you and Blade starting this coming week," Marianne said, seemingly uncaring of the duke's glower. "Do you have any preferences?"

"I don't care which of them comes on what days," Cecile said, directing her words at the marquess while surreptitiously pinching herself. Hard.

No, she definitely wasn't sleeping.

She met Carlisle's amused gaze and gave him a freezing look. "Just make sure you are here at ten o'clock on the dot on your assigned day."

Rather than look frozen, the marquess—or she supposed she should become accustomed to calling him *Guy*—looked delighted. "With pleasure, ma'am."

Cecile ignored him—or at least tried to because it was the only way she could keep sane—but it was like trying to ignore something awe-inspiring, like a volcanic eruption or a visitant sent by God.

The duke cleared his throat and gave Marianne a pointed look. "Don't forget that other matter we discussed, Miss Simpson."

Marianne's forehead furrowed, but quickly cleared. "Oh yes. That." She turned to Cecile. "Neither of them will be in the actual performances until we begin the tour. The third one, Smithy he is called, will be available if you have need of him."

It was obvious to Cecile why neither of these two men could set foot on stage.

Although . . . with Staunton's distinctive ash-blond hair dyed almost black and wearing spectacles, the duke *might* go unnoticed by the aristocratic members of their audience.

But it would be impossible to disguise the Darling.

"I'll tell my uncle that you'll be using Basil now that Donald is no longer needed," Marianne said.

Basil was the stagehand who filled in for all the women's acts whenever necessary. He was so phlegmatic that he wouldn't have jumped or squeaked if ten women shot pistols at him. The only problem with Basil was that his imperturbable nature didn't lend itself to the comedic parts of her routine.

The Darling, Cecile decided with a smirk as she allowed her eyes to wander up and down his magnificent body and then linger on his bedroom eyes and full, smiling lips, would add new zest to her rather stale routine.

Not to mention the rest of her life.

"Good God, she's a beauty," Guy said, striding down the slush-filled, crowded street beside Sin.

"She is quite . . . appealing," Sin murmured, sounding almost grudging.

"Appealing?" Guy repeated. "She's bloody gorgeous, man! I saw her once before—but only from the audience—and thought her merely lovely. But up close she is a stunner." He frowned. "One would never guess that she is a woman in her thirties."

"What are you talking about?" Sin asked. "She is twenty."

Guy turned to his friend. "I was talking about Miss Tremblay."

Sin's eyebrows arched in surprise and a faint red stain darkened his already cold-flushed skin. "Oh."

"Who were *you* talking about?" Guy asked, not that it took a genius to guess.

Sin shrugged.

Hmm. That was interesting.

"If you find her so entrancing perhaps *you* can do all the *volunteering* for her," Sin said, his tone more than a bit peevish.

"Have you seen her shoot? I am not nervous."

Sin gave him a look of disbelief.

"What?" Guy demanded. "The woman is the most skilled marksman—er, markswoman—" He paused and thought a moment. "Actually, she's the most talented shot I've ever seen, full stop. Do you know any man who can shoot like that? No, you don't," Guy added because it looked as if Sin was going to run through all their bloody acquaintances. He could be stubborn that way. "She is damned amazing."

"Guy—" Sin broke off and clamped his jaws shut.

"What?" Guy asked.

"Nothing."

"No, go ahead and say whatever it was you were thinking."

"You do understand that we will be traveling across France with these two women—and the rest of Farnham's employees—for as long as eight weeks, don't you?"

"Yes, Sin," Guy said with exaggerated patience. "I know that we are engaging in this entire façade for serious reasons, not for a lark. Or don't you recall that I was there when we discussed all this? Do you think I'm not committed to our mission? That I don't want to help you rescue Benjamin?"

"I'm not suggesting that at all, Guy. I know you are as eager as I am to help ransom my brother and get him back to England safe and sound. However, I think you, er, underestimate the effect you're likely to have on Farnham's employees—the *female* ones, for certain—and I think you don't fully comprehend that if you dally with any of these women, we shall have to contend with the repercussions for weeks, perhaps even months."

"Repercussions," Guy repeated.

"Yes, you know what I'm talking about."

"These are all adult women, Sin, not schoolgirls."

"All your lovers are adults, Guy, but that hasn't stopped some of them from"—he flung up his hands—"Devil take it, man! You know what I am trying to say."

"Yes, Sin. I know what you mean."

Unfortunately, there was some truth to the other man's concern.

As hard as Guy worked to avoid it, sometimes the women he sported with surprised him. And not always in a good way. Sometimes, they fancied themselves in love with Guy, which was not only inconvenient, but ludicrous. While he might be loveable—his mother and sisters thought so, at least—he never spent more than a few hours with any of his paramours and he always, always, always avoided emotional intimacy.

Sin cleared his throat. "As attractive as you find Miss Tremblay, perhaps you might want to keep matters between you on a business footing? At least until we've rescued Benjamin and brought him home. Once we've completed our business in France and are back in London—well, then you may do what you like with her."

Guy laid a hand on Sin's shoulder, stopping him, because this topic was too important to discuss while striding down the street.

Once they were face-to-face, he said, "Sin, I know these next months are critical—I know that we are going to Europe for Benjamin, *not* so I can enjoy a long-delayed tour of the Continent."

Sin smiled at that last part, as Guy had hoped.

"I won't do anything to jeopardize our mission or Ben's life," he promised.

Sin huffed out a breath. "I know that, Guy, and I don't mean to hector you. It is only that you have a tendency to, er, leave a trail of brokenhearted women in your wake."

Guy wanted to argue that there weren't *that* many women who pined for him, but the man had a point. Guy was lighthearted when it came to his amours and always hoped that his lovers—he never dallied with maidens, only with women of experience—would see their time with him for what it was: temporary sensual pleasure. But often women began angling for marriage—even if they hadn't wanted to marry him at the beginning. Even women who *were* married sometimes developed terrifying obsessions.

In his experience, the only way to avoid crushing a lover's expectations was to leave long before she could develop any. And *that*—unfairly enough—was why he'd earned a reputation as a heartless libertine, all because he'd tried to avoid heartbreak.

A drop of moisture hit him on the nose and shook him from his thoughts. He saw that Sin was still watching him, his brow furrowed in concern.

Guy smiled and clapped him on the shoulder. "You have not offended me, old man. Truth be told, the last thing I need to be doing right now is indulging in erotic adventures. Not after the conversation I had with my grandfather last week."

Sin winced. "Bad news?"

"Yes. His Grace told me that matters on the ducal estate have taken an abrupt turn for the worse."

"Guy—are you sure you want to go to France right now? I won't blame you if—"

"Don't be daft. Of course, I'm going. Besides, my grandfather said that the end of the year would be soon enough to announce a betrothal. The marriage itself I might put off until the middle of next year."

He didn't need to explain the subtext of that statement to his friend—they both knew what he meant. Once a man was betrothed to an heiress, his creditors suddenly developed both patience and a willingness to extend yet more credit.

And the Fairhurst dukedom was critically in need of both patience and credit.

Sin made a sympathetic noise. "Anyone in mind?" he asked as the rain began to fall more heavily and they resumed walking.

Guy laughed, but there was no amusement in it. "No. But my mother and grandfather have been conspiring on a list."

He had planned to tackle their list once after Easter, but now that he would be away from England until at least the end of April, he'd have a few months' reprieve.

Guy knew this journey across France was not without danger, nor was it undertaken frivolously. Indeed, it was deadly serious, but that didn't mean he didn't look forward to spending time with his two best mates.

Sin, he already saw far too rarely.

And Elliot Wingate—the other man who would accompany

them—he saw even less, even though Guy shared lodgings with Elliot. But his friend worked for the government—an agency so secretive it didn't have a bloody name—and had been run off his feet these past few years.

Hopefully that would change now that the war was over and the Corsican Fiend was caged on Elba.

When they reached the small, inconspicuous town house they were using while they prepared for their mission, Sin turned to him. "Want to come inside and get dry?"

"No, I need to be on my way."

"Shall I see you and Elliot for dinner at the club tonight?"

"I can't speak for Elliot as I've not seen him for two days, but I'll be there."

"Excellent."

"Oh, and Sin," Guy said as his friend turned to go.

"Yes?"

"Taking advantage of women who labor for their crust is not something I do. I shan't tamper with Miss Tremblay or anyone else who works at Farnham's. You have my word on that."

Guy didn't know it then, but that promise would come back to haunt him in the not-too-distant future.

Chapter 3

Guy yelped yet again as Cecile Tremblay's bullet ripped the playing card from his fingers. But at least he didn't jump this time.

"I'm sorry," he said reflexively.

"Don't be," she said, commencing to reload the six pistols she'd just used on him. "The audience will love hearing a big, strong man squeal like a little girl."

Rather than be insulted—no doubt her intention—he was tickled by her acerbic response.

Guy hated to admit it, but women generally giggled a lot around him, even older, more sophisticated women. Why that happened, he didn't know. Yes, he was aware that he was considered attractive, but so were Sin and Elliot, and yet neither of them appeared to reduce seemingly intelligent women to giggling.

Cecile Tremblay, rather than giggle, had no qualms about giving him the rough part of her tongue—often—and cutting him the most delightfully derisive glares.

What a woman!

She was the first female he'd met in God knows how long who appeared to be immune to his charm.

Guy loved a challenge.

"I'm flattered," Guy said, sauntering over to her reloading table.

"Flattered about what?" she asked, not bothering to look up, her attention on her work.

"That you think me big and strong."

Her head whipped up and Guy was elated to see a flush spread from her disappointingly high-necked gown upward, tinting her cheeks a fetching pink.

So, not immune to him after all.

They locked gazes and he unabashedly took advantage of the opportunity to study every detail of her lovely face: sinfully full red lips, brown eyes that were so dark they appeared black, a saucy retroussé nose, firm chin, and wickedly sharp cheekbones. And best of all, that haughty look she always had for him.

Her hand fumbled with the ramrod as she pushed the patch and lead ball down the barrel. "Why are you staring at me?"

"Because you're beautiful."

Her eyes widened, her lips parted, and Guy heard the softest exhalation of air. All that took about half a second to transpire before her mask of cool derision was back in place.

"If you are trying to charm me, do not waste your time," she said in her clipped, charmingly accented English.

"Oh, darling. Nothing that has anything to do with you could ever be a waste of my time."

Her forehead furrowed and he could see she was thinking about what he'd said and trying to look for hidden meaning.

When she found none, she scowled and jerked her chin toward the other end of the stage.

"Go and stand in front of the straw bales again. I am not done shooting at you."

A week later . . .

Cecile smirked as chunks of pulverized apple went flying, secretly impressed when Guy—she thought of him that way easily now—did not so much as twitch.

If he'd been any other man—meaning one that she'd not had the most disturbingly erotic dreams about every night for a week—she would have complimented him. But the last thing a man with his titanic self-confidence needed was more petting and praising from anyone—especially a woman.

So instead, she turned and said without looking over her shoulder, "You may rest for a few moments while I reload."

This was the sixth time he'd come to her for rehearsal, and she had done well keeping their conversation to a minimum.

She had also cut her rehearsals shorter and shorter, something that had attracted a comment or two from Barnabas, who'd had the temerity to ask if she wasn't taking an unnecessary risk by skipping so much practice.

Not only that, but he'd also had the utter gall to force Cecile to get permission for the new part of her routine—the part with the blindfold.

"I am serious, Cecile," Barnabas had barked when she had ignored him. "Shooting at my employees is one thing. Doing it blindfolded is another matter entirely, and I cannot force them to participate."

Cecile hadn't bothered to explain to Barnabas—yet again—why this was no more dangerous than anything else she did.

Barnabas Farnham was not a man to listen to other people—especially not women, something that was more than a little ironic given that he made a fine living off his all-female circus.

Still, plenty of men made their living off women's labors, so his obstinacy and arrogance weren't exactly unusual.

Just look at her wretched, thieving cousin Curtis, for example.

Don't even start thinking about him, she chided herself.

It was good advice. If she wanted to think about unhappy things, she could think about asking the gorgeous Marquess of Carlisle for his *permission* to participate in the blindfolded portion of her routine. She hated the thought of asking him for anything—especially a favor.

"Why the heavy sigh?"

She jumped at the sound of his voice—which was so close she felt his hot breath on the crown of her head—and spun around.

"What are you doing creeping up on me so quietly?"

He gestured to his heavy boots. "Sweetheart, I couldn't creep wearing these if I tried. You just didn't hear me because you were off in your own world."

"Don't call me that," she snapped, turning back to her guns.

He walked around to her side and leaned against the table. "What has you in such a foul mood today?"

She ignored his question. "We will practice with the blindfold next."

When he didn't answer immediately, she risked a look at him.

His eyebrows had lowered and a deep notch had formed between them. "Blindfold?"

Cecile shoved the ramrod down the barrel of the pistol with unnecessary force. "Yes, it is a new part of my act that I wish to rehearse today. Do not worry, you will not need to learn anything challenging or difficult."

He snorted at that.

"You will stand there and hold things for me to shoot, just like always. It is nothing new—except that I will wear a blindfold."

He chuckled. "That's actually quite new, darling."

"Don't call me that," she said, the automatic words coming out with more heat than she liked.

Why it bothered her, she didn't know—he said the same things to every female he spoke to. Maybe that was why she found it so irksome; maybe she didn't care to be lumped in with the herd.

You're infatuated with him.

She gritted her teeth at the internal taunting, put down the gun, and turned to him. "If you do not wish to do it, you—"

"No, no, I didn't say that. I just want a few more details first."

Cecile crossed her arms and glared up at him, even though what he was asking was reasonable. Even Basil, the most placid of men, had balked when she had first mentioned the blindfold.

"I will be able to see through it. A little," she added reluctantly.

He just stared.

Cecile sighed. "It is a special weave. I had it made for the blind-fold." She reached into the sleeve of her gown and pulled out the thin silk scarf. "Put it over your eyes and you will see what I mean."

He took the scarf, looked at it skeptically, and then held it up to his eyes, his hands fumbling with the ends, as if he'd never tied a knot in his life. Well, she supposed he had a valet to do everything from shaving him to buttoning his dance slippers.

"Here! Let me do it," she snapped, snatching the scarf from his elegant but clumsy fingers.

Not until her hands were against his silky soft hair and her body close to his did she question the wisdom of her actions.

God! He smelled so good. A blend of cologne or shaving soap, or perhaps shampoo along with a faint saltiness that was sweat on clean skin.

Cecile wanted to lick the strong column of his throat.

You are weak and pathetic, Cecile.

Yes, she was. She most certainly was.

Her fingers fumbled and she struggled with the simple knot.

"Should I bend down?" he asked.

"No, it's fine," she muttered, finally getting the damned knot tied. She put her hands on his shoulders, her eyelids fluttering as she realized the breadth of them, and then turned him around.

"Open your eyes," she said gruffly, reaching up to shift the blind-fold until the special weft—which ran right down the center, al-though you couldn't see it—was in his line of vision. Then she strode to stand where he would be. "There. You can see me, can't you?"

His lush lips pulled down at the corners. "Er . . . see? Not ex-actly. It's more of a lighter smudge of darkness—an outline."

Cecile rolled her eyes, even though he wouldn't be able to see that. "Yes, that is all I need."

He hesitated a long moment before asking, "And what shall I be holding? Please tell me it will be bigger than an apple or playing card?"

"It will be a hat."

"I'll be holding a hat?"

She snorted. "You will be wearing it on your head, you fool."

His jaw went slack. "You want to shoot at my head while blind-folded?"

"Yes, that is what I said."

He laughed.

Cecile strode toward him. "What is so funny?"

He reached up and pulled off the strip of black silk, the action mussing his hair in a way that made her think of rumpled sheets, tangled, naked limbs, and sweaty skin.

You're standing far too close to him, Cecile.

She took a furtive step back, and then another, until her breathing got easier.

The look in his honey-brown eyes was warm, but rueful. "You feel confident you can hit the target?"

"I wouldn't suggest such a thing if I was not *confident*."

He pursed his lips and twitched his mouth from side to side, his expression contemplative. "Very well," he finally said. "I will allow you to do it today—one time."

She scowled. "I need more than one shot to practice."

"We shall start with one," he said. He was still smiling, but, for once, there was a surprisingly firm expression in his melting brown eyes.

Well, it was more than she'd hoped for.

Cecile turned to her guns and resumed loading them.

"And I will only do it in exchange for a favor," he added.

She whipped around. "A favor? What do you mean?"

"I believe your command of English is excellent. Don't you know the word?" he teased.

She cut him an irritated look and he chuckled.

"Does your *favor* require any part of my body touching any part of yours?"

The way his eyes widened told her that she had shocked him.

He gave a low, wicked laugh. "Er, no. But I wish I had thought of that."

"What favor?" she repeated, annoyed by how her belly fluttered at his laughter.

"I want you to talk to me."

"We are talking."

"No, I mean talk *to* me. Not *at* me. As much as I adore being insulted by you—called a fool, an oaf, and so forth—I am interested in a more meaningful transaction."

"Meaningful? What are you babbling about? Just come out and say what you mean."

"Specifically, I want you to answer some questions."

She narrowed her eyes. "What sort of questions?"

"Why do you look so suspicious?" he asked, a half smirk curving his sinful lips. "Just what have you heard about me that has put you so much on edge?"

"The women have been talking," she admitted, and then wished she'd kept her mouth shut.

"Well, they can't have been saying too much because I have been on my best behavior."

That was what she'd heard, too—that he'd been *disappointingly* gentlemanly and courteous and oblivious to the blatant lures that several of Farnham's employees had dangled to bring him into their beds.

Cecile had seen them flirting with him, calling on him to help carry things they normally would have carried themselves, summoning him for pointless errands, and lots and lots of *giggling* when the women of Farnham's were *not*, normally, gigglers.

Everyone had noticed, even Barnabas, the least observant man in England.

The Fayre's owner had complained about it at dinner, chiding Marianne for engaging the man.

"The other two aren't so much of a distraction," Barnabas had groused, "but that Darling fellow is a bloody menace to women."

Cecile had been hugely amused that Barnabas didn't appear to have guessed the true identities of his three newest employees, which meant Cecile wasn't the only one Marianne wasn't confiding in.

As diverting as Barnabas's ignorance was, Cecile wholeheart-edly agreed with the normally clueless man when it came to the Marquess of Carlisle.

Neither the Duke of Staunton, who was a very handsome, im-posing man in his way, nor the third man—a dark-haired, slimly built, and rather mysterious-looking gentleman named *Smithy*, whose real identity continued to elude her—caused as much havoc among the female employees as Lord Carlisle.

When Cecile had looked at Marianne to see what her reaction was to her uncle's comment on the Darling, the younger woman had just stared at her food.

Marianne had become quieter and quieter lately and had been avoiding Cecile. They used to go for tea every Tuesday afternoon, just the two of them. But they'd not done anything together since the day of Cecile's birthday almost a month ago. Which was, coin-cidentally, *right before* Marianne had engaged the three aristocrats.

Yes, her friend had changed a great deal since the men had en-tered their lives.

Cecile's life had changed, too.

Even though she'd done everything possible to avoid the mar-quess, she'd not been able to banish him from her thoughts *or* her dreams.

Even now, as she stood looking right at him, she couldn't believe he was the Darling—who'd been mentioned in *The Daily Exam-iner* as riding in Hyde Park yesterday afternoon with some Prussian princess—and also the same man who was going to allow her to shoot at him while blindfolded.

"Well?" Guy asked, interrupting her thoughts. "Do we have a bargain?"

She blinked, momentarily confused. "What bargain?"

"I'll allow you to shoot at me wearing a blindfold and you an-swer some questions."

Questions? What in the world could he want to ask her?

"Is aught amiss?" he asked, his warm eyes glinting with amuse-ment, almost as if he could look into her head and knew about the dream that had woken her up that morning, her body taut and sheened with sweat, her hand between her thighs—

Cecile recoiled from the intoxicating image and hastily banished it from her mind.

"Fine," she snapped rudely. "But I shoot first and *then* you get your question."

"That's hardly fair—if you shoot me in the head, I'll never get my questions. How about this—I ask one question before and one question after."

"Why do you get two questions and I only get one shot?"

"I'd say two questions are a fair price for getting shot at by a blindfolded marksman. Er, marksperson," he corrected with the faint smirk that made her heart pound.

Ugh. Everything about the wretched man affected her body in one way or another.

She heaved an exasperated sigh, hoping to conceal her pleasure that the Darling wanted to ask *her*—plain Manon Cecile Tremblay Blanchet—a question.

"Well," she said gruffly. "Get on with your question."

"Why do you do this sort of work?"

She snorted, both relieved and disappointed by his rather pedestrian question, one she'd been asked times beyond counting.

"I do it because it is easy and pays well."

"Yes, but—"

"Sorry," she said, not feeling in the least bit sorry, "but that was your one question."

He frowned, for once looking distinctly unamused. In fact, it was the first time she'd seen any hint of aristocratic hauteur in his demeanor. He looked positively . . . lordly. And thwarted.

Good.

"That's—" He broke off and bit his sinfully lush lower lip with white, even teeth.

It was Cecile's turn to laugh. "Were you about to say that it was not *fair*, Mr. Darling?"

Judging by the faint flush over cheekbones that would make an artist weep, that was exactly what he'd been about to say.

"Go stand in front of the bale and put on the hat," she ordered, pointing to the hat the costumer had created, an extra high-crowned top hat that was made of plain black fabric instead of expensive beaver pelt. It had a little surprise inside and she had to suppress a smirk at the thought of what his lordship would make of it.

She quickly tied on the blindfold, careful to position it in such a way that it didn't need tweaking—because an adjustment of that sort would surely alert the audience members that there was trickery afoot, no matter how raucous and intoxicated the men usually were.

Cecile took her mark and lifted the pistol, able to see Guy distinctly, if not clearly, which was all she needed before she pulled the trigger.

"Very amusing," Guy said, shaking the tiny bits of confetti from his hair, eyebrows, and even his eyelashes.

She chuckled, pulling off her blindfold and grinning at him— the first time she'd looked at him with anything other than suspicion or dislike.

Guy's cock responded instantly to her joyous smile, considerably uplifted by what, in its rather limited experience, was a sign of a woman's desire to become better acquainted.

Guy's brain, however, knew better.

She strode to where the hat had fallen when she'd shot it and picked it up, examining it briefly before holding it up for Guy to see.

He couldn't help feeling a bit impressed—and relieved—that the hole was smack in the middle of the hat.

"Dead center," she said, her smug, confident tone doing nothing to diminish his cock's opinion of the situation.

"Yes, well done," he said. "Now, I get another question."

Her full lips pulled down into a frown, and she tossed the hat onto the table where she kept her guns. "I am finished with you for the day. You may go."

"Not without my answer, I won't."

She made a sound that was remarkably like a *growl*.

"Get on with it," she ordered, her hands deftly cleaning and oiling the pistols.

"Tell me how you came to be in England."

"By boat."

Guy couldn't help laughing. "I don't think so, sweetheart. I shall require a bit more detail than that."

Her lips curved into a slight, self-satisfied smirk. "You asked a question and I gave you an answer."

"I want a genuine answer."

"That is the only answer you'll be getting."

"If you want me and Sin—or Smithy," he added, recalling that Elliot had also rehearsed with her, although only once thus far, "to allow you to shoot at us wearing a blindfold, you'd better be more cooperative."

Her head whipped up. "Why are you asking me these personal questions?"

He recoiled at the anger sparking in her dark eyes. "Because I'm curious about you."

"I am not an item for curiosity," she retorted, her accent heavier than he'd ever heard it. "If you wish to be curious, go find somebody else. I am not a toy for you to play with. Do you understand me?" She didn't wait for him to answer before going on, the words coming faster, her accent thicker. "In fact, I do not need you—or your friends—to perform my act, so you needn't bother coming to my rehearsals any longer." She turned back to her guns, her hands shaking as she resumed cleaning them.

Her fury momentarily robbed him of words.

"I'm sorry," he said after a long, fraught silence. "I didn't mean to make you angry." He lifted a hand to her shoulder and then—thinking better of it—dropped it to his side. "I asked those questions because you are unlike any woman I've ever met and I find you interesting. I didn't mean any disrespect."

She ignored his apology.

Guy looked at her tense shoulders and taut expression and felt a pang—more than a pang, actually—that he was responsible for making her look so strained and unhappy.

"I shan't ask you any more personal questions," he said quietly. "And I'll be here again on Tuesday, as usual, and you may shoot at me as often as you like, with or without a blindfold."

A nerve ticced in her tight jaw and she gave an abrupt nod.

Guy was at the door that led to the back of the stage when her voice stopped him.

"It was never my plan to work in a circus. My father was Michel Blanchet, the royal gunmaker to Louis the sixteenth, as was his father before him, and his before him—back to my great-great-grandfather, who made guns for the Sun King." She turned to face him. "I was my father's only child and he trained me the way he'd been trained, teaching me his craft."

She shrugged and glanced down at her hand, absently wiping away some of the gun oil with a cloth. "It is doubtful the next king would have engaged a female gunsmith, but my father had nobody else. He taught me everything he knew. I am an expert gunsmith," she said, her chin lifting, her voice as proud as her posture.

Guy doubted there was an English peer alive who didn't yearn to possess a Blanchet firearm—either a pistol or a fowling piece—which were works of art as well as exceptional guns.

"Why aren't you producing guns?" he asked in amazement. "I would think—"

"I have no right to do so. My cousin Curtis Blanchard owns the rights to manufacture Blanchet firearms in Britain," she said, the words clipped and abrupt, and clearly not a subject she was interested in discussing with him.

Guy left the matter alone, instead saying, "My grandfather has a Blanchet fowling piece. It is his favorite gun."

She smiled faintly at that. "How did he acquire it?"

"It was a gift from the king—Louis the fifteenth—who gave it to him when my grandfather was on his tour of the Continent, something young aristocratic males did back before the War."

"That would have been made by my grandfather."

"There are initials on the gun—M.C.B."

"Every Blanchet male has borne the same name—Michel Charles—so there is no way to distinguish the guns by name, but there should have been a number?"

"Yes—I actually remember it because he has allowed me to use the gun on occasion. It's a 1747-19."

"That is the year it was made and would have been the nineteenth gun my grandfather finished that year."

Regardless of the promise he'd just given, Guy was on the cusp of asking why her name didn't begin with an M if her father had trained her to be his successor.

But her next words stopped him. "What I just told you is something I've not told anyone else—not even Marianne."

It was clear to see the two women were close, even though separated by at least a decade. Guy felt both startled and honored. "I won't tell anyone."

She turned back to her table. "I will see you next week, Mr. Darling."

This time she didn't stop him when he left.

Chapter 4

"*Clean the dressing room from top to bottom and make sure all the costumes that are jumbled on the settee are returned to the wardrobe mistress. Give the stove a fresh blacking and fix the leg of the wobbly stool,*" Guy muttered in a high voice that—admittedly—sounded nothing at all like Marianne Simpson's. "*And don't forget to wash the mirrors and clean out the drawers in both dressing tables. And while you're about all that, make sure you take time to turn water into wine.*"

Somebody snickered behind him, making him jump.

Guy turned to find Elliot. "Good Lord! I thought it was her behind me."

"I doubt *she* would have laughed," Elliot pointed out.

"Could you at least make some noise if you're going to sneak up on me?" Guy demanded pettishly.

Before his friend and roommate could answer he accused, "I thought our all-powerful employer-slash-overlady gave you dispensation to leave today, so why are you still here?"

"Look who got out of bed on the wrong side this morning."

"That's because it's six thirty in the bloody morning."

Guy, Elliot, and Sin had just left the crack-of-dawn twice-weekly meeting that Marianne insisted upon. It was not an event that put Guy in a good mood.

"Who gets up this early?" Guy demanded.

"Pretty much most of the population of London."

"Yes, well, they don't usually stay up until five, do they?" Guy yawned so hugely that it threatened to dislocate his jaw.

"I told you not to go to the Hershaw ball last night," Elliot said in a prim way that made Guy want to punch him.

Guy prudently refrained from taking a swing at the other man for two reasons. First, Elliot was one of his best friends.

And second, Guy might get one punch in, but it would likely be the only one.

Although Elliot was four inches shorter and a least a stone lighter than Guy, he was a damned fine pugilist who'd won the championship every year at Eton.

"For your information, my dear *Smithy*," Guy pointed out, "I had to go to Hershaw's bleeding ball last night because my mother and Lady Hershaw were bosom beaus when they were girls."

"Ah." Elliot, the son of an earl, immediately comprehended the meaning beneath Guy's words: When one's mother's closest girl-hood friend invited you to a ball, you went and you danced. A lot. There were no two ways about it.

Guy saw no reason to admit that he'd only stayed an hour at the insipid event. Nor did he feel any reason to mention that he'd gone to Mrs. Adele Murphy's house upon departing the ball.

He had been delighted to receive a message from his erstwhile lover just as he'd been leaving home for the Hershaw party. It had seemed serendipitous and he decided he'd pay her a visit before he left London.

He'd not seen Addy in ages. She was the widow of a wealthy window maker—try saying that three times quickly—and perhaps a decade older than Guy.

Addy was not the sort of woman to be invited to a *haut ton* function like the Hershaw ball, nor did she aspire to attend such events, which was one of several reasons Guy enjoyed their time together.

Another reason was her free and easy attitude toward sexual pleasure.

Guy wasn't Addy's only lover and she didn't expect him to remain constant, either. An arrangement which suited him down to the ground.

"Well, I'd best be off." Elliot pulled worn workmanlike gloves from the pocket of his equally worn coat.

"How is it that you're escaping demeaning physical labor today?" Guy demanded, unashamed of the fact that he sounded like a sniveling twelve-year-old boy chafing beneath his chores.

"I'm not. I have to take the laundry over."

They both groaned.

The washer woman—Mrs. Bascom—hated all men with a vengeance and let them know it often with loud verbal harangues whenever they had the misfortune to enter her domain.

"After I leave the delightful Mrs. Bascom, I have to pay a visit to the man who is supposed to be providing us with caravans but is apparently a month and a half behind schedule."

Guy didn't envy his friend *that* particular errand, either. He'd met the obstreperous Prussian wheelwright, who was given to throwing tools and chunks of wood when he became irritable.

Perhaps cleaning the dressing room wasn't so bad, after all?

Guy knocked on said room's door. "Anyone in there?" he called out. Receiving no answer, he opened the door and winced at the mess inside.

"Suddenly enduring one of Mrs. Bascom's harangues doesn't seem so bad," he muttered, turning to Elliot, who'd followed him. "I don't suppose you want to change jobs with me?" he asked without much hope.

Elliot just laughed as he pushed past him into the room and took his battered overcoat off a coatrack that was so overloaded with garments, Guy wasn't sure how it managed to stay upright.

"Are you going to Alastair's dinner party tonight?" Elliot asked as he pulled his flat cap from the coat's pocket and clapped it onto his closely shorn head.

Guy grimaced. "Lord. Is that tonight?"

"If you miss it, he will kill you," Elliot said.

Guy glanced around the shambles that was the dressing room. "I'll be lucky to finish in here before midnight. And she also wants me to clean the orchestra pit."

Elliot whistled softly. "She must dislike you almost as much as she does poor Sin."

It was true that Marianne seemed to save a special antipathy for the duke. Guy supposed that was because it was Sin who'd forced her to hire the three of them—and to go along with his plans to rescue his brother.

"In any case," Elliot went on, "you'd better be there tonight because Ally has an important announcement to make." He wrapped a mottled scarf around his throat.

With his three-day beard growth and too-colorful, tatty clothing, Elliot looked more like a disreputable cockfight fixer than the fourth son of an earl. Guy doubted even his own mother would recognize her son.

"As if we can't all guess what Ally's announcement is," Guy groused.

Lord Alastair Scorton was a friend of theirs from school—not as close a mate as Elliot or Sin, but still a good friend. His betrothal to Lady Lily Melson had been planned by their parents since the two were still in their cradles.

Lily was a good friend of one of Guy's sisters and had spent many a school holiday at Darlington Park. In fact, Guy had rolled around in a hayloft with Lily one memorable Easter break.

She had been unsentimental and pragmatic even at eighteen, not expecting anything more from Guy than a bit of sensual pleasure, her life with Alastair already mapped out before her. What they'd done was no secret from Ally, either; he'd been engaged in a rather torrid affair with an opera dancer at the time.

There was no doubt in Guy's mind that Lily and Alastair would marry, reproduce, and then go back to their separate entertainments just as soon as Lily provided her new husband with his heir and spare.

Guy had always envied Ally and Lily's easy friendship and had often wished that his parents had stitched him into a betrothal when he was still in the cradle.

As it was, he'd need to expend energy to find a suitable heiress. If the woman was not one of his acquaintances, which was highly likely as the downiest debutantes came from the emerging merchant class, then he'd run the risk of marrying somebody whose notion of marriage and fidelity was not so elastic as Lily's was.

That would lead to disharmony in the household—which was what had happened in his own parents' marriage, when his bourgeois mother's expectations of marital fidelity had run headlong into his aristocratic father's equally firm expectation that his only responsibility to his new wife was to elevate her socially and give her offspring.

It had not made for a happy marriage.

"Guy?"

"Hmm?" He looked up from his uneasy thoughts.

"You'll be there tonight, right?" Elliot said, pausing on his way out the door.

"I'll be there."

"Good." Elliot glanced around the pigsty. "Enjoy your cleaning."

"Go to the devil," Guy muttered as Elliot's laughter echoed through the quiet theater.

Farnham's performers worked late, so most of them would not begin wandering in until midday, which was just as well because Guy could do without a herd of females mucking up the dressing room before he could even get it sorted.

He stared around at the room, his mind reeling at where to start.

Look at you: Lord Carlisle, heir to a dukedom, wondering how to commence cleaning.

Guy scowled. *I'm doing this to help Sin—to help save a man's life, in fact.*

What a glorious way to spend your last year of freedom, cleaning up after circus folk. Surely there must have been some better way to have engineered this rescue effort?

Guy banished the disloyal thought from his head—even though

it had certainly popped into his mind more than a few times in the weeks since he'd begun insinuating himself into Barnabas Farnham's Fayre—and gazed around the shambles of a room.

His attention settled on the settee—or, more accurately—the huge pile of garments that covered every inch of the settee.

Had none of these women ever heard of hangers or clothes hooks?

Marianne had said she wanted proof there was a settee in the room.

And that she wanted all the clothing and costumes returned to their proper places.

Then she wanted the room scrubbed until it *gleamed*.

Yes, she'd used the word *gleamed*, her eyes doing a bit of gleaming as well as she'd smirked at Guy.

At that moment, Guy had wanted to strangle Sin for getting him into this bloody predicament, but then Marianne had given the duke the job of cleaning up the night-soil closet and Guy had decided to shut his mouth and be grateful.

But looking around the cluttered room, he felt utterly overwhelmed. Where did a person even start with such a mess? He'd never cleaned a thing in his life. Well, except his fowling piece, on occasion—but usually even *that* had been done by somebody else. Some servant.

God, how he missed all his servants.

His gaze wandered to the dressing tables and he blanched. He knew nothing about all the tubes and tubs of face paint. And nothing about all the shoes and boots lying in various stages of disrepair since this was where the cobbler came to do the monthly mending. And then there were hats and masks and feathered headdresses and—

His harried gaze landed on a tidy stack of newspapers in the corner of the room and Guy blinked.

The stack sat on a tiny table tucked into an odd-shaped enclave that must have been a broom cupboard before somebody removed the door.

The newspapers were especially conspicuous because they were the only neat thing in the entire room.

It only took two steps to get to the table; he tilted his head so he could read the top page.

And then he squinted and leaned closer.

"No," he murmured.

Just what were the chances?

He flicked through the first newspaper—not an entire paper, just a few pages—his gaze running over a few columns about the interminable peace negotiations in Vienna. Next there was the Court section, and finally there was the part people generally called the gossip or society column.

Guy's name jumped out of the small print and he gave a startled laugh.

"What in the world . . . ?"

Forgetting about cleaning for a moment, he shoved a pile of garments off a nearby stool and sat, pulling the stack of papers into his lap.

He'd made it halfway through the pile, his jaw sagging lower with each new gossip section—when the door opened and he looked up to find the knife-thrower, Josephine Brown—or Blade as she was commonly called—with her pet bird, Angus, on her shoulder.

"Hallo," she said, fixing him with her opalescent gaze.

Her raven stared at Guy as intently as his mistress, but with black, shiny eyes rather than pale gray ones.

"Oh, hello," Guy said, feeling slightly guilty for sitting and going through newspapers when he was supposed to be working. Even though he was *not* getting paid for it.

He shook aside the pointless thought as she closed the door behind her.

"Do you need me to leave?" he asked hopefully.

"No."

"Oh."

Instead of doing . . . anything, she just stood in the middle of the cluttered room and stared, not at Guy—thankfully—but at the newspapers he was holding.

A slow smile curled her lips, which were such a pale pink they were hardly any darker than her skin.

She was, Guy realized, almost entirely colorless—like a drawing composed of whites, grays, and blacks with only the merest whisper of pale, pale pink.

"Reading about yourself?" she asked.

Guy blinked. *"What?"*

She chuckled and the sound was strangely rusty. "Don't worry, I won't tell anyone about you, His Grace of Staunton, or the Honorable Elliot Wingate."

"You know who we really are?" Guy said stupidly.

"I doubt I'm the only one to have figured it out."

Well. That was interesting.

Guy could understand her recognizing him and Sin because they'd both been immortalized in satirical cartoons—Guy because of his amorous antics and Sin thanks to his crusade against child labor—but how she'd learned Elliot's identity was a mystery.

"Who else do you think knows?" he asked.

She merely shrugged and turned toward the pile of clothing on the settee, which she began digging through, as if she were no longer interested in Guy or his friends.

As if she found herself in the same room with a masquerading marquess every day of the week.

Guy—who'd been dreading all the prying questions she was going to ask about the three of them and what they were doing—couldn't help being offended that she had no interest in the matter *at all*.

"How did you know who Elliot was?" he finally asked, irked by his own curiosity but unable to resist.

She appeared not to hear him and kept digging.

Really, the woman was beyond strange. In the weeks that Guy had been working at Farnham's, Marianne had *volunteered* him to rehearse with Blade and her bird four times.

The lethal woman probably hadn't said more than a dozen sentences, most of which had been of the two-word variety: "Hold this. Stand there. Don't move." And so forth.

Quite honestly, she was one of the oddest people he'd ever met. More than a little disgruntled by her lack of curiosity, Guy turned back to the newspapers.

They didn't all contain stories about him or mention his name, but enough of them did to surprise him. He hadn't read the society section in any newspaper in years and he was shocked by just how closely they reported every little thing he did. *And* how often they either made up things entirely or embroidered on events until they were all but unrecognizable to him.

Indeed, if a person were to form a picture of him based solely on the contents of the numerous references in the society sections, that person would conclude he did nothing but carouse, womanize, and engage in dangerous or foolish wagers.

"Learning anything new?" Blade had moved to the end of the settee that was closest to him and was still rooting through the garments like a truffle-hunting pig.

"I have, actually. A great deal of it is nothing but fiction."

He flicked through the papers and brought out an issue of the *London Chronicle*, a newspaper he knew for a fact his mother read.

"Look here," he said, holding up the paper.

She stopped her digging and came over to look. "Swimming nude in the Serpentine?" She looked at Guy. "Who is the C___ of N___?"

"The Countess of Neath."

"And you're saying you didn't go swimming in the nude?"

"No, I'm saying I didn't go swimming in the nude with *her.* Betsy—the countess—is happily married, and the last time I saw her was at dinner at her house, with her husband and parents in attendance. And everyone was fully clothed, by the way."

"But you *did* go swimming nude with somebody?"

"Well, yes. But that's hardly the point, is it?"

She snorted and then went back to her digging.

Guy was peeved by her dismissive attitude. Indeed, he'd moved past annoyed into the neighborhood of downright irritated.

Just what was it with the women in this circus, anyhow?

Marianne either ignored, mocked, or laughed at him, Cecile openly despised him, and here was Blade pretending that his antics weren't enough to fascinate half the population of England, behaving as if stories about Guy didn't sell more newspapers than articles about Boney!

"What are you looking for?" he asked.

"Angus has been taking things and hiding them," she said, a hint of annoyance in her normally flat tone.

Guy looked at the bird, who'd flown over to the dressing table when his mistress had begun digging.

The raven seemed to be staring at him, although it was difficult to say since his eyes were so black one couldn't distinguish pupil from iris. In fact, did birds even have an iris or pupil? Guy had never been in close enough proximity to one to know.

He shook the thought away and asked, "What kinds of things?"

"Have you misplaced or lost anything lately?"

Guy frowned. "As a matter of fact, I haven't been able to find my fire—"

She yanked on the corner of something brightly colored, and several items clattered to the floor.

"Why, there it is," Guy exclaimed. "My fire piston."

He bent over and picked up the slender rod that he usually kept in his pocket.

"My cousin gave me this for my twentieth birthday and I thought I'd lost it," he said, inspecting the simple tool for any damage before turning to glare at the bird. "How the devil did he get it out of my pocket?"

Angus was looking elsewhere in a way that appeared almost . . . studied.

"He is very skilled," Blade muttered, staring at something in her palm before dropping the item into her pocket far too quickly for Guy to identify it.

"Aha," she said, reaching under the settee to pull out something sparkly.

"Is that an earring?" Guy asked.

She ignored him yet again, instead turning to her bird and scowling. "What have I told you about taking valuable things, Angus?"

The huge beast made a soft *quork quork* that actually sounded apologetic and—Guy was mortified to admit—quite adorable.

"That won't work," she retorted, apparently not as charmed by Angus as Guy was.

The raven's wings sagged at her words and Guy *swore* the beast looked guilty.

"Whose is that?" Guy asked as she pocketed the piece of jewelry.

"It's Cordelia's and apparently it is *not* paste. Why she wore such a valuable item to work I don't understand," she added under her breath.

Cordelia Black was the woman whose small theatrical troop performed a harlequinade for the circus. She was quite lovely and had made her interest in Guy quite clear. Only his promise to Sin had kept Guy from misbehaving with her.

Blade stood and brushed off her skirt, which had become dusty when she'd bent to collect the pilfered items.

When she was finished, she pointed to the newspapers that had slid to the floor as he'd reached for the fire piston. "You'd better not mess those up or Cecile will be most displeased with you."

"Cecile?"

"Yes, they're hers and she keeps them arranged in a particular order."

"*Order*," Angus repeated, his voice so much like Blade's, it was unnerving.

Guy sat back hard in his chair at Blade's words. "They belong to Miss Tremblay?"

The haughty Frenchwoman insisted that Guy call her that even though she allowed everyone else to use her Christian name.

"Yes, she collects them."

"Well, isn't that interesting," Guy said.

Blade either didn't hear him or didn't think his comment worthy of acknowledging. Instead, she dug around in one of the dressing table drawers, slipped something else into her pocket and then nodded to her bird. "Come along, Angus."

The massive raven gave an almost soundless flap of his wings and landed on her shoulder, where he immediately snuggled up to her neck.

Woman and bird left without another word.

Guy picked up the papers and straightened the edges before returning them to the table, a grin pulling at his lips and his smile growing the more he thought about the abrupt, intimidating Frenchwoman reading society pages and then actually *collecting* them as a hobby.

It made him snicker to think how thrilled she'd be when he told her—

And then his smile fell.

It was a damned shame that Guy would never be able to tell her who he really was.

Damn! It was going to be bloody agonizing passing up such a priceless opportunity to tease her.

Chapter 5

Dover
February 28, 1815

Cecile watched the three noblemen as they coaxed the draft horses up the ramp that led to the packet ship that would take them to Calais.

These were the last animals that needed to go onboard and the men had already loaded both their own caravan and the one Cecile would be sharing with Marianne and Blade.

Cecile glanced around at the milling employees who were coming to board, looking for the other women, but didn't see either one.

She'd not seen Blade since the last show they'd done in London a few days earlier, but she'd briefly spotted Marianne last night at the hotel when she'd arrived with her uncle Barnabas and Sonia Marchand, who was Barnabas's housekeeper and lover.

It had surprised her that Marianne had ridden down from London in her uncle's carriage. Sonia by herself was a chore, but Sonia and Barnabas together were often unbearable.

That might have explained why Marianne had looked so out of sorts when she'd arrived, barely saying hello before going up to her room and not coming out again.

When Cecile had knocked on her door and asked if she wanted to go to dinner, Marianne had said she wasn't hungry.

That was when she'd known something was wrong; Marianne was *always* hungry and she ate like a horse. It was infuriating that she could eat so much and remain so slender. Cecile had to be careful with what she ate as it had a tendency to attach itself to her hips and bottom.

In any event, Cecile hadn't seen any other employees in the hotel dining room last night except Sonia and Barnabas and had ended up eating her meal with them, an activity that had put her in a vile mood.

Although she'd been a tenant in Barnabas's house for almost four years, she made it a practice to avoid both him and his lover. She avoided Barnabas because she already had enough of his company during the day at work.

And she avoided Sonia's company because the woman was an unpleasant, jealous cat who believed every female was on the hunt for Barnabas. Her jealousy over the man had been laughable at first but had grown old over time.

Also, Sonia seemed to delight in vexing and sniping at the younger woman about everything under the sun, behavior that bothered Cecile far more than it did Marianne.

Although Marianne's aristocratic employees hadn't been in the dining room last night, they must have stayed in the hotel because she saw all three at breakfast—not that she'd talked to any of them.

After pouring out the details of her family's past to the marquess that day several weeks earlier, Cecile had taken care not to make the same slip again. He had made that easier by not asking her any more personal questions. He'd also stopped teasing her or lingering after her rehearsals. She told herself she was grateful that he'd become more reserved with her, but, in fact, the less time he spent chasing her, the more time she'd spent furtively watching him socialize with the other Fayre employees.

He was personable and polite with both the male and female staff, and people of all sorts seemed drawn to him. He possessed that special knack of being friendly to the females without being *too* familiar, which was something many other male workers had not been able to achieve.

A contest to bed him had begun between some of her unmarried coworkers. It was that sort of unapologetically earthy behavior that had attracted the unwanted attention of reformers to theatrical companies, an attitude that was infuriatingly hypocritical given that many peeresses of the realm behaved just as freely—if not more outrageously—than the women she worked with. Cecile probably would have entered the competition for the marquess herself if she hadn't known his real identity.

Unfortunately, Cecile *did* know who he was. Not only that, but she'd developed an excessively strong, and exceedingly unwanted, attraction to him. She could only attribute her giddy reaction to him to the fact that he was something of a celebrity. It shamed her to behave in such a fashion, but there was no denying she had been smitten by him before ever meeting him. The man was simply too dangerous to her peace of mind to spend any time around him.

Although his two friends—Sin and Smithy—were every bit as handsome in their own ways, she felt no spark of attraction for either.

All three men were surprisingly good employees for all that none of them had likely done even one day of manual labor in their lives.

They arrived on time for their scheduled rehearsals, did what she asked of them with a minimum of fuss, and never balked at carrying out even the most menial of tasks.

In the four weeks since the three men had come to work for Farnham's, Marianne still hadn't explained their presence to Cecile.

It astounded her that nobody in the circus seemed to recognize the trio. Not because their disguises were so perfect, but because most people wouldn't believe that men of that stature would be working in a circus—especially not the way Marianne treated them, as if they were drudges.

If there was a vile, difficult, or boring job, one of the men was going to get it. The worst tasks went to the duke, for whom Marianne seemed to reserve a particular animus.

Cecile had watched in open-mouthed amazement as they'd hauled laundry, cleaned the front of the house—an excellent job for the three of them since it was *their* cohort who spilled, spit, slopped, and generally behaved like swine—swept, scrubbed, and even washed the pail closet a few times when the night-soil men had made a mess of their job.

And they'd done it all without complaint.

Whatever they were up to at the circus hadn't seemed to cut into their nighttime activities, either. At least not when it came to the duke and marquess.

Both men made regular appearances in the newspapers. The duke not as often as his friend, and usually in regard to matters of state or simply because his name was printed on dinner lists.

Guy, on the other hand, was described as dancing until dawn almost nightly and driving different heiresses in Hyde Park in his high-perch phaeton during the fashionable hour. There were also murkier rumors of him engaging in less innocent activities with several of society's most notorious widows as well as at least three married women.

Cecile wished she could stop reading the stories about the wretched man, and she hated herself for joining the pushing throngs who gathered outside Humphrey's print shop daily to see what new scandalous illustration might be up, but she couldn't seem to stop herself.

Thankfully the man himself had no clue about her obsession with his outrageous activities.

More than ever, Cecile burned to know why the three men were working in a circus but by this point it had become a matter of pride not to ask. If Marianne didn't want to confide in her, she wasn't going to force the issue.

Cecile looked up from her thoughts and noticed that the other employees were already boarding; it was time to get on the packet and return to the country she'd fled over twenty years before.

Cecile was watching the water churn a short time later when the man who'd been occupying so much of her thoughts came strolling toward her.

"Marianne is looking for you," she said before he could open his mouth.

He gave her a wry look and settled his forearms on the railing beside her. "Don't fret yourself, darling, she already found me and had me drudging for her."

"Hard work builds character," she retorted.

He laughed. "Well, she has turned her attention to Sin for now, so I am safe from her machinations. At least until we reach Calais."

Cecile ignored his comment, both willing him to go away and wanting him to stay.

He fidgeted, glancing from his hands to the water and then back before cutting her a speculative look.

"Where did you work before coming to the Fayre?" Cecile couldn't help asking, wondering what amusing falsehood he'd concoct.

"Oh, here and there."

"Doing what?"

"Whatever was necessary."

It was her turn to laugh. "If one is going to embark on a masquerade, it behooves one to concoct a believable story."

"What do you mean?"

Quite suddenly, Cecile could bear the deception no longer. "I know who you are . . . *Lord Carlisle.*"

Rather than look displeased or at least surprised, as she'd expected, he looked disturbingly . . . amused.

"Oh, do you? How long have you known?"

"Since the first day I saw you." She smirked at him. "I know *all* about you."

Again, he didn't look surprised by her admission. "And what, exactly, do you think you know about me, Miss Tremblay?"

"I've read about you in the society pages and seen countless illustrations and satires in print shop windows."

"And both those are such a reliable source of information."

"Are you denying that the stories printed about you are true?"

"I don't know—which one do you mean?"

"Oh, there are so many!"

"Then it should be easy for you to pick one."

"How about one of the more well-known stories—the one about you and the Duchess of Leicester?" she blurted, goaded by his blasé attitude.

His lips curved into a wicked smile. "Ah, yes, the most famous— or perhaps infamous—image of me."

Cecile's heart pounded faster just thinking about the drawing in question, which depicted Guy and the duchess naked in a well-appointed bedchamber, sprawled out on a canopy-covered bed.

An older man peeked in through a window, the cartoon drawn from a clever perspective that made it look as if the man was clinging to a ledge outside the building.

The cartoon had attracted such a huge crowd that the Watch had read the Riot Act outside Mr. Humphrey's print shop, where over three hundred people had gathered to view the new satire, jostling and pushing until a massive brawl had erupted.

The Darling slid a step closer to her, his big body dwarfing hers. "You must have hurried to see that particular drawing, Miss Tremblay because it wasn't in the window long."

Indeed, it had been removed the same day it had gone up. Because in addition to a riot, it had also triggered a morals inquiry.

Cecile cleared her throat, refusing to step away from him and demonstrate how much his proximity was making her perspire. "So, my lord, was it an accurate depiction?"

Her pert question surprised another laugh out of Guy. "Actually, the artist rather understated my attributes."

Her brow furrowed, as if she were trying to discern his meaning.

Guy knew the instant she did because her cheeks were tinted a delightful pink and she huffed. "*That* wasn't what I meant."

"Oh? It wasn't? What *did* you mean then?" He actually knew very well what she'd meant.

"I meant is it true that the duke caught you in bed with his wife?"

Guy was familiar with this sort of question, although usually only men were brave enough to ask it so directly. Normally, it irritated him to talk about all the stories that circulated about his exploits. But he found that he was most eager to satisfy Miss Tremblay's curiosity. After all, it was the only interest she'd shown in him after almost five weeks. She'd become something of an anomaly in his experience: a woman to whom he appeared practically invisible. Which was ironic given that she had all those newspapers tucked away in the dressing room.

Guy was sorely tempted to tell her the truth—which was far more deviant than the cartoon—that the duke *had* watched them, but through a peephole rather than a window. And that Guy hadn't cuckolded the man—at least not without his express invitation.

Indeed, the duke and duchess together had invited Guy into His Grace's bedchambers to participate in one of their erotic games, apparently a favorite, in which the duke observed while another man pleasured his wife.

His Grace had never become angry or made a scene. In fact, Guy hadn't even seen the duke that night as the older man had been behind the wall viewing from a priest hole the entire time.

It had been a first for Guy and had, strangely, left him feeling like a prostitute as the duke and duchess were very much in love and obviously using his presence to titillate themselves. It had been an interesting feeling, and quite singular in his experience.

One of the duke's disgruntled servants had sold the lascivious story to a newspaperman, and Guy's reputation as a cuckolder of dukes had been born.

One look at Cecile's lovely face made it obvious that she was panting to hear all the filthy details.

Guy smiled. "A gentleman never kisses and tells, Miss Tremblay."

She gave an unladylike snort. "From what I've read, my lord, you have never allowed your behavior to be proscribed by what *gentlemen* do."

"You sound like quite a specialist where I am concerned."

"It would be impossible to avoid knowing about your antics since they are noised about everywhere."

"If by *everywhere* you mean gossip columns and print shop windows, then you are correct." He cocked an eyebrow. "Perhaps you need to spend your time and attention pursuing more elevated subjects, Miss Tremblay."

"I could say the same about you, Lord Carlisle."

"Please tell me you don't believe everything you read in the newspapers?"

"I am not so gullible. However, I think where there is smoke—as there is in your case—there is probably fire."

"By *fire* I assume you mean that I encourage women to be unfaithful to their husbands?"

"I'm not so sure who does the actual *encouraging*, but I do believe you have an exceedingly, er, elastic notion of what is moral behavior."

He chuckled. "Well, it may surprise you to know that I am not so debauched as I'm painted."

She gave him a saucy look and then said. "How disappointing." And then she pivoted on her heel and sauntered off, leaving Guy alone to ponder what she meant.

And what he should do about it.

Chapter 6

Lille, France
March 5, 1815

Guy was not, by and large, a praying man. But as he held the playing card a mere inch above his head, he offered up the most heartfelt plea he could muster.

Silently, of course.

"Should I use a blindfold this time?" Cecile called out in French to the loud and raucous crowd.

"*Blindfold!*" the crazed audience yelled in almost one voice.

"Oh God," Guy muttered under his breath.

This next part of the act was not one he'd been relishing, even though they'd practiced it often during the month of rehearsals.

But this was the first time he'd been on stage during an actual show, and there was something about being dressed like a bloody court jester in front of two hundred screaming Frenchmen that made the experience infinitely more harrowing.

Cecile grinned at the yelling audience in a way that caused Guy's cock to perk up. And why shouldn't it enjoy itself? It wasn't his cock that she was going to shoot at, was it?

She pulled the black silk scarf from the extremely low-cut bodice of her gown, causing the theater to thunder with shouts and wolf whistles.

Guy swallowed as she tied the blindfold on.

He knew the bright lighting behind and above him would help to throw him into relief and make him a clearer target, but knowing that didn't stop him from worrying every time they got to this part of the act.

"Quiet now!" She had to raise her voice to be heard above the crowd. "I need complete silence to concentrate. I cannot miss this shot—Monsieur Darling is my third assistant this year and I don't want to have to hire another one."

The audience thought that was hilarious.

Once the crowd grew silent, she lifted the pistol and took aim with one heart-stoppingly smooth motion.

Guy barely had time to be terrified before she squeezed the trigger.

Thank God the report of the pistol was too loud to hear the high-pitched squeaking sound he made when the hat flew off—as if a fierce wind had streaked through the theater—and exploded in midair, showering him with bits of glitter and foil.

The crowd erupted in cheers and Cecile turned and took a bow, as did Guy, but far more shakily. Thankfully the blindfold shot was her encore so he could wobble off the stage.

The first thing he was going to do was ingest a fortifying glass of the strongest spirits he could find. Perhaps even two glasses. Who knew that the addition of two hundred or so people could make the experience of being shot at so *fraught*?

"You did well tonight—better than you've done in rehearsal."

Guy stopped and turned at the sound of Cecile's unprecedented praise, his lips parted in shock.

Because they'd ridden in the same caravan together from Calais to Lille, they had spoken more in two days than in all the weeks before. But except for that brief conversation aboard the packet, their conversation had been only about impersonal matters—most especially the improbable rumor they'd heard two nights ago that Napoleon had escaped Elba and was gathering an army.

Once they'd reached Lille, she'd resumed her prior behavior, pretending that Guy didn't actually exist.

Guy smirked at her. "Oh, are you actually speaking to me now, Princess?"

"You must be mistaking me for somebody else. I think the term you are searching for is 'my queen.'"

He laughed.

"And I never stopped talking to you," she said.

"No, you never stopped barking orders at me, but that's not the same thing at all, sweetheart."

She clucked her tongue. "Poor *Mister* Darling—so unused to encountering a female who doesn't throw herself at his feet."

"Actually, *My Queen*, if you're going to throw yourself at my body, my feet would not be the first choice of appendage."

She snorted and pushed past him, closing the distance between the stage door and dressing room in long, loose-limbed strides.

"Care to have dinner with me?" he called after her.

Her derisive laughter drifted back over her shoulder.

Guy wasn't surprised by her rejection; why should anything change between them just because they were in a different country? She'd been rejecting his overtures of friendship since the very first day she'd shot at him. He watched her until she disappeared into the dressing room and then sighed. Lord, but he liked to watch her walk. Or stand. Or bark orders at him. And—yes—he even would put up with being shot at if he could look at her.

He'd really hoped the drive to Lille would have eased the barriers between them. They'd discussed—well, argued would probably be a better way to describe their exchanges—not just Bonaparte's alleged escape from Elba, but books, plays, food, and a dozen other subjects. Yet never had they come close to talking about themselves.

Cecile was a fascinating woman, but she'd erected a barrier between them that Guy forced himself to respect, no matter how badly he wanted to scale her walls and discover the woman who lived behind them.

"So, how was your first evening on the stage?"

Guy turned at the sound of Sin's voice. "For a moment I thought I might need to change my breeches after the show."

Sin gave one of his rare laughs.

"Go ahead and laugh, my friend. It will be your turn to face the smoking end of her pistol tomorrow night, won't it?"

"Don't forget that I already *volunteered* to have knives thrown at my head and be mocked by a bird earlier tonight."

"At least Blade doesn't throw them at you while blindfolded."

"I wouldn't be surprised if Cecile's show inspired her."

Guy groaned. "Lord, I hope not, one blindfolded weapon-wielding woman seems like more than enough. I'd actually hoped to watch your show earlier but Mademoiselle Tremblay decided that she needed *another* of her countless trunks from the caravan, and no other lackey but me would do."

"I've noticed she enjoys having you fetch and carry for her."

Guy had noticed it, too. Actually, it was the only thing that made him think she might like him at least a little.

"Are you hungry?" Guy asked his friend. "The ostler at the inn said there was a café on Grand Place that stays open late to cater to theater people."

Sin winced. "Lord, Guy—did you never practice your French when we were at school?"

Guy shrugged, already accustomed to being mocked for his atrocious accent after only a few days in France. "Are you hungry or not, Sin?"

"I ate there earlier," Sin said, pulling out his watch. "They are closing in half an hour, so you'd better hurry."

"Blast! That doesn't give me any time to change."

Sin looked at the burgundy velvet and gold-trimmed costume it amused Barnabas to make his few male performers wear, and grinned. "You don't need to change, Guy; you look like some wealthy old woman's favorite footman."

"Very droll."

Sin had to wear a similar costume, so he was hardly in a position to mock. Guy turned away and headed toward the cloak room.

"If you stop to change your clothing, you'll miss dinner," Sin called after him.

Guy just waved a dismissive hand at him.

He wasn't going to change and miss out on eating. Being shot at was surprisingly hungry and thirsty work, so food was more important than his reluctance to traipse through a French city looking like a court jester.

Cecile hurried through the quiet streets, wrapped in a heavy wool cloak against the chill of the evening.

She didn't like walking alone, but all the other women had already eaten, and the only place that served late meals was closing soon.

Because discretion was the better part of valor—or some such English saying—she'd also taken the precaution of buckling her gun holster over her gray wool gown after she'd taken off her black silk costume.

Lord Carlisle asked you to go to dinner with him.

Cecile laughed out loud at that thought.

Yes, she knew *exactly* what the gorgeous peer had in mind, and it hadn't been merely food. The days she'd spent riding in the caravan with him had worn away at her reserve until she'd almost given in to his charm. What she needed to do now was put some distance between them.

One would have thought that spending *more* time with him would have made him seem more mundane, but it hadn't. There was something about the man that made her feel like a fourteen-year-old girl: dizzy, breathless, and awed. The last thing Cecile needed was the complication of a man in her life. Especially one that would end in disappointment, if not actual heartache.

She was no fool; Guy would one day be a duke and she was a circus performer. Cecile could never be anything other than a temporary dalliance to such a man.

You could tell him the truth—that you are a duchess in your own right.

She actually laughed out loud at that.

Yes, because he would surely believe such a tale. And even if he did believe her, impoverished French aristocrats were literally a ha'penny a dozen these days.

Cecile recalled meeting a French duke and duchess operating a pawnbroker's shop when she first moved to England. Twenty years ago the French community had swelled so rapidly that most Englishmen, especially the upper echelon, had considered the émigrés flooding their shore a nuisance at best and a plague at worst.

Cecile had borne the brunt of such derision often over the years, although it had become less of an issue of late, especially now that she worked for Barnabas. As an émigré himself—albeit one who'd come to England years and years before the Revolution—he had no tolerance for such abuse, and at least half his employees were French.

But a man like the Marquess of Carlisle would look down his nose at an impoverished Frenchwoman who'd entered into a white marriage with a dying duke in a prison. Not that she had any proof of the alliance.

No, that was a part of her life best left exactly where it was—buried somewhere in the English Channel.

Nothing could come of her attraction to Lord Carlisle, and she would do well to remember it.

Are you saying that you want something to come of it? Since when did you want anything more than a roll in the sheets?

Cecile's lips flexed into a scowl. *I don't want marriage. But neither do I want to be used and cast aside like a piece of rubbish.*

No, if there is going to be any casting aside, then you like to do it.

Cecile couldn't argue with that; it *was* far better to be the person in control of the affair, something she'd discovered after the first, and only, time she'd fancied herself in love—years and years and years ago, when she'd been an innocent and foolish girl of nineteen. She'd had many lovers since then—why not, she had only herself to please after all—and she'd been in control of each and every relationship. That was the only way she would—

"Hello, sweetheart," a low voice said in French as a thick male arm snaked out of the doorway she was passing and grabbed her wrist. Two arms as thick as tree trunks slid around her torso and pulled her back, clamping her against a broad chest.

"Help!" Cecile shrieked, immediately kicking back with her

heel, which must have made contact with something because her aggressor screamed.

"*Sacré bleu!*" he shouted when she kicked him again, shoving her forward so hard she tripped and slammed into the alley wall, barely catching herself in time to keep from smashing her nose against the rough brick. Suddenly free from his grip, she spun and bolted for the alley entrance, her feet skittering on the slick cobblestones.

"Not so fast, girly," the man snarled, snagging her heavy cloak and yanking her back hard enough that he almost pulled her off her feet.

"Help me!" she yelled, having the foresight to yell the words in French, this time. "Please—somebody—"

A massive, not so clean hand clamped over her mouth and Cecile fumbled with her cloak tie while writhing and thrashing in his grasp.

But then his arm snaked around her waist like an iron clamp and pulled her tightly enough to him that she could feel the hard ridge of an erection against her lower back.

Terror shot through her like a bolt of lightning, reinvigorating her rapidly tiring muscles. "*Mmmph! Mmmmmmmggrh!*"

His meaty fingers muffled her screams so thoroughly that even she could barely hear them.

He chuckled, holding her arms pinned against her body with horrifying ease as he groped her with his other hand. "This is a nice little body you've got under here," he said, cupping a breast and then sliding his hand down her belly, until he encountered her holster. "Oooh, and what's this?" He traced the line of the belt to her right hip. "What the hell?" he muttered, loosening his grip for a fraction of a second so that he might turn her and inspect what he'd discovered.

That fraction of a second was all she needed, and Cecile slammed her head back as hard as she could.

There was a sickening but highly gratifying crunching sound.

He screamed and released her. "*Aaaargh!* You bitch!"

Cecile scrambled forward but, yet again, he caught her cloak and yanked her back as easily as reeling in a fish. "You just wait! I'm going to—"

"You're going to take your hands off her, you bounder, or I'll take you apart piece by piece," a calm voice declaimed from the alley entrance.

It was the most execrable French accent Cecile had ever heard. It was also the most welcome.

The man holding her grabbed her wrist but didn't pull her any closer. "I didn't know she was your woman," he said, as if that excused his actions.

"Let. Her. Go," Guy said with so much menace dripping from his words that his incorrect pronouns, tense, and bad pronunciation somehow didn't matter.

"Fine—take her." Her captor shoved her forward. "She's not worth fighting over."

Guy caught her and kept her from falling, the light behind him hiding his face in shadow. "Are you all right?" he asked softly.

Cecile nodded, too rattled to speak.

Guy turned to her aggressor and snarled in French, *"Tu pars en enfer avant que je t'apprenne une leçon!"*

You get the hell out of here before I decide to teach you a lesson.

Or at least she *thought* that's what he wanted to say.

"Fine, fine!" The man threw up his hands and eased around them, then backed out of the alley, keeping his distance

"Are you hurt?" Guy asked once the attacker had disappeared around the corner.

Cecile shook herself from her terror-fueled fugue, disgusted that her first impulse was to either swoon or launch herself into his powerful arms. What in the world was wrong with her?

"Release me," she said coolly, placing her hands on his chest and firmly pushing him away before brushing off her person with shaking hands.

"Release me," he repeated in a flat voice.

"What do you want—a reward?"

"A *thank you very much, Guy,* would be nice."

Her face heated in the darkness. She *was* being churlish. She had taken a deep breath to say *something* to him, she wasn't sure what, when she realized her reticule was no longer attached to her wrist.

"He stole my money!" she shouted, bolting for the alley exit.

"Wait! Where the devil are you going?" he demanded.

Cecile skidded to a halt outside the alley, her head whipping both ways. The thief had paused beside a streetlight and was riffling through her reticule.

"Give that back!" she yelled.

The man looked up, made an extremely rude gesture, and yelled back, "Come get it!" He laughed and returned to his riffling.

Cecile slid a pistol from its holster and took aim.

Behind her, Guy gave a startled squawk. "Good God! You're not going to actually shoo—"

The loud *crack* was instantly followed by a blood-curdling howl of pain.

Cecile sheathed her pistol and marched toward where the man was now screaming and hopping up and down on one foot.

"Are you mad?" Guy demanded, trotting beside her as she stalked toward the wounded thief.

"I'm not mad, but I am angry," she admitted.

"Bloody hell, Cecile! You can't go about shooting people!"

"I just did."

He made a strangled sound. "Wait here and I'll run and fetch your reticule."

Cecile ignored him. Instead, she took out the second pistol, and called out, "Drop my reticule and get away from it or I will shoot something more critical this next time."

The man gave a piteous yelp and half hopped, half dragged his injured foot down the street.

Cecile smirked and slid her pistol back into the holster.

"Good God! That was *terribly* illegal—or didn't you know that?"

"Why are you still here, Guy? You may go."

"Oh, *may* I? You might have killed him."

Cecile scoffed. "Please. I aimed at the toe of his boot and that is what I hit."

When they reached the lamppost, Guy dropped to his haunches to help pick up the contents of her reticule. "You're mad. Completely and utterly mad." He held out a handful of items. "And why are you walking around by yourself at this time of night?" He pushed to his feet and then helped her to hers before planting his fisted hands on his hips. "Cecile?"

She pulled the drawstring on her reticule, tied it, and then slid it over her wrist and continued on toward the café.

"Where are you going?" he demanded, falling into step beside her.

"To eat."

"I just came from there—they closed early tonight."

Cecile scowled. "I'm hungry." Her stomach growled as if to support her claim.

His lips twitched into a smile. "So I hear. Elliot told me it is possible to get some bread and cheese and a bottle of wine from one of the maids for a few sou. I will fetch us something when we return to the inn."

She squinted up at him, her pulse pounding from either her recent brush with danger or at the sight of his too-perfect face. "Just food. Nothing else."

He snorted. "Don't flatter yourself, darling. I might not be the brightest star in the firmament but I'm smart enough to know when a woman isn't interested in me. Come," he said, holding out his arm. "Let me escort you back to the inn."

When she hesitated, he smiled down at her and his lids drooped over his warm eyes, the expression robbing her of breath.

"You've got one bullet left, sweetheart—you can always shoot me if I don't behave like a perfect gentleman."

Cecile realized she was smiling before she knew what she was doing. She quickly schooled her face into a frown and ignored his arm. "Fine. I'll go back with you, but only for dinner."

"I give you my word that I shall restrain my baser instincts."

Cecile didn't bother explaining that it wasn't *his* baser instincts she was worried about.

Chapter 7

Guy topped up Cecile's wineglass and then nudged the platter toward her. "More cheese?"

She shook her head, her mouth too full to speak.

One of the housemaids had allowed them to eat in the empty dining room for considerably more than a few sous, but it was quiet and private and worth the money after what had been a hectic day.

Guy's body was still humming from the confrontation in the alley. His heart had almost stopped when he'd seen that brute groping Cecile.

It had almost stopped again when she'd calmly shot the man.

He grinned at the memory. *Lord. What a woman.*

His stomach had been churning too savagely to be hungry, but he'd forced down some bread and cheese, not wanting to make her feel uncomfortable about eating alone.

What he probably should have done was have the food sent up to the room she shared with Marianne and then gone to the room he shared with Elliot.

He should *not* be sitting at a candlelit table for two at one in the morning.

But the opportunity had been too appealing to pass up. Besides, surely a late supper couldn't cause any trouble?

Cecile took a sip of wine before asking, "What do you think will happen?"

She didn't need to explain what she meant.

"I don't know what Bonaparte will end up doing," Guy admitted. "But what I *do* think is that this tour will probably end early."

"I heard Barnabas arguing with the theater manager this afternoon," she said. "The man told him he might exercise some clause in the contract if hostilities commence."

"Doubtless he means a *force majeure* clause."

"Yes, that was the phrase."

Guy racked his brains to recall what he knew of the legal term. "I think it means a contract can be broken if some catastrophic and uncontrollable event makes the performance of it impossible." He snorted. "I suppose a war would qualify as both catastrophic and uncontrollable."

Her eyebrows rose.

"Why are you looking at me like that?"

"I just didn't expect you to know such a thing."

"Why? Because I've only got fluff in my head?"

"Not only fluff—probably women, fine horses, and your own pleasure."

Guy laughed. "Well, it just so happens that I went to university and attended a few classes." Not many, that was true, but she hardly needed to know that. "I've also managed both my family estate and the ducal affairs for several years, so I'm not utterly useless."

Her dark eyes flickered over him, the look leaving a trail of fire in its wake. "I never thought you were useless."

He was foolishly pleased that she'd admitted to thinking of him at all.

"What will you do if the tour is canceled?" she asked him.

He opened his mouth, and then closed it and shrugged.

"You still won't tell me what you and your friends are doing—even though we are on the brink of war?"

"It's not my story to tell, Cecile. What about you?"

"What about me?"

"Will you go back to England? Or will you stay in France for a while?"

"Why would I stay here?"

"You are from here. Don't you still have family here? Friends?"

She looked away. "No."

"Cecile."

She turned back and the scowl she seemed to reserve solely for Guy was on her full lips. "I never gave you permission to call me—"

"Don't."

She blinked at the quiet word. "I won't become your lover."

It was Guy's turn to blink. "I'm not asking for that."

She arched one elegant black eyebrow.

"Fine, so I've been thinking about that. A lot. But I said earlier that this was only going to be dinner and I'm a man of my word. Don't be so suspicious. I'm just interested in you—true, I'm interested in you as a woman," he admitted when she cut him a jaded look. "But I'm also interested in you as a person."

She inhaled deeply, an action that did distracting things to the snug bodice of her gown—not that he allowed himself to look. Much.

"I already told you something about me," she said. "Tell me something about *you*."

"I saw the stack of newspapers you keep in the dressing room in London. You already know plenty about me."

Cecile's jaw sagged. "Who told you about those papers?"

"I found them."

"What were you doing digging in my—"

Guy held up a staying hand, astounded when she stopped talking. "If you recall, Marianne enjoys using the three of us like her own personal serfs. She *made* me clean that room from top to bottom."

"How do you know those were mine?"

He didn't want to tattle on Blade, so he asked, "Are you denying it?"

She made a sound like an angry badger. "There were stories about lots of people."

"Yes, but the great majority were about *me*."

"That's hardly my fault!"

He chuckled. "Fine, fine. So, what do you want to know about me?" He allowed his eyelids to droop low. "Although I should point out that some things are better *demonstrated* than talked about."

As Guy had hoped, she laughed at his ridiculous boast, and the sound was more delicious than the finest champagne.

"You are relentless," she said when she'd stopped laughing. "Tell me how you came to be called the Darling."

"What do you mean?"

"Why are you so . . . frenetic in your amours?"

"I'm not—"

She made a rude but expressive *pffft* sound. "Don't try to deny it; I can see it for myself in the stories about you. You pursue women with a single-mindedness that is frenetic. Tell me the truth, Guy."

Guy felt a pleasing tingle in his balls at the sound of his pet name on her tongue. He loved the way she pronounced it: *Ghee*. Nobody else had ever called him that.

True, now that he was in France, everyone pronounced it that way, but none with the same inflection as Cecile. Almost as if she was challenging him to something when she said it.

"You can trust me," she added, mistaking his hesitation for reticence. "I won't sell your story to a newspaper man. You say you want to know things about me; prove yourself worthy of my confidences and tell me what makes you the way you are."

Guy opened his mouth to say he didn't want to know anything badly enough to spill his guts out before her, but then decided that wasn't true. What did it matter if he told her the truth? It might be shameful and even a bit sordid, but it wasn't a great secret, after all.

Cecile ignored the voice that told her to go up to her room—to get as far away from Guy as she could. He'd behaved himself just as he'd promised. Where was the harm in enjoying some wine and conversation with an interesting man?

I'll remind you of that, later, the annoying voice piped up.

"This isn't a very interesting story, you know," he said. "That's the main reason I hesitate to tell it."

"I'm listening."

"There is a tradition in my family—not a noble one, so perhaps I should call it more of a curse—that the oldest sons always marry for money. Not because they wish to, but because the dukedom is like an unquenchable thirst—there is an incessant need for money, money, and more money."

For once, there was no hint of a smile on his face. And he made no effort to charm, his attention on the wineglass on the table, which he turned in restless circles.

"It's possible the curse might have bypassed me," he said. For a long moment he just played with his wineglass. But then he glanced up. "You see, my grandfather, the current duke, married one of the greatest heiresses of her generation. For many years the dukedom was healthy and robust." A nerve in his jaw jumped and he leaned back in his chair and heaved a sigh, his broad, powerful chest flexing beneath his worn coat.

"My grandfather had three sons. The eldest showed every sign of following in his father's footsteps—which meant he would have been a responsible and diligent caretaker for the dukedom." His lips curved into a small, unhappy smile as he looked up. "But he died before his twentieth birthday and the next son to inherit was—" He laughed, but the sound held no amusement. "Suffice it to say that my uncle Henry would have been a disastrous duke. Fortunately for the dukedom, he killed a man in a duel—and not just any man, but a peer. My grandfather had to get him out of the country. The plan was to let the scandal settle for a few years and then bring him back."

"How could such a thing ever *settle*?"

"Money, my dear." He shrugged. "In any event, that never happened. Uncle Henry went a lot of places. In fact, he enjoyed his banishment so much that when my grandfather sent for him five years later, he refused to come home. The next time my grandfather sent a man to bring him home rather than just sending a letter. That's when he discovered that my uncle had simply disappeared. Over the decade that followed, my grandfather sent probably a dozen inquiries. Finally, about eighteen years ago, one of his agents returned with an answer: My uncle had died—ironically—in a duel."

"So, your father was next in line?"

"Yes."

"How old were you?"

He took a sip of wine and turned his attention back to the table. "I was fourteen when I learned that my life wasn't going to be my own." He pulled a face. "I know that sounds melodramatic and self-pitying."

"You didn't want to become a duke?" she asked, allowing her amazement—and no small amount of disbelief—to show in her tone.

"Lord no! Up until that time I'd hoped my father would purchase a commission for me and I could join the army. That became impossible after learning of my uncle's death. To be honest, my father wasn't much better for the dukedom than my uncle Henry would have been—maybe he was even worse. Who knows? I won't go into the gory details, but he accumulated a great deal of debt. A whopping, crushing, mind-numbing amount of debt, to be honest."

Cecile heard the restrained fury beneath his wry tone.

"Because he had been managing the dukedom's business, as well as his own properties—Darlington Park, a house in London, and a smaller estate in Yorkshire—my grandfather and I had no notion of the extent of the debt he'd accrued until after he died three years ago. We had to sell off everything that wasn't entailed, but even that isn't enough."

His hand, which was resting on the table, had clenched into a fist.

Guy tracked her gaze and he stretched his fingers and smiled at her. "I don't know why I can still be upset about something that has already happened. It is not only illogical but such a waste of time."

Cecile knew the feeling; it was the same emotion she felt whenever she thought of her cousin Curtis.

★   ★   ★

"So what you are working up to saying is that you have to marry a wealthy woman?"

Guy took a sip of wine and considered her question. This conversation was more irksome than he would have imagined. Not until he'd begun talking did he realize just how bloody grim the story was. He had never articulated it to anyone before. His friends—and everyone who made up the *ton*—just *knew* without needing to be told.

But Cecile was not of the *ton*, and he could only imagine how grasping, shallow, and immoral his family and, indeed, his future plans, must appear to her.

He forced himself to look at her when he answered. "Yes, I have to marry a wealthy woman. An extremely wealthy woman."

Guy couldn't read the look in her eyes, but it made him feel itchy, anxious.

He shrugged. "But then that is hardly uncommon. With a great landed estate comes great responsibility." He forced a chuckle. "I didn't coin that phrase, by the way. Anyhow, your question was why am I so *frenetic*. Why do I take so many lovers? Why are they always widows or—so the papers claim—married women?" He couldn't help smirking at the blush his words triggered. He leaned an elbow on the table and dropped his chin in his hand, bringing them closer.

"The newspaper stories about me aren't all true, Cecile. One of the reasons I don't read them is because it used to infuriate me to read the lies—about how I'd cuckolded this or that man. You want plain speaking? The truth is that I don't bed married women." He met her skeptical gaze and was goaded into adding, "At least not unless their husbands ask me to."

Her jaw dropped.

"As to why I never take the same young woman driving in my phaeton more than twice or why I only waltz with married ladies? Because there is no point in getting to know young women or spend time with them. Because when I finally marry, it won't be the sort of girl you'd find dancing at Almack's. When I marry, I shan't be able to wed a genteel heiress. No, I shall need to do what both my father and grandfather have done and marry outside my class. I shall need a monstrous amount of money—the sort of money I'll only be able to find in the vulgar daughters of the merchant class, some poor girl who'd never get an invitation to an *haut ton* function. Somebody who will marry into my world and spend the rest of her life regretting it. Somebody who will always be an outsider—even to her own children once they are old enough to recognize exactly who she is. Somebody who will never belong no matter how hard she works to fit in. In fact, she will be looked down upon as too pushing if she tries too hard."

He gave a bitter laugh. "If it sounds like I'm an expert on this, that is because I *am*. I grew to adulthood witnessing two miserable marriages. And soon I shall have my own. In fact, as we sit here talking, my grandfather is compiling his list of potential brides. With any luck I shall be betrothed by the end of the year. Foolishly, I had hoped for a few more years—until I was five and thirty—but I've no right to complain since I've managed to prolong my reckless youth for years longer than most of my cohort."

He stopped and blinked, as if astounded by his emotional soliloquy.

Cecile was astounded, as well. And impressed. She'd suspected there was more beneath his beautiful veneer than fluff, and now she had proof that a passionate, troubled soul occupied that gorgeous body.

He stood and his chair made a jarring screech as he shoved it back. "Come," he said abruptly. "Let me escort you to your room."

Chapter 8

"Ah, there you are."

Guy turned at the sound of Sin's voice. He'd been watching from the wings as Blade and her raven rehearsed their routine, making Elliot the butt of their jesting.

Sin looked from Guy to Elliot and frowned. "I thought it was your honor to have knives thrown at your head this week—didn't you two decide to alternate?"

"Er, we did—at first. But we finally decided to split up the routines. To specialize, as it were. From now on I'm working only for Cecile and he's taking all Blade's shows."

Sin's eyebrows shot up. "Hmm."

Guy felt his face get red. He wanted to deny what the other man was thinking, but he and Sin had known each other since the cradle; his friend knew him better than he knew himself.

"We thought it was a good idea since you handle all the boxing," he added.

Sin just stared.

For one agonizingly long, silent moment he thought his friend would demand the truth.

And the truth was that there must be something wrong with Guy. Because he wanted Cecile more than ever since the night they'd shared bread and cheese and a little of themselves, too.

What sort of idiot was he after he'd watched her shoot off a man's toe from fifty paces?

"Any news?" Guy asked before Sin broached any uncomfortable subjects.

"I just came from the town square, where it seems that more news—and plenty of rumors—comes in every hour. All of it points toward Bonaparte's army getting bigger. Quickly."

"Bloody hell," Guy muttered. "This is a complication we could have done without. Any news from Vienna? The Allies will have to do something about this."

"One would think," Sin said dryly.

"What does Farnham think? I know he's been whining about the ticket sales plummeting."

"I don't think he knows what to do."

"You think he's waiting for war to be declared before he goes home?"

"Who knows? This entire thing has a certain air of unreality about it."

Guy had been thinking the same thing. It felt as if the world had been at war all his life. And just when it seemed that they'd left the madness behind, the lunatic came marching back—with apparently nobody to stop him.

"It's a bit ironic that we haven't finished hammering out the bloody peace treaty after the *last* time we stopped Napoleon's rampage," he muttered.

"At least the Allies are all together so it will be convenient when it comes to declaring war."

They shared a grim chuckle over that.

Guy didn't bother pointing out the obvious to his friend—that he, Sin, and Elliot would be considered hostiles in France if war broke out.

Instead, he asked, "What are your thoughts?"

"I don't have a choice; I *need* to get to Metz by April first, Guy."

"I'm going wherever you're going, Sin."

Sin gave him a faint but grateful smile. "Thank you."

Guy scratched his jaw; he'd believed that not shaving every day would be a relief. Instead, he'd discovered the new growth itched like mad. "Is there anything we should do to prepare? I mean if we end up needing to leave quickly?"

"Yes, and I was just coming to talk to you about that. I think you should move our caravan closer to the inn."

"I'm not sure I can find another place where we can keep it locked up inside a building."

"Then one of us will have to stay with it every night."

"I can do that," Guy said.

"The three of us can take turns."

"Please," Guy said, meeting Sin's gaze. "Let me do this. You need to be at the inn or the theater if things go to hell, and Elliot does his best work slipping and sliding through the shadows. So it only makes sense that I stake out the caravans and make sure they are ready to go."

"Good thinking."

Guy pushed off the wall. "I'll go look into moving them right now."

"I'm going to go find Farnham and let him know our plans."

Guy watched him go, uneasy about the dark circles he saw beneath the other man's usually vivid green eyes. He was more than a little concerned for his friend; Sin was the sort of person to keep all his worries bottled up, rather than ask for help. Although they never talked about it, Guy knew the news that Sin's brother might still be alive was causing his friend both stress and joy. But the joy was a guarded sort of happiness because not one of the three of them believed that Baron Dominic Strickland—the man who was ransoming his brother—would actually deliver on his promise. It simply seemed too fantastical that Benjamin could have survived the brutal ambush that had killed all the others who'd been with him.

The trip was already going to be nerve-racking enough before Napoleon broke out of his island prison. With France falling to pieces around them, things were likely to become more than a little dangerous in the days and weeks to come.

★　★　★

Cecile heard the door open and looked up from the trunk she'd been digging through to see Marianne had entered the room they shared.

"Ah, there you are," Cecile said. "I need a bag from our caravan. Do you know where Sin is keeping them?"

Marianne laughed as she stripped off her gloves. "I thought you'd had Guy bring up every single bag you brought on the journey, whether you needed it or not."

"I thought I had, too," Cecile admitted.

Marianne grinned. "You're quite cruel to him."

"You're one to talk! You had all three of them cleaning chamber pots and scrubbing floors."

Rather than look guilty, Marianne only chuckled.

"Do you know where the caravans are?"

"Guy will know. He's downstairs in the coffee room—I just saw him talking to the innkeeper. If you hurry, you might catch him."

Cecile ignored the foolish fluttering in her chest as she hurried down the stairs. Since that night in the dining room, she and Guy had scarcely exchanged a word outside of her performances. She avoided him and, to her chagrin, he seemed to have stopped seeking her out.

The man in question was just getting to his feet when she entered the coffee room, and she heard him say something that sounded like, "I'll move it tonight, then?"

The innkeeper winced and nodded.

Guy's face lit up when he saw her, and he smiled down at her. "Hello, darling."

"You know, if you have business to conduct in French you might want to have Barnabas, Marianne, or me help you. Our two countries are already verging on war—having you slaughter the French language might not be the best thing to do at this point."

"Ha! You are so amusing, Miss Tremblay. Instead of shooting at people for a living, you should be on the stage in comedic productions. Now, what can I do for you—other than serve as a scratching post for your claws?"

"I need to get a small trunk from our caravan."

His eyes widened in mock surprise. "You mean there is a piece of luggage that you *haven't* had me tote up three floors? How shocking!"

"Well, this should be the last one. Unfortunately."

"If you can wait a bit, I'll bring it *to* you, my queen. I actually have to move both caravans to a closer location."

"Are you going right now?"

"Why?" he asked, looking interested. "Would you like to come with me?"

"You know that Barnabas told us we shouldn't go out alone," she chided. "Especially those of us who are so very, very English." Already some of the crew had encountered hostility from the locals. Even without a declaration of war, relations had quickly worsened.

Guy gestured to her. "But you have no weapon; how will you protect me?"

Cecile reached through a slit in the side of her skirt and extracted a tiny pistol from the pocket in her petticoat.

"Good God!" He glanced around the coffee room, which was empty at this hour of the afternoon. "Can you put that away, please."

She shrugged. "You asked."

"Run along and fetch your cloak," he said. "In addition to your bodyguard duty you can drive the second caravan so I only have to make one trip."

Guy watched Cecile disappear up the stairs and couldn't help smiling.

He'd been employing a new method with the beautiful woman—ignoring her. And it seemed to be working because here she was, coming to *him*.

Because she wants one of her trunks.

Oh, he didn't believe that excuse for a minute. He'd seen the way she'd been looking at him—with interest rather than derision—since their tête-à-tête that night.

But his interest in her company today was not all for frivolous pleasure.

He'd been serious about her helping with the caravans. He'd seen Cecile drive the caravan and had to admit she was better at it than he was. In fact, all the women in Farnham's Fantastical Female Fayre could pretty much do anything men could do and often better.

It was quite humbling.

As an only son with five sisters, he'd grown up believing women desperately needed his help. Now he was beginning to question that belief. Indeed, he was starting to wonder if his sisters might not have been *indulging* him. Indeed, perhaps they'd even been manipulating him!

A shocking thought.

Not only was Cecile self-sufficient, but she also wasn't a dawdler. When she said she was going to fetch her cloak, that's all she did—not change her gown, tidy her hair, or whatever it was his sisters did that took hours.

Instead, she came striding down the stairs only moments later.

"So, now that you've been back in France for a little over a week, how does it feel?" Guy asked as they set out at a decent clip. He didn't even need to shorten his stride because Cecile was a tall woman, easily five foot eight, and did not have a mincing step.

"It's ironic that I waited over twenty years to return, only for peace to unravel the very day I set foot on French soil."

"Yes," Guy said, in an exaggerated, musing tone. "I was wondering about that connection."

She laughed, the sound both pleasing and rare. She was, by and large, a serious woman who didn't spend lots of time chatting and socializing with her coworkers. Or at least she didn't with him.

Most of the other people who worked at Farnham's hung about together after their shows and rehearsals. But Cecile kept to herself.

Or who knew? Maybe she had a lover she went to see?

Guy found that he didn't care for *that* thought at all.

"I never thought I would come back here," she said.

Before he could ask why, she turned to him and said, "You think Napoleon's escape from Elba will lead to war?"

"I didn't at first," he admitted. "But the fact that he seems to be drawing soldiers to him like flies to honey makes me realize just how little we English understand this country."

"I'm not sure the French people understand it, themselves."

"You know," he said, "you don't need to wait for Barnabas to decide to go home before you do."

"I'm not so terrified yet. Besides, I can always blend in. What about you—and Sin? Aren't you worried about being caught and exposed for who you really are?"

"I notice you don't mention Smithy?"

"That man could probably blend in better than I could. His French is impeccable and he has a surprising ability to . . . disappear."

"Doesn't he, though? I asked him to teach me how to do it and he just laughed."

Cecile laughed, too.

"What?" he demanded.

"You would have as much luck blending in as a peacock."

He gave her a mock scandalized look.

"You know it is true," she continued, her eyes sparkling with humor.

As much as he would have liked to continue the discussion, they'd reached their destination.

"It's in here," Guy said, turning down a narrow alley. "I'll have to harness the horses."

"I'll help," she said, going immediately to the tack room without needing any instruction from him.

They harnessed the two teams in companionable silence. Once again, he couldn't help admitting that she was more efficient at the task than Guy, who'd always had servants to tend to such matters.

Thanks to Cecile, they were soon rumbling toward a livery that belonged to yet another of the innkeeper's relatives.

While Guy made arrangements with the ostler, Cecile climbed into the caravan to look for whatever it was that she wanted.

A few moments later he poked his head into the glossy red caravan the women shared.

He gave a low whistle. "Very nice! I'd not seen inside here before," he said, running a hand down the highly polished wainscoting beside the door.

"Yours looks much newer than this one," she said in a muffled voice as she dug through something at the other end of the caravan.

"Ours is newer but it's mostly unfinished inside and rather basic. But then, we're mere servants, so that's more than we deserve."

She gave one of the throaty chuckles that went straight to his groin.

"It's good that you've begun to accept your place in life."

Guy snorted.

"Drat," she muttered, yanking on something.

"What is it?" he asked.

"The handle is stuck beneath Blade's trunk."

"Here, let me help, since brawn is about all I have to offer."

"Poor Lord Carlisle—is it wearing on you to work for your crust and take orders from women?" She turned to him, her flashing eyes just a few inches below his.

Guy hovered above her, captivated by her dark brown gaze; he'd never seen irises so dark before. They were almost as black as the pupils they surrounded, and he kept feeling an impulse to lean closer to see where the colors changed.

He was wise enough to quash that impulse as he suspected that she wouldn't appreciate it.

She cleared her throat and pointed to her valise. "The bag."

Guy wrenched his gaze away and then bent to tug the bag from beneath the trunk. He grimaced when it finally came free and he could lift it, his grunt only partly feigned. "What did you put in here—bricks?"

"The severed heads of all the men who've displeased me."

He laughed. "I would think that would take a much bigger trunk."

"I can carry it if it's too heavy for you."

"No, no, you must allow me to do my job." He reached down to take the trunk by both handles, stood, and then took a step toward the door beyond her.

She didn't move to let him pass. Instead, she just stood there staring up at him with the most . . . *intense* look.

Guy cocked his head. "Is aught amiss?"

She muttered something beneath her breath, slid a cool, slightly rough palm around his jaw, stood on her toes, and captured his mouth with hers.

Chapter 9

Cecile! What are you doing?

The voice in her head was so loud that Cecile actually jolted.

"Mmm," the man beneath her murmured, bending just enough to let the trunk fall to the floor with a dull *thud* before sliding his hands around her waist.

Stop what you are doing this instant! You know what will happen if you continue this madness!

She did know, but she didn't care.

Instead, she pressed her torso against his and deepened the kiss. His mouth was hot and tasted slightly of brandy. Big hands gripped her bottom and pulled her against his hips, where an even bigger erection proclaimed his body's highly excited state.

Cecile groaned at the feel of him, shamelessly grinding against him. Why not? She'd already taken one reckless step, why not take another? And another. What was the point of pretending she didn't want him?

He stroked up her body slowly, caressing and exploring, until his fingers slid around her jaw, holding her head in a masterful way that caused her body to turn to water. Lord, but she'd dreamed about kissing his full, shapely lips; reality was far, far better than her dreams.

He knew what he was about, his hot tongue confident without being obnoxious, stroking into her in a way that lured her deeper.

Cecile was beginning to get light-headed, but was reluctant to come up for air, when Guy pulled back with a groan.

"I would ask why you've changed your mind now—after rejecting me for weeks—but I find that I don't care what your reasons are. I want you, Cecile," he murmured against her temple, his words yanking her from her erotic daze.

"I have waited this long because that is how long my good sense held out," she retorted. "But now, apparently, it has fled."

He grinned. "Cause for celebration."

"I have one rule—only one."

"Anything," he muttered, his hands spanning her waist and gently squeezing, his thumbs sliding down the front of her body, caressing up and down over the sensitive bones of her pelvis.

"It is over once we set foot on English soil again. Do you agree?"

"Mm-hmm," he hummed, trailing kisses down her temple and stopping near her earlobe, which he nibbled.

Cecile shoved him back so that his treacherous mouth was nowhere near her while they established their rules. "Repeat what I just said," she ordered.

His mouth curled up on one side, the smile so wicked her knees threatened to buckle. "It's over the minute we set foot in England."

His easy agreement left her momentarily nonplussed.

He caressed her jaw with his elegant fingers, his eyes smoldering and his normally pleasant expression nowhere to be seen. Instead, he looked like a predator who'd finally cornered his prey. "I want to take you right here," he muttered, his dark eyes flickering around the inside of the caravan, which was small and cramped and messy. "But if you desire a bit more ceremony for our first time, you should speak up. Now."

Cecile—who was more than ready to climb on top of him right there and then—didn't know whether to be pleased or insulted that he was in control of his passions enough to wait until they were in a more appropriate environment.

She opened her mouth to tell him to forget the whole thing, but he didn't give her the chance.

"Strike that," he muttered. "I've changed my mind. I don't want to wait." He pointed to the narrow built-in bench off to one side. "Get on the bed."

Cecile gave Guy one of her haughty, feline looks—the one that sent his blood boiling—and, for a moment, he thought she'd tell him to go to the devil. But then, amazingly . . . she obeyed his order.

And she took her time about it, too, turning her movements into a performance, stretching her long body out on the narrow bed and then propping her head on her hand and smoldering up at him from beneath her thick, black lashes. "Strip."

Guy's jaw dropped. "Excuse me?"

"You heard me."

"You just want me to—"

"Are you a virgin, *my lord*? Should I be moving more slowly?"

He couldn't believe it when his face heated. Damn this woman and her saucy mouth!

He adored her.

"Is that something you would like to do—pretend I'm a virgin you could deflower?" He opened his eyes wide and fluttered his eyelashes in an expression of innocent virtue. "Oh, Miss Tremblay, that's just not the sort of boy *I am*."

She laughed. "As intriguing as that game sounds, what I would like is to see you naked. Now."

"Yes, ma'am." He grinned and toed off his boots, his fingers fumbling as he unbuttoned his waistcoat. "Anything you say."

"Tell me why you, the duke, and your other friend—whoever he is—are on this journey."

His fingers froze. "Er . . . that isn't my story to tell. You might want to ask Marianne."

"I'm asking you."

He shook his head and gave her a look of genuine regret, dropping his hands to his sides. "I'm sorry, darling, but if what we are about to do is contingent on knowing that, then I'm afraid—"

"Did I say you could stop stripping?" she demanded. "Quit dragging your feet and get on with it."

He smirked and happily resumed his labor. "Yes, mistress."

Guy had stripped for women dozens of times but never had one looked at him as carnivorously as Cecile Tremblay.

"I have another question," she said.

"Hmm?"

"It's about what you said the other night—about your impending marriage."

Guy groaned and his hands froze. "Lord. Now there is a question devised to kill a man's ardor." He wasn't jesting. Marriage was a subject he liked to keep far from his thoughts at all times, but especially when he was taking off his clothing in front of a beautiful woman. "Do we have to talk about this right now, darling?"

"Yes, we do. And I never said you could stop undressing."

He laughed. "Are you always this bossy?" he asked, shrugging out of his waistcoat.

"Always."

"Fine. What is it that you *need* to know on the matter?"

"You said you will have to marry for money?"

"Yes."

"Does marrying for money naturally preclude love and affection?"

Guy pulled his shirt over his head and tossed it onto the growing pile of clothing, gratified to see that her eyes were fastened to his torso, her lips parted, and her throat slightly flushed.

He smirked at her reaction, enjoying it for a moment before she wrenched her gaze from his chest and met his eyes, her own narrowing.

"Yes, you are a fine physical specimen," she said. "No point in gloating about it."

"No point in *not* gloating either," he pointed out, amused by the way her gaze flickered to his shoulders when he shrugged.

"Answer my question."

"Oh. I was hoping you'd forgotten."

"Why is marriage so difficult to talk about?"

"Let's talk about you, Cecile—or do I need to call you Miss Tremblay even when I'm naked?"

"I don't know," she said. "Because you aren't naked yet. Keep going."

His hands dropped to the catches on his breeches. "Why aren't *you* married?"

"Why should I be?"

He blinked at the unexpected answer. "Er, I don't know—because women like to get married?"

"What a typically male response."

"I have five sisters, Miss Tremblay, three already married and two looking forward to it. Trust me, I know plenty about women and their attitude toward marriage."

"Has it ever occurred to you that women might not *want* to marry but are forced to do so?" Her eyes dropped to his breeches, where his fingers had, once again, paused. "Surely you can think and get undressed at the same time?"

He laughed, flicked open the catches, and then reached for the five buttons that held his fall closed, hissing softly when he grazed a hand over his erection.

"What do you mean *forced* to marry?" he asked through clenched teeth, less and less interested in their conversation.

"I mean a woman alone in England is vulnerable. She needs a man for almost everything. She has few legal rights over her person or—" Her eyes followed his hand as he unfastened first one and then the second button and the breeches slid lower on his hips.

She swallowed audibly as he flicked open the last three and allowed the breeches to slide to the floor, leaving him in only his smalls and stockings.

Guy settled a hand over the obscenely tented muslin of his drawers and squeezed his shaft lightly.

Cecile sat up on the bed. "Come here," she ordered, every bit as imperious as a queen.

Guy shuffled toward her, purposely leaving himself hobbled with his breeches, which of course made her chuckle. And God, did he love hearing her laugh.

"You fool," she chided, her body shaking with mirth. "Kick them off—and the drawers, as well—and come stand here."

Guy did as she bade him, sloughing off both drawers and stockings in one motion while he bent low, and then stood and stepped out of the bunched clothing.

She made a sharp hissing sound, her chest swelling as she filled her lungs, her black gaze fastened to his erect cock.

His penis—a shameless exhibitionist—jumped at the hungry look on her face and Guy hastened to obey and step closer, intensely aware of his state of undress and the fact that she was fully clothed.

How was it that he'd never noticed the power one's clothing afforded one? Possibly because he was usually on the other side of the equation—the one ordering the stripping.

Her throat flexed when she swallowed, and her eyes traveled slowly from his prick up to his abdomen, lingering on his chest for a long moment before meeting his gaze.

"I have to agree with you."

"What have I done to bring on such an unprecedented statement from you?" he teased, unable to resist sliding a hand around the soft curve of her jaw.

"I'm agreeing that you have plenty to gloat about."

"I'm glad that I please you, because you are the most fascinating woman I've ever met, Cecile."

Predictably, she scoffed. "Why? Because I resisted your advances for six entire weeks?"

"That's certainly part of it."

She made a disgusted huffing noise, and it was his turn to laugh.

"I'm sorry, darling—but it's the truth. I simply haven't encountered many women who haven't thrown themselves at my feet."

"Not that it has made you arrogant."

"Is it arrogant to admit the truth?"

She rolled her expressive eyes.

"Here is another truth, Cecile," he said, the smile sliding from his face as he traced the curve of her lower lip with his thumb.

"Oh—what is that?"

"There is more to my fascination than your elusiveness. You are simply *different* from anyone I've ever met. You are so utterly, intriguingly . . . self-contained. Do you need anyone for anything?" he asked, genuinely curious.

Her lips curved into a smile that was a little sad. "Of course, I need people—just like anyone else." Her eyes dropped to his bobbing cock, and she set her hands on his hips. "But if you mean do I need a man for a husband, then the answer is *no*." She leaned forward and flicked the tiny slit in his crown with the tip of her tongue.

"My. God." A shudder rocked Guy's body from his toes to the tips of his ears.

"But men are good for a few things," she went on, cutting him a wicked smile, while she stroked his hips and buttocks, kneading his flesh with strong fingers.

He made a low purring sound. "Lord, that feels divine."

"Yes, it does," she agreed, her breath hot on the head of his cock, which was brushing ever so lightly against her pillowy lower lip.

If she kept up this way, he'd go off like one of the fireworks at Vauxhall Gardens.

"I want to see your hair down," he said in an embarrassingly raspy voice.

"Then take it down."

His fingers fumbled with the myriad pins that held the heavy plait in place.

Her eyes met his as she took his thrusting cock into the hot velvet of her mouth.

Guy whimpered as she slid her hands between his spread thighs, cupping his heavy balls with an expert, confident touch.

"My God, Cecile," he muttered through clenched teeth as she sucked hard enough to hollow her cheeks. "Are you trying to make me shame myself, woman?"

Naturally, she laughed, the mocking sound vibrating tauntingly up his shaft.

As entertaining as it was to torment and wreck the Darling of the *Ton*, it was becoming increasingly difficult to keep her own passions in check.

Not only was Guy's face perfect, but his body was a work of art: Michelangelo's *David* had nothing on Lord Carlisle.

She was vacillating between climbing him like a tree or sucking him until he shattered and cried out her name, when he took the dilemma out of her hands—quite literally.

"Enough of that for the moment, sweetheart," he said, his jaws clenched as he gently slid his impressive erection from her mouth.

His eyes moved over her still-dressed person and a look of frustration flickered over his face. "I want to see your body so bloody badly, but I'm so damned hard for you, a breeze is probably enough to set me off, and I *really* don't wish to shame myself our first time out."

"We have until nine o'clock," she reminded him, amused and flattered by the raw need in his voice. "There will be time for more finesse . . . after."

"Right," he said, his perfect features turning hard and stern. "Lift your skirts."

When he spoke to her in that tone, with that look in his eyes, she couldn't think of a playful retort: She obeyed.

"Damnation," he muttered, his expression fierce as she raised the hem of her dress over her knees and thighs, not stopping until she exposed her sex.

Moving so quickly he was like a blur, he leaned over, slid his hands beneath her bottom, and lifted her with breathtaking ease.

Cecile held his neck with one hand and reached between their bodies with the other, positioning his thick shaft at her entrance. And then she held on to his shoulders and lowered herself slowly, taking him inside her inch by delicious inch.

"I think you're trying to kill me," he accused gruffly.

Cecile heaved a sigh of pure ecstasy and wiggled her hips slightly to take him that last bit deeper.

He groaned, giving her time to adjust to the exquisite stretch before he shifted her into a more comfortable position.

"Cecile," he whispered, her name sounding like a desperate prayer, and he claimed her mouth with a deep, penetrating kiss.

She met his tongue, thrust for thrust, exploring him with a hunger that stunned her.

It was Guy who pulled away first, their chests both heaving.

He stared deeply into her eyes, his brown irises sliver-thin coronas surrounding the velvety blackness of his pupils. "Please don't judge me by the next few minutes, darling."

Cecile couldn't help laughing at his plaintive tone.

She'd never had a playful lover before. It was rather lovely to laugh with a man when he was deep inside your body.

He flexed his hips, nudging something deep inside her—something that was almost painfully pleasurable—and she gasped, all her laughter gone in a heartbeat.

"Too much?" he asked, his voice strained.

She shook her head. "More."

Cecile was not a small woman and she'd never had a lover hold her in his arms without so much as her toes grazing the floor.

But Guy's powerful body undulated beneath her hands and tightly clenched thighs as he worked her in slow, unhurried thrusts, the only sign of any strain the sweat that beaded on his forehead.

She tilted her head back and closed her eyes, luxuriating in his measured stroking, the angle of his pelvis grinding against her sensitive flesh in a way she knew was not accidental. She was in a state of partial arousal just standing across from him, so it didn't take long for her climax to build, her pleasure escalating, but only to the edge, where he kept her erotically balanced, teasing her until she thought she'd go mad.

"Guy," she begged, rocking her hips to take him deeper—or trying to as he held her in a viselike grip.

He gave an evil chuckle. "Open your eyes and look at me, Cecile," he whispered, trailing light kisses over her lips. "And then maybe I'll give you what you need."

She forced her heavy lids up and glared into his smug, lust-flooded gaze.

"That's a good girl," he praised, his lips curving in the most infuriatingly erotic smile, his breathing raspy and harsh.

He began to pump his hips, giving her the deep, hard thrusts she'd been craving.

And then he stopped on an outstroke, leaving only his fat crown inside her. "Now beg me for what you want, darling."

Cecile wanted to hit him over the head with something heavy and blunt.

But she wanted to orgasm more.

She flexed her legs, squeezing his waist and digging her heels into him until he gave a grunt of pain.

But still he didn't move.

"*Please*," she ground out, not caring how wanton she sounded and no doubt looked.

Guy chuckled. "That's a good start—now tell me what you're begging for."

Something exploded in Cecile's head at his words—she heard an actual *pop* and *hiss*—and weeks and weeks of pent-up, frustrated yearning for the maddeningly irresistible man collided with overwhelming hunger.

She wouldn't have believed herself capable of the animalistic sound that tore from her tight throat. "Fuck me, you bastard."

And then she bit him.

"*Ow!*" Guy shouted, every muscle in his body tightening at the sudden, sharp pain in his chin.

She pulled away at his agonized, unmanly squawk, a wicked smirk on her lips—along with a smear of his blood.

The desire he'd been holding by a tenuous lead snapped at the glorious, savage sight of her.

Guy spun her away from the bench and slammed her up against the built-in cupboard on the opposite wall. The loud *crack* of wood splitting filled the caravan but was overwhelmed by their raw, primal grunting as he drove into her, giving her every inch, and giving it to her hard.

Her blunt fingernails dug into his back like ten tiny bullets. "Harder."

Somebody laughed insanely, and he thought it might be him.

Guy gave her the pounding she demanded, the muscles in his hips, thighs, and arse screaming as he plowed her.

Her climax, when it came, was almost enough to crush his cock and Guy lasted four more strokes before surrendering to his need, emptying himself deep inside her, his body spasming violently as he filled her time after time.

All the strength drained out of him, and his legs were like water as he staggered toward the front of the caravan, to the only actual bed, which was, predictably, mounded with garments.

Guy barely made it before his knees buckled and he dropped with a grunt, Cecile's legs still tightly twined around his body.

She gave a half whimper, half growl as she released him and rolled onto her back. Guy slumped down beside her, the two of them jammed tightly together on the narrow bed.

He must have dozed because when he opened his eyes again the light that slanted through the narrow window across from him was the watery gray-gold of twilight.

Guy turned his head to the side and encountered a pair of hooded brown eyes. He'd noticed—while he'd been hilt deep inside her—that he could finally see where black met the beautiful dark chocolate brown.

Her expression was, for once, slack and relaxed, the look of a well-fucked woman. His favorite expression on a woman, as a matter of fact. And it looked especially well on Cecile, who rarely appeared either relaxed *or* happy.

"What are you smirking about?" she asked.

"Am I?"

"You know you are."

He allowed his grin to grow larger. "That's because I'm perfectly, utterly content."

She snorted and turned to face the ceiling.

"What? Are you not content?"

"I'm an idiot."

He saw the corner of her mouth turn down and wanted to groan. He *hated* post-coital guilt above all things.

Guy took her chin in his hand and turned her to face him. "Please don't regret this, Cecile."

She rolled her eyes. "Don't worry, my lord. I'm not wallowing in guilt."

"But you regret it?"

She opened her mouth, met his gaze, and something in her eyes softened—not much, but it was something. "No."

He felt his lips curving and made no effort to stop his smile.

"Shut up," she said, her cheeks flushing at whatever she saw on his face.

He laughed.

Her eyes dropped to his chin, and she winced.

Guy reached up and felt where she'd bitten him. His slumbering prick stirred at the memory.

Her eyelids lowered and he saw the answering hunger in her gaze. Lord. How in the world had he got so damned lucky? A woman who looked like she did, *and* she didn't require delicate handling when it came to bed sport.

"Remember that it ends when we get home—whether that's next week or at the end of the tour, months from now. It ends."

"It ends when we get back home," he repeated.

"Good."

Guy carefully turned his body on the narrow bed and propped himself up on his elbow. She held his gaze with the steady, challenging look that was already becoming a necessity to him. Her skirt was rucked up to her knees and he used his free hand to pull it higher, exposing the dark curls of her sex.

She let her legs fall open as wide as the narrow bed allowed.

"Christ, Cecile. You *are* trying to kill me."

"Maybe."

He smirked, tickled by her wicked, sensual stare. "I can't think of a better way to die," he said, loving the startled snort of surprise that slipped from between her shocked lips and the way her body shook with laughter under his hand.

"I think I might take you with me," he muttered, and then pushed a finger between her swollen lips.

She stopped laughing and hissed when he stroked from her engorged clitoris to the entrance to her body.

"Mmm," he hummed, gently probing her while massaging her little bud with his thumb. "Too sore to take me again?"

She shook her head.

The gush of slickness he encountered when he shoved his two middle fingers into her tight sheath reminded him that he'd just spent inside her.

Guy paused. "What about—"

The sleepy, sensual expression that had begun to settle on her beautiful face fled and she stiffened like a board. "You don't need to worry about that—I'll make sure there are no reminders." Her sharp tone told him better than any words that there was no more to say on the topic.

Guy resumed his stroking, only relaxing when the tension drained from her limbs.

He should have felt relief that they'd had such an easy meeting of the minds. There'd be neither tears nor recriminations—nor any fear of unwanted children—when things ended between them.

Instead, Guy felt the oddest heaviness in his chest.

It was almost like regret.

Part III

The Present

Chapter 10

London
1816
One year later

Guy gawked at the man who had entered his study ten minutes ago and then immediately set about tearing down his entire world.

"This is most . . . unexpected," he finally managed to spit out.

The stranger chuckled merrily—as if he hadn't just destroyed another man's entire world using only a handful of words.

"*Unexpected*," his unwanted guest repeated. "I recall my father used to be a master of understatement, too. I didn't realize it was a national characteristic."

"I don't suppose you possess any documentation or proof of who you claim to be?" Guy asked, proud of himself for not yelling.

"I was wondering when we'd get to that, old man."

"Yes, well forgive me for not taking only—"

"No, no, not at all." He reached for the satchel he'd set beside his chair earlier.

Guy took the opportunity to study this—this usurper.

He was tall and broad and bore an uncanny resemblance to Guy himself. There was no denying they were related. But whether he was who he claimed to be—the son of Guy's long-lost uncle Henry, the man who would have inherited the dukedom before Guy—was another matter.

Guy thought it was entirely possible the other man had been born on the wrong side of the blanket—probable, even. After all, the Darlington men were well-known for sowing their seed far and wide.

Barrymore Darlington—or *Barry* as he'd introduced himself—stood and handed Guy a slim sheaf of papers. "Here you are."

It took Guy a shockingly brief amount of time to discern that his uncle had, indeed, married and produced a son. Said son was born on the island of Réunion, off the coast of Africa, in 1775.

He read through the marriage lines and certificate of birth a second, and then a third time, as if repeated perusal might alter the contents of the documents.

"And just who is this . . . Sarah Norton?" Guy finally asked.

Rather than appear offended, Barry looked tolerantly amused. It was an obnoxious expression and Guy wanted to punch it right off his smug, handsome face.

"I take it you are inquiring into my departed mother's lineage. She was the daughter of a sugar plantation owner—the biggest heiress on the island. So, you see, my father—blackguard and murderer—actually took a step up when he married dear mater. I never knew her as she died bringing me into the world, but she left my father a wealthy man and the means to become even wealthier." Barry pulled a face. "My father, being who and what he was, failed to seize the opportunity to change his ways. Instead of making a go of the plantation, he died when I was a mere sprig of fifteen, shot in a duel over a game of cards."

"Well, at least he was consistent," Guy said, and then immediately felt cruel.

But Barry merely laughed. "Indeed, he was. He was also a dreadful father, and I suspect he was a horrid husband. Not to mention a rotten cardplayer."

"And apparently a poor shot."

"Yes, that was his assessment, as well. He once told me that the man he'd shot and killed—the reason our grandfather banished him from Britain—actually died of a freak complication from a minor flesh wound in his elbow, of all places."

That was the story Guy had heard, as well.

He sat back in his chair—or Barry's chair, rather—and tried to absorb what all this meant.

But he must have been in shock because he couldn't make himself believe it.

"Why did you wait so long to come back to England?" he asked.

Barry shrugged. "As far as I knew, I'd be coming back to a host of relatives who despised me, so I was in no hurry."

"By that reasoning, why are you here *now*?"

"Pure happenstance, old boy. I was planning to make only a brief stop on my way to the Americas and—"

"I may not have been the best student of geography, *old boy*, but I'm pretty sure England is *not* on the way from east Africa to Boston."

Barry gave another of his smug chuckles, a sound Guy suspected he would come to hate in short order.

"I left Réunion ages ago—shortly after my father died."

"You didn't want to operate the plantation?"

"Oh, that was long gone. He'd frittered it all away, you see, and left me with nothing but debts. And so I made my way to Europe, inflated my age to eighteen, and joined on with the *régiment de Châteauvieux* when I was fifteen."

Guy's eyebrows shot up. He'd read about the Swiss mercenaries—who hadn't?—when they'd made the front pages of English newspapers for their volatile role in the early stages of the French Revolution, a role that had ended in many of them being court-martialed and then executed.

"Were you in—"

"Yes, I was in Nancy during the mutiny," Barry confirmed, his smarmy smile slipping briefly. "But I was not one of the mutineers, dear Cousin. In any case, I've spent the past two decades either chasing *after* Boney or running *from* him, so I decided when it was all over—for the *second* time, when he was safely on his way to St. Helena—that it was time for something new. I sold out and have been meandering my way west. When I got to Dover, I thought, why not stop awhile and take a gander at the family estate, see what I'd been cast out of." A grin spread slowly across his face. "And that's when I heard the happy news." He chuckled again. "Well, happy for me, not so happy for you, I suspect. But never fear, Cousin—I won't throw you out into the cold, cruel world."

Guy struggled with disbelief as he glanced around at his familiar library—no, *Barry's* library—searching for something—anything—that could wake him from this nightmare.

This simply could not be happening to him.

And yet . . .

The irony of the situation was not lost on him.

For years—ever since his oldest uncle had died, leaving Guy in line to inherit the dukedom—he had hated the responsibility that awaited him.

Last year, after his grandfather had succumbed to a severe influenza and Guy had found himself Duke of Fairhurst, he'd felt as if life as he knew it was over. His future had stretched before him as one distasteful duty linked to another.

And now that was no longer true.

Instead of feeling as if somebody had cracked open his chest and scooped out his organs, he should be embracing Barry and thanking him! Indeed, he should be chuckling and grinning like the annoying bastard sitting across from him.

And yet . . . he was *grieving.*

He glanced up and the gleeful, almost derisive look on the other man's face sent a spike of unease through him.

But then Guy blinked, and Barry was grinning again.

So maybe Guy had just imagined the expression?

"Look here, old man," Barry said, "I know you're worried that I'll step in and upend everything—your life, the life of your widowed mother, your unmarried and dependent sisters—"

Why did those words sound like such a threat?

"—but I promise you, Guy—I may call you Guy, mayn't I?"

"I believe you just did."

Barry chuckled. "You're a witty . . . Guy, aren't you?"

As if he'd not heard some variation of *that* tired jest several hundred times in his life.

"For your information, *Barry*, my mother has her jointure and a life estate in the Dower House at Darlington Park; she only lives at Fairhurst because I live here. You needn't be concerned that she will require your support.

"As for my sisters," Guy went on, speaking over the other man's demurrals, "they will live with my mother until they marry."

Which would likely be never once the *ton* discovered that Guy was no longer a duke betrothed to the second wealthiest heiress in England.

And his heiress—Miss Helena Carter—*would* jilt him, of that he was certain.

Not because Helena was cold or callous or because she *wanted* to jilt him. No, she would do so at the behest of her father. Because it was Mr. Carter—the man responsible for the hundreds of thousands of pounds his daughter would inherit—who'd been the force behind their betrothal. Mr. Carter wanted a *duke* for his daughter, not the impecunious cousin of a duke.

Barry gave that annoying chuckle again. "Don't be hasty, Cousin. There's no need for anyone to be moving anywhere."

Oh, yes there was; Guy feared he'd come to blows with Barry if he was forced to spend too much time in close proximity.

Barry waved an arm to encompass the room around them, or perhaps the house. "There's plenty of room for my tiny family in this huge pile." His smile grew larger. "Just me and my poor, motherless child rattling around in this enormous house like two little peas in a pod."

"Yes, your son." The man had mentioned having a child when he'd first arrived, but Guy had forgotten all about it while listening to the rest of his story. "How fortunate that you were able to have a family while you were so busy following the drum."

"Ah, well—never too busy for love," he said, his smirk grating more every second. "I met and married poor Jenny five years ago." He pulled a wry face. "I'm afraid she hadn't the lineage necessary for our grand family, but it is too late to do anything about that. She was the daughter of a captain in my regiment. It was love at first sight."

Somehow Guy doubted that. He'd known the man less than an hour and had already surmised that everything he did was done with one motivation: personal gain.

"Alas, poor Jenny caught a putrid fever when Alan was still at the tit—oh, I mean still an infant." He grimaced. "Lord, I suppose I'll have to watch that rough soldier talk now that I'm a . . ." He trailed off, as if he were afraid to say the word.

"How old is your son?" Guy asked.

"Not yet five."

Guy wondered if he'd married *poor Jenny* at the end of her father's saber. Not that it mattered. Barrymore was the duke and his son, no matter his age, was Marquess of Carlisle.

That meant Guy was, for the first time in years, plain Gaius Darlington. He'd been stripped of his home, responsibilities, and name in less than an hour. Quite remarkable, when one thought about it.

"—although I wonder if that will be possible."

Guy realized the man had been talking while he'd been gathering wool. "I beg your pardon?"

"I was talking about the dukedom's properties."

Guy's eyes narrowed. "What about them?"

"I understand they are in rather delicate condition."

"If by *delicate* you mean in need of money and repairs, then you are correct."

"Hmm." Barry sat back in his chair and laid an expensively booted foot over his knee. "Everything entailed, is it?"

"Yes."

Guy could practically hear the gears turning in the other man's head. Mainly because he'd had all the same thoughts himself in his quest to find a way to save the dukedom without whoring out the title—and himself—to the highest bidder.

Although he'd worked through the identical process that Barry was now feeling his way through, there was something viscerally repellent in this newcomer doing the same thing.

"You and the old man never considered trying to break entail?"

"No, we never discussed such a thing."

"But there *is* a way to do it," he persisted. "It's called common recovery, or some such?"

He met Barry's melting brown eyes—so much like his own, it was like looking in a mirror—and forced a smile. "I believe so," he said vaguely.

A small, vindictive spark of pleasure warmed him when he thought about how amusing it would be to watch the other man learn that the law of common recovery—the legal fiction aristocrats had used to break entail—would not work for the new duke. At least not until his son was of age.

Barry began talking about the logistics of moving his possessions and child from London, where they'd been lodging, to Fairhurst.

Guy stopped listening and stared sightlessly before him, his thoughts not on the arse sitting across from him, not even in this country.

Instead, he was back in France, lying in a cramped, uncomfortable bed with the first and only woman he'd ever fallen in love with.

He'd just enjoyed the most delicious sex in his life and had decided—in direct contravention of his agreement with Cecile—that he didn't want what they had to end when they returned to England.

Guy could clearly recall his thoughts that day as he'd looked at her sated face and sleepy eyes. He'd had the maddest urge to not get on the packet the following day. They could stay in war-torn France and keep running, and never, ever go home.

They could live like vagabonds, happy and free, just the two of them in their caravan.

Of course, he'd never made such a foolish suggestion.

But, in retrospect, it would have been better if he'd proffered that option, rather than the one he *had* ended up making to Cecile.

God. What a bloody mess he'd made of something beautiful.

And now, ironically, it seemed that he'd destroyed what they had for nothing.

Wasn't life grand?

★   ★   ★

Cecile was wading through the endless paperwork that went with managing a theatrical company when the door to her office swung open.

Before she could chide the intruder for not knocking, she saw it was Blade and her raven, Angus, holding a copy of the *Times*.

Blade was holding the newspaper—not Angus. Although the bird could do almost everything else, so Cecile wouldn't have been surprised if he read the newspaper, too.

The other woman's unusual colorless eyes dropped to the newspaper that lay on the desk in front of Cecile. "Oh, I see you've already read it." She turned to leave.

"Did you just come to say *that* and then leave?"

"Yes."

Cecile sputtered.

"Why, what else am I supposed to do?" Blade asked, looking genuinely perplexed.

"You are supposed to comfort me! That is what friends do."

"We're friends?"

Cecile could only laugh. "Sit down."

Blade shrugged and obeyed, tossing the newspaper onto the small end table before lowering herself into a chair.

Once she was seated, she reached up and scratched her raven's head in a habitual gesture. The big black bird ruffled his neck feathers to allow better access, making cat-like purring noises as she stroked him.

"What do you want me to do?" Blade asked.

"I want you to comfort me," she said, amused by Blade's blank expression. "Surely you've *heard* of the word? I'm not a native English speaker and even I know it."

"I don't have any experience in that area," she said, as if Cecile couldn't have guessed as much.

"It is time for you to learn new skills."

"I think you'd have better luck getting comfort from Angus."

The raven *quorked* softly at the sound of his name.

"Besides, why should you need comforting?" Blade asked. "I thought you were done with Guy after we returned from France last year. What do you care if he is betrothed or not?"

"*Pffft!* You English have all the passion of a biscuit. You should comfort me because our love affair has now entered the ranks of true tragedy."

"How is that?" Blade dropped her hand and Angus fluffed his feathers before settling them into a tight, glossy black shield. And then he tucked his huge head beneath his wing and went to sleep.

"Because it has transpired that Guy could have offered me an honorable arrangement, after all. But because he insulted me, we are forever separated instead."

Blade's smooth, pale brow furrowed. "That makes no sense. He's free to marry you now—if you want him, you can have him."

She spun a knife in lazy circles around and around her hand. Blade could not be still for more than a minute before a knife materialized in her hand.

Cecile clucked her tongue and shook her head. "Sometimes I wonder if you are truly a woman."

Blade snorted softly. "You're not the only one."

Cecile wanted to ask her what she meant by that, but she wanted to finish the point she was making first—if not for Blade, then for herself.

"Guy rejected and insulted me. I could never forgive him for choosing another."

"Not even if he groveled?"

Cecile frowned. "Grovel? I don't know that word."

"It means that he would do things to try to show he was sorry— he would, er, abase himself to you."

"Abase—yes, I know that word." Cecile perked up at that; she wouldn't mind some abasing where Guy was concerned.

She pondered the other woman's suggestion for a moment before shaking her head.

"Now that I think about it, I'm not sure there is enough groveling in the world to make up for what he did."

"But it would be amusing to watch him try, wouldn't it?"

The women shared a grin.

But Cecile sighed and shook her head. "No, it wouldn't be enough. I cannot forgive him."

"Doesn't it weigh with you that he only did what he did to save his family from ruin?"

"Of course, it matters! But it still makes no difference. Or, actually, it might even make it *more* tragic: He is being punished even though his motives were admirable."

"That makes no sense."

"*Love* makes no sense."

"You love him?"

Cecile opened her mouth to deny the ridiculous claim, but then paused. Had she loved him? She didn't think so. Not because he was unlovable—he was the most irresistible man she'd ever met—but because she'd been too wise to allow such a thing to happen.

But she had *liked* him far too much for comfort or sense.

"So, let me see if I understand you," Blade said. "You'll reject him because he once rejected you for honorable reasons." A second knife had appeared, and Blade twirled them in opposite directions. It made Cecile's eyes cross just to watch.

"No, I'll reject him because he did not choose *me*. Not that I will have an opportunity to do any rejecting," she pointed out.

Blade chuckled—true, it was closer to a quick snort—perhaps the first time Cecile had ever heard the other woman even come close to laughing. "You're right," she said dryly. "If that is female logic, then I'm not a woman."

She palmed both knives and tucked them into the reinforced sheaths that were hidden in the pockets of her skirts. When her hands came away, the knives were gone.

"Doesn't he ever hurt your shoulder?" Cecile asked, gesturing to Angus.

"Sometimes. But he's worth it." She stood and her bird woke from his brief nap. "In any case, I hope my visit has brought you some comfort."

"*Comfort,*" Angus echoed, sounding so much like his mistress it was eerie.

"Yes, I am immeasurably comforted. By the way, I need to find somebody to replace Gerry—do you think your Nigel would agree to work with me until I can find a replacement?"

Nigel was one of the stagehands who earned handsome wages by agreeing to allow Blade to hurl knives at his head.

"I'll ask him. I thought you were going to hire an apprentice?"

"I have potential candidates coming, starting on Monday."

Cecile was *not* looking forward to the process of interviewing her replacement. But if she was really going to have a business that supported her into her dotage, she needed to find an able assistant, sooner rather than later.

Chapter 11

"This is an irrevocable step, Guy. Are you sure?" Sin asked.

Guy met the other man's concerned gaze. "I know selling an estate that has been in the family for generations is irrevocable. But it is all I have to sell now that I, personally, am no longer of any value." He gave a bitter laugh. "I'm exhausted, Sin. I feel as if my entire life has gone toward fixing a mess that simply will not be fixed."

He gazed down at the glass of whiskey—his second since coming to Sin's house after signing the papers. "Selling Darlington Park is the only thing that will allow me to take care of both Claudia and Diana. I know a generous dowry won't ensure that they get decent husbands, but at least they won't have to settle. Besides, I think Claudia just wants to marry Donald Hemmings," he added.

Hemmings was a gentleman farmer of respectable means. Unfortunately, Guy's mother didn't think he was good enough for a duke's sister. She couldn't say that now.

"Hemmings is a good man," Sin murmured.

Because Sin's property ran with Darlington Park on the southwest side, they knew all the same people.

"As for Diana?" Guy went on. "Well, she told me yesterday that she never wants to get married. She says she wants to study rocks."

"Your little sister is a force of nature," Sin said.

"She is indeed," Guy agreed proudly. Diana was his favorite sibling, even though they were the farthest apart in years.

"This money will allow her to study rocks or any other damned things she wants," Guy said, and then threw back the rest of his drink and didn't protest when Sin stood and poured him another.

"If you had to sell to anyone, you made a good choice," Sin said, breaking the brittle tension that Guy knew was his fault. "Baron Westfield is a good man and will take care of Darlington Park."

Guy knew that. Westfield was one of the new crop of peers to come out of the War. Men who'd served their country with money and ingenuity and received a title—without any land to go with it—from Prinny as thanks.

"He is a good man," Guy agreed. "And he was very kind about the terms he offered."

Westfield had been embarrassingly kind. Guy had looked into the older man's face and known that he understood the pain of parting with the property.

"He offered to keep Diana's three hunters in the Darlington stables and encouraged the girls and my mother to make use of the library and anything else they wanted. He said he will not reside there full time—this is at least the fourth estate he's acquired in the past few years—and he told me that Mother should avail herself of the property as if it was still hers."

Guy's mother, he'd been ashamed to see, had treated the gregarious industrialist as if he were something she'd brought in on her shoe.

Westfield was a pleasant older man—a bachelor—and he'd clearly found Guy's mother's chilly behavior amusing. In fact, Guy suspected Westfield was rather taken with her.

He laughed at the thought of the rough-and-tumble ironmonger breaking through the foot-thick ice barrier his mother had always kept around herself. It didn't matter that her background was far closer to Westfield's than it had been to Guy's father. She was as starchy as any of the Almack's patronesses when it came to matters of lineage.

"The Dower House is a nice little property," Sin said, clearly trying to cheer him up.

"It is very pleasant," Guy agreed.

Especially since he'd poured so much of Darlington Park's precious revenue into it since his father's death. Even though his mother had lived with him at Fairhurst, Guy had known that one day, when he married, she'd need to move into the Dower House. She was simply too strong a personality to live in the same house with his wife.

If he'd married a woman with any will, they would have clashed. And if he'd married a sweet, gentle thing, his mother would have rolled over her like a mail coach.

Guy hadn't been well-enough acquainted with Miss Helena Carter to know if she'd been in the first or second category.

"So, what are you going to do, Guy?" Sin asked quietly.

He glanced up from his thoughts and met his friend's apprehensive look, suddenly feeling guilty for visiting with such depressing tidings.

"I will land on my feet, Sin—you know I always do. But enough about my issues—they are over now, and it is time to move past them. How are things with you and Marianne?"

Sin's stern features softened at the mention of his wife. "She is taking to her new life surprisingly well." He gave an almost shy smile. "Well, it's not so surprising given the fact she is a born fighter."

Guy chuckled at his friend's obvious pride. Who would have believed the serious, proper Duke of Staunton—the man everyone called Lord Flawless for both his appearance and impeccable behavior—would have fallen in love with a female pugilist? And then married her.

"Is she ready for the Season?" Guy asked, not wanting to think about how he might have been happily married to Cecile—had he been braver.

"She says she is—so does my aunt Julia. The two of them get on so well, I sometimes feel as if *I* am the one to have married into *their* family."

Guy could tell that thrilled his friend.

"You are going to Trentham's ball next week?" Guy asked.

The Countess of Trentham's ball was an annual event that signaled the beginning of the Season proper, although there had been 'lesser' functions for weeks. Invitations to the gala were highly prized. Guy had been shocked to discover he'd received one this year—addressed to Mr. Gaius Darlington, which meant Lady Trentham had *meant* to send it to him.

"Yes, that will be her first big function." Sin paused. "Are you—"

"No. I already sent my regrets."

"You know that most people don't think the less of you for what happened, Guy."

"That doesn't mean they won't stare at me like a novelty if I were foolish enough to show my face. Can you imagine the scene? Me appearing at the same ball where the current Duke of Fairhurst is dancing with his betrothed—my former fiancée?" He laughed. "No, I think it would be best to avoid that sort of farce."

"I do hope you'll make an exception for our first ball," Sin said. "Marianne and my aunt have been plotting and planning, and you should get your invitation soon. It would make both of us happy to see you."

"I wouldn't miss it for the world," Guy said, pleased when his little white lie made his friend smile.

"I think you might be surprised how many people are happy to see you for *you*—not because you are a figure of speculation. Who knows? It might be the beginning of a new life for you."

"No, your ball will be the only one I attend this year. But perhaps in a few years, once the dust has settled, I will accept an invitation or two."

Although by that time, Guy doubted he'd be receiving invitations.

No, by that time, he hoped to be so far beyond the pale that he'd receive the cut direct from just about everyone he knew, with the exception of Sin and Elliot.

★　★　★

"Are you ready, Miss Tremblay?"

"Yes, send the next person in." Cecile forced herself to smile at Richie, the young stagehand who was keeping an eye on the three dozen women who'd shown up today to interview for the position. It was only the third day of interviewing, and already she'd spoken to over forty applicants.

Some of the women might have done in a pinch, but nobody stood out.

Because her new employee wouldn't just train with pistols but would also serve as her new stage assistant, part of each interview was to hold a playing card while Cecile shot it out of the applicant's hand. At least a third of the women declined to participate and left at that point.

And of those who stayed, another three-quarters screamed even louder than Gerry.

She sighed, shuffled the papers on her makeshift desk—two saw-horses and a plank of wood—and looked up when the stage door opened.

Gaius Darlington, the Duke—no, just Gaius, now—stood in the doorway, filling it as if he were a second, more attractive door.

"Hello, darling," he said.

Guy might have lost a dukedom and been publicly jilted by the second richest woman in England, but he wore the same irresistible smile that charmed birds from the trees, and his whisky-colored eyes sparkled with good humor.

And sensuality.

Cecile scrambled to her feet as he sauntered toward her, his big body garbed in a criminally well-fitted black clawhammer coat and skintight fawn pantaloons whose fabric was stretched to within an inch of its life to cover his powerful thighs.

How dare he look like a god while she resembled a frazzled washerwoman with the sleeves of her old gray gown rolled up and her hair curling like corkscrews from humidity and exertion!

"What are *you* doing here?" she demanded.

His smile widened, the dimples in his cheeks sending twin flares of desire and annoyance through her body. "I've come to apply for the position."

"Very droll. What do you want, *Mr.* Darlington?"

"Ah, you've heard of my recent, er, demotion, then?"

"I should think all of Britain knows your business."

"Good, then you should know I am no longer a man of leisure. I require a job."

Cecile enjoyed a hearty belly laugh at that. And then she saw he was serious.

"Have your wits gone begging?"

"Not at all. You are hiring and I need a *position*."

She scowled at the slight emphasis he put on the word, even as her body responded in ways she couldn't control. Which only served to madden her even more.

"You can seek your *position* somewhere else, Mr. Darlington. This is a female circus, in case you hadn't noticed."

"I've been part of your act and Blade's in the past. Both of you employ male assistants because it's far better for ticket sales if you shoot at men."

He was right. It often increased the comedic factor in both their acts if a man was the one being shot at or dodging knives.

Cecile crossed her arms. "What are you really doing here, Guy?"

His smile slid away, leaving an uncharacteristically grim expression on his face. "I need help, Cecile." He raised his hands when she opened her mouth. "No. I don't want money or charity—I'm willing to work. I *need* to work—just for five-and-a-half months."

"What happens in five-and-a-half months?" Cecile asked.

Guy thought it was a good sign that she was asking questions rather than summoning burly stagehands to throw him out in the street.

"The only property that is still in my name will come out from under lease and I will have somewhere to live."

"I thought you sold Darlington Park."

Guy couldn't help laughing—both at her comment and the

bright flush that colored her cheeks. "Still reading those parts of the newspaper, I see."

Her mouth tightened.

"Yes, I sold Darlington Park. I'm talking about another property. This one is in Massachusetts."

Cecile stared at him as though he'd just said or done something foul and unpleasant.

"Lord, why do you look so horrified? It just America, not the moon."

"America, yes," she said, her voice strangely faint. "So, you are going to Massachusetts. Boston?"

Her question surprised him for some reason. "Er, no. The property is in the western half of the colony, er, I mean state."

"But there is nothing *in* the western half of the state."

"You sound almost as if you are speaking from exp—"

"I lived there—in Boston."

It was Guy's turn to gawk. "You lived in America?"

"Yes."

Judging by her expression, it hadn't been a happy experience.

Why was he so stunned that she'd lived there? It wasn't as if he actually knew much about her past—which was all thanks to the stupid vow they'd made never to share the details of their lives in case they became emotionally *entangled* during their brief affair.

"What sort of property is it?" she asked before he could formulate a smooth way to pry.

"It's a farm. It belonged to an uncle on my mother's side who died several years ago. He'd lived there for decades, even before the colonists broke away. It's been leased out since his death, but in six months it will be available. Until then, I need a job."

Why not tell her the real reason you want to work here?

Oh, and she'll be so thrilled and receptive to me declaring my undying love for her now that I've been cast aside by another woman, thrown out of my home, and left virtually penniless?

Guy grimaced. When stated so brutally, it seemed like a very poor idea.

No, what he *needed* to do was earn her respect, trust, and love, not stroll in here and tell her he loved her as if he were doing *her* a favor.

He was going to do it correctly this time. For the first time in his life.

Tell her about your idea—about how you can triple ticket sales . . .

No need to be hasty, he chided his imaginative inner voice. He'd save *that* suggestion until it looked as if he was losing the battle.

"Surely you can find a job that pays more than I do," she demanded.

Guy's head whipped up and he met her gaze, thrilled and encouraged by the question because he'd expected her to simply throw him out.

He suddenly felt lighter than he'd felt in ages—since that last morning in France when he'd made a muddle of his life.

Perhaps this wasn't so hopeless, after all?

This was hopeless.

Cecile couldn't believe she'd just asked him that question. The minimal pay was the least of the reasons he couldn't be working for her.

She opened her mouth to do what she should have already done—tell him *no* emphatically—but then he said, "I also need somewhere to live."

"What do you mean? Don't you live with Elliot? Has he thrown you out?"

"No, of course he hasn't. Sin and Elliot have offered me their places, but I don't want to be a burden on them."

"You'd rather be a burden on *me*."

He smiled, but it was strained. "You know I'll pull my own weight—and then some."

Cecile inhaled deeply and held her breath.

What he said was correct: He worked hard and didn't shirk or balk at doing nasty, dirty, or menial jobs—she'd had ample proof of that last year. He was strong, smart, and intuitive in a pinch—skills that made for a good all-around worker.

But he was also . . . *Guy*. Her ex-lover. A man who—if he'd not exactly broken her heart—at least left a few bruises and lacerations.

In fact, it hurt just looking at him. What would it be like if—

"I know you're still angry and hurt over—"

"Je ne suis pas blessée!" she snapped, and then scowled and re-peated herself in English. "I am *not* hurt!"

The slight, infuriating smile on his sinful lips told her that he knew she was lying.

He knew she always lapsed into her native tongue when she was emotional.

And nobody made her more emotional than Guy.

"If you're not angry . . . or hurt, then why not hire me? What difference could it make to you if you're not angry?" He smirked. "Or hurt."

"Quit saying that," she ordered.

"Unless you're lying about that—are you lying about that?"

She reined in her temper and forced herself to speak in a level, un-angry, un-hurt tone. "I wanted to hire an assistant to train. *You* may be a convenient beast of burden when it comes to mindless drudgery—"

He barked a laugh, his eyes shining with amusement.

Cecile scowled. Really, there was something wrong with a man who reveled in being insulted.

She gritted her teeth and continued. "But you are *not* a female and I remind you, yet again, this *is* a female circus."

He shrugged, momentarily distracting her with the sight of his muscular shoulders flexing and stretching the seams of his tightly fitted coat.

"If you hire me to do all your mindless drudgery, then your assistant can concentrate on learning the important duties—like shooting well enough not to injure anyone."

"I can't afford to hire *two* new employees."

"Jemmy is quittin' and movin' back 'ome at the end of this month, Miss Tremblay."

She whipped around to find Richie leaning against the door. "I thought you left!"

Which just went to show how much Guy had scrambled her wits already.

Richie straightened up and swallowed hard enough that she could hear his gulp.

"What are *you* doing in here?"

"Er—" His wide blue eyes slid beseechingly to Guy.

"You took money to allow him in here, didn't you?" Cecile accused, her eyes narrowing. "Perhaps I might have a job opening for a *stagehand*."

Richie's Adam's apple bobbed frantically. "I'm sorry, Miss T. I didn't—"

"He was just trying to be helpful."

Cecile whirled on Guy. "You have not even been here ten minutes and already you are subverting my authority."

"I didn't—"

"You think you can just waltz in here and charm my employees into disobeying me?"

"No, I wouldn't—"

"If you work for me, then you must take *my* orders. You must obey *me*." She wanted to scream when she realized what she'd just said.

A tiny smile curved his lips. "If I worked for you, I could do that." His eyelids drooped. "Obey you in every way."

The suggestive words and heated glance sent desire arrowing through her body.

Cecile could not believe this was happening.

Was it a dream? Was that where she was? In her bed, dreaming?

"Please," he said softly, no longer smirking or confident.

In fact, Cecile saw an expression on his face she'd never seen before: worry.

"I promise I will give you excellent value for money. I will work hard, and I will do *anything* you tell me to do."

Cecile latched on to that word. "Anything?"

Guy opened his mouth, closed it, visibly undergoing an internal struggle before he nodded and said, "Anything."

Cecile felt an unpleasant smile curve her lips. "I will want you to be onstage—every time I perform."

So much for holding that idea in reserve, Guy thought.

He opened his mouth to say he'd do whatever she wanted when the voice in his head stopped him.

Don't give in too easily or it will make her suspicious.

He grimaced and shuffled from one foot to the other, trying to look as if he wouldn't willingly get on stage every night—in front of men he'd gone to school with—stark naked and covered in marmalade, if that's what she wanted. "Er, you mean I have to be in your act all six nights? That seems a bit—"

She cocked an eyebrow.

"I suppose that sounds fair," Guy said, struggling to hide his elation.

"And Blade's routines, too."

That gave him a genuine moment's pause, although why he hadn't expected her demand, he didn't know.

She gave a wicked, throaty laugh. "To have the Darling of the *Ton* as the butt of our jests will sell tickets," she said, her eyes sparkling at the thought of all that money. "A great many tickets."

Guy knew that. He wasn't conceited—all right, so perhaps he was a *little* conceited—but his erstwhile contemporaries would flock to see him. They would find a morbid sort of glee in seeing him brought so low. It was a thought that had hovered at the back of his mind ever since he'd come up with this plan, but this was the first time he'd looked the idea square in the face.

All his mates from school, his relatives, men he liked, men he didn't like, men whose wives he'd cuckolded . . .

It would be excruciating.

"Yes," she said, her black gaze riveted to his face. "I see you understand what I meant."

"Oh God." Guy pinched the bridge of his nose as he realized what he'd committed himself to.

"Have you changed your—"

"No!" His head whipped up and he met her mocking smirk. "No, I have not changed my mind. I will be your assistant. I will clean chamber pots. I will do whatever you contrive." And he knew quite well just how much she could *contrive* when left to her own devices.

Her gaze was heavy and brooding, but guy knew that she would agree to it. Not just because she was a savvy woman of business, but because she was only human, and who *wouldn't* want to exact their pound of flesh after what he'd done to her?

"Very well, *Mister* Darlington. I will hire you—but on a trial basis. After thirty days, if you do not obey and give satisfaction, you will have to find another job. Understood?"

"Understood."

"You will earn the same money as Jemmy, but you are *not* to touch a hammer this time."

Jemmy was a junior carpenter, so it wasn't as insulting an offer as he'd expected.

As for the comment about the hammer? Well, he couldn't blame her for that. The last time he'd attempted to do some carpentry— when they'd been traveling through France—he'd accidentally nailed the corner of the main curtain to some stage light rigging and had almost set the entire theater on fire.

"You will work when Blade needs you and you will fetch and carry and assist the cleaners and do whatever else I can find for you."

"Yes, ma'am," he said, struggling to hide the joy inside him.

Had any man in history ever been this happy selling himself into indentured servitude?

She made an abrupt gesture to the stage door. "Now get out— I still have interviews. You can move your things into the smallest room at the back of the house—the one closest to the outhouse."

If she'd thought such information would dampen his spirits, she'd mistaken him.

"Right away. Thank you, ma'am."

"Don't make me sorry for this decision, Guy."

"You won't regret it. I promise, Cecile."

"You will call me *Miss* Tremblay," she retorted.

Oh, they were back to that, were they? He smiled in a way he hoped was humble. "Thank you, Miss Tremblay."

Cecile snorted and turned back to Richie, who was hovering nervously near the door.

She jabbed a finger at him. "You, I will talk to later about bringing him in here without telling me. For now, show the next applicant in."

As Guy strode through the familiar backstage area, he felt hopeful for the first time since the afternoon when Barry had barged into his life and turned it upside down.

While it was true that Cecile had hired him to make money and make him grovel rather than out of any real affection, at least he had a chance with her.

Out on the street he hailed one of the hackneys that always could be found in the environs of the Fayre.

"Thirteen Piccadilly Terrace," he told the driver, and then settled back onto the worn, cracked leather seat.

Guy glanced at his watch and saw he was running a little ahead of his schedule.

He'd asked both Sin and Elliot to meet him at his lodgings—well, his soon to be ex-lodgings—this afternoon. When he'd made the plans, he'd had no idea whether or not Cecile would hire him. He'd intended to tell the other men what his future held, regardless of which way things fell. If she'd not hired him, it was likely he would have been purchasing his passage to Boston this afternoon, rather than packing his things to move into Cecile's house.

Guy was so busy with his thoughts that he didn't notice when the hackney stopped outside the building that had been his home for almost seven years.

The porter opened the front door before he reached it. "Good afternoon Your—er, I mean Mr. Darlington."

Guy was used to that stuttering and stumbling when it came to his change in status.

"I'm expecting a guest in a few minutes—"

"The Duke of Staunton already arrived and your man, Chamberlain, let him in. Mr. Wingate just got home a few minutes ago."

Guy nodded his thanks.

Good, they were both already there. He could get it all over with at once.

When he thought about Chamberlain, he grimaced. The man would give him that *look* when Guy told him what was going to happen over the next six months.

Well, Chamberlain could take his *look* to visit his brother, a man who still worked as underbutler at Darlington Park. Guy wasn't so skint that he couldn't pay his servant, but he hardly needed the man at Cecile's house. Chamberlain could enjoy a protracted paid holiday and think about whether or not he would follow Guy to America at the end of six months.

Sin and Elliot were already comfortably settled in the book room by the time Guy had divested himself of his coat, hat, gloves, and stick.

"You're early," he said to Sin, nodding at Elliot, who was lifting up the brandy decanter.

"I can count the number of times I've come to visit you two on one hand," Sin said. "So, it seemed that this might be a momentous occasion and I should get here on time."

Guy turned to Elliot. "Have we really had him here so rarely?"

The shorter man nodded and handed Guy his drink. "I think we prefer Staunton's fine brandy and far more comfortable library to our humble offerings."

Guy laughed. "Elliot is right, Sin—you do have superior taste in spirits. But I wanted you to come here today because—well, it feels a bit like the end of an era."

"You're still determined to move out?" Sin asked.

"Yes."

"I don't know why you won't stay at Staunton House. There are so many bloody rooms, there might very well be families living there whom I've never seen."

Sin had extended this same offer repeatedly over the past weeks. While Guy appreciated the gesture, he could not, in good conscience, accept. Especially when Sin was a newlywed. Besides, one did *not* impose on one's wealthy friends if one wanted to continue being friends.

Elliot cut him a quick, sympathetic glance that said he understood Guy's reluctance to take advantage of their rich, generous friend.

Elliot had survived on the meager allowance of a younger son all the way through university. The moment he'd gotten out, he'd found himself a job. He would never sponge off a friend's generosity.

"I see you two exchanging glances," Sin said. "I can almost understand why you don't want to accept my offer of somewhere to stay while you find your feet, but I *cannot* comprehend why you refuse to take my advice and have this—this *interloper* investigated to verify the truth of his claims."

While Guy appreciated Sin's support, the other man's words left him more than a little exhausted.

"Barry is the heir, Sin. He had my uncle's papers, his signet, and he knew all sorts of details about our family and his father's history here."

"Papers can be stolen and those stories are things he might have heard anywhere." Sin turned to Elliot. "Tell him—this is your métier."

"What? Long-lost relatives?" Elliot asked with a humorous look, which he quickly masked when he saw how serious Sin was.

Elliot turned to Guy and made the offer he'd made six weeks ago, when Barry had first arrived. "Are you sure you don't want me to engage somebody to check into this for you?"

By *somebody* he meant one of his cronies from the Home Office.

"I'm sure."

"Lord, Guy! He could be anyone."

"Possibly, but have you seen the man, Sin?"

Sin nodded, his expression grudging. "Yes."

"And he looks a great deal like me, doesn't he?"

"There is a resemblance."

"A resemblance?" he repeated. "The man could be my twin." A fact which upset Guy more than he wanted to admit.

It had been unnerving to sit across from somebody who might have been his double, to watch the expressions flitting across Barry's face and know exactly what he was thinking.

Lord, he was an irritatingly smug-looking bastard! Guy couldn't believe that more people hadn't punched him in the face if his smirk was that annoying.

"I still think it is worth investigating," Sin said.

"I need to move on, Sin."

The other man held his gaze for a long moment and then sighed and nodded. "I can understand that."

It was surprising how much relief Guy felt at his friend's words. Some part of him had felt guilty for not wanting to fight harder to hang on to the title, and it shamed him that he was actually relieved to no longer have those burdens on his shoulders.

"In any case," Guy said, putting the issue of Barry behind him and moving toward a subject that was likely to rile his normally calm friend even more, "I've taken care of all I can over the past weeks. My mother is settled at the Dower House—comfortably, if not exactly happily. I've sold Darlington to a man who is already pouring money into the house itself as well as repairing the badly neglected tenant cottages; Claudia is betrothed to her farmer—in spite of my mother's objections—and happier than I've seen her in years; and Diana is tickled to be allowed to spend all her days with her rocks, not to mention having exacted my promise that she won't be forced into a Season if she doesn't wish to be."

Sin's eyebrows rose. "How did your mother respond to that?"

"She was most . . . unhappy."

That was an understatement; his mother had been livid, even going so far as to bring out the ever useful *just what would your grandfather think of this* cudgel and beat Guy over the head with it.

"But Diana's joy and relief more than made up for my mother's displeasure," Guy assured him.

Guy didn't tell the other men what Di had said to him after he'd assured her that she had a comfortable, if not wealthy, competence and her future was her own.

"I never wanted you to marry just so I could have frocks and go to stupid balls, Guy. Neither did Claudia. We couldn't say anything to you because—well, you were so *intent* on saving us all. But you are our brother, and we want you to be happy the same way you want us to be happy. You wouldn't be happy marrying some woman for her money, even though Helena seemed like a nice enough girl."

His sister's words had moved him more than he would have believed.

"Can you be happy, Guy?" she had asked. "I mean, without the dukedom and all that goes with it?"

"Of course, I'll be happy," he'd assured her, not wishing to talk about what he hoped for.

He hadn't told anyone what he was going to do.

Quit dragging your heels; this news will not get less shocking the longer you wait.

He looked from Sin to Elliot. "I just came from Newcastle Street."

Sin's pale green eyes went wide. "You went to the Fayre? But . . . why?"

Elliot just watched him, a strange, almost knowing expression on his face.

"Yes. I went there to ask for a job."

Sin goggled. "You can't be . . . you *are* serious, aren't you?"

It wasn't a question, but Guy nodded.

"Good Lord," Sin whispered. "What happened?"

"She hired me."

Sin sat back in his chair; his expression not dissimilar to that of a person watching a carriage collision.

Guy turned to Elliot. "Well?"

Even though he'd lived with Elliot for years, he could never read the man.

"I don't blame you," he said. "I'd go back to work there if I thought I could get away with it."

Sin made a disbelieving noise.

Elliot turned to him. "What? You didn't enjoy the time we spent with them?"

Sin opened his mouth . . . and then closed it, pressing his lips together.

"I thought so." Elliot turned to Guy. "You can keep an eye on Josephine while you're there."

Guy laughed. "Ah, so that's why you don't have a problem with my decision."

"No, I really do understand what you are going to try to do and I wish you good luck with it—with her," he added quietly, something like pity flickering across his face.

"I'm surprised you need me to watch Blade, er, Josephine. Haven't you been keeping an eye on her?" In France it had seemed as if Blade and Elliot had engaged in spying as some bizarre sort of courtship ritual.

"Well, yes, but I can't watch her all the time," Elliot admitted.

"My God! Do you mean you have somebody spying on her?"

Elliot merely shrugged.

"You two."

Guy and Elliot turned to Sin.

"What?" Guy demanded.

"Why can't either of you just come out and do things directly? If you want Cecile, which I'm assuming is your motivation, why not beg her to forgive you and ask her to marry you?" Before Guy could answer, he turned to Elliot. "As for you. Just what went on between you and Blade last year? I've never asked because I've tried to respect your privacy, but you know everything the four of *us* were doing, so—"

"Not everything," Guy interjected quietly.

Sin gave a soft laugh of surprise before turning back to Elliot. "Very well, so perhaps you don't know everything that we got up to. But can't you tell us if you are serious about this woman? We're your friends, after all."

Elliot hesitated so long, Guy thought he wasn't going to answer.

But then he said, "Unfortunately—unlike you and Marianne and Guy and Cecile—there isn't much to tell." Elliot smiled faintly. "At least not what I think you're hinting at."

Sin's cheeks flushed. "I didn't mean to pry or ask about personal matters like—"

"I did," Guy said.

Elliot laughed softly. "Suffice it to say there is no future for the two of us. At least not together."

Guy and Sin looked at each other, their brows furrowed.

"Josephine is still very much a mystery to me," Elliot said.

"You love a mystery," Guy pointed out.

"Sometimes that is true," he murmured, suddenly looking uncomfortable with the turn in the conversation.

"Well, back to me," Guy said, earning a quick, grateful look from his more reserved friend. "Working for Cecile won't be like it was the last time."

"What do you mean?" Sin asked.

"I mean there won't be any anonymity. The reason she agreed to hire me is because she knows I will send ticket sales soaring by assisting both her and Blade in their routines."

"I can already imagine the satirical cartoons in Humphrey's windows," Elliot said.

So could Guy. He could only be grateful that his mother wasn't coming to London any time soon.

"To what end are you doing this?" Sin asked.

"I want Cecile to forgive me and take me back." Guy could not ignore the disbelief he saw on both his friends' faces. He sighed. "I know you're both thinking that she is *still* furious with me and will probably never forgive me."

"Er, I'm not sure furious is the right word," Elliot said.

"I'm not speaking out of turn by relating what Marianne has said on the subject," Sin said. "Cecile never ceased being angry at you because reading about you with a multitude of females week in and week out for the past year kept her anger fueled and stoked."

Guy grimaced. "Yes, well, there isn't anything I can do about all that, is there? I already know how angry she is. Trust me—that was evident today."

"You know she never opened your letters."

He was referring to the half dozen letters Guy had sent last year trying to apologize for what he'd done—for the way he'd gone back on his word—as well as several other matters.

"I didn't know that she never opened them, but it doesn't surprise me. I expected her to just throw them away."

"She did."

Guy frowned. "How do *you* know that?"

Elliot shrugged.

"Lord, if you're snooping around and prying into things you shouldn't, you need to stop now, Elliot. You're risking life and limb spying now that Cecile owns the Fayre. She keeps a loaded pistol beside her bed, you know."

Elliot merely smiled.

"I know you don't need me to tell you this," Sin said, "but if you do this—"

"If I get up on stage in front of all and sundry, I shall put myself beyond the pale," Guy said. *Far* beyond the pale.

Both Sin and Elliot nodded.

"I no longer care. As for my family . . . well, they are all taken care of in every way that matters. They will doubtless experience embarrassment at their association with me, but that cannot be helped at this point."

Sin hesitated a moment before saying, "Have you asked Elliot about finding you work?"

"Can you imagine me doing what Elliot does?"

Even Sin—ever serious—smiled at that. "Well, not precisely. But he does have numerous connections. There are all sorts of government jobs, Guy." He turned to Elliot. "Tell him—tell him you can find something suitable that won't be nearly so . . . drastic."

"I've already made these same suggestions," Elliot said. "But Guy is adamant."

Sin gave a frustrated *tsk*. "To what purpose, Guy?"

"If she won't have me, I'm leaving Britain," Guy said.

"*What?* To go where?" Sin demanded.

"You recall my mother's brother—my uncle Phillip?"

"The one who had the cranberry bog in America?"

"Yes, cranberries among other crops."

Sin was already shaking his head. "Surely you're not—"

"After I work in a circus, nobody here will want anything to do with me, Sin. You know that."

Sin opened his mouth, closed it, and then made an expressive growling noise. "Why are you doing this? You don't have to work for her, Guy. You could ask her to marry you—grovel, do whatever is necessary. But why, in the name of God, do you need to get up on stage in front of everyone we know?"

"First off, I *want* to work with her." He snorted. "Well, *for* her if you hear her tell it. Second, I want her to know I'm not ashamed of her and what she does to earn her crust, Sin. Because that was how I treated her last year."

Sin hadn't been there that last morning and heard what Guy had said to Cecile. His words came back to haunt him over and over again. They still made him cringe.

"As for going to America. Well, I won't want to stay in England if she won't have me. Not to mention there is nothing else for me here. And don't say my sisters or mother. Soon Claudia will be happily married to her farmer and if Diana wants to join me in Massachusetts, I will gladly take her. Besides, it is not as if I am leaving to live in a tent, Sin. The farmhouse is said to be quite nice and there are six thousand acres. I've read the quarterly reports for years and know there is great potential there."

"If the farm is so successful, then you could sell it and buy something here."

"I don't want to sell it and live here. And even if I did, a farm in the wilds of Western Massachusetts would never fetch enough money to buy much more than a cottage and garden plot here and you know that. Trust me, if selling the place would have made any difference, I should have done it to save Darlington. But the property is worth more for what it can produce than what it would fetch in a sale."

Sin heaved a sigh, looking profoundly unhappy. "You are my best friend—closer to me than even my brothers were. I don't want you to move halfway round the world."

Guy was touched by the other man's unprecedented show of affection. Sin was often a hard man to read, though Guy had always known that his friend loved him.

He forced a grin. "I will come back in a few years a wealthy man. People will call me the Cranberry King and *ton* hostesses will fall over themselves to fling their daughters at me."

"So you're assuming she will say *no* and you'll go there by yourself, then?"

Guy shoved a hand through his hair. "God, I don't know, Sin. She's very angry with me—very. The only reason she's giving me this job is to humiliate me. And to make me grovel. Well, and because she will make a good deal of money. If she ever cared for me, I shall need to work damned hard to remind her of it."

A long, uncomfortable silence inserted itself.

Elliot cleared his throat. "So, she hired you. Congratulations— you weren't expecting that, even," he said, his smile somewhat forced.

"Yes, she hired me."

Guy didn't bother telling his friends that it had been a bloody uncomfortable meeting today. They all knew Cecile well enough; they could guess how things had gone.

It had physically hurt to be in the same room with her and not touch her. God, she was a beauty! Even more than her body and face, her fire drew him, although he knew better than most how dangerous it could be to give in to her seductive lure.

Guy had fallen in love with her hard and fast, like a tree felled by a fierce storm.

That was Cecile—a storm in female form.

Had she loved him or even cared for him? He could never be sure. Hell, he'd not fully understood just how deep his own feelings were until after she was gone.

Cecile was a mystery to him. She kept the greater part of herself hidden away, not just from him, but from everyone in her life. They'd spent entire days together last year, but there'd been an unspoken agreement never to open up to each other on personal matters—that had been true on both their parts—and so he knew little about her.

Other than that she was the most mesmerizing, sensual woman he'd ever met.

Deep down he knew it was probable she'd never forgive him for what he'd done. Guy didn't blame her. Whatever she'd felt for him, his actions would have destroyed not only any finer feelings, but also her not inconsiderable pride.

If he could change one thing in his life it would be to go back to the moment he'd offered her his carte blanche. The words hadn't even been out of his mouth before he'd regretted them.

And he could never, ever take them back or make her forget.

He couldn't have offered her marriage at the time—not the way things had stood—but he shouldn't have insulted her with anything less.

"So," Elliot said, once again breaking the awkward silence that had pervaded the room while Guy wallowed in his misery. "When do you start your new job?"

"I was going to move my things in tonight."

They both looked nonplussed but nodded.

"You'll need to have dinner," Sin said. "Why not come dine with us at the club before you begin your packing?"

"I gave up my membership just a few days ago," Guy said. It was an expense he could ill afford. And now that he'd be working for Cecile, he wouldn't want to go there.

"You can dine there as our guest," Sin said.

Guy wanted to say *no*. He wanted to just leave his old, painful life behind and start his new—probably equally painful—life. But these two men were his best friends—the brothers he'd never had—and from now on, he'd rarely see them. Especially if he moved half a world away.

Guy forced a smile. "Dinner sounds grand."

Chapter 12

"I cannot believe you hired him!" Blade laughed so hard that tears ran down her cheeks.

And Cecile could not believe that she had once thought it would be nice to hear the serious, almost grim-faced woman laugh.

It was bad enough being laughed at by her employee, but Blade's beast, Angus, was chuckling right along with her.

Cecile was being mocked by a bird, and the sad part was that she deserved both their mockery. What had she been *thinking* to allow Guy not only into her life, but into her business and even her home?

She was an idiot, and a coward, too, because she was hiding in her office rather than going home—afraid to encounter her newest tenant.

It had been Blade who'd informed her—with eyes as big and round as an owl's—that she'd just encountered Guy in the book room all Cecile's tenants and employees were free to use.

When Cecile had confessed that she'd hired him, Blade had begun to laugh. And laugh.

"Are you finished?" Cecile asked icily, when it seemed Blade might be winding down, although Angus was laughing just as hard as ever.

Blade clamped her mouth shut and reached up to scratch Angus's belly, an action that shut the bird up, too—or at least replaced his chuckling with the far less grating *quorking* sound he made when he was content.

"I'm sorry," Blade said, looking and sounding very *un*-sorry as she wiped the tears from her cheeks. "I shouldn't laugh; it's just—"

"Just?" Cecile prodded against her better judgment.

"I've always admired your resolve and strength," the younger woman admitted.

"Well, now you know I am as weak-willed as any other female when faced with a handsome man," she retorted.

"It makes you more human."

"I've not noticed you giving in to such *humanity*."

Blade only grunted at that, the last of the good humor draining from her face.

Cecile knew that Blade had spent days and weeks in France with Elliot Wingate, but she wasn't sure what had transpired between her employee and the mysterious spy. They could have been lovers; they could have been enemies. They might be both. The one thing she knew for certain about them was that Blade would never share her feelings for the man.

Cecile made a mental note to ask Marianne if she could winkle anything from her husband about Elliot and his feelings for Blade.

She grimaced. Of course, the next time she saw Marianne—at their weekly tea on Tuesday—she'd probably be far too busy explaining her recent madness to her friend to do much prying.

Cecile shoved that unappealing thought from her mind and turned back to Blade, who was watching her with quiet speculation.

"I'm sorry to disappoint you, my dear Josephine, but I've made the offer and can hardly go back on my word now." At least not without looking like a fool. Cecile pointed at Blade. "But the first time he refuses to obey me I will cast him out like a dirty rag."

Blade nodded, but Cecile could see the other woman didn't believe her threat. Cecile couldn't blame her; she didn't believe it, either.

Well, that was fine—the only person who needed to believe it was Guy, and she would make *certain* he did.

"I want you to use Guy in all your shows. Don't worry, I'll pay him," Cecile added, earning raised eyebrows from the other woman. Generally, the acts she employed paid for their own assistants, but the more she put Guy on stage, the more money she'd make.

And she refused to feel guilty for that, either.

Cecile studied the extensive scheduling calendar she kept tacked to the wall in front of her desk.

"Guy can also fill in as knee man for Lucy and Nora," she said, more to herself than Blade.

Lucy and Nora were the Fayre's two female pugilists—the most lucrative acts after Cecile and Blade.

She also had a magician, some tumblers, and a theatrical troupe, but they took care of their own assistants as they were often highly skilled.

Cecile smirked at the thought; Guy was highly skilled, but not in a way that would earn money on stage.

Stop thinking about those skills! she ordered herself.

"That still leaves him with plenty of time," she mused, brushing her chin with the quill as she studied the long list of tasks that always needed doing.

And then grinning when she spotted one particularly unpleasant job. "He can take over the laundry, too."

Blade barked a laugh. "Basil will appreciate that."

Nobody liked hauling the laundry. It was heavy, dirty, thankless work. And at the end of toting bag after bag of dirty linen, the person had to deal with Ginny Bascom, their laundry woman.

Ginny made Vlad the Impaler seem like a Sunday school teacher by comparison. She held anyone who delivered laundry personally accountable for all the stains on the garments she washed. She especially disliked men, and her harsh haranguing was enough to send even the stoutest of them running scared.

Cecile watched absently as Angus sidled up to Blade's neck and made a purring sound, nuzzling his head against her jaw.

"That bird has an unnatural attachment to you."

Blade ignored her criticism, her gaze on nothing in particular as she spun a knife.

Cecile had never seen the woman angry, upset, scared, or sad, and no insult seemed sharp enough to pierce her aura of impenetrability.

Angus, on the other hand, gave Cecile a hostile glare from his glossy black eyes and made an aggressive snapping sound with his giant beak. The raven protected his mistress and loved her.

Maybe Blade had the right idea when it came to keeping other people out of her life and just sticking with her bird—after all, it was difficult to see Angus discarding Blade so he could marry a wealthy raven.

Cecile dropped her head in her hands and squeezed her eyes shut.

Good Lord, she was envious of a bird's affection. Clearly Guy's influence was already scrambling her wits.

As Guy stood surrounded by a few hundred or so of his erstwhile good chums and mates—all shouting, stamping their feet, and guffawing loudly—he struggled to remind himself why he'd signed up for this especially agonizing brand of humiliation.

You did it to get close to Cecile, and you are now close to her—living in her house, right down the corridor from her, in point of fact.

Fine, fine. That was true. But was anything worth this humiliation?

Blade bowed to the wildly clapping audience and then strode toward Guy, the black leather breeches, black tailcoat, and top boots she wore provocative enough to draw even Guy's gaze.

Jo Brown was an attractive woman—her body slender but shapely—but she was far too strange for him to feel any attraction to her.

And after what she'd done in France last year—essentially rescuing the rest of them single-handedly—he held a great deal of respect, and no small amount of awe, for her.

But that didn't mean he wanted to get to know her.

No, he'd leave that to his friend Elliot, whom Guy would swear was in love with the woman. Not that you'd ever have known it from Elliot's cagey behavior.

"You'd better smile or Cecile will have your head," Blade hissed through her teeth as she plucked several razor-sharp knives from the thick wooden board behind Guy's head, juggled them in a showy fashion that garnered hoots from the audience, and then tucked them into the tightly fitted vest beneath her tailcoat.

The first time Guy had seen her do that, he'd been shocked by the seemingly dangerous gesture. But then he'd learned there were bone-lined pockets all over her costume, even in the bodice, so she'd not cut herself. Well, unless she missed the pockets entirely. And Blade *never* missed anything she was aiming for.

"*Smile*," Angus echoed, bobbing up and down on Guy's shoulder before nipping his ear.

"Dammit!" Guy yelped, his startled cry driving the crowd of drunken aristocrats to almost hysterical levels of mirth.

Guy forced a smile that was probably more like a death rictus and glared at the part of the theater that was too high and too dark to see clearly—the part of the house that theatrical folk called the gods. He bloody well wished he were up there. Even the gods had sold out now that word had got out that the former Duke of Fairhurst was working in a female circus.

To be honest, he was more than a little appalled by how much of an attraction he was.

When he'd taken the job, he'd been thinking of how things had been when the Fayre toured France last year.

But Guy hadn't grown up in France.

And Guy didn't know every member of the French aristocracy and wasn't related to at least half of them.

In France, Guy hadn't stood in front of enemies and *former* friends and earned his living being shot at, tormented by a raven, and nearly stabbed in the forehead.

That part about the stabbing was actually unfair. The only good thing about the wretched job was knowing both Blade and Cecile were among the most skilled people—male or female—in the entire country in their respective specialties.

He didn't really mind the bullets and blades whizzing past his head, but he'd forgotten about the little flourishes both women had worked into their routines; flourishes calculated to get laughs from their audience, usually at the expense of their assistant.

Guy was getting laughs, all right. He was bringing down the bloody house.

"Ticket sales are up by eighteen percent already," Cecile had told him after his first week on the job. "It is possible that you might actually earn your keep."

Instead of being mortified that he was generating profits by serving as the butt of *ton* jokes, he'd actually been proud to know he was financially viable.

He needed to get his bloody head examined.

"Perhaps we should add your name to the marquee?" Cecile had mused. "Are there legal repercussions if I mention the *former* Duke of Fairhurst is appearing live and in person?"

When his jaw had dropped in horror, she'd merely laughed at him.

"Don't worry, I am only jesting with you. For now, at least."

Thankfully, Blade was moving toward the last portion of her routine.

Guy sighed through his smile, tolerated Angus plucking a prop purse from his coat pocket and then pecking Guy in the arse when he bent over to retrieve it, took his bows—three curtain calls tonight—and then breathed a sigh of relief when it was all over—until tomorrow night.

That relief lasted all of thirty seconds after escaping from the stage into the dressing room, where he was scraping off the face paint Cecile—oh, beg your pardon, *Miss Tremblay*—made him wear whenever he went on stage, when he heard the woman herself shouting his name.

"Guy! Guy! Come out here at once!" Her voice easily penetrated the flimsy dressing-room door. As always, he couldn't help smirking at the way she pronounced his name in the French fashion, which sounded like *Ghee*.

But his amusement was short-lived when he stepped out of the dressing room to find her glaring at him.

"You bellowed, Mistress Tremblay?"

Her eyes narrowed dangerously at his mocking words and tone. Guy couldn't help allowing his gaze to travel the exotic scenery that was her magnificent body. She'd been the first act tonight but was also the mistress of ceremonies between the routines, so she still wore her costume, a wicked black satin gown that was so scrumptiously tight and cut so deliciously low it grazed her nipples. And she had lovely nipples. Guy knew that from firsthand—and mouth—experience. Thoughts of her body—naked and sweaty beneath his—woke him up nights with agonizing frequency.

"Dogs have pulled over the rubbish bin in the alley again. I thought you put bricks in it to keep it from tipping?"

"I did."

"Well, put more!" she shouted, and then spun on one slippered foot and sashayed away.

Guy took a moment to enjoy the sight of her lush bottom swaying from side to side, until she disappeared from view. The roar of the all-male audience was deafening as she strode on stage to announce the final act of the night, which was Nora, one of the pugs.

Guy couldn't blame the men for making fools of themselves over Cecile—he was doing it himself, wasn't he?

He quickly stripped off his costume and dressed in the rough work clothing that he wore to carry out the endless menial tasks Cecile had found for him to do these past two weeks.

Out in the alley, Guy groaned when he saw the rubbish strewn all over, the bin on its side.

"Goddammit," he muttered. How in the world had dogs managed to—

Out of the corner of his eye he saw something move, and Guy's head whipped around.

Yes, there was a dog, all right, but there was also a grimy little urchin digging through the various bits of rubbish, making an even larger mess.

"Oi!" Guy barked, striding toward the child—male or female, he couldn't tell—and then stopping when the medium-sized cur beside the miniature vandal bared sizeable fangs and rumbled threateningly.

"You'd better stay back. He'll bite you," the urchin said mildly, the high voice either that of a female or a younger male.

"Are you the one who has been pushing this over every night?"

The urchin ignored him and continued sorting through the rubbish.

"What the devil are you searching for?" he demanded.

The child glared up at him and spat one word: *"Food."*

Guy felt like an idiot at her answer. He knew the streets were full of hungry children, but this was the first time he'd ever actually spoken to one. He'd always had servants to carry on such conversations for him in the past.

You are *the servant, now, my dear Gaius,* his mental voice noted, sounding disturbingly like Cecile.

He decided that he'd worry about that frightening new development later.

"There won't be much in there," Guy said rather lamely.

"I know." The words dripped with disgust, as if Cecile's business and household were criminally negligent because they didn't waste food.

Guy sighed. He was tired, humiliated, and ready to have a few pints and then fall into his narrow, hard, pallet-like bed in his monastic cell of a room and forget what his life had been reduced to.

He shoved a hand in his pocket and pulled out a few coppers. "Here. Take this and buy yourself some food."

The child's head whipped up, and so did the dog's, suspicion gleaming in both pairs of eyes.

"Look, you needn't come near. I'll toss it over there." He motioned to the far wall and then gently threw the coins.

He'd not even finished the sentence before both the child and dog moved like a blur, the urchin quickly discovering the coins in the near darkness.

Guy got to work putting the bin upright and collecting the contents.

When a piece of rubbish that he'd not thrown landed in the bin, he turned to find the child helping.

"I'm not going to pay you again," he warned.

"Didn't ask you to, did I?" the feral-looking little beast snarled.

"Are you a boy or a girl?" Guy asked.

"What're you?"

The sharp retort startled a bark of laughter out of him. "I'm a *boy*. Now, what about you?"

"Tisn't any business of yours!"

Well, that was true enough.

Guy shrugged and turned back to his work.

There hadn't been much in the bin to begin with, and none of it was especially disgusting, so the area was soon tidy. He'd find more bricks tomorrow to weigh down the bottom. But right now, he was knackered.

He pounded on the door and waited for somebody to open it and let him back inside.

Child and dog stood and watched him.

"You should get home—it's past midnight."

"Don't have a home."

The door opened and Richie poked his head out. "Oh, it's you, Your Grace."

Guy just rolled his eyes. "Just *Guy* is fine, Richie," he reminded the lad for at least the dozenth time.

The employees of Farnham's Fantastical Female Fayre thought Guy's life was a source of constant amusement and called him anything from Your Grace to Your Highness to whatever else suited their fancy.

Well, who was he to chouse them out of a free laugh?

Richie's eyes slid to the urchin and dog and they narrowed.

"You again! What'd I say the last time you came lurkin' about? I'll set the Watch on you!"

"Kiss my arse!" the child shouted.

The dog barked, as if to second that suggestion.

Guy choked on a laugh and seized Richie's collar when the lad lunged toward the filthy duo as if he might thrash one or both of them.

"It's fine, Richie. Leave them be."

"But Miss Tremblay says not to—"

"I'll handle her," Guy said with more conviction than he felt.

To his credit, Ritchie snorted at that. "Oh, *aye,* Yer Grace. It's yer 'ead on the block."

Indeed, it was.

Cecile was making her final walk-through before locking the theater for the night when she heard voices.

Her skin prickled, goose bumps forming up and down her body, and she froze and listened until she could isolate the sound; it was coming from the cupboard where the laundry was stored while awaiting a trip to the washerwoman.

Cecile swallowed down a lump of fear and snatched up a push broom that some lazy employee had left leaning against a wall rather than returning it to the broom closet.

She stared at the cupboard door and hesitated.

Perhaps she should go and get help?

Although most of the crew had gone to a late supper at a restaurant that catered to theatrical people, she knew Guy had gone back to his room.

And how do you know that, *Cecile?*

She scowled at the taunt.

So what if she'd watched where he'd gone? She watched all her employees. Besides, he'd looked so exhausted and beaten down that she'd—briefly—felt guilty for working him so hard.

But then she'd remember that he'd thrown her away to marry an heiress and treated her like a whore, and any guilt she'd felt had burnt away.

While it might be amusing to wake him up and drag him here to help, that would also be admitting that she needed his help to sort out problems with her own business.

As she was dithering, the door to the cupboard creaked open and a filthy little face peeked out.

The child—for that was obviously what it was—saw Cecile, squeaked, and pulled the door shut.

Cecile frowned and set the broom aside. "Come out of there."

The theater was silent but for the creaking of old timbers.

"If you make me go in there—"

The door opened again and this time a furry face joined the childish one. "We weren't doing nothing bad—just sleeping."

"How did you get in here?"

"His lordship let us in." The voice now sounded challenging—braver.

Cecile's mouth pulled into a grim smile. "His lordship, eh?" She noticed something glinting on the child's cheek. "Is that jam on your face?"

"We didn't steal it! His lordship gave it to us."

Cecile muttered some curse words in her native tongue. "Your dog better not have piddled in there—or you either."

The child looked outraged by her accusation; so did the dog, for that matter, baring its teeth and growling low.

Cecile picked up the broom again.

The urchin flung skinny arms around the cur and hugged it tight. "Don't hit him, please! He won't hurt anything."

Cecile sighed; she was going to strangle Guy.

She was going to wake him from the tiny, uncomfortable cot she'd allowed him to have and strangle him.

"Please, missus, we didn't hurt anything. We'll go. Don't call the Watch."

Cecile decided the voice belonged to a female—a young one. She watched in silence as the dirty creature gathered a few possessions and put them in a burlap sack. The girl's shoulders were spindly and narrow, her bones as delicate as a bird's. Even the scrubby cur's shoulders seemed to slump.

Cecile groaned and she heaved a sigh. "Fine. You can stay—for tonight."

The girl gave a breathless little sob that did more to touch Cecile's heart than anything in a long, long time.

"Thank you, miss," she mumbled, her chin wobbling dangerously.

"What is your name?"

"Cat."

"That's not a name—it's an animal."

Cat bristled, just like her namesake. "It's the only one I've got."

Cecile grunted; *that* sounded like a lie. "How old are you?"

The girl shrugged.

Cecile took a step closer and then recoiled. *"Mon Dieu!"* she gasped as the smell hit her.

"What?" Cat snapped.

"You smell like—like—" Cecile gagged.

"It's not my fault," Cat retorted.

Cecile decided that was probably true.

"Do you and the hound have fleas?" She raised a staying hand before the girl could answer. "Never mind. You both will take a bath before you spend a night in my house."

"A bath?" Cat sounded as if Cecile were speaking a foreign language.

Oh God. Had the child never even heard of a bath? How many years' worth of filth would Cecile discover beneath the layer of dirt she could see?

And why was she doing this?

She should just take the girl—*and* her dog—and drop them in Guy's room. If he wanted to take in filthy urchins, then *he* should have to tend to them.

Cecile scowled, getting angrier by the second. Wasn't it just like a man to put a child and dog in a cupboard?

What? He should have left them on the street, as you would have done?
She flinched, her face heating at the truth of the accusation.

"Come," she said shortly, heading for the door that led from the
theater to the building on the backside, which was Cecile's home.

The girl and dog trotted after her and Cecile paused. "Is your
dog going to do his business inside? Because if he does—"

"No, George is a good boy. He knows how to behave."

Cecile laughed. "George? You named your cur after the king?"

"No," Cat scoffed. "I named him after *Saint* George. And don't
call him a cur."

Cecile found the key she needed on the heavy ring and unlocked the door, ushering the child and dog into the short corridor
before locking it behind them.

"A saint, hmm? The dog is that well behaved, is he?"

"Not because of that." Cat rolled her eyes. "Don't you know
anything?"

Cecile laughed, amused by the girl's fire. "Apparently not. Tell
me about this saint."

"He slayed a dragon to protect England. George is valiant like
that, too."

"There's no such thing as a dragon."

"You don't know that."

"I've never seen one."

"Have you seen a bald eagle?"

Cecile stopped and turned to stare down at the girl. "A *what?*"
She'd lived in Boston, so of course she knew the bird the Americans
had adopted as their emblem. But she was stunned that a London
street urchin would know such a thing.

"It's a bird that lives in America. Have you seen one?"

"No, I haven't seen any bald birds. I think you just made it up,"
Cecile teased, resuming guiding her guests toward the kitchen.

"I did not! It's a real bird."

"Why would a bird be bald?"

"It only *looks* bald because the feathers are white and its body is
darker."

"How do you know about this bird?"

The question cut off the girl's loquacity. Cecile couldn't help noticing that the child's accent had shifted subtly, and there were fewer grammatical lapses the more she talked. It was an impressive attempt at subterfuge for such a small child. Somebody must have taught her well.

"Tell me more," Cecile demanded as she lit the lamps in the kitchen. "How do you know about this bald bird—have you been to America?"

"It doesn't matter."

"Don't do that."

"Do what?"

"Don't give up so easily. You were making a point in an argument, were you not?"

Cat nodded.

"Well—finish what you started."

Cat heaved a put-upon sigh. "Just because you haven't seen something doesn't mean that thing doesn't exist."

Cecile raised her eyebrows. "That is a very good point."

"Why are you looking at me like that?" Cat asked, her blue eyes narrowed with suspicion.

"Because I was thinking the same thing—just because I can't *see* a little girl, doesn't mean there isn't one under all that dirt. Now come, you help me haul some water from the pump. While it heats for a bath, I'll give you something more to eat. I just so happen to know where Cook keeps her secret supply of shortbread."

Chapter 13

The banging in Guy's skull was deafening.

Christ! He'd barely had anything to drink the night before, scarcely two glasses of—

"Wake up, Guy!"

Guy forced his eyes open. Hangovers might pound, but they didn't shout one's name. And they didn't call one *Ghee*.

He glanced out the window; dawn had just broken, the light a pale, watery gray. Since he'd not even gone to bed until three, that meant he'd barely had two hours' sleep.

He groaned and swung his feet to the floor.

"Guy! Don't make me throw a bucket of water on you."

"I'm awake—I'm up." He tripped over something—a shoe—and stubbed his toe on the nearby wing chair before slamming against the wall.

"Aaarrgh!" He squeezed his throbbing toe, hopping across the room and biting his lip to keep from groaning.

"What is going on in there?" Cecile demanded.

"Nothing!"

"Have you got *company* in there? You'd better not have."

"What? *No.*" He gingerly lowered his foot to the floor and whimpered.

And then frowned; was that . . . *giggling* he heard?

"I'll give you one minute to get out here."

"I'm hurrying," he called out in a raspy voice, struggling into his work clothes.

"*One* minute. And then we are coming in."

Guy paused; *we?*

He hurried, suddenly much more awake. Who the devil did she have out there? He could hear voices. Had something gone wrong last night? He'd not touched any hammers or saws, so it couldn't be that he'd wrecked anything.

"Your time is up." The door swung open just as Guy was tying a simple knot in his neckcloth.

It was Cecile and—Guy squinted—a little girl. And a dog, a very familiar dog.

"Holy hell!"

"Guy!"

Guy winced. "Do you have to yell, Cecile?"

"It is *Miss Tremblay* to you. And yes, I have to yell when you use inappropriate language in front of a child."

"Oh, sorry." He couldn't stop staring at the pretty little girl— her hair was golden blond, not a muddy, grayish brown.

He looked at Cecile. "How—what—er . . ."

Cecile snorted. "That sounds similar to what I said last night when I opened my laundry cupboard."

Guy grimaced. "Oh."

"Oh, indeed."

"It was cold out and I just thought—"

"That you would store a child in a cupboard—as if she were dirty laundry?"

Guy shoved his hand through his hair, staring down at his feet. Well, when put that way, it sounded *bad*.

He forced himself to look up and meet Cecile's dark gaze. "I was only keeping her there until I came up with something better."

"I have something better."

He perked up. "You do?"

"Yes. Cat and George will stay in your room from now on."

"Erm, Cat and George?"

Cecile ushered the girl and dog into the room. George—at least he assumed the dog was called George and not the girl—bared its not inconsiderable fangs at him.

Guy backed up until his legs hit the cot. "Cecile—er, Miss Tremblay," he amended hastily. "There's not enough room in here—and just the one bed. And George doesn't look pleased to share the space, either."

Cecile reached down and scratched the dog's head; the dog stopped growling and rubbed against her leg.

Why, the ungrateful cur! You'd think he'd remember who it was who rescued him.

"It is just a dog, Guy. Surely you can charm a dog? You will have to exert some of that famous charisma of yours."

"Ha, ha. Very droll."

"As for just one bed—you may fetch one of the boxing mats. That should suffice for you and George to sleep on. That way Cat can take the bed."

"But—"

"Children require regular meals, so you will need to make arrangements with Cook."

"Arrangeme—"

"And Cat will need schooling—either you may teach her, or perhaps you might inquire at an establishment that provides such services."

"*Teach* her? Lord, Cecile! The only things I could teach are—"

"Not in front of the child, Guy."

He ground his teeth. "You can stop, now. I understand what you're doing."

"I may stop? And do what, pray? Throw Cat and George back onto the street?"

Child and dog glared at Guy.

He raised his hands. "No, no, of course not. But I'll get in touch with Marianne. You know she's wild about this sort of thing. In fact, that was where I was planning to take the girl all along—to one of Marianne's whosey whatsits."

Cecile gave him a withering look. "This is *your* responsibility, Guy. Take charge of it instead of shuffling it aside."

Guy thought his head might explode. "Look, darling, I just wanted to—"

"Play the hero, but at no cost to yourself?" she asked innocently.

"Er . . ." Guy looked from Cecile to the girl—Cat. She was quite a taking little thing now that she was all cleaned up. Seeing her looking like a real little girl made it even more appalling that she'd been digging through rubbish for food. Had he only taken her inside because he wanted to be a hero?

His gaze flickered to Cecile, and something uncomfortable unfurled in the pit of his stomach.

The love of his life stared back at him with an unyielding look. She didn't need to say anything—he could see the truth in her eyes. She thought he was a dilettante and that taking Cat off the street was yet another of his thoughtless, careless actions.

Lord, was she right?

Guy sighed again and yanked his gaze away from Cecile, forcing himself to smile at his new responsibility.

He gestured to the tiny room. "Welcome to my humble abode."

Guy learned many, many things over the next few hours.

Cat was eight, or perhaps nine—she couldn't quite remember. Her father had died when she was little, and she'd lived with her mother until she was seven, of that she was positive.

Guy still didn't know what had happened to her mother and was afraid to press the matter when Cat's eyes grew huge and glassy and her lower lip trembled.

She had met George the first month she'd lived on the street, when he'd bitten a man who was trying to drag her into a scary house.

Horror, fury, and shame swirled inside him when she'd told that part of her story.

Cat had been *very, very* lucky to last as long as she had, unmolested. Although she had not said it explicitly, life became somewhat easier for her when she got so dirty that her gender was no longer apparent; fewer people had tried to lure, entice, or capture her.

An old woman had taken pity on Cat and George not long after the harrowing experience with the man, and she had given them little bits of food and allowed them to sleep on her porch on the coldest nights.

But the woman had died a few weeks ago and Cat and her dog had been scavenging full-time since then.

"Nobody hardly came into your alley, so me and George didn't have to hide," Cat confided over a breakfast of porridge swimming in cream, currants, and honey.

Guy suspected nobody came into that particular rubbish alley because the pickings were so slim. Judging by the way girl and dog devoured their food—yes, Cook had even found a meaty bone for the trusty hound, not to mention the food that made its way from Cat's bowl down to the floor—both were half-starved.

Amazingly, Cat knew how to read, having been fortunate enough to attend a day school in a small village whose name she couldn't recall.

Guy suspected her mother had come to London seeking better wages, like many agricultural and rural folk. There had been constant waves of disease in the poorer parts of London, and the poor woman must have succumbed to one without making any arrangements for her daughter.

Cat's last name was Smith, a singularly unhelpful surname when it came to tracking down relatives. According to Cat, her mother was a princess and her father a knight who'd died while fighting trolls.

Since the girl had been living by her wits for the past two and half years, Guy couldn't blame her for creating a more satisfying life.

That said, he suspected tracking down such people might prove more difficult than one would think, given the dearth of either princesses, knight protectors, or trolls.

★ ★ ★

Cecile spent the day swinging from one extreme to another. She'd felt righteous this morning when she'd woken Guy and forced him to face his responsibilities.

But as the hours passed, she questioned whether she'd done the proper thing. After all—what did he know about taking care of a little girl?

Actually, he probably knew more than Cecile. At least he had younger sisters. Cecile had never been around children—not even when she'd been a child herself. She'd spent her days in her father's workshop, learning the rudiments of gunsmithing from the time she could walk and talk.

The evening before had been something of a revelation when it came to children. It had astounded her that such a small child could converse so easily. The more she'd spoken, the more Cat's accent had changed from a street urchin's to that of a little girl whose parents must have taught their daughter to speak properly.

Though Cecile did not believe that Cat was the child of a princess and knight protector, she wouldn't have been surprised if Cat's mother and father were educated servants or tradespeople.

Cecile knew all too well how people of a certain status could become easily lost and forgotten in a city like London. Although she'd been years older than Cat when her own father had died, she'd faced a whole new world with strangers who spoke a different language.

She'd had her cousin to take her in, of course, so she'd not had to sleep on the street or forage for food like Cat, but Curtis had caused her other problems soon enough.

Cecile pushed those unpleasant memories away and thought instead about Guy's stunned face this morning. She couldn't help smiling; it was bad to tease him, but it was so amusing. He was so big and strong and yet there was something about him that was so—so innocent—although she knew well enough that he wasn't the least bit innocent.

But when it came to understanding how harsh the world could be, Guy was naïve. He had led a charmed life.

Until recently.

Beneath the anger, humiliation, and pain that he'd caused her, Cecile actually felt sorry for his recent losses.

He loved his sisters and mother and had an unshakeable sense of duty when it came to his responsibilities toward the dukedom. He'd been prepared to sacrifice his personal desires by marrying for money.

Or perhaps he had fallen in love with his heiress?

Cecile scowled at the unwanted thought. But as little as she cared for it, perhaps it was true. She suspected that—given his scores of lovers—he was the sort of man who loved lightly and often.

But then, what did she know about love? She'd never loved at all, even though she'd had more than a few lovers herself, several of whom had begged her to marry them.

But none of those offers had been compelling enough to sacrifice her freedom.

Would she have said yes to Guy if he'd—

Cecile made a noise of disgust and shoved back her chair, giving up on her unending paperwork for the time being.

Instead, she loaded her pistols, strapped on her holsters, and headed for the stage, which, according to the rehearsal schedule, was available.

Employees waylaid her often to ask questions, but she didn't mind the interruptions. She was happier operating the Fayre than she'd ever been in her life.

Except for those weeks in the caravan with Guy.

Cecile ignored the insidious thought and pushed open the stage door, grateful to be able to shoot something.

She shoved the straw bales out onto the stage and wedged the heavy slate and wood barrier between them.

Thanks to the combination of the straw, the six-inch barrier, and the small caliber of her pistols, she could fire indoors without having to worry about damaging the building.

She clipped several playing cards into a wire spring-holder and set it bobbing wildly before taking her position behind the mark.

As always when she practiced, she thought about nothing except hitting her target.

Once the first batch of playing cards were nothing but confetti, she reloaded, and attached more cards to a wheel and gave it a spin.

She'd reloaded three times more and had just fired the last shot when the sound of clapping made her turn.

Guy was standing with Cat and George.

"You are so *good!*" Cat said. "You hardly missed at all—only once."

"I shouldn't have missed that one either," Cecile groused. She glanced at Guy, who was watching her with the amused glint that always made her want to slap him or kiss him.

"How did you get so good?" Cat asked.

"Practice, practice, and more practice."

"Can I try?" the girl asked, bouncing excitedly on her toes.

Cecile paused to look at her.

She had begun shooting when she could barely stand, but then, she'd also grown up around guns and understood the danger inherent in them.

She looked into Cat's imploring eyes. "There is much to learn before you fire a gun. I will teach you, but it will take some time. Perhaps tomorrow you can come to my office, and I will show you how to take apart a pistol."

To her surprise and relief, Cat nodded rather than argued.

"Where did you two go today?" Cecile asked.

"We went to a *duke's* house."

Pistols and target shooting were instantly forgotten as Cat babbled about the grand house where Guy had taken her.

Cecile cocked her head at Guy, and he raised both his hands. "Don't look at me that way—I only went to see Marianne so I could ask a few questions, not to fob off, er, my responsibilities."

"The duchess gave this to me," Cat said, spinning around to show off her dress. It was not the dress she'd left the house in that morning, and it doubtless cost more than most of Cecile's employees made in a year.

Cecile gave Guy a pointed look. "What was wrong with the dress from Cook's daughter?"

He shrugged. "Nothing. But why can't she have these, too?"

"These?"

"Yes, there were closets full of gowns. Marianne said they belong to Sin's nieces and the girls had just left them there. They're too small for them now. She said she was going to give them away to one of the schools she's so fond of, so—"

"She said I could take as many as I wanted," Cat interrupted, gleeful. "I was going to take all of them, but Guy said I *couldn't*."

Judging by the girl's scowl and Guy's pained look, there must have been a disagreement over that point.

"I told her she could take a *few* because I only have a small clothes cupboard, and we'll have to share—"

Cecile gave a dismissive flick of one hand. "You can keep your cupboard. I had Mary and Susan clean out the room that is right next to my chambers. It used to be part of a two-bedroom suite so it was full of furniture beneath all the crates."

Guy's smirk was growing larger as he realized that she, too, had been charmed by their diminutive guest.

Cecile narrowed her eyes at him in warning and turned to Cat. "You'll have your own room."

Rather than look excited, as she'd expected, the girl cut Guy a yearning look—the same look that females from eight to eighty always gave the gorgeous erstwhile lord—as if she'd been looking forward to being roommates and plaiting each other's hair.

Cecile snorted; he'd won the girl's heart in less than a day— probably in less than an hour.

It was disgusting how easily the man could charm people of all ages, male or female.

Not that Cecile had any room to talk—she'd allowed him into her bed after barely a month. The man was . . . insidious.

"Are you hungry?" she asked when she noticed they were both looking at her and waiting for . . . something.

"Yes!" Guy said.

"Not you." Cecile looked at Cat, who smiled and nodded eagerly.

Cecile took her bundle of keys from her petticoat pocket and held up the key with the filigree handle. "Here is the key. Take your hound to the kitchen—Cook made something special for you."

They watched the girl skip off, George trotting along at her heels.

Once the door closed, Guy turned back to Cecile. "I take it you wanted to get me alone? What can I do for you, *Mistress* Tremblay?"

Cecile ground her teeth; she *had* wanted to get him alone. But she hardly wanted to admit it. Instead, she turned away from him and busied herself with her guns but could feel the weight of his gaze. "Are you finished practicing? Or would you like my assistance?" he offered.

"That's probably not wise right now." Cecile felt the dull thud of his boots on the stage and then the heat of his body when he stopped beside her.

He traced a finger from the corner of her eye down her jaw.

Rather than slap his hand away or tell him to stop it, she froze like a startled rabbit and reveled in even this barely-there touch.

"How long are you going to keep me at arm's length, Cecile? How many times do I need to admit I was wrong and beg your forgiveness?"

"I'll tell you when it's enough."

"I was terribly, terribly wrong. And conceited and stupid."

"Keep going."

Warm, slightly calloused fingers slid beneath her chin, his thumb brushing her lower lip.

Finally, she did what she should have done right away and slapped his hand away. "I didn't mean keep going with your touching; I mean with your apology."

Rather than look offended or hurt at being rejected, he said, "I never should have made such an insulting offer. It was wrong, but it would be a mistake for you to believe that I did it because you weren't good enough for me or because I didn't value you." He stroked her jaw with the back of his knuckles. "I did it because I couldn't bear to give you up."

"And yet you *did* give me up."

He groaned, the sound so low and intense that she felt it in her own chest.

"I was wrong—terribly wrong. I realized, almost immediately afterward, that I'd never felt about anyone else the way I felt about you."

She shoved his hand away and pushed past him, prudently leaving her pistols on the cleaning table and thinking to put some space between them, but he followed her.

Cecile spun around, only to discover he was standing so close they were almost touching. At five-foot-eight she was tall for a woman, but he was tall for a man, and she had to crane her neck to glare up at him.

"This is a business relationship, Mr. Darlington. Or have you forgotten what you promised already?"

"No, I haven't forgotten. I lied to you when I said that."

She gave a bark of laughter. "You lied about what, exactly? Wanting to work? Wanting this job?"

"No, I lied about my reason for wanting this job, about its being only business. I'm here because of you, Cecile. Only you."

Her lips parted, but no words came out.

His normally pleasant features were brooding and intense, the deep commas around his full lips and the lines at the corners of his eyes the only evidence that he had ever smiled. His jaw flexed as his dark gaze traveled over her face, settling finally on her mouth, the raw, hot need in his brown eyes intoxicating.

He had the most beautiful eyelashes of any person—man or woman or child—that she'd ever seen. Lush and dark and so long the upper set often tangled with the lower.

"I was wrong, Cecile, so very wrong. I can see that, now—"

"You were *betrothed*, Guy!" she hissed, and then wanted to bite off her own tongue for allowing those words out. But now that she'd begun . . .

"If not for the arrival of your cousin, you would be married right now instead of standing in front of me declaring how much you want me."

A muscle jumped in his temple, and he nodded. "That is true. I would have married her."

"You sent me a letter after I read the announcement of your betrothal in the newspaper," she said.

"A letter you never answered," he retorted.

"Because I didn't read it!"

"Well, you should have, Cecile. If you had, you would have known that I regretted what I said in Calais."

"And is that all that letter and the others you sent said?"

His composure cracked, and he thrust a hand through his hair and looked down at the stage floor. "No, the letters contained more than just an apology."

"What did they say?"

"It doesn't matter now."

She gave a bitter bark of laughter. "You *still* wanted to make me complicit in your infidelity, didn't you?"

"It's not what you think." The words sounded as if they'd been squeezed from his chest.

"What do you mean?"

"The two of us—Helena and I—made a—a bargain, a pact, for lack of a better word."

"Helena?"

"The woman I was betrothed to—Helena Carter."

"What kind of bargain?"

"She is in love with a clerk who works for her father, but he would never permit the match. Instead, he threatened to punish the man if she pursued what she wanted. Carter said he'd sack the clerk and ruin his chances for employment. He threatened her with disinheritance if she fought him. So, Helena came to me and confided the truth. She told me she could not marry me in good conscience without telling me that she wanted another. I—I told her I felt the same. About you." He paused, staring at her, his flush darkening the longer she stared. "I know what you are thinking, Cecile—"

"I doubt it."

"All right, all right," he conceded. "I probably don't know the *whole* of what—"

"The two of you decided you would marry and then carry on separate lives."

He nodded.

"What did her lover think of this plan?"

Guy's gaze flickered away. "Er, Helena said he wasn't exactly happy about the idea, but—"

"Imagine that! Because I don't care for it, either."

"Yes, I know, Cecile—neither did I. Neither did Helena. But sometimes in the adult world we live in, we *can't* have everything we want."

She poked him in the chest with a finger. Hard.

"Ow!"

She poked him again and opened her mouth.

"What?" he asked when she didn't speak.

She inhaled deeply and then said in a rush, "Don't you *ever* tell me about the adult world and what we are *forced* to do. I know plenty about being forced into things."

Cecile instantly wished she could take the words back but the determined expression that settled on his normally happy face told her there was no chance of it.

Guy caught her hand when she dropped it, holding her gently but firmly. "What do you mean? What were you forced to do?"

"Nothing. It is none of your business."

"I want to make it my business—I want to make *you* my business. I want to know every single detail about you, Cecile, no matter how small or insignificant. Of all the things I regret in my life—perhaps even more than the insulting offer I made to you—I regret not pushing past your wall of reserve in France and learning who you really are."

"What difference would that have made?"

"Because you are worth knowing, Cecile." He rubbed his thumb over the thin skin on the back of her hand. "Is what Helena and I planned immoral?" He shrugged, his expression more than a little wry. "Probably. But then commonly accepted principles of morality have rarely influenced my decision-making. I wrote those letters to you because I was greedy, and I wanted to have you *and* rescue my family." He sighed. "It is not the stuff of Gothic romance tales, I'm afraid. I did not do the noble or honorable thing—I am no romance hero. But neither am I a villain. I am just a flawed man who wants to be with you more than anything I've wanted in my life."

Cecile pulled her hand away and he let her go. She turned, unable to look at him and think at the same time, struggling to wrap her mind around his words. She did what she always did when an emotional issue was before her: She imagined that a friend— Marianne, for example—had come to her for advice.

What would she say if Marianne had laid out the mess Guy had just confessed to her?

He'd not just thrown her away and forgotten about her. He'd had a plan—a stupid one—but at least the person he was going to marry wouldn't have been hurt by his behavior.

Indeed, looked at objectively, and with bourgeois standards of morality stripped away, everyone would win in his scenario. His sisters and mother would be taken care of, the hundreds of people relying on the Duke of Fairhurst would prosper, his wife and her lover would get to be together—as would Cecile and Guy, at least part of the time.

The only thing Guy could not have given her was respectability. Or a family. Two things she'd never believed she wanted.

Until Guy.

The truth was that Cecile never could have accepted such a compromise, and it infuriated her that he could.

Jealousy would have eaten her from the inside out.

She looked up to find him waiting for her. "And would you have taken her to your bed, Guy?"

He hesitated, but then nodded and said, "Yes, but just for an heir."

Cecile threw her head back and laughed. It was either that or hit him.

His big hands settled on her shoulders. "I see now that might have been difficult for you to—"

"Difficult?" she shouted, knocking his hands away. "Is that what you said? *Difficult?*"

"Very well, perhaps that was the wrong word."

"Here is a better one: unbearable."

He inhaled deeply, let it out, and then nodded. "I agree. But none of that matters now that things are—"

"No!"

"Cecile—"

She raised a hand. "I don't wish to know how *things are* as you put it. That might be how things are for *you*, but not for me, Guy."

"But—"

"You think I can just forgive you for this past year and take you to my bed?"

He gave her a hopeful look. "Maybe if you took me to your bed, I could *help* you forgive me."

Cecile gave a squawk of disbelief. "Can you really be so arrogant? So thoughtless?"

"I've been told more than once that I really can be," he admitted.

"If I take you to my bed, it will be because I want you in my bed—not because I want anything more—"

A smile—no, a grin—spread across his face, cutting her rant short.

Cecile bit her tongue; she literally bit her tongue, and blood flooded her mouth as the realization of what she'd just said flooded her brain.

Why had she said that? *Why?*

He stepped toward her. "If you'd only—"

"Of course, I won't!" she snapped, stepping back. "Not ever again!"

His lips twitched, but he didn't smile.

"If you smirk in that obnoxious manner, Guy, so help me—"

"Sorry!" He pressed his lips together into a frown, or at least he attempted to. "No smirking here—see, only serious frowning." But his smile would not be suppressed.

Cecile knew how to erase his smile. "There is a cupboard full of laundry that will not clean itself. Once you've taken that to Mrs. Bascom, you can help Basil mop the house since your contemporaries have been especially filthy of late. I want you to do *all* of it, from the pit to the gods. Nobody has cleaned the floor up there in far too long."

The gods were cramped and dark and had a tendency to be neglected. It was bound to be nasty up there.

He grinned, his spirits clearly unbowed by the threat of a visit to Bascom and an afternoon spent with a mop and bucket.

The determination in his gaze was that of a predator stalking its prey. And it told her that the little bit of hope she'd just inadvertently let slip had strengthened his resolve in such a way that he'd never give up.

"What are you waiting for?" she snapped.

"Yes, Miss Tremblay, right away."

When the stage door shut behind him, Cecile sagged against it.

Lord, she needed to stop speaking to the man, because every single time she did she lost more ground to him.

Chapter 14

"I can't do it right now, Guy—I have to go to Paris, and I'll be gone at least two weeks," Elliot said.

"That's fine. I'll just look into the bloke who owns Blanchard guns myself—how hard can it be?" Guy lifted his almost-empty pint and then smiled and nodded at a nearby serving wench, who leapt up from the customer's lap where she'd been lolling, and hurried toward the bar.

Elliot chuckled and Guy blinked. "What?"

"You don't even notice, do you?"

"Notice what?"

"How women practically throw themselves at your feet and beg to do your bidding."

Guy frowned. "What are you talking about?"

"That serving girl who just about broke her foot rushing to fetch you another pint of ale."

"That's her job, Elliot."

"Yes, that's true—but she didn't hurry to get *my* drink with quite so much enthusiasm."

Guy gave a dismissive grunt. There was only one woman he'd like to see eager to please him, and that wasn't going to happen in this lifetime.

"But back to the other matter," Elliot said. "Digging around

in somebody's business isn't as easy as you think. If you start indis-
criminately poking into things, this Blanchard bloke will hear about
it—I promise you."

"What? You don't think I can be inconspicuous?"

Elliot coughed and glanced around the room.

"What the devil is that supposed to mean?"

"Look around this pub, Guy."

Guy looked around, nodding to the other customers, most of
whom seemed quite friendly and all of whom were smiling at him.
He turned to his friend. "So?"

"Do you think they stare at me that way—adoringly—when I
come in here alone?"

"They're not staring adoringly."

"Oh, yes they are. Look again."

Guy lowered his lashes and drank off the last of his pint, his gaze
flickering around the room at the other punters.

They *did* seem to be watching him rather . . . raptly.

He set down his empty glass. "I'd say they're watching with
interest rather than adoration."

"You are splitting hairs. The truth is that people read the society or gossip sections of the paper to escape their dreary lives. The
women want you and the men want to *be* you."

"Do *you* want to be me, Elliot?" he teased.

"I'm the exception."

Guy laughed.

But Elliot wouldn't be distracted from his point. "They *all* know
who you are—every single one of them. Sketches of you flood the
newspapers and print shops. Stories of your antics—*from duke to door-
man! The peer is now a porter!* are everywhere. Have you seen Humphrey's window lately?"

Guy was feeling less and less amused. "Is that a serious question?
I avoid those places like the plague."

"If you *had* seen it, then maybe you'd understand why you are
the last person who can perform an investigation into anything. At
least not unless you want that investigation to end up a newsworthy

event. Even before you lost your status, title, and money, you were fodder for the masses: Lord Darlington, the Darling of the *Ton*. The man who—"

"All right, all right—that's enough, I get your point. So, then what *can* I do?"

"I'll be back in two or three weeks."

"Well, damn it, Elliot, I don't want to just sit here for two or three weeks doing nothing." He leaned across the table, not bothering to hide his urgency. "I *need* to find some way to make Cecile forgive me."

Elliot made a scoffing sound. "And you think prying into her past is the way to go?"

"I think something rotten happened with her cousin, but Cecile won't tell me the details. The one time I asked why she wasn't making Blanchet guns—she's an artist, for pity's sake!—she cut me cold. That tells me something is wrong."

"Just because something is wrong doesn't mean there is anything legally actionable. Or anything you can do about it."

"She said *I can't* make guns. Something about that makes me feel as if she tried, but Blanchard stopped her. You didn't hear how proud she was of her father and her own skill, Elliot. I don't think she'd give up her family's heritage easily. Something bad must have happened to her."

"So, this is all conjecture on your part."

Guy sighed. "Yes, it's desperate flailing, if you really want the words with the bark on them."

"This seems a Byzantine way to get information, Guy. Can't you just talk to the woman? Do what normal people do and ask her?"

"Good God, Elliot, don't you think I've tried?" Cecile had been more distant than ever with Guy after their encounter last week. "She'll hardly speak to me. It's all I can do to get her to pass the saltcellar at the breakfast table."

"You must have really, really gotten under her skin."

"I did," Guy admitted. "So now I need to find some way—some *thing*—to make her believe I'm sorry and that I've changed."

"I fail to see a connection between making her believe you're sorry and digging into her past."

"How can I help her—and thereby get into her good graces—if she won't tell me anything about herself?"

"And you think digging into her relationship with Blanchard is the *thing* that might help you?"

Guy flung up his hands. "I don't know, but it's all I've got."

"Won't she be angry that you've pried into her affairs?"

"That's a risk I'm willing to take." Hell, she couldn't be any angrier at him than she was already.

Could she?

Elliot didn't immediately respond, but Guy saw signs of calculation behind the other man's flat gray gaze. "What are you thinking?"

"I'll be gone for a few weeks, but you've got somebody just as good." He stopped, muttered something beneath his breath, and said, "You've got somebody *better* than me right under your nose."

"Wait. You mean I should ask Blade to investigate for me?"

"Yes."

Guy grinned. "So, she's better than you, hmm?"

Elliot looked pained. "In some ways—sneaking around is one of those ways."

"How can *she* go unnoticed? She's hardly average looking. In fact, I'd say she was downright—"

Elliot's eyes narrowed.

Guy changed the word he was going to use—*odd*—to something less offensive. "Er, unusual."

Elliot's pensive stare stoked Guy's suspicion that his emotionless friend had finally fallen to Eros's arrow. Or he'd fallen to *something*— maybe it was just professional admiration? Who knew with Elliot. Guy had never met anyone who held their cards closer to their chest than his former roommate.

Actually, that wasn't true. The woman they were discussing, Josephine Brown—if that was her real name—was even quieter and more mysterious than Elliot.

She was almost abnormally reserved and quiet. Guy doubted

she'd spoken more than a hundred words during the weeks they'd been traveling companions. Hell, her raven talked more than she did.

"Do you want me to ask her to help you?" Elliot volunteered, the faintest, minutest, tiniest speck of color staining his cheeks.

Guy grinned and opened his mouth to tease his friend.

"Don't," Elliot warned, holding up a deceptively gentlemanly looking hand—a hand Guy knew could kill quicker than most men could sign a document.

"I would be most grateful if you broached the subject with her," Guy said, throwing the poor man a bone by giving him an excuse to talk to the elusive woman.

Elliot nodded, only the slightest curve of his thin lips giving away how pleased he was to have a reason to speak with Blade.

Guy had given up wondering just what went on between the two mercenaries/spies/agents or whatever they both called themselves. For all he knew, the remote and reserved duo hadn't even come close to each other. Maybe it was all professional respect between them?

Besides, he was scarcely one to talk when it came to conducting his love life in a way that made any sense—not to mention made him a walking, talking butt of *ton* jokes.

"Here you are, luv." The attractive brunette placed his pint on the table, taking care not to spill a drop.

Guy gave her a genuine smile—people who brought you good things always deserved genuine gratitude, in his opinion—and a generous bit extra to go with it. He enjoyed the view while she sashayed back to the bar, and then he turned to Elliot.

"Why no, I won't have another—but thank you, Guy."

"Sorry. I could get her to—"

"No, actually—I do need to be going."

Guy pulled a face. "I probably need to hurry, as well. I'll need to swing by and pick up fresh towels on the way back to the theater."

Elliot grinned, the rare expression lightening his normally stern features. "Cecile's still running you ragged, is she?"

"Ha! Did you think she would suddenly stop?"

"No. In fact—never mind." Elliot's pale face suddenly flushed.

Guy laughed bitterly. "You bet against me, didn't you?"

He didn't need to explain what he meant. The way Elliot was looking around the room—anywhere but at Guy—told him all he needed to know.

"So," Guy said, sitting back and crossing his arms, "what are the odds?"

"Er, it depends which book—at White's, they're behind you. But at Brooks's . . ." Elliot shrugged.

"My own club—er, ex-club—has lost faith in me?"

"Well, the members know you better there, don't they?"

Guy scowled. "What are you saying, Elliot?"

"Just that everything that has happened to you is a *lot* to manage. And working for Cecile seems, er, both unnecessary and unwise for your peace of mind."

"This job might make me the butt of jests and wagering, but it is the only way I stand a chance of getting her back, Elliot. I might be the *ton* fool right now, but at least I'm my own fool."

Elliot looked as if he wanted to say something more, but then settled for nodding.

Guy scratched his jaw, the loud sound reminding him that he'd forgotten to shave that morning. Lord, how his mother and sisters—not to mention his valet—would scream or faint if they could see him now. No doubt they'd be able to see him tomorrow in Humphrey's window. He could just picture the headline: *Scruffy Scoundrel Seduces Siren Shootist . . .*

"Do you know what year Cecile came to England?" Elliot asked.

"Er, no. But she mentioned once that she was fourteen."

"How old is she now?"

Guy's face heated. "I have no idea how old she is," he admitted bluntly. "In fact, I know almost nothing of her life both up to those weeks in France and afterward."

Elliot opened his mouth and then closed it.

"What is it?" Guy asked warily.

"Not to be indelicate, but the two of you spent solid days—and nights—together in a tiny caravan. Just what did you talk about?"

Guy was sorely tempted to quip something about how there wasn't much talking, but that would have been a lie.

"We talked about Bonaparte, what he'd do, how France would react, whether we'd have difficulty getting to Calais, and a hundred other daily details."

They had also speculated endlessly on what was transpiring between Elliot and Blade and Sin and Marianne, but he decided to keep that bit to himself.

"Whenever I tried to ask her anything personal, it led to an argument," Guy admitted. "She told me she didn't want to talk about the future or the past. She told me we had a few weeks to enjoy ourselves and then it would all be over, and we'd never see each other again." He met Elliot's gaze. "And so I never asked her any questions. Of course now I know that I should have persisted—I shouldn't have behaved like such a coward. But I didn't. From the first day to the last morning, I acted as if I were the one doing her a favor. I treated her like just another woman in a long line of many. And I couldn't be any sorrier for my behavior than I am. What terrifies me is that there is nothing I can do to atone. That no amount of apologizing will make her forgive me."

Guy could see by Elliot's expression that the other man agreed with him.

Chapter 15

Cecile struggled to absorb the information one of her maids, Mary, had just delivered: that Nathan Whitfield was in the book room, waiting for her to receive him.

It was their usual night to meet, but Cecile had forgotten all about the man—something she'd never done before and which was unforgivably rude.

"Er, tell him I will receive him shortly—I will ring for you to bring him up when I am ready. No more than ten minutes."

Not that she knew what she'd say to him in ten minutes.

Cecile had begun seeing Nathan perhaps six months ago. They met once a week when he was in the city. He was an industrialist from Bristol and sometimes he did not come to London for weeks on end. Which was why she'd forgotten all about him, because she'd not seen him for a month, not since before Guy had come to work for her.

She'd never forgotten one of Nathan's visits in the past and didn't like how guilty she felt. She also didn't like what she was going to have to do—which was send him away.

What a mess this was; and what a potential for farce.

Cecile went to the mirror to assess her appearance, her mind racing as she tried to come up with something to say to him.

Fortunately, she was wearing one of her nicer gowns as she'd had to meet with her man of business earlier. And because she'd not been engaged in any bookwork—which usually caused her to savage her hair until it resembled a bird nest—her hair was sleek and tidy.

Quit thinking about your hair. Nathan will be up here in less than ten minutes and you need to think of a polite way to put him off. How could she phrase the fact that she needed to cancel any future meetings between them until . . . well, she wasn't sure when, if ever, they would resume their affair.

It simply wouldn't be right to entertain a lover with Cat living in the house.

Oh, is that the only reason?

Cecile frowned. No, it was not—there was also the fact that it would be a bit farcical having one lover in her bed while an ex-lover slept down the hall.

So, you're going to allow Guy's presence to disrupt not only your house, but also your life? You're going to allow—

The door to her private sitting room opened and the disruptive man himself walked into the room.

Cecile shot to her feet. "Don't you ever knock?"

Guy recoiled at her angry tone. "I'm sorry. Do you want me to go out and knock?"

"No! I want you not to have done it to begin with."

He smiled. "I know you think highly of me, but I don't have that sort of time-traveling ability, I'm afraid."

"What do you want?" she snapped.

"What is Whitfield doing in the book room?"

Cecile's temper—not calm at the best of times—flared. "Who are you to ask about my guests?"

"I—"

"Don't you have work to do? I know Wilfred was looking for you earlier." She narrowed her eyes. "Where were you? Don't you work here? Do you think you can wander off whenever you choose?"

He opened his mouth.

"Get out of my private room," she ordered before he could speak, charging toward him and making a shooing motion with her hands, as if he were a chicken.

"Fine, fine, I'll leave. I just wanted to tell you I found a school for Cat, not far from here."

Cecile paused. "I can't imagine any school in this area would be a place she should go."

"Well, you need to broaden your imagination, then. This is operated by the Society of Friends. Marianne assured me it is—"

"You have friends who run a school?"

He chuckled. "No—the Society of Friends is a religious group— they are nonconformists."

Cecile had no time to listen to his bizarre babbling. "I will go and see this school before we make any decision. You are not to be trusted with such matters."

Rather than look offended, he smiled. "Good. I was going to take her to see it tomorrow."

Cecile realized that she'd been staring at his mouth—which was surely one of God's great creations—and wrenched her eyes to meet his, yet another impressive creation. "Is that all you wanted to tell me?"

He hesitated, and then said, "Yes."

"Good. Then go."

He sighed and turned, taking such a long time, she wanted to shout at him.

Once he'd gone, she yanked the servant pull. When Mary opened the door she said, "Show Lord Whitfield up."

"Here?" Mary asked.

Cecile couldn't blame the girl for her confusion; she'd always shown Whitfield to her boudoir in the past.

"Yes, here."

Cecile smoothed her skirts as she waited, taking several deep, even breaths so that when the door opened a minute or two later, she was calm and smiling.

She held her hands out to him. "I'm sorry to make you wait, Nathan."

He smiled, his sharp eyes flickering over her person. "You are worth waiting for," he said, kissing the backs of her hands and pulling her toward him, until their bodies touched from knees to chest. He bent to kiss her properly—and he was a very good kisser.

Cecile allowed it but did not prolong or encourage the embrace.

When she pulled away, he groaned and set his forehead against hers. "Why do I feel that you are going to send me on my way, Cecile?"

"Because I must—tonight is not a good time. I am terribly sorry I did not send word earlier and you've made this trip."

He brushed away her apology with a casual wave. "Must I leave immediately—or can we at least have a little time to chat?"

She would have preferred him gone, but that was hardly polite.

"Of course, I have time for you." She forced a sweet smile—well, as sweet as she could ever muster—and they sat on the settee that faced the fireplace.

He took her hand in his and idly played with her fingers. "I suspected this would happen when I heard Darlington was here."

She opened her mouth to demand what he meant, but he was not finished.

He gave a derisive laugh. "What a buffoon. The man has no pride, coming—"

Cecile pulled her hand away. "What? He has no pride to work for a woman?"

"No, of course that wasn't what I meant. I just meant that it is a known fact that he wants you and that you have denied him repeatedly over the past year."

Cecile's jaw sagged. "It is *not* a known fact! Is it?" she demanded a few seconds later.

"Well, perhaps *known* is an overstatement," he admitted.

Other than Marianne, Blade, Sin, and Elliot she had *never* said anything about her involvement with Guy to anyone and she was certain he hadn't spoken of their time together either.

At least he'd better not have done.

"How do you know such a thing?"

"Please, darling, I have my ways."

"You mean you bribe my employees?"

He shrugged. "I do whatever is necessary to get what I want."

He smiled at her, but the glint in his icy blue eyes was dangerous. "For example, I know he sent you letters that you didn't open, and I know you were lovers at some point in the past."

Cecile stared for a moment, sorely tempted to slap him—hard—and then throw him out of her house.

Instead, she smoothed her already straight skirts, wishing she could smooth her temper as easily.

"This is work; he is not my lover now. Not that it is any of your concern," she added sharply. "Do I interrogate you about your lovers, past or present?"

"No, you don't," he said, using the irritatingly soothing tone he might also use on a child or an animal. "And no, our arrangement is not . . . exclusive, so it is not, in fact, my concern."

"I will leave the issue of your spying, *for now*, but suffice it to say that I am most displeased that you would bribe my employees."

"All is fair in love and war, my dear."

"But we are neither in love nor is this war," she pointed out. "I thought I made that clear from the outset."

"You did, you did." He hesitated, and then added, "But given the history you share with Darlington, I would have thought that he'd have looked elsewhere for employment." He chuckled. "It's not as if he has any experience in this sort of work—surely he could have found something more suitable to do."

"Suitable, how?" she asked evenly.

Nathan sighed and took her hands, holding them tightly when she would have pulled away. "Don't rip up at me, you little termagant, I only meant it is a strange trajectory—from duke to circus employee. I don't think you could argue with that, could you?"

"No, no, of course not. You are right." She struggled to regain control of her temper. "But I do not wish to talk about him."

"Good, because I'd rather talk about the two of us."

Cecile didn't like the sound of this.

"Nathan, there is no *us*. I told you when we began this that it was nothing more than pleasure."

"Yes, you did tell me that," he said, his handsome face wearing

the bland mask she'd come to recognize as concealing an exceptionally stubborn man who always got what he wanted. "But, for some
time now, I have wanted . . . more."

"I will not become your mistress and go—"

"I want you to marry me, Cecile."

Cecile knew that the expression on her face—eyes goggling and
jaw hanging—was not especially attractive, but she couldn't seem to
close her mouth.

He chuckled. "Why do you look so surprised?"

"Because you are a wealthy peer, and I am a circus worker!"

"My title is so new it still pinches, I continue to earn money in
trade, and—most importantly—I don't give a damn what anyone
else thinks about me. What's the point of being screamingly wealthy
if one conforms to the expectations of others?"

Cecile couldn't help smiling. "That is, I must admit, an excellent philosophy, Nathan."

"So?" he said, his eyelids lowering and his clever hands sliding
up her arms and then around her shoulders in a way that made her
hiss in a sharp breath. "Will you marry me, my dear? Will you allow me to dress you in silk and velvet and furs and spoil you with
diamonds and emeralds?"

What about love?

The voice was so quiet that she barely heard it. It wasn't her
voice—that much was certain. When had she ever thought about
love?

"But—Nathan, this is so—"

"Don't say it is so sudden, Cecile. You must know how I feel
about you?" His normally lazy, mocking gaze was suddenly sharp
and possessive. "I don't like thinking of you working so hard, and I
hate thinking of you with other men."

Was the man mad? They'd shared a few dozen meals and engaged in sex perhaps the same number of times and he fancied himself in *love*?

*You've been his lover for nearly five months; that is more than twice as
long as you were with Guy.*

The thought was rather shocking. Mainly because she felt nothing for the handsome man beside her.

A man she'd forgotten about as she sat there thinking about Guy. Again.

She smiled at Nathan and said, "I am honored."

"I want you all to myself, and I want to take care of you."

Did Cecile want to be taken care of? There was some appeal, and yet—no. At least not by Nathan.

"I'm afraid my answer is *no*."

He gave a wry chuckle, but she saw a flash of displeasure in his beautiful blue gaze. Nathan Whitfield did not like being denied. "I reserve the right to ask you again, my dear."

Cecile opened her mouth to tell him this was probably a good time to end things between them, but a loud rapping on the door spared her that uncomfortable announcement.

Before she could say *come in* the door opened.

Guy stood on the threshold, his charming smile fixed in place but his warm brown eyes flat and hard.

"Hallo, Whitfield."

The baron lounged back on the settee, still in possession of Cecile's hand.

"Well, look at you, Darlington." He grinned and gave Guy—who was dressed in his simple, old work clothing—a deliberate once-over.

Cecile allowed herself a good look at Guy, too, even though she could have drawn him from memory if she'd possessed any artistic skill.

Nathan would hate to hear it—and he would disbelieve it—but Guy, in his worn old buckskins and battered boots, emanated almost suffocating waves of masculinity. And that was just the lower half of his body. Even dressed for manual labor, he was far more mesmerizing than Nathan with his closely molded coat, skintight pantaloons, and spotless Hessians.

She wrenched her gaze away from Guy before she got distracted by the upper half.

"Dressed for a night at a bowsing ken, are you?" Nathan drawled.

Cecile frowned. "Bowsing ken?"

"It's thieves' cant for a public house," Guy explained, flashing his teeth at Nathan. "Were you wanting to enjoy a pint or two at my local public house with me, old man? Or just making a statement on my attire."

Nathan laughed.

Guy turned to Cecile. "I'm sorry to interrupt, but Francine has accused Angus of—well, I'm sure you can guess. She is refusing to go on until the item in question is located and returned."

Cecile gave him a hard look. "Why hasn't—"

"Beryl is busy with an issue in the trap room or I would have taken the problem to her, of course."

This ongoing war between Angus and several of her other employees was an almost nightly occurrence, so Cecile's mediation skills were hardly necessary to soothe ruffled feathers—or fur—or whatever.

Guy's motivation for interrupting her was painfully transparent.

Still, she wanted Nathan gone . . .

She turned to the handsome, wealthy young industrialist and smiled with regret. "I must see to this, Nathan." She gave his hand a gentle squeeze before pulling him close and kissing him.

This was not the kiss of friends; tongues were involved, and the stroking of hands, or at least fingers.

In fact, just when it was apparent his lordship was preparing to lift her onto his lap, a throat cleared, and Cecile felt the movement of air and a looming presence.

She pulled away, taking care to ignore Guy, not easy to do when he was practically standing on top of them.

She lavished a smile on Nathan. "I shall look forward to next Wednesday," she lied, and then wanted to kick herself. Oh, it was pleasant to tweak Guy, but now she had only protracted what would be a parting between her and Nathan.

The baron did not look pleased at such a dismissal, but, thankfully, neither did he seem inclined to make an unpleasant scene.

Cecile turned away from the younger man and glared up at Guy, who was glaring at the baron.

"Why are you still here?" she demanded. "You've delivered your message—now go!"

Petty enjoyment and shame swirled in her at the brick-red flush that spread up his neck. He was a proud man and his pride had taken one blow after another over the past weeks. It was cruel to pile more humiliation on him by treating him like a dog in front of a man he knew was her lover.

And yet she could not seem to stop herself.

After holding her gaze a moment longer than any other employee would dare to do and grinding his teeth almost audibly, Guy turned on his heel and strode from the room.

Nathan chuckled. "Really, Cecile. You are taunting a tiger on a leash, aren't you?" His fingers slid beneath her chin, and he tilted her face until she was forced to meet his bold blue gaze. His lips pulled into a mocking smile. "Just don't try to keep two tigers leashed, my dear. You might very well find yourself in the middle."

As threats went, it was far from subtle. If she wasn't careful, it would be inevitable that two masculine, possessive males would give in to their baser passions and fight. One of them might end up badly injured or worse.

Rather than answer, she merely smiled at her soon-to-be-former lover, easily reading his thoughts on his handsome, arrogant face.

He was young, rich, and women beyond counting had set their caps at him.

Guy was poor, disgraced, and without financial prospects.

No doubt Nathan was confident of her choice.

Cecile doubted that he'd believe just how easy it was for her to decide which tiger to keep, and which to turn loose.

Chapter 16

Guy wanted to smash something—some*one*—as he strode out of Cecile's private rooms.

It had taken every ounce of self-control he possessed to leave her in the same room with Whitfield. *Everything.*

He could not go back to the Fayre without becoming violent.

So, instead of heading back through the corridor that connected the house to the theater, he thundered down the main staircase and snatched his work hat and overcoat off the wooden coat-tree that groaned beneath the weight of untold garments.

He rammed his fists into the armholes as he strode out into the night, only pausing to lock the door behind him.

It was bloody cold and there was enough humidity in the air to suggest there would be rain or sleet later tonight. Well, it was the tail end of winter, after all. He would take his chances with the weather; right now, what he needed was to burn away the anger inside him.

Guy had only gone a few steps down the street when he encountered Cordelia Black and two of her employees. Cordelia operated the Fayre's harlequinade and shared a large house close by with all eight of her employees.

Her smile faltered when she got a closer look at his face. "Trouble? Should we turn around and go back home?"

He knew she was only half jesting; all the Fayre employees knew to make themselves scarce if Cecile was displeased.

The last thing Guy wanted to do was talk, but he could hardly ignore her. "Francine and Angus."

It only took those three words to describe the situation.

Cordelia pulled a face, but her shoulders lost some of their tension. "Oh no. Not again?" She laughed. "Angus seems to enjoy bedeviling her more than any of us."

That was unfortunately true. Angus was smart—Guy suspected he was more clever than Francine Gordon, the Fayre magician—and the raven also had light fingers, or claws and beak, rather. Things disappeared all the time and most of the employees just accepted it and stopped leaving their possessions lying about. But Francine was something of a scatterbrain and couldn't seem to keep track of her valuables. Not that the thing Angus was accused of stealing—a carved wooden carrot belonging to her rabbit, Henry—was valuable.

"Well, I can't blame you for running away," Cordelia teased. "I won't keep you." The other two nodded their goodbyes and all three went past.

As Guy strode away it struck him how quickly he'd fallen into his brand-new life. He worked at the Fayre, socialized with Fayre employees, and even lived with several.

In addition to the two housemaids and Cook and her young daughter, there were five Fayre employees living at Cecile's—six, including Guy.

And there was also Cat, now, which brought the number of people occupying the house up to an even dozen when you added Cecile in.

While it was a huge old shack, Guy sometimes felt as if they were all living on top of each other.

Because I'm spoiled—at least that's what she *would say.*

That was probably true enough. He'd been accustomed not only to an enormous suite of rooms at each of the ducal residences, but he'd also had dozens of other rooms that few people entered except Guy, his sisters, and his mother.

Cecile had the only suite of rooms in the house, all the others having been carved into smaller accommodations and storage for theatrical items too valuable to leave next door.

The book room, by far the nicest of the common areas, was never empty, either filled with Fayre employees who were all allowed to use it, or visitors waiting for tenants, or tenants using one of the two desks to write letters.

In other words, the only place Guy could be assured of privacy was in his tiny cupboard of a room. Even that wasn't entirely safe as people were always knocking on his door. People like Cecile.

Cecile.

Guy growled just thinking the name. The wind whistled down the narrow street, but Guy hardly noticed the cold as he recalled the proprietary manner in which Whitfield had held Cecile's hand.

And kissed her.

Guy had always been a mild mannered, almost placid man. He'd been friendly with all the social cliques at school, able to move easily between the divisions that grew up between young boys who were jockeying for power.

And yet in Cecile's sitting room he'd been almost floored by his desire to kill Whitfield. The sensation had been violent, like an influenza Guy had once suffered. His body had burned, his skin on fire, his head so hot it felt as if it might split apart, and it had been difficult to suck air into his lungs—not to mention the strange crackling noise in his head, as if a blaze was burning.

Whitfield had been touching *his* female.

No, not yours—you gave her up, Guy. Or have you forgotten?

No! He bloody well hadn't forgotten, which only made what he was feeling worse. All of this was happening because he had thrown her away. He'd thrown away what they'd had. In short, he'd thrown away love.

But how in the world could he have known that? At the time they'd gone their separate ways, he'd merely felt vaguely uneasy, as if he'd just lost something valuable.

Not until several days, perhaps a few weeks, had passed and he'd felt more and more . . . anxious had he comprehended what he'd done. He'd not only missed her dreadfully, but he'd been utterly uninterested in new lovers. He'd not gone more than a week or so without a lover in decades!

Initially he'd believed lack of sexual intercourse might be the source of his malaise, so he'd accepted one of the blatant invitations he received daily and had gone to visit a woman he'd not been with in years. Dorothea Maxwell was ten years his senior and had been one of his few long-term—well, three months—lovers back when he'd still engaged in more lengthy affairs.

It had been Doro who'd cleared up the mystery for him. At the time of their discussion, they'd been lying in her bed and Guy had just put in one of the least impressive performances of his life. Not catastrophic, mind, but damned close.

"Is this why we stopped seeing one another, Doro? Because I was so useless?" he'd teased, but only half jesting.

"No, darling, we stopped because you're terrified of becoming attached," she'd said without hesitation. "And don't bother arguing with me," she'd added when he'd opened his mouth to do just that.

"What is it, Guy?" Doro had teased, not unkindly. "Has some woman finally stolen your heart?"

Guy knew he was an idiot because it wasn't until that exact moment that he'd truly understood what had happened to him.

He had fallen in love.

Doro had looked almost as stunned as he had, easily reading his expression. "Lord, who's the lucky woman, Guy?"

He'd merely shaken off her question with a lighthearted jest, not that she'd believed him. But the last thing he'd wanted to do was discuss one lover with another.

Besides, he didn't need to discuss what he'd discovered that night; he now knew what had happened to him.

But if he'd believed knowing it and accepting it would make him feel any better, he'd been terribly wrong.

Because acknowledging that he loved Cecile hadn't meant that he could *have* her.

No, last year he'd not been able to follow his heart due to a surfeit of family obligations.

Now he couldn't follow his heart because the woman he loved obviously hated him. Or wanted to cause him pain, or both.

Not only that, but it appeared she'd moved on from him in every way and had already taken a new lover.

Perhaps she'd not fallen out of love with him at all; perhaps she'd never been in love to begin with. Perhaps, for the first time in his life, it had been *Guy* who'd been left wanting more when an affair ended?

Guy gritted his teeth. No, he couldn't think about that. At least not now. He might consider it by the time his six months at the Fayre were over. But until then, he needed to keep his spirits up. And he also needed to find some way to get through to Cecile.

If you love her so much, then why aren't you back at the house talking to her instead of hiding from her?

"Ha!" He startled himself with the bitter bark of laughter and then glanced around to see if he'd been overheard. But the chilly, windswept streets were mostly empty at this time of night and the only traffic was a shocking quantity of rats scurrying in the shadows.

As little as he wished to consider it, Guy was beginning to wonder if Cecile really was as adamant about not wanting him as she sounded. Had he ruined things between them forever? Or had there never been anything to ruin?

No, that latter thought could not be right. He'd felt something between them—some frisson that had been special. He was simply too hasty and hadn't given her enough time. If their situations were reversed—if *she'd* tossed *him* aside to marry somebody else, like Whitfield, for example—he'd be beyond bitter.

Whitfield.

Guy's hands clenched at the thought of the younger, richer, still titled man.

He'd heard rumors of Whitfield casting lures out to Cecile—he'd made it his business to keep up with matters at the Fayre, although most of the information he gleaned was general in nature—but he'd not believed that Cecile had succumbed to Whitfield. Tonight had been a shock, to say the least.

That kiss . . .

Good God. It was lucky he'd been too paralyzed with astonishment to jump on top of Whitfield. But he'd give no guarantees if the man had the nerve to show his face again next Wednesday.

The thought of Cecile with another man was more than he could bear. If he were wise, he'd move out of her house immediately. He'd get on the next ship leaving for Boston and put Cecile firmly in his past.

But he couldn't.

A blast of wind made him realize that it had got *cold* since he'd begun his walk. He looked up and took in his surroundings, frowning at what he saw. Lord! He'd almost walked all the way to his house on Hanover Square.

No, not your house, Barry's house.

Guy stared; was that a *light* in the library window? At this time of night and with no knocker on the door that he could see?

He'd just have a quick look . . .

The rumble of carriage wheels on cobbles drew his attention, and he paused in the middle of the street to watch as a wagon rolled out from the mews that served Fairhurst House. Two men sat on the bench seat, the wagon behind them piled high with—he squinted—furniture? Paintings? And something that looked suspiciously like the longcase clock from the library.

What the devil?

"You there!" Guy shouted, jogging toward the wagon. "Stop."

The man driving whipped around, his eyes widened, and his hands snapped the reins before he even turned to his team. "Haw!" he yelled, and the two old nags leaped forward so quickly they almost dislodged the longcase clock from its precarious perch.

Guy ran after the wagon, shouting for the driver to stop. He knew he was behaving like a madman—it wasn't his house, after all—but he chased the men for two streets, the wagon getting smaller and smaller as it pulled ahead.

Finally, he had to stop. He dropped his hands to his knees and fought to catch his breath.

Obviously, the men were thieves. Why did the servants—Jerrod, the butler—not do something? Surely, they couldn't have slept through men hauling out clocks, furniture, and portraits?

What if the thieves had hurt the servants?

Grimly, Guy started back toward the house.

But just as he reached the corner, a carriage turned onto the street.

Guy gawked at the escutcheon on the side of the big black coach as it rumbled past him. It was the bloody Fairhurst traveling carriage—the newer family coach that was kept in the country, not in town!

He had no chance of catching it, of course, so he continued on to the house.

Never had he gone around back before—to the servant's entrance—but he surmised that would be the quickest way to summon the staff.

Guy cranked the bell and waited. And then cranked it again.

Finally, after the fifth time, the door opened a sliver and a man he'd never seen before stood in the entrance.

"What the 'ell do you—"

"Where's Jerrod?" Guy demanded.

The fellow was a scrawny, pointy-nosed man who looked like a rat. "'Oo?"

"Jerrod—the butler."

"Ain't nobody but me. And 'oo are you to be—"

"This house was just *robbed*. Did you sleep through that, too, you fool? Or were they mates of yours?"

The man's squinty eyes turned mean. "Those men was sent by the duke."

Guy laughed. "At midnight?"

"Wot business is it of yorn?"

"I—"

Guy broke off when he realized it *wasn't* his business, at least not if Barry really had sent the men. And there was no disputing that was the ducal coach. Perhaps Barry had even been inside it, as bizarre as that would be.

The servant, or whatever he was, slammed the door before Guy could formulate a response.

Guy's brain was like a wild horse trapped in a cramped paddock—bolting and darting and charging in all directions, going nowhere.

Who should he tell about this? If it was Barry selling off the contents of the house, could he do anything about it? He knew that some items belonged to the dukedom—like the Fairhurst sapphires—but others . . . well, to be honest, Guy didn't know what exactly could be sold. It had never occurred to him to strip the family homes of their furniture or to sell the portraits of his ancestors.

Guy would have to go to the Fairhurst solicitors first thing in the morning. While it was true that he had no real legal rights when it came to ducal affairs, he was still part of the family and had an interest in seeing the estate wasn't plundered, if that was what was happening. Surely somebody could stop the man?

He turned and began the long trudge back to Newcastle Street.

He'd not gone very far when the light rain turned to flakes of snow, but Guy kept walking, even though he had miles to go before he got back home.

Home.

Guy snorted. He didn't have a home with Cecile—he was an employee.

But Fairhurst House wasn't his home, either.

And he no longer owned Darlington Park.

He had nowhere to call home.

For the first time since Barry's return, Guy understood just how dire his situation was. He must be the thickest man in all England. Why had it taken him so long to understand just how far he'd fallen?

It struck him quite suddenly, and quite horrifically, that Cecile had probably offered him the job not because she loved him or wanted him back in her life. She'd offered him the job because she'd seen his situation clearly.

Because she felt sorry for him.

He was a public joke and had no real future to offer any woman. Rather than pester her, he should have just tucked his tail between his legs and boarded the first ship to Boston.

You could leave tomorrow.

He could do, except he'd committed to working for Cecile for six months. If he left now, he'd look like an even bigger failure. Indeed, he'd look as though he'd run away.

No, Guy had to stay and keep his word. It would hurt to be near her, but it would hurt worse when he had to leave.

The snow turned to sleet, but Guy didn't even notice.

Chapter 17

Cecile glanced at Guy from beneath her lashes. After last night she had not believed that he would be ready and waiting to escort her to look at the prospective school that morning.

And yet he'd been dressed and waiting when she'd come down to breakfast.

At least it *looked* like Guy, but it was as if a different man inhabited his body. Gone was his mischievous smile, his teasing manner, and warm, admiring looks. He'd not called her *darling* or *sweetheart* or anything other than Miss Tremblay, and without the mockery that was his wont.

Cecile suddenly noticed things about him she'd never seen before—signs of age on a face that had seemed perennially boyish. How was it that she'd never seen the harsh grooves that bracketed his ridiculously sensual lips or the network of lines on his brow and around his eyes?

He seemed to have aged in a matter of hours.

Whether it was seeing her with Nathan or something else, she didn't know. But he'd become a different person in less than twelve hours.

Cecile knew he'd been out late because she had waited for him to return home last night, lurking in the book room so she could hear the front door when it opened, ready with a scold because scolding him was always a perfect excuse to seek out his company.

Last night's scold had been about summoning her away from her guest to mediate a dispute that her stage manager could have easily handled. In fact, that was Beryl's job, and her employee had looked hurt when Cecile had arrived on the scene, as if she didn't trust Beryl to sort out an argument between an excitable magician and a knife thrower who barely had a pulse.

Cecile had stormed back to the house afterward, both furious that Guy had possessed the audacity to disturb her, and relieved that she'd not had to tell Nathan to go home.

She had become even more furious when she realized that she didn't want Nathan anymore. Indeed, had she ever *wanted* him? Or had he merely been a sop to her damaged self-esteem after Guy had cast her aside and she'd been forced to read about his exploits in the newspapers for weeks on end?

Cecile sighed. How in the world could she break off matters between her and Nathan without making an ugly scene? Ugh. That was why she always established limits for her lovers in advance. Who would have ever believed that Nathan—who was almost a decade younger than she—would offer marriage to a circus entertainer?

But she would have to speak to him—before next Wednesday came around and he arrived on her doorstep—and sort out the situation before matters got worse.

As for Guy . . .

After discovering that Guy had gone out into the vile weather, she had been unable to sleep last night. Instead, she'd stayed awake for hours, awaiting his return.

He'd finally returned shortly after three o'clock and, judging by his bearing, he'd not been drunk.

His coat and hat had been encrusted in a thick shell of ice and she'd hovered in the darkness of the book room, on the brink of going to him—of stripping off his frozen clothing and warming him. Of wrapping herself around his big body and easing the dejection she'd seen in his posture.

Of course, she had done no such thing, even though she knew she was at least partly responsible for his drooping shoulders.

Why was she making him so miserable when all she wanted was to take him into her bed?

She cast a surreptitious glance at him as he strode along beside her, silent and grim-faced.

Cecile honestly didn't know what made her continue to hold him at arm's length. Every single time she considered forgiving him, she would remember his casual, insulting insouciance that last morning in France—when he'd offered to make her his whore and set her up in a London house—and then it would be all she could do not to slap him.

They stopped at a busy corner to wait for the traffic to thin so they could cross. Cecile couldn't help noticing that there was a rut in the street that was deep enough to submerge a good six inches of wagon wheel.

She glanced down at her ankle boots and frowned. They were sturdy enough, but they would surely be ruined if she marched through such a mess.

The traffic paused and the crowd of people began to cross the street.

But before she could move to walk around the rut, Guy turned to her and matter-of-factly took her by the waist and lifted her over the sludge, then set her down lightly before striding on.

Cecile stared at his receding back for one stunned moment. She was not a small woman—in fact, she was both tall and solidly built—and yet he'd picked her up as if she were as slight as Cat.

Guy stopped and turned, a querying expression on his face. "Yes?"

"Nothing," she muttered, hurrying toward him.

Cecile delivered a silent scold to herself as they marched onward.

So what if he could lift her easily? He would have done the same thing for Cook or one of her maids or, indeed, the contumacious laundry woman, Mrs. Bascom.

He was a gentleman, bred to the bone to be honorable and

thoughtful. It was as much a part of him as his melting brown eyes or perfect bone structure.

Until meeting Guy, Cecile had believed chivalry was a myth. But chivalry was a coin with two very different sides. After all, Guy's chivalry toward his mother and sisters had meant rejection for Cecile, hadn't it? Doing the *right* thing could often have uncomfortable results, as she well knew.

Guy stopped in front of a large two-story gray stone building. "This is it."

Cecile studied the building, which looked fairly new—perhaps built in the last fifty years. The windows were without drapes, and she could see the orderly desks in the ground floor rooms.

"It is nondenominational," he said. "Although the gentleman who founded it is a Quaker. The school operates six days a week and costs eight pence a month. I wanted us to walk, rather than take a hackney so you could see it is an easy distance, even in inclement weather." He turned to her, his warm brown eyes strangely cool. "If you like, we may take a tour of the facility, although I have already done so."

"And you approve of it?"

He hesitated and then nodded.

"What were you going to say?"

"If my situation were different, I would engage a governess, as we did for my sisters. But this is certainly better than nothing."

"How much is a governess?"

He turned to face her fully. "It's not only the wage; you must also house them."

"I know that. How much?"

He pushed his hat aside and scratched behind his ear, his expression thoughtful. "I'm afraid I never paid the bills myself—I had a secretary. But I should think somewhere between forty to seventy-five pounds per annum, depending on the woman's education and breeding."

Cecilia chewed on that sum as she stared at the building across the street. She could afford it—even the high end of the pay—and she could always empty out one of the three remaining storage rooms to house the woman.

But such a step was . . . well, it smacked of permanence. But wasn't that already the case? Cat had only been with her two weeks and already it was hard to remember what life had been like before her.

"What do you think?" she asked him.

"It might be better for her to be with other children," Guy said. "And she'd—"

"What are we doing, Guy?"

He blinked and for a long moment Cecile thought he might not know what she meant.

He sighed. "She is already settling in, Cecile. It would be cruel to turn her out at this point."

"I would never do that!"

"No, I didn't think you would. I wanted to tell you that I would write to my mother about her if you decided that you can't keep her here." He gave a wry smile. "Although I can just imagine what she would think."

"That Cat is your lovechild?"

"That is what everyone will think, Cecile—about one or both of us."

"Disregarding the fact that she looks nothing like me, there is also the fact that I don't care what anyone thinks."

Guy smiled, and it was his usual smile, not the ghost of a smile he'd been wearing all morning.

"But what I *do* care about is doing right by Cat now that I have her," Cecile went on. "She should have a chance to be a young lady—as Marianne was raised, even though she ended up going into the Fayre. I think perhaps a governess is better. I never had one and I have often felt the lack of an education."

"You didn't go to school?"

"My father had me in the shop from the age of five—that is the way it is done in my family," she said, aware that she sounded more than a little defensive.

"I wasn't going to criticize."

"People have in the past." Her cousin Curtis had, for one. The fool should have understood that she never could have recreated her father's gun plans from memory if she'd not grown up working at the bench alongside him.

Guy didn't speak, but merely held her gaze, his expression serious and very un-Guy-like.

Also very unnerving.

"She will live with me," Cecile said, only realizing as she said it how calm she now felt. Cecile had nobody of her own. And Cat had only George. The three of them could now have each other.

"I am glad to hear that," Guy said, his smile gentle.

"I will engage a governess for her," she said. "Cat will have to earn her own way in life; the least I can do is equip her."

"I think that is the right decision." He raised a hand to hail a hackney.

"I would prefer to walk back."

Surprise flickered on his face, but he nodded.

"Richie says you have more applicants to interview this afternoon," he said after a moment or two.

"Yes, but I am not optimistic. I am beginning to think I am searching for someone who doesn't exist. Most of the women have been so clumsy I'd never trust them with a spoon, not to mention a loaded pistol."

He laughed, the sound warming her far more than it should and sending flutters through her chest.

"It's true," she insisted. "I had a girl—a pastrycook's assistant who I think must have set fire to her last employer's business—and when she discharged the pistol—after I'd demonstrated the process extensively—she shrieked, her arm jerked up, and she shot the ceiling, thankfully one of the panels rather than the chandelier."

Guy chuckled.

Ugh. That intoxicating sound again.

"Well, there are women who know how to use fowling pieces and hunt—my sisters do—but you'll not find them among the laboring classes, I'm afraid."

"Maybe I should be advertising in the society section of the papers," Cecile reflected gloomily.

They walked for a while in companionable silence.

"I want to ask you something. Something that is personal in nature," Guy said a few moments later. "But I don't want you to get angry with me."

She cut him an amused glance. "Since when have you cared about anything like that?"

"You'd be surprised," he muttered.

Whatever that meant.

Cecile considered his question while he gave a coin to the lad who'd cleared a path through the rapidly melting slush.

Although they'd been lovers for weeks, they'd rarely spoken of personal matters. Their lives had been filled with so much drama and excitement, they'd had plenty of other things to discuss, like dodging French mercenaries, demented deposed kings, and unscrupulous barons.

Cecile had discouraged personal questions and hadn't asked any of her own. She'd known all along their liaison was temporary. Why make parting an even more painful business?

But here he was, back in her life.

Despite what he claimed—that she was what he wanted—Cecile knew he would never settle in to working in a circus for the rest of his life. Something, or likely some*one*, would come along who would be suitable for a man of his background and status.

The one thing she knew for certain about aristocratic men was that they were forgiven any folly if they were handsome and charming. Guy's stint at the Fayre would be a story he could tell at *ton* gatherings for years to come.

That same generous attitude was *not* extended to the women of his class. Or the women of any other class, for that matter.

Cecile eyed his patient, handsome face, and her impulse to protect herself at all costs wavered.

He would never use her past against her, so what would it hurt to share a bit of her life with him? She'd already told him who she really was—something she'd never told anyone else—and he'd kept the story to himself.

Cecile nodded. "Ask your question."

"I want to know about your journey to Britain."

"It's not very exciting."

"I'd still like to hear it if it is not painful to talk about?"

Cecile considered his question and realized her heart no longer hurt when she thought about that horrid night.

"It is no longer painful." She inhaled deeply, exhaled, and began.

"It was storming the night we left—badly—and we shouldn't have sailed, but my father was afraid to linger in France. You see, he'd spent most of his money to visit his patron in prison. By the time we stepped onto that boat, we had only coins left to us. His plan was to go to my cousin in England and work for him."

"So he was acquainted with your cousin?"

"They had never met, but they'd exchanged letters for years. The Blanchard family had made guns for a long time, but they were never of the caliber"—she laughed—"pardon the bad pun, of those the Blanchets made. From time to time my father helped them, as had my grandfather, by sending them some of the improvements in his designs."

They walked in silence for a moment, the past and that night gradually coming back to her.

"My father was not well. I think he contracted something when we went to La Force to visit his former patron, who was dying." She glanced at Guy and saw he was looking at her, his brow furrowed with concern. "He was very ill before we left France, and he actually died on the boat journey to England."

"Good Lord," he murmured. "Didn't you say that you were only fourteen?"

"Yes."

"Did you have anyone else with you?"

"No, it was just the two of us."

"You must have been terrified."

She gave a humorless laugh. "There should be a new word for

what I felt. I spoke almost no English, and I discovered right before the boat capsized in the middle of the Channel—in a violent storm—that my father had died while sitting right beside me. When the boat went over, I managed to cling to it, holding on for hours. As for the two men who'd been rowing, one moment they were there, the next they were gone. I don't know if they survived or if—"

Cecile shivered as she recalled those long, freezing, terrifying hours in the darkness.

Guy stared at her in horror. "My God, Cecile."

"When I washed up the next day, there were a great many people on the shore. It seemed another ship—a real ship—had broken apart during the storm. It was an English vessel, so those helping the survivors assumed I was another passenger and gave me shelter and food while I recovered. My father had always insisted I learn a little English, so I could understand just enough that I knew I needed to pretend I was mute rather than attempt to speak." She gave him a wry smile. "It was not a good time to be a French émigré as they were flooding England's shores."

The guilty look on his face told her he knew what she meant. So many French people had come to England in so short a time that the populace—from poor to wealthy—had viewed them as a nuisance, at best, and a dangerous menace at worst.

It was interesting how emotional the story was making her, she thought, rapidly blinking her eyes to clear her vision.

It occurred to her that she'd never told it to anyone in its entirety. Curtis and his wife hadn't wanted to know the details; they'd wanted her to become as English as possible, as fast as possible, and had pretended her past didn't exist.

Marianne had asked her, but Cecile had put her off with a few vague details, not wanting her best friend to know what a pitiful creature she had once been.

Was it significant that yet again it was Guy in whom she confided?

She shrugged off the thought and continued. "Everything was lost when our boat capsized: my father's plans, what little we had left in terms of family valuables, our small amount of money, and all our documents."

Not a day passed that Cecile didn't regret losing her father's bag.

"All I had in my possession was my cousin's name and direction and a few coins that had been in my skirt pocket. My father had told me to go to him if I was ever in need of help."

She snorted, remembering how stupidly hopeful she'd been.

"Curtis wasn't so difficult to find," Cecile said, not wanting to dwell on those nightmare weeks when she'd been adrift in a foreign country with hostile strangers, afraid to speak the language. As for the French émigrés she'd eventually encountered, well, their attempts to manipulate or use her had been even worse than the disdain of the hard-eyed Englishmen and women.

"That is . . . well, that is quite a harrowing story," he said after a long moment.

"I am one of thousands who have similar tales, although perhaps without the shipwreck. It might sound bad, but it was still much better than staying in France."

"Did your father's position as royal gunmaker make him a target of anti-Royalists?"

"That was part of the problem," she admitted. "But there was also the fact that we'd lived for many years in the household of the Duc de La Fontaine, who served as my father's patron. Their association was a close one and we were—well, let's just say it wasn't safe for us after things began to fall apart."

"And your cousin is your only relative?"

At her raised eyebrow, he added, "I recall you saying when we were in France that you had no relatives."

Not for the first time did she consider telling the man beside her that she was a duchess in her country.

She held her peace at the painful memory of Curtis's and his wife, Martha's, reaction.

Guy would probably not call her a liar as her cousin had done, but without those precious papers in her father's bag, her marriage to the duke might as well have never taken place.

"No other family that I know of," she said, which was the truth. "My father was an only child. I suppose there might be people on my mother's side, but she died in childbed, and I never met any of her relations growing up. My father always seemed content to train me in his craft even though I was not a son. Perhaps if things had been different, he might have taken another wife in time." She shrugged. "But then the world went mad, and nobody was buying expensive, handcrafted pistols, so having a male heir was the least of his worries."

"You mentioned your father visiting the duke in La Force Prison? Wasn't that dangerous?"

"Very."

"Why would he take such a risk?"

"I'd grown up in the castle, not a daughter of the house but not a servant, either—always apart. The duke was old even when I was a child. He had one son who'd died years before, as had his duchess. Really, we were his family, and he was ours. My father helped the duke escape, and he helped *us* with the money he brought with him. Even though we were no better than tradespeople, those distinctions suddenly didn't matter during the Revolution."

"How long did you hide?" he asked, picking her up again to lift her over the same deep rut in the road.

This time the memory of those dark days robbed her of any appreciation of his minor chivalrous action.

"We lived deep in the country, and the duke had always been a well-liked landlord and master, so the discontent came more slowly there. Not until men came from the city did the trouble start. We were all fortunate that they were so busy ransacking the castle for valuables, they had no time to spare for us. Aided by one of the grooms, Papa took an old farm wagon, and the duke dressed up in ragged clothing."

Cecile could still recall her shock the first time she'd seen the magnificent duke stripped of his wig and jewels and brocades. In rough homespun and sabots, he had resembled a skinny old peasant— so long as one didn't look at his soft, white hands.

"We stayed in sizeable towns where people were less apt to ask questions than they would in small villages. We were just more of the displaced peasantry roaming the country, a middle-aged man taking care of his young daughter and aged father.

"Even so, we could never stay for long before people began to be suspicious and we would have to move—we did so often. The duke had taken some money and jewels with him when we fled, so we sold bits and pieces here and there. My father worked when he could—repairing weapons or clocks or anything requiring a skilled touch."

Cecile had been excited at first and had looked forward to being on the run. It had seemed so romantic and much more interesting than living in the boring countryside. "I thought it was a game at first, moving from town to town. But as the weeks turned into months turned into years, I started to understand that we might need to hide forever—or at least until the money ran out. The stories one would hear about Paris"—she shivered—"it was hard to know fact from fiction. It was impossible to know who might be in charge from one day to the next. When we'd hear the Royalist factions were gaining ground, the duke would begin to hope. But only days later we'd hear of some new atrocity perpetrated against the aristocracy or church.

"After we learned of the king's execution, the duke went into decline. I think he simply lost hope. He would not leave the country with us, so my father and I stayed because there was nobody else to take care of him."

When Guy stopped walking, Cecile looked up from her thoughts to discover they were back at the theater.

"Well, here we are," she said lamely, feeling flustered at how much she'd revealed.

He set a hand on her shoulder before she could escape into the familiar comfort of her business.

"I'm sorry you had such a wretched time," he said when she risked a glance up at him.

She shrugged, but he didn't release her. "It's hardly your fault."

"I know that, but I wish I could have spared you the pain."

Something odd unfurled in her chest at his words and the gentle expression in his brown eyes, which were no longer distant as they'd been earlier that morning.

Her stomach twisted almost painfully at the unwanted kindness she saw.

Fear spurred anger and she lashed out. "You mean instead of adding to my unhappy experiences?"

He flinched away and his hand dropped to his side.

Good.

Cecile turned and escaped into the safety of the theater. As usual, there were employees with questions, but she brushed them all aside.

"Later," she muttered over and over, almost breathless with the need to get to her private sanctum.

Once inside her small office, she threw the latch and sank into the chair in front of her cluttered desk.

In the center of the desk was the early mail delivery.

On top of the pile of cheap onionskin that signified bills was a rectangle of thick cream parchment, her name scrawled across the front in a familiar, commanding hand.

Nathan.

She snatched up the missive, already guessing what was inside.

There was a timid knock on the door.

"What is it?" she snapped, sliding a letter opener beneath the thick blob of blue sealing wax.

The door handle jiggled.

"Just tell me through the door," she ordered, spreading the expensive parchment out on her desk to read.

My dearest Cecile,

I'm sure you can guess at my displeasure regarding Wednesday night. The more time I've spent pondering the matter, the more I think it is not wise to allow Darlington to continue working for you and living in your house.

While I am willing to accept your past, I do not wish my

future wife to be known as the sort of woman who would live with a man out of wedlock.

I wish to see you and I do not want to wait until next Wednesday. Nor do I wish to meet at your house, for obvious reasons.

Come to my house tomorrow night—I know your show is first on Friday—come to me immediately afterward and we shall discuss what is to be done and make our plans for the future.

Your servant,

Nathan

Cecile snarled and crumpled up the paper.

Richie's hesitant voice came through the door. "Your first interview is waiting, Miss Tremblay. Er, she's half an hour early."

Cecile raised her voice to be heard through the door. "Tell her she will have to wait until her appointed time!"

"Very good, Miss Tremblay."

Cecile turned away from the door and took several deep breaths, her anger threatening to get the better of her again—as it had outside with Guy.

Bloody Nathan! Just who did he think he was to be giving ultimatums?

She whipped out a sheet of paper and dashed out a response, one that was both short and to the point. She had thought to spare his feelings on the matter of the marriage proposal, but as he had no thought to spare *hers*, she would end their liaison immediately.

Guy was repairing a section of pinrail—which Basil the carpenter had painstakingly showed him how to fix—and brooding about Cecile and her angry reaction that morning.

He was no longer surprised when she lashed out at him, and much of the time he had to agree that he deserved it. But this morning? What had driven her into such a rage?

"Guy!"

He looked up from his work and grinned as Cat came flying

toward him, screeching to a stop almost on the toes of his boots. George was dancing around her, just as excited as his mistress.

"Hello, Kitty-Cat," he teased, tying off the new line.

"Where have you *been*?" she demanded.

"I told you I was taking Ce—Miss Tremblay to look at the school today."

Her expression told him just what she thought about that.

"You needn't look so mulish—she's decided it's better to engage a governess for you." Guy gave her a moment to absorb that news as he held out his hand to the small terrier mutt. Clearly the jury was still out when it came to Guy, but George unbent enough to allow Guy to give him a quick scratch behind the ears.

"Well, what say you?" he asked when Cat remained uncharacteristically quiet.

She shrugged, her face long. "I like spending the day with Cook and Nancy in the kitchen."

Nancy was Cook's daughter, who at eleven was a few years older than Cat, but—thankfully—the two girls got on very well.

"Yes, well, the kitchen is a good place to learn, er, housewifery skills, my girl, but there are many other things you must learn."

"You mean bookish things?"

"Just so."

"Why can't you and Cecile teach me bookish things? Why do we need somebody else?"

Guy dropped to his haunches, met her eye to eye, and set his hands on her fragile shoulders. "We have to work, darling. And you need somebody who knows all the things you've been missing out on. I'm afraid if you relied on me to teach you maths, you'd end up using your fingers and toes to count."

She scoffed and giggled. "You're so silly."

"I am." He brushed a stray curl from her forehead and tucked it behind her ear. "You'll see us plenty—we live together." Although he wasn't sure how long he'd be staying if Whitfield came into the house again. Cat could always visit him in Newgate after he throttled the man and was sentenced to hang.

"Chances are that you shall be good friends with your new governess," Guy continued. "My younger sisters had a governess they simply adored, and Diana cried when she left."

Of course, his older sisters had been terrorized by an old crone who'd smacked their knuckles with a ruler and tied a board to their backs for posture correction. Still, no point in mentioning that . . .

She nodded, but he could see she wasn't convinced.

Guy held out his hand. "Come on—you can help me in the dressing room. Let's see if we can find the settee rumored to be beneath that mountain of clothing." It wasn't the settee Cecile was worried about so much as costumes lost in the huge pile of garments the staff tended to fling into the dressing room.

Cat skipped alongside him. "Can I put on some face paint?"

"Er, that's probably not a good idea."

"Why not?"

"You're not old enough."

She frowned, and Guy sensed that wasn't the end of the discussion, by any means.

The theater was virtually empty, as it was that strange time of the day between rehearsals and the start of the first performances. That meant—hopefully—the dressing room would be unoccupied.

But when he opened the door, he saw Blade standing on a stool while Marie, the wardrobe mistress, did something to the hem of an unusual black skirt.

"Oh. We can come back—"

Marie waved him in. "'Most done," she said through a mouthful of pins.

Guy glanced at Blade. "Do you mind us coming in?"

"No."

"Er, new costume?" he asked.

She nodded, her strange pale eyes on Cat.

"Have you met Cat and George?" Guy asked, looking around for Blade's familiar when the terrier's ruff stood up and he began to growl.

"George—be a good boy," Cat chided, her eyes all but glued to the same thing her dog was glaring at: Angus.

The huge bird was perched on the heavy wooden chandelier that lighted the small space. Somebody, Blade, probably, had removed two of the candles at some point so he could roost without setting himself on fire.

"We've not been formally introduced," Blade said with a faint smile, nodding her thanks to Marie when the older woman finished chalking and pinning and stood.

"Er, Cat, this is Miss Brown."

Blade smiled down at the little girl, her expression unusually open for the reserved woman. "Hello, Cat. I'm Josephine, but everyone calls me Blade." She gestured to the raven, who appeared to be watching the proceedings with interest. "And that is Angus."

Cat glanced at Guy, and he knew she was asking permission to call an adult by her first name. Or, in this case, her nickname. Guy's mother would have been outraged, but things were more relaxed among theatrical people.

He nodded.

"It's a pleasure to meet you . . . Blade." Cat turned to Angus, her eyes widening.

"Er, Cat—can you make George stop snarling, please?" Guy asked. "I don't think Angus likes being growled at."

Indeed, the huge bird turned its glossy black gaze on the terrier and ruffled its feathers, making itself appear three times larger and prompting George to growl even louder.

Blade stepped behind the screen just as George barked.

"Stop it, George!" Cat scolded. "You mustn't—"

Angus leaned low, his black beady eyes on the dog, and then *he* barked—the sound deeper, more of a mastiff than a terrier.

George yelped and backed away.

Blade chuckled as she changed out of her costume. "You want to meet him?" she asked the girl.

"Yes, please!" Cat nodded so vigorously it made Guy's head hurt just watching.

"Let me finish changing and I'll introduce you."

Cat turned to her dog and crouched down beside him, giving

him some reassuring strokes while she waited. "It is fine, George, Angus is not going to hurt me. I want you to sit and be nice."

To Guy's surprise, the dog sat.

"Good boy." Cat scratched behind his ears and George gave her a deliriously happy canine smile.

Blade came out from behind the screen, wearing one of the gray wool dresses many of the women seemed to favor, and handed the black gown to Marie.

"I'll have it back by the end of the week," the Frenchwoman said, leaving the small room.

Blade looked at her bird and gave the slightest of nods. For all that Angus had to weigh at least a third of a stone and was a good two feet tall, he moved quickly and soundlessly, landing on Blade's shoulder in a soft flurry of feathers.

Blade sat in a chair in front of one of the mirrors. "Come closer," she said to Cat. "He won't peck you."

Cat didn't look convinced, but she went toward the huge bird, which was easily half as tall as she. Angus seemed to realize it was a time for gentleness because he stood still, his feathers tight and his posture unthreatening.

"He's a common raven," Blade said, reaching up and scratching the bird below the chin, as Guy had seen her do countless times.

Angus immediately melted, his feathers fluffing to allow her fingers better purchase. "He likes being petted right here—it is his hackles. You can pet him if you like."

Cat's small body was tense, but she was a fearless little thing and she reached for him. No doubt a bird wasn't half as terrifying as living on the streets for the last few years.

She laughed when her fingers touched his feathers. "He's so soft."

Blade smiled—the first Guy had ever seen on her, and he'd known her over a year—the expression transforming her strangely featureless face and making her look pretty and almost girlish. "That's his body down."

"Like a goose," Cat said, her expression trancelike as she stared at the bird.

"Yes, the same idea."

"I've never seen a bird like him before. He's so big!"

"There used to be many ravens, and they were very helpful to farmers. But perhaps a hundred years or so ago, people decided they were pests, so they hunted them to near extinction. I haven't seen a single raven in Britain although I understand a few still live here."

"Where did you get him?" Cat asked, the tension leaking from her small frame as it became obvious the bird wasn't going to hurt her.

"He found me," Blade said simply. "Where did you get your dog?"

"We found each other," Cat said, and then laughed when Angus purred. "He's purring like a cat!"

"*Cat*," Angus echoed.

Guy, Angus, Blade, and possibly George, too, all winced at Cat's high-pitched squeal. "He *talks*!"

"He does," Blade said, turning to the bird. "What's the weather like today, Angus?"

"*It's a pea souper,*" he said in his strange voice, which sounded like a slightly raspier version of Blade's.

They all laughed.

"What do you want for supper, Angus?"

"*Pork pie and peas.*"

Cat laughed so hard it was a joy to watch.

Guy narrowed his eyes at the bird. "He also steals."

Angus snapped his beak at Guy and cut him a filthy look.

"Does he really?" Cat asked.

Blade nodded. "Don't leave anything of value around because Angus likes pretty things. Or even just things."

"Why?"

"He gives them to me."

"He gives you presents?"

"Yes. It's his way of showing affection. Or at least one way. The way he's purring for you is another."

Cat was transfixed.

Blade turned to Guy. "I found one of his caches yesterday." She took a folding penknife from the pocket in her gown. "It has your name engraved on it."

"Ah, thank you. I thought I'd lost it. It was a gift from my grandmother when I was a boy." He took it and slipped it into his pocket. "Is this part of last night's excitement?"

Guy turned to the settee and began to sort the abandoned garments into separate piles.

A glint of humor shone in Blade's opalescent eyes. "It started out as one thing and led to another. Francine was not . . . happy."

"So then Angus *did* take Henry's toy?" he asked.

Henry was Francine the magician's rabbit, a fluffy white creature with startling pink eyes. Henry's favorite toy was a carved carrot.

Guy held up something that looked like a medieval gown.

"Yes, I'm afraid that Angus has developed an attachment to the wooden carrot." Blade looked at the garment he was frowning at. "That belongs to one of Cordelia's people."

"Ah." Guy grunted and made up yet another pile. Cordelia Black's actors kept charge of their own costumes—or at least they were supposed to. He doubted Cordelia would be happy to learn somebody had just left one lying about in the dressing room.

"You're handy with knives. Why don't you just whittle him another carrot?" he asked, momentarily transfixed by a skirt that was so filmy surely one could see through it. Lord, who wore this and why had *he* never seen it?

His willful imagination immediately pictured Cecile wearing it.

"I have done, several times."

Guy looked up from the skirt. "I'm sorry, what did you say?"

He put the diaphanous skirt in a whole new pile—one he'd bring to Cecile. Because . . . why not dream?

"I said I've whittled Angus several toys." She sounded frustrated. It was unlike Blade to show any emotion.

Thinking about not showing emotion made him think of Elliot.

"Did Elliot talk to you about doing something for me?" He glanced at Cat, not wanting to bring up the sensitive subject in front of her since he knew from his sisters that little pitchers had big ears.

But Cat had become bold enough to employ two hands and was giving Angus a proper rubdown. The raven's beak was hanging open in an expression of corvid ecstasy.

"Elliot mentioned something to me," she said, her face once more a mask of reserve. "I can work for you as long as it doesn't interfere with any of my nights here." Her gaze hardened. "Elliot indicated this might be about our employer?"

Guy nodded.

"She has enough trouble on her hands right now without my adding to it."

"I'm not trying to add to her troubles," he shot back. "I'm trying to *help* her."

Blade looked unconvinced.

"Besides, Elliot said you'd be careful enough that nobody would find out anything."

"That's true," she agreed. "But he also said you'd mentioned having a look about yourself."

"No. I changed my mind about that after he pointed out the obvious disadvantages." He glanced at Cat.

Blade nodded. "We can talk about exactly what you want to do later." She turned to Cat and Angus. "We have to go now, but I can bring Angus over to see you at the house." She glanced at George, who was still cowering in the corner. "He can become acquainted with your dog, too, so they get along better."

Cat bounced up and down on her toes. "Oh, could we? Is that all right, Guy?"

"I'm sure Cecile wouldn't mind." He winked at her. "Blade can bring Angus sometime when Cecile's not home and we can turn him loose on all her things."

Blade clucked her tongue. "Oh, Guy."

"*Oh, Guy*," Angus echoed, making the same clucking sound.

Cat laughed so hard he worried she'd do herself harm.

"I'll get back to you within the next few days," Blade said, and then left with her bird.

"Here, you can help me sort," Guy said to Cat.

As he sorted clothing and costumes and Cat jabbered to him and George, Guy thought about the other matter he'd seen to today.

After the unhappy end to his conversation with Cecile, Guy had required another long walk to settle his temper, and so he'd gone to visit the offices of Ashe and Ashe, the solicitors who'd managed the ducal affairs for decades.

The visit had done nothing to alleviate his rotten mood.

Instead of being met by one of the senior partners of the firm—as was usually the procedure when the solicitors called on him—he'd been passed off to a mere clerk.

"I'm sorry, Mr. Darlington, but I'm afraid I can't talk to you about matters pertaining to the dukedom."

"Well then, how about Ashe or his father? Can *they* speak to me?"

"Neither of them are in the office, sir."

That was a bloody lie because Guy could hear Ashe senior shouting at a subordinate in the back office.

So there was a blow to his dignity he'd not been expecting. That was the way things were now—he wasn't even important enough to merit a visit with a bloody solicitor.

He would talk to Blade about *that matter* as well when he saw her.

Guy might no longer be duke, but he was bloody well still a Darlington, no matter how many people might wish that he'd simply disappear.

Chapter 18

"I have finally hired an apprentice," Cecile declared upon entering the kitchen a few evenings later.

It was early and Guy was keeping company with Cat and George, who were eating their dinner.

"Congratulations," Guy said, setting aside his spoon to stand, and quickly being waved back into his seat by his employer.

"Sit, sit. I will eat, too." She glanced at Cook, who was already filling a bowl with stew.

Since the occupants of the house kept such odd hours, everyone tended to eat when they had the time, and the kitchen was generally considered the social center of the big house.

"And you want to know the really good news?" Cecile asked Cat, whose mouth was so stuffed with fresh-baked bread that her cheeks looked like a squirrel's.

Cat nodded.

"This woman is also your new governess."

Guy choked on his stew. "You found a woman who could fill both positions?" he asked once he could speak, not bothering to hide his disbelief.

Cecile gave him a haughty look. "What? You think women cannot possess more than one skill, Mr. Darlington?"

He rolled his eyes. "Obviously, I'm not so ignorant as to think such a thing, Mistress Tremblay. And I'd be criminally stupid to admit it out loud if I *did* think it," he added under his breath, earning a glare from his employer. "So, who is this paragon?"

"Her name is Miss Helen Keeble."

"Keeble? That's an odd name," he said, resuming his meal.

"Says the man whose last name is *Darling*ton."

Guy ignored her dig. "So, when does Miss Keeble start?"

"She is moving into the corner room tonight. In fact, you will be clearing out the room after you finish eating."

"Yes, mistress."

She cocked her head at him. "You might think that is sarcasm, but your quick, respectful obedience is pleasing to me and demonstrates that you are finally learning your place."

Guy laughed. "You just keep right on thinking that, sweetheart." He stood and fetched a glass, then gestured to the bottle of wine on the table.

Cecile nodded. "Yes, please."

"When do I have to start lessons?" Cat asked, her mulish expression telling Guy that at least one person in the room wasn't happy at the news.

Guy handed Cecile her wine and she nodded her thanks. "You will have to ask Miss Keeble since she is in charge of all that."

"Where is she from? What is her background?" Guy asked.

"Her mother was a governess and her father is a vicar in some tiny village—I forget the name. She went to a school for young ladies, whose name I've also forgotten, but she said it is quite a fine establishment. I think it was—"

Blade and Angus appeared in the doorway and Guy stood.

"Please, sit," Blade murmured to Guy, her pale eyes drifting to the pot of stew.

"Have a seat and eat," Cecile said, pushing out the chair beside her.

"Oh." Blade glanced around the room in the dreamy way she had, her gaze flickering over Guy and Cat to settle on George, who was bristling, staring at Angus, and growling.

"Maybe some other time," she finally said.

Cecile heaved a sigh, grabbed Blade's hand, and yanked her down into the chair beside her. "Another bowl, please, Cook. George, you—" Cecile issued a rapid stream of French words too quickly for Guy to follow.

The dog must have comprehended, because he sat back down on his haunches and shut his mouth. But his gaze remained fixed on the raven.

"Wine?" Guy offered.

When Blade hesitated Cecile answered for her. "Yes."

He busied himself fetching another glass.

"Did you hear about your former fiancée?" Blade asked.

Guy paused in the act of pouring the wine. "Do you mean me?"

Blade turned to Cecile and asked her, with no apparent sarcasm, "Were you ever betrothed?"

"She means you, Guy," Cecile said flatly.

"No, what about Miss Carter?"

"I take it that you knew she was betrothed to your cousin?" Blade asked, taking the bowl of stew from Cook and nodding her thanks.

"Do you think there is anyone in Britain who doesn't know that piece of news?" he asked, not caring if he sounded shirty.

Blade and Cecile exchanged an amused look, which further annoyed him.

Before he could open his mouth to say as much, Blade said, "Well, Miss Helena Carter has disappeared."

"Disappeared?" Guy repeated.

"Yes." Blade blew on a spoonful of stew and then lifted it to Angus. The raven eyed the contents of the spoon for a moment and then delicately selected a piece of carrot.

Blade ate the rest.

Cecile made a hissing sound. "That is not sanitary."

"Angus's mouth is cleaner than any human's," Blade demurred.

"May I feed George from my spoon?" Cat asked.

"No, you may *not*." Cecile glared at Blade "See what you've started?"

"Back to your story," Guy interrupted, before things got ugly. "Disappeared how?"

"Her father hosted a betrothal dinner for her and your cousin the duke and she didn't appear."

"How did you hear about this? It wasn't in this morning's paper."

"No, it wasn't," she agreed, buttering some warm bread and then tearing off a small chunk for her bird.

"Then how do you—" He stopped, rolled his eyes, and said, "Never mind."

Whoever she really was and wherever she came from, Josephine Brown was every bit as sneaky as Elliot and always seemed to know things that she shouldn't.

"Well, that's an interesting development," Guy said a moment later, feeling a pang of concern for his ex-betrothed. He didn't love Helena, of course, but he'd come to like her quite a bit in the time they'd been conspirators.

"Apparently, she didn't want to marry your cousin," Cecile said.

"I can't blame her," Guy retorted.

"Why? What is he like?"

Guy's impulse was to say he was an ignorant arse and as sneaky as a weasel, but he tried to answer more objectively.

"He's handsome and gregarious enough. I wouldn't have thought that he'd repel a woman."

"What would you know about what women like?" Cecile demanded.

Guy counted to ten before answering. "You are correct, *Miss Tremblay*. As always."

"Maybe she just didn't care to be traded from man to man like a horse," she suggested.

Rather than feel insulted by her comment, Guy actually happened to agree with it.

It wouldn't have been Helena's choice to marry Barry any more than it had been her choice to marry Guy. She'd been a pawn in her father's quest for power and influence. He hoped that wherever she ended up, she could at least choose whom to spend her life with.

He finished his last mouthful of stew, threw back the remains of his wine, and stood.

"Well, I'd better get to work on that room if she is coming tonight. If you ladies will excuse me?"

"Oh," Cecile said. "Will you put all the paste jewels from the storage room into the counting room?"

"Of course." Guy turned to the hook on the wall where the key to the counting room was usually kept. "The key is not here."

"I wasn't the last to use it!" Cook called over her shoulder without even turning.

"Don't look at me," Guy said when Cecile looked at him.

"I know it was on the hook this morning because I put the silver back in there after polishing it," Cook said.

Everyone turned to Blade.

She finished chewing and set down her spoon before turning to Angus.

Some sort of silent communication passed between woman and bird and then Blade sighed and began patting at the various pockets sewn all over her clothing. Her hand paused on her upper arm and she stuck her fingers into a slit in the fabric that was only a few inches from Angus's beak and pulled out a small silver key.

"You thieving beast!" Cecile hissed, glaring at the bird.

Guy had to bite his lip to keep from laughing as the raven and Frenchwoman locked gazes. If he'd had to lay money on the confrontation, he couldn't have decided who'd win.

"What's the counting room?" Cat piped up, oblivious to the tension in the room.

"I'll show it to you when you've finished your dinner," Guy promised.

"I'm finished now."

"No," Cecile said, wrenching her gaze away from the bird and directing it to Cat. "You are not. If you take bread, then you should eat it." She eyed the thick slice Cat had put on her plate.

Guy thought that was a bit draconian, but then he'd been raised in the lap of luxury compared to Cecile, so he kept his mouth shut.

He held out his hand and Blade gave him the key.

"I'm free after my set tonight if you want to talk," Blade said.

He looked quickly at Cecile, but she was discussing something with Cat in a heated undertone.

"Here?" he asked.

"I think it would be better at the Greedy Vicar."

Guy nodded; he knew the place, an ancient pub not far from the Fayre. It was a favorite haunt among theatrical folk.

The box room he was supposed to clear was right next to his room. Amazingly, it was even smaller.

Like everything in the house, it was neatly organized and stacked with crates that were filled with costumes and props. He assumed they were left over from the days when the prior owner used to host his own productions.

The first thing Guy did was find the jewels Cecile had mentioned. They weren't hard to locate since they were in a gaudy gold cask encrusted with paste jewels, which must have once been a prop, itself.

Inside it was a tangle of sparkly stones that would only fool people from a distance.

Guy thought he might ask Cecile if it would be all right to let Cat play with them. She'd already given the little girl a fairy costume that was no longer in use. Guy recalled that his sisters—young and old—had a mania for paste jewelry, dressing up in fancy clothing, and playing pretend.

By the time he'd moved all the crates into another box room at the far end of the corridor, he was sweaty, covered with dust, and looking forward to washing up, even if it was in the basin of frigid water in his room.

One of the things he'd learned quickly when he'd gone from duke to laborer was that somebody—usually several somebodies—had *worked* to provide him with all the lovely steaming baths he'd enjoyed in his life and never gave any thought to.

He'd taken one bath thus far—hauling and heating the water for himself—and that was in the kitchen, which was where the only tub lived. It was difficult to find a time when the kitchen wasn't crawling with people, so Guy normally washed his body using the poor man's method—a sponge bath.

He'd just decided to go down to the kitchen and fetch some hot water when Cat charged up the stairs toward him. "Did I miss going into the counting room?" she demanded, breathless from her run.

"Almost!" he teased. "Where were you?"

"Cecile said I should help Cook with the dishes since Mary is out sick today."

"That was nice of you." He would never think about getting a child to do something like that; clearly Cecile was much better at this parenting business. He was fairly certain that none of his sisters had washed a dish in their lives. Neither had Guy, for that matter— not until coming to work at the Fayre.

While he did not enjoy many of the tasks Cecile made him do, he *did* like knowing how to take care of himself.

Still, he'd be bloody grateful to have his valet back.

"I like drying dishes," Cat said. "And Cook gave me a biscuit after," she added.

Guy chuckled at her reluctant honesty.

"I've never seen a secret room before."

"Well, I hope you aren't disappointed," he said as he shoved aside the thin, moth-eaten tapestry that hid the door.

"I didn't even know this was here," she said, gazing at the door with round eyes.

Once he'd pushed open the door and lighted the two candles in the wall sconce, he turned to Cat, who was hesitating outside the room. "Come in."

She stepped inside, looked around, and frowned.

He laughed at her crestfallen expression. "What? Isn't it everything you'd hoped for?"

"It's just a small room."

"Why, yes—that's right. What were you expecting?"

"I don't know . . . just, *something*. But it doesn't look special at all, so why is it hidden?"

"I don't know for a fact, but if I had to guess, I'd say this house belonged to people who made coins. Years ago, before the mint took over, there were people all over Britain who did such work. My guess is they needed somewhere to hide their wealth. Or perhaps the house belonged to people who were *not* supposed to be making coins—*counterfeiters* such criminals are called."

He could see her sharp mind turning it over. "So people used to hide coins in here, then?"

"That is only my guess."

"So why don't you call it the coin room?"

Guy laughed. "I don't know. That's a very good question. Perhaps you might ask your new governess about such matters," he said, not so subtly dodging any other questions.

One of the housemaids, Susan, poked her head into the room. "The governess is here, and she's got a trunk with her. Can you bring it up?"

"Of course, my dear."

"Oh! I want to go and meet her," Cat said, tearing from the room with George fast on her heels.

"There's someone who's excited," Susan said with a chuckle.

"Indeed." Guy smiled at Cat's receding form. "I've cleared out the box room, but I think it could use a bit of a dust and polish."

"I'll see to it immediately, Your Grace," she said, cutting him a cheeky look that made him laugh. Guy rolled down his sleeves and slipped on his coat before heading down to the foyer, where he could hear the sound of female voices.

He slowed his steps as he listened, recognizing not only Cecile and Cat, but the third voice, as well.

Guy frowned. No. It couldn't be.

Three female heads turned to him when he reached the bottom step.

"Ah, there you are, Guy. This is my new assistant and Cat's new governess, Miss Keeble," Cecile said.

Guy merely stared at the newcomer, his jaw hanging open.

"Hello," the woman said, her eyes wide and pleading as she took a few steps toward him and thrust out her hand. "Pleased to meet you. I'm Miss Keeble."

Guy took the proffered hand and bowed over it, his body so trained to courtesy that it could carry on without any assistance from his brain—which, in this case—was spinning.

"It's a pleasure to meet you," she said, her gaze becoming a bit frantic.

Guy nodded, still clinging to her gloved hand.

"His name is Guy Darlington," Cecile finally interjected in an exasperated tone when all Guy could do was stare at his former betrothed.

"Mr. Darlington," Helena Carter repeated, her eyes imploring him to keep her identity a secret.

"Miss *Keeble*," he mumbled, taking in her hair—which had once been blond and very long and was now a dark chestnut shade and almost as short as his. She also wore spectacles—who knew, perhaps she always had?—which he'd never seen before.

"Is Miss Keeble's room ready, Guy?" Cecile urged when it became clear he had nothing else to say.

"Er, Susan is just giving it a few final touches. I should think it will be ready in a little while."

"You can take the trunk up, and Miss Keeble will come with me to the kitchen and have some tea."

Guy watched them walk down the narrow corridor beside the stairs, which led to the kitchen.

Just before Helena disappeared around the corner, she turned back to him and mouthed *thank you.*

Guy just stood staring, unable to gather his wits.

As things turned out, Guy got to the Greedy Vicar a little later than he'd wanted thanks to Beryl, who'd summoned him to the theater to see to a rodent scare.

Fortunately, it wasn't a rat, but a *cat* that had somehow sneaked into the dressing room and then burrowed beneath the ever-accumulating pile of detritus on the settee.

Guy had brought the cat to Cook, who'd just mentioned a few days earlier that she wanted a new mouser now that the old kitchen cat had gone on to its reward.

How George and the new cat were going to cohabitate was a mystery to Guy, but it wasn't his concern, so he gratefully left the matter with Cook and hurried to meet Blade.

"Good evening, Your Grace."

Guy turned at the sound of the feminine purr and smiled down at the barmaid. "Hello, Cora. How are you this evening?"

"Better now that you're here, Your Grace."

He chuckled, accustomed to her flirtatious manner, which she assumed with all the men who entered her domain.

"Now, Cora, you know that I'm a mere commoner now."

"You're not a *mere* anything and you couldn't be common if you tried."

He lifted her work-worn hand and gave the back of it a smacking kiss. "Thank you, darling."

"Cook's gone home but I could bring you some bread, cheese, and a bit of cold ham?"

"Just a pint of home brew, please."

He felt something move at his side and turned to find that Blade had seemingly sprung from the wooden floor.

"What would you like?" he asked her.

"I'll take the same as His Grace," she said, smirking slightly as Cora laughed.

Cora went off to fetch their beer and Guy led Blade between tables crowded with both men and women, most of whom gave them friendly nods as they made their way to the corner of the room.

Guy waited until she sat to ask, "Where's Angus?"

"I dropped him off at home after my act."

"Er, does he mind being awake at night—aren't his sort daytime dwellers? I thought most birds went to bed with the sunset?"

Guy realized he was babbling when he saw the faint smile on her lips.

Truth be told, Blade always made him a bit nervous. She rarely spoke and seemed to awe even his friend Elliot—who'd been the most private, self-sufficient, and cleverest person of Guy's acquaintance before Blade.

The way she'd handled herself in France last year had been bloody intimidating. If there was anything the woman couldn't do, he'd yet to find out what it was.

She fixed him with her strange, almost opaque, gaze and said, "Angus isn't like most birds."

Huh. Well, that much was true.

Guy cleared his throat and wisely changed the subject. "Did you meet the new governess?"

"You mean your ex-betrothed."

Guy made a mortifying squawking sound. "Bloody hell!" He grimaced and muttered, "Sorry, please forgive my language. But *how* do you know that?"

Blade just shrugged.

"Here you are," Cora said, setting down their two glasses.

"Ta, Cora," Guy said, handing her the money.

Blade took a sip from her glass and then wiped the foam from her lip with the back of her hand in a way Guy found strangely charming. "Elliot said you wanted me to look into something in Cecile's past."

"That's it?" Guy said, exasperated. "We're done with the subject of Helena Carter? You're not going to say anything more about one of the richest women in England coming to work for a circus?"

"She's not really a rich woman if her father controls all the wealth."

Guy hesitated, and then said, "Good point."

"I'm not sure I want to pry into Cecile's past," Blade said.

Guy blinked at the change of subject. "And I respect you for that, Blade. But I'm not asking you to gather prurient or private details of her life."

"Why don't you tell me what you want, and I'll tell you whether I can do it."

"Fair enough." He sighed, shoved his hand through his hair, not

sure where to start. Well, he wanted to know about the guns, so that
seemed as good a place as any.

"Her father's name was Michel Blanchet. He was—"

"A gunsmith."

"Ah, so you've heard of him?"

"Yes."

Guy waited for more and should have known better.

He continued. "When she came to England—which was about
twenty-two years ago—she approached a cousin of hers, Curtis
Blanchard. Apparently, he has managed to exclude her from making
and selling her father's designs. Or something to that effect."

"So you want me to find out why that is?"

He nodded.

"Why?"

"I feel that there is something not right about all this. I can't
help wondering if her cousin took advantage of her. The reason I
wonder that is because the two times we spoke about the subject she
seemed . . . angry."

"Why don't you just ask her?"

He sighed. "You know why."

She stared at him and sipped her beer.

And stared.

And stared.

Guy was just about to squirm right out of his skin when she nodded. "I'll look into it."

"You will?" he said, more than a little surprised after all that
staring.

"Yes. But I will only pass along information if I feel it wouldn't
offend Cecile." She lowered her piercing, unnerving gaze for a moment. "She's—well, she's tried to be a friend to me, so I don't want
to repay her by hurting her."

"I don't want to hurt her, Jo. I love her."

Her eyes slid slowly to his and widened. "Have you told her
that?"

He snorted. "You think she would believe me?"

"You could try."

"If I declared my love for her at this point—now that I'm home-less, jobless, and penniless—she'd think I was manipulating her."

To Guy's disappointment, Blade didn't argue with him.

Instead, she said, "What do you think looking into this cousin will do?"

"If there was anything crooked on his part . . . well, I still have enough influence left in London to do something about that."

"Very well. Is that all?"

"Actually, now that you ask, I'd also like you to look into my dearest cousin Barrymore."

"What about him?"

"I don't know—anything suspicious. Like him selling off family property, for example."

Guy explained what he'd seen the other night—about the wagon full of furniture and paintings he'd watched rolling away from the duke's London residence.

"Is that illegal? Doesn't it all belong to him?" Blade asked when he'd finished.

"Not all of it—the land and house do not, I know that for sure. As to the contents of the house?" He shrugged. "I don't know. I went to see my family solicitor but now that I'm no longer head of the family, they didn't have time for me."

He shook the unpleasant memory away. "I've written them a letter and we shall see if I can get any response, *that way*. Of course, there might be nothing left to salvage by then."

She made a low humming sound and lifted her glass, emptying the contents in four big swallows before standing. "I'll go see what I can find."

"You're going *now*?"

"No time like the present." She wrapped her cloak around her more snugly and pulled on a pair of battered leather gloves before taking a knitted cap out of her cloak pocket and pulling it over her distinctive hair. By the time she was done arranging herself, she looked like a woman of the laboring classes, dressed in blacks, browns, and grays.

Without another word, she turned and left.

Guy's brow furrowed as he watched her depart. If there was a stranger person in London, he'd yet to meet them.

He put on his own hat and gloves and headed back to the house.

Nobody was loitering in the book room when he got home, but then it was quite late, and Blade's act had been the last of the night.

Guy hesitated outside Helena's door, sorely tempted to knock and ask her what the devil she was about. But all he needed to do was frighten the poor woman and have her scream down the house. He could just imagine how delightful that would be to explain to Cecile.

As it happened, when he opened the door to his room and saw a person sitting on his bed, *he* almost screamed down the house.

"Bloody hell," he hissed under his breath after making a very unmanly squeaking sound. He closed the door with exaggerated care. "What are you doing in here, Miss Carter?"

She raised a finger in front of her mouth. "Shh, please don't use that name—here, I am Miss Helen Keeble."

Guy heaved a sigh, crossed his arms, and leaned back against the door since she was sitting on the only thing in the room a person could sit on.

"I suppose you are wondering what is going on," she said.

"Yes, a bit," he said, not bothering to hide his sarcasm.

Her cheeks flushed and she chewed her lower lip. Interestingly, she looked more attractive with her short haircut, although he wasn't sure the dark color suited her. Her rather plain, severe gown looked better on her, too. In the past he'd only seen her covered in ruffles with her hair in sausage-like ringlets.

Yes, this pixie-like cut suited her slender face and fine-boned looks.

But no matter how good she looked, Guy didn't want her in

his room—or in this house, masquerading under a different name. Because if anyone was going to get blamed for the impropriety, it would be *him*.

He cleared his throat when she didn't begin speaking. Every second she was in his room was another opportunity for Cecile to catch her there. The woman knew *everything* that went on under her roof.

"I came here because I read about Miss Tremblay hiring you. And I knew that the Duchess of Staunton once lived and worked here, too. If that was the case, then it must be a respectable place. And of course you spoke so highly of Miss Tremblay, too. It seemed like a—a safe place for a woman with few options."

Well, Guy couldn't argue with that logic.

"Tell me what happened—why you decided to run away."

"You know I, er, well—"

"Became betrothed to my cousin after publicly jilting me?"

Her flush deepened. "I'm sorry, it's not—"

"Shh," he said, feeling a bit ogreish for being so sharp with her. "I know your father is making those decisions." He frowned. "But why here? What about the man you loved and wanted—"

Her delicate features shifted into a scowl. *"Him!"*

"Ah," Guy said. "You've had a, erm, falling out, I take it?"

"He is utterly spineless," she spat, her voice rising.

"Shhh." He jerked his chin toward the corridor.

She grimaced and then whispered angrily, "He accepted a position in my father's Newcastle factory."

Guy considered his next words carefully. "Well, as a young man who is dependent—"

"A position that came with a *wife*."

Guy kept his mouth shut; after all, what could he say?

She glared at something—or somebody—not in the room. "It was better I found out his true colors now rather than waiting."

"So, if he's no longer a consideration, then why, er . . ."

"Why did I jilt your cousin?" she asked tartly.

"Yes."

Revulsion flickered across her face. "There is something . . . not right about him." She cut him a quick glance. "Not meaning to give offense—"

"Please, say whatever you like about him—it shan't offend me. Did he, er, do something?" he demanded, not sure he wanted to hear the answer, which might mean he'd need to meet the bounder at dawn.

"Oh, no, nothing like that. But—and I know you probably will think this female foolishness—but he gives me a bad feeling."

As it happened, Guy didn't think that foolish at all. "I think that is self-preservation at work. Did you say this to your father?"

"Father believes I am just willful. That I wanted to marry Gerald and would do anything to get what I wanted. But that isn't true. I'm not foolish—I know life is not easy for most people."

"That makes you smarter than me." At her curious look, Guy explained. "Not until I took a job with the Fayre did I realize just how difficult life is for the average Englishman. And woman." And child, he could have added, thinking about poor Cat and her miserable existence.

"So," he said, "do you have some sort of plan—other than to work as a governess the rest of your life, that is?"

"I don't know. But I *do* know I will no longer marry whomever my father chooses."

"Couldn't you have told him that and remained in your own home?"

"I *did* tell him that. You don't understand," she said. "He would wear away at me day in and day out until I capitulated."

Guy knew the type—his mother was something of an expert at the erosion approach, too.

"Cecile needs to know the truth."

"So soon?"

"Yes. I owe her that much and I do *not* wish to anger her any more than I already have. You know how I feel about her."

"I know. And I don't wish to cause problems between the two of you."

"Yes, thank you for that because I can cause plenty of trouble on my own. You do realize that your father probably has every Bow Street runner in London hunting for you?"

"I know. I took . . . precautions when I left."

"You mean the hair and glasses."

"No, I mean I left a trail leading elsewhere. He is looking for me—I know that because my old nurse is the one who helped me, and she still lives in my father's house—but he believes I've gone to Newcastle to try to stop Gerald's impending wedding. He would never imagine that I would come here—especially not with you here."

He chuckled. "Yes, that was good thinking. But the Newcastle ruse probably won't occupy him for long."

"I know. I've taken care of that. I promise I won't jeopardize Miss Tremblay."

"If your father discovers you here, there is no saying how angry he might be or what he might do to punish her."

The way she looked at him told him she knew exactly what he was saying. Her father was one of the most feared, heartless, and vindictive men in business. Guy would never want to cross the man, and he certainly wouldn't want to involve Cecile in such trouble.

"Can we wait a few days, at least?" she asked.

Guy *almost* gave in to her request. But the strident critic in his head screamed so loudly, he thought it might be in the room with them.

"No. We tell her first thing tomorrow."

Have you no bloody sense, Guy? You should march down the hallway, wake up Cecile, and tell her right now!

It was late and he honestly could not bear to face this new problem without at least four or five hours' sleep.

"Will you be with me when I tell her?" Helena asked.

"I don't know what good you think that will do." Afford Cecile a larger target, for certain. "But I'll be with you."

"Do you think she will make me leave?" Helena asked, her brow furrowed with worry.

"If there's one thing I can honestly say about Cecile, it's that I never know what she'll do next."

Cecile was coming back from the kitchen with a glass of warm milk when she saw her new assistant/governess slipping from Guy's room.

She froze at the top of the stairs, openmouthed as Miss Helen Keeble tiptoed back to her room.

Once her door had closed, Cecile marched directly to Guy's room, raised her fist to pound on the door, but then hesitated.

What could she say to him? That he wasn't allowed to have a lover in the house? She'd never said anything of the kind to any of the other employees who lived in the building.

Cecile chewed her lip furiously, her hand tightening on the heavy glass tumbler until her fingers ached. Her head spun and pulsed, and her eyes were hot: what a *dog* the man was!

Why was she even surprised? Miss Keeble was young—*far* younger than Cecile—and if she was not exactly beautiful, she was attractive. And of course, *nubile*.

She ground her teeth.

Why was she such a fool? She'd almost begun to believe he really might care for her and regret how he'd treated her.

He wasn't coming out of her room; she was coming out of his.

The thought gave Cecile pause. That *was* odd.

Something else teased at her brain; Miss Keeble had been fully dressed.

Perhaps there is something more here? she thought.

Besides, what can you do to him? Throw him out for taking a lover?

That was true. What hold did she have over him? Nothing except a stupid, blind hope. A girl's dream of a knight who would come along and be true.

She was such an idiot it was physically painful.

Cecile dropped her hand to her side and turned toward her room. Thankfully she'd not done anything she regretted—like take him into her bed.

When she reached her room, she set the glass of milk on her dressing table; she'd lost her appetite.

Cecile climbed into bed and blew out the candle and then stared into the dark, her mind racing. She liked Helen Keeble and had been optimistic for the first time that she'd be able to find not only an able assistant, but somebody she'd instantly been drawn to.

Of course, that wasn't over, just . . . muddled. She could only hope that if Guy was dallying with the young woman, he would move on quickly.

She could hardly dislike Miss Keeble for falling for a man she'd fallen for herself, could she? But that didn't mean she wanted to watch the progression of their affair. She recalled her own time with Guy far too clearly.

Cecile forced her eyes shut and breathed deeply. Nothing had really changed—except she now had Cat in her life, which was the only good thing to come out of Guy's return.

Chapter 19

Guy glanced down at Helena—*Helen*, he reminded himself—and asked, "Are you ready?"

She nodded, her expression grim. Neither of them had seen Cecile that morning, and Cook said she'd not come to breakfast, which wasn't like her, so they'd left Cat with Cook and gone to seek her out.

Guy rapped on the door of her office.

"What is it?"

The voice from beyond sounded . . . Well, it sounded like Cecile yet *not* like Cecile.

"It is Guy. May I come in?"

"No."

He was rendered speechless for a moment, but then regrouped. "Cecile, I need to talk to you."

"Go away."

He tried the door, but it was locked.

"Please let us in."

"Us?"

"It is Miss Keeble and I."

There was a long pause and then the door opened suddenly.

Cecile stood in the opening, her cheeks flushed and her eyes snapping. "What took you so long?"

"Er, I just got up and ate breakfast and here I am. Why? Was I supposed to do something this morning?"

She ground her teeth audibly.

"What's wrong, Cecile?"

"What do you two want? Are you leaving already?"

"Leaving?" He looked down at Helen, who looked blankly back at him.

"No, we just wanted to get something out of the way this morning, and then we'll both go to work."

"Oh, is that what you think?"

He frowned. "What's the matter? Can we come in? This is hardly a subject I wish to discuss out in the open."

"Of course, you don't! Although I'm sure everyone will find out about it in Mr. Humphrey's window."

Guy's mouth opened, but he wasn't sure what to say.

"I think Miss Tremblay might have the wrong idea."

He looked down at Helen's flushed cheeks and then at Cecile.

Her eyes were black, her dark hair wild, and her lips a deep red, as if she'd been chewing them.

As if she'd been kissed.

Lord but the woman was bloody gorgeous!

Still, Guy had to admit she looked a bit . . . deranged.

Helena cleared her throat. "Mr. Darlington," she said in an urgent tone.

"Ah, yes." Guy pushed past Cecile into the room, firmly shutting the door once he'd ushered Helen inside. "Before you build up anything in your fertile imagination, let me explain."

"It is none of my business." Cecile crossed her arms, which only made her heaving chest more noticeable.

Good God; she was jealous.

Guy perked up. That meant she must at least like him a little?

True, jealousy was no true sign of love. But people weren't jealous of what they *didn't* want. Were they?

Guy's first impulse was to leap and yell *huzzah*.

Fortunately, his second impulse was to conceal his enjoyment of her current predicament.

"Did you see Helen going into or coming out of my room last night?" he asked.

Her mouth tightened and it seemed that actual flames licked from her eyes.

Again, it was a challenge not to grin like a fool.

Instead, he said, "Cecile Tremblay, let me introduce you to Helena Carter."

For a moment Guy thought he might need to repeat himself because she was so furious that she didn't appear to hear him.

Helen took a step toward the other woman. "I am so terribly sorry for lying to you, Miss Tremblay."

Cecile turned slowly and unwillingly toward the other woman as if her head were being pulled by a winch.

Once she was no longer scorching Guy with her fiery gaze, he, too, turned to Helen, who was getting her first taste of Cecile's Glare of Death.

Well, everyone got it eventually, some more than others, as Guy could attest.

Cecile inhaled until it looked as if she'd burst the bodice of her plain work gown.

"Sit and explain," she finally snapped.

They quickly took the two chairs she kept in her office—both uncomfortable to dissuade lingerers—and Guy gestured that Helen should speak first.

"Guy didn't know anything about this, Miss Tremblay. I came here because, well, because he always spoke so highly of you."

Cecile cut him a quick, cold glare.

"Now wait a minute," Guy said. "Why are you looking at—"

"It is not your turn to speak now." Her voice was as soft as a snake's hiss and about as menacing. She turned back to Helen. "Go on."

"I believe Guy told you that I was in l-love—or at least I fancied myself in love—with a clerk at my father's London factory?"

Cecile nodded.

"I foolishly hoped that I might bring my father around to my way of thinking about marriage." She scowled suddenly. "Although my inconstant suitor has, in fact, made me wonder if my own judgment could be any worse than his."

"What do you mean?"

"I'd hoped to marry the man after repudiating my betrothal and leaving my father's house. But when I went to his lodgings, I discovered that he'd accepted a job in another city and would"—she squeezed her eyes shut but not fast enough to catch a tear—"he assented to my father's demand that he marry a woman. A woman who is not *me*."

Guy handed her his handkerchief.

She dried her cheeks and continued. "My father will not relent when it comes to marriage. He is . . . obsessed about linking our family to the peerage. And—and I find that I simply cannot live with his expectations any longer, even though it means I will have to earn my own crust. Don't misunderstand me," she added hastily. "I took the position you offered because I fully expect to work." She glanced at Guy. "But last night it was brought home to me that you may be the focus of my father's displeasure if he discovers me here. Guy insisted I tell you of my identity first thing this morning. I will understand if you don't want me in your business or house." Once she finished, she sat back in her chair.

None of them spoke for a long moment, the only sounds those of other employees moving about beyond the door.

"I am not afraid of your father," Cecile said, no longer angry eyed and red cheeked. She slid a glance at Guy, but he couldn't decipher it. "If I gave in to fear every time a man threatened me, I'd be a quivering heap hiding in a closet. If he discovers your whereabouts, however, he will have the legal right to make you go home—will he not?"

They both looked at Guy, who nodded. "I'm afraid he will, Helen—you're only twenty. But let us not borrow trouble; as of right now you're here." He looked at Cecile. "And she may remain here?"

She nodded. "I hired you because you are the best candidate to fill both positions. I do not wish you to leave. Guy is right. When it comes to your father, we shall take things as they come."

Guy knew he'd be waiting a long, long time if he expected Cecile to apologize for misjudging him.

Besides, he didn't care if she apologized. It was worth being accused of lechery to find out that she at least cared for him.

Not that she demonstrated her affection in any way in the days after Helen joined the household.

No, instead she just avoided him at all times except during performances. Even their rehearsals had been cut in half now that Helen had assumed some of the assistant responsibilities.

"You really want to do this?" Guy had asked her the first time she'd shown up to rehearse Cecile's routine. "I'm sure she'd let you out of this part of the job. Lord knows you've got your hands full with Cat."

As ambivalent as the little girl had been about having a governess, Cat had fallen in love with Helen and shadowed her steps from morning until night.

"I want to do this," Helen said, her face set in firm lines.

He smiled.

"What? Why are you looking at me that way?"

"I was just thinking that you've changed a great deal since, er, well, since our betrothal."

"I've grown up, you mean."

It wasn't a question, so he didn't answer it. But he thought she was right; she had grown up. They both had. Guy was ashamed that maturity had taken so long to find him, but better late than never.

Perhaps a week or so after the confrontation between Helen and Cecile, Blade sought out Guy one morning.

He'd just finished swabbing the night-soil closet—a job he hated so much that he was surprised he didn't incinerate the vile box just by looking at it.

"Aren't you the fortunate one," Blade said, wrinkling her delicate nose. Even Angus appeared to be holding his breath.

"What? Does she need something else done? A stall mucked? Chamber pots scoured?"

"I don't know," Blade admitted. "She might."

"What do *you* want?"

"I have some information for you."

Guy stilled the mop and looked up. "About which thing?"

"Both."

Guy put the mop in the battered bucket and gestured for her to follow. He unlocked the door to the alley and held it open.

Once they were outside he shut the door and then leaned against it. "I'm all ears."

Angus suddenly took flight, drafting sharply upward before he made it to the busy street.

"Where's he going?" Guy asked.

"Wherever he wants," Blade said, leaning against the rough brick wall, a knife already in her hand. "Angus is his own bird."

Guy snorted. "Very well. So what did you learn?"

"I'm not going to tell you everything I found out."

"Is this a standard response to the people who pay you?"

"Oh, are you paying me?" she asked, looking mildly amused.

"I assumed I was."

Blade reached beneath her cloak and pulled out an oilskin-wrapped packet, which she held toward him.

He looked at it and frowned. "What is it?"

"It's the contract for the sale of the Blanchet designs."

"She *sold* her father's designs to him?" Guy demanded. "How the devil did you get your hands on the actual contract? Did you break in somewhere to steal this? Will somebody be laying an information against me for hiring you to do this?"

"You needn't worry—it wasn't me. Angus did it."

Guy's jaw sagged. "*Angus?* He—No, that's impossible." He stared at her expressionless face. "Isn't it?"

She laughed, the sound rusty, as if it wasn't something she did often.

"You're bamming me, aren't you."

"Just a bit," she said, smirking. "After Cecile signed the contract, she moved to Boston."

"Why?"

"That's something I'm not telling you."

Guy swallowed his annoyance and said,. "Fine. Go on."

"Cecile lived in Boston for almost ten years. She returned to England because Blanchard stopped sending her payments for her part of the gunsmithing business."

"Because he closed it?"

"That was what he claimed. But really, he stopped making guns almost immediately after Cecile left."

Guy shook his head. "Why would he do that?"

"Because Curtis and his wife didn't want to soil their hands with trade."

"How do you know all this?" Guy asked, more than a little awed.

"Blanchard's servants hate him, which means they aren't exactly loyal."

"Why do they hate him?"

"He's clutch-fisted, pesters his female employees, and his wife is a harpy."

"He sounds like quite a prize."

Blade spun the knife around the back of her hand and fixed him with an unblinking stare.

"So, is that . . . it?"

"No."

Guy let his head fall back against the door with a *thud*.

When he heard her chuckle, he looked down at her. "You're tormenting me on purpose."

"I can't help myself," she admitted. "It's just so . . . easy."

"Very droll. So, if Blanchard sold the gun business, then how does he make his money?"

"Do you know the story of Blanchet and Blanchard?" she asked. "I know they both made fowling pieces and pistols and that the English guns were relatively inexpensive and nowhere near the same level of craftsmanship as the French."

Blade nodded. "Cecile's grandfather and his twin founded Blanchet in France but had a falling out. The brother moved here and changed his name to Blanchard. As you say, Blanchard never produced the sought-after collector's pieces that the French gunsmiths did. Perhaps that was because of a lack of royal patronage—who knows?" She shrugged, slid one of her knives into a coat pocket, and continued. "Since closing the business, Curtis moved his family to a house on the edge of Mayfair, his wife patronizes only the best shops, and his two sons attended Harrow. He's also a member of White's and has aspirations to run for a seat in Commons."

Guy stared, confused. "Your story doesn't make any sense. Curtis was only modestly well-off before he closed his company, but now he's wealthy? Where is all this money coming from?"

"Curtis sold a patent for a percussion cap to an armament maker—J. T. Guthrie's."

"Guthrie's has several big government contracts if I'm not mistaken. So . . . are you telling me that Curtis Blanchard conceived of this percussion cap?"

"No, Blanchard didn't come up with the idea; *Cecile* did."

"Cecile?"

"Yes, Cecile. I spoke to one of Blanchard's ex-employees, a man who worked alongside Cecile in her cousin's shop. The man admitted—albeit grudgingly—that she was the best gunsmith working at Blanchard's. He also said that Cecile was always working on improvements for the guns and that production quality soared during the few years she worked there. Before she began working there, Blanchard designs were decades behind other English gunmakers and the company was struggling. After Cecile had worked there only a year, Curtis made enough money to hire another six employees."

Guy shook his head. "This is making less and less sense. She was making him money and yet he forced her to sell him the rights to her father's designs and then closed the company?"

Blade nodded.

"So, what about this patent? Was it mentioned in the contract?"

"No."

Guy frowned. "Are you telling me that Curtis stole the patent?"

"The employee said he thought Curtis tricked her out of it. He said—" She paused and cut him a look.

"What? Or is this another thing you won't tell me?"

"No, this is something I'm guessing you won't want to hear."

"If it's about Cecile, then I want to hear it."

"He said he thought Cecile was in love with Curtis and the two were having an affair."

Guy swallowed down the poisonous surge of jealousy that threatened to choke him and asked, "So, what did your informant think? That Blanchard used her affection to get her to sign?"

"Something like that."

He wanted to yell and smash things. "Blade, what the devil aren't you telling me?"

"Blanchard was married at the time and he's quite a bit older than Cecile. Though she might refer to him as a cousin, the age difference between them was more that of an uncle and niece. Keep in mind she came to him at fourteen . . ."

Guy felt sick at the thought of a fourteen-year-old girl in the hands of an exploitative, unscrupulous man, which Blanchard must certainly be if he'd stolen her idea.

"What do *you* think happened?" he asked, not sure he wanted to know.

"I think you need to tell Cecile what you are doing and ask her these questions."

"You are right." He could see by her startled expression that his answer had surprised her. "And I will do so, I promise. I just wanted . . . *something* to give her." He glanced down at the packet in his hands. "I'll look at this contract and see if I can make anything of it. I know there are ways to get out of a contract," he said. "But I'm not sure what exactly they are."

"Contracts with minors aren't enforceable," she volunteered.

Guy was going to ask her how old Cecile was when she signed, when Angus glided into the alley, slowing his speed to a hover before landing on Blade's shoulder.

He winced. "Lord, don't his claws hurt?"

She didn't appear to hear him, her gaze pensive.

"What is it?" he asked.

"Blanchard turned around almost immediately after filing for the patent and sold it to Guthrie. It is the reason Guthrie's company won the first of their big government contracts."

"So you think the two are conspirators to defraud Cecile?"

"I don't know. But I'm going to poke around a bit more."

"Good idea," Guy said. "Unless, er, does that mean you're going to break into his business or house?"

"The less you know, the better."

He opened his mouth to argue, and then decided that was probably true. "Did you find anything out about Barry?"

"Not about Barry, but about the child. He's not your cousin's son."

Guy's jaw dropped—something it seemed to do a lot in conversations with Blade. "How—what—"

"Did you ever see the fellow who serves as his batman?"

Guy had to think a moment and was ashamed to admit that he rarely noticed servants.

"He's hard to forget—he's got an eye patch."

"Ah, yes, I did see him. He's Barry's valet?"

"In name, he is. But he is also in charge of the stables, and the servants in the house seem to go in fear of him, even the butler."

"Hodge is afraid of him?" Guy asked, stunned.

She nodded.

"Good God! I was always in awe of Hodge. He was my grandfather's butler before he was mine and I think even Grandfather feared him." Guy snorted. "Lord, this man—what did you say his name was?"

"John Norton."

"He must be terrifying." He frowned. "But what does this have to do with Barry's son—isn't his name Alan?"

"Yes. Except Alan is Norton's son, not your cousin's."

Guy's head was spinning. "But I don't understand. Why would—" He gave a sharp, unamused laugh. "He thinks to use an action in common recovery to break the entail."

It wasn't a question, but Blade nodded.

"The heir needs to be of age before he can legally agree," Guy said. "But who will object if he isn't?" he asked, more of himself.

"Indeed," Blade said.

Guy shook himself. "How did you find out about the boy?"

"Norton's wife is very unhappy that the boy's father—they are not husband and wife, by the way—has taken the boy and put him under your cousin's care. There have been . . . arguments. Loud ones that more than a few of your cousin's servants have overheard."

"Zeus! You really are quite amazing," Guy said, his mind spinning at what he'd just heard. "I'll need to get in touch with some other members of my family and let them know that Barry is up to something. Maybe they can take action since the solicitors don't seem inclined to pay any heed to me," he added, more to himself.

Blade scratched her bird, clearly uninterested in what he was saying.

"I want to pay you for—"

"I don't want your money," Blade said.

"Er, why not?"

"I'd rather have you owe me."

"You want me to owe you money?"

She made an exasperated sound. "No. You can owe me a favor."

This sounded . . . ominous, and Guy envisioned her dragooning him to go on her next housebreaking adventure. "What sort of favor?"

"Whatever I want."

Guy stared.

"Don't worry, it won't be monetary or sexual."

He barked a startled laugh and heat surged up his neck. Good God! She'd made him blush.

Blade smirked, turned, and without so much as a farewell, strode out of the alley.

Chapter 20

"You shouldn't come here," Cecile said, happiness and concern warring in her chest as she looked at her dearest friend.

"What is the point of being a duchess if I can't visit the people I like?" Marianne asked, shifting on the uncomfortable chair. They were in the office at the theater, where Cecile had been working when Marianne knocked on the door.

Her friend looked so out of place in her gorgeous carriage costume that it was as if a tropical bird had just flown into the room.

"Are you sure you don't want to go next door and have some tea?" Cecile asked.

"No, no, this is fine. I can't stay long. I have a rather grueling evening planned. Or, should I say, Sin's aunt Julia has planned a grueling evening for me."

"How is your baptism into the *ton*?" Cecile asked, struggling with the envy she felt at her friend's opportunities to meet the *haut ton*. It just wasn't fair; especially since Marianne didn't *want* to engage in the pleasures the Season had to offer, while Cecile would have loved it.

"It is going as well as can be expected," Marianne said with a slight grimace. "I'm thrilled we had such a small wedding, even if it only delayed my entrée into the *ton*." Her expression softened.

"Both Lady Julia and Sin have been lovely, and thank heavens, my presentation is behind me."

"I still want to see your gown and hear all about your meeting with the Queen," Cecile reminded her.

Marianne smiled. "Gladly. I can't have tea this coming Tuesday, but shall we meet the next?"

"You don't need to keep that appointment. I know you are—"

"It is one of my favorite hours of the week."

"Mine, too," Cecile admitted.

"Good, then that is settled. Now, the reason I'm here today is that I'm giving my first dinner party and ball." She reached into a lovely beaded reticule and pulled out a thick cream envelope with the distinctive crest of the Duke of Staunton. "And you are invited."

Cecile gave her friend a startled look. "But, Marianne—"

"If you say even one thing about not being suitable, I shall be extremely vexed with you, Cecile."

Cecile felt her face heat at her friend's fierce, affectionate expression, and she was unable to keep her yearning gaze from the elegant invitation; an invitation into a life she'd only ever seen from the outside, like an urchin peeking into a sweetshop window.

"Promise me that you will come," Marianne begged, leaning forward and clutching the hand that wasn't holding the invitation. "Please."

"You *know* I will come. But I can't help questioning the wisdom of your husband and his aunt." Her eyes widened. "Please tell me they know I am coming—this is not some surprise that—"

"Of course, they know you are coming!" Marianne looked hurt and more than a little angry.

"I'm sorry, naturally you wouldn't do such a thing."

"I don't think you understand my position, Cecile. Yes, I am the Duchess of Staunton and wife of *Lord Flawless*. And yes, the Prince of Wales himself granted me a title, so people are forced to accept me or insult Prinny. But trust me when I say that *nobody* has forgotten where I come from. Julia says I must embrace my past and make it part of my reputation—which is that of an *original*." She frowned. "Apparently, being an original means—"

Cecile laughed. "I know what that means!"

"That's right. How could I forget you probably know more about fitting into the *ton* than I do, with all your many years of research. In any case, as an original, I'll be expected to do things like invite my friends to functions. Not that I needed such permission, but if you are concerned about ruining my entrée into society, you needn't be. Understood?" she asked, cocking an eyebrow.

"Very well. I will go to the ball, Marianne. But I cannot attend your dinner."

Marianne opened her mouth, no doubt to scold and nag, but she must have realized that Cecile was not merely fishing for assurance in this instance.

"Fine. I can see that might be a bit . . . nerve-racking. You are excused—but only on this occasion. So," she said briskly, "now that *my* business is out of the way, let us talk about *yours*. You hired him."

There was no doubt which *him* she meant.

Cecile shrugged.

"Oh no! You cannot get away with that, Cecile. I've been forced to miss an entire month of our Tuesday teas, and I'm positively burning up with curiosity."

"It was just good business. Can you imagine how thrilled Barnabas would have been to have the Darling on his stage?"

"Yes, my uncle would have loved it." Marianne's smile was sad. Cecile didn't know what had transpired between Marianne and her uncle before he'd died last year, but she knew there'd been bad blood on her friend's side toward the end.

"So, Guy is living in the house with you?" Marianne asked.

"Not just me, I have almost a dozen people living there."

"I met the little girl—Cat. She's a darling, and it was so kind of you to take her in."

Cecile knew her face was as red as a boiled lobster.

"Ah, well," she muttered.

"Don't feel bad for being softhearted, Cecile."

"Softheaded, you mean."

"Whatever you want to call it, I'm happy for you both. She is a little charmer."

Cecile felt a burst of pride in Cat that she'd done nothing at all to earn. "She is. And clever, too."

"So, are you going to forgive him?" Marianne asked, suddenly serious.

"What do you think?"

Marianne grinned and clapped her hands. "You are!" She leaned forward and lowered her voice, "But you want to make him grovel a bit more, don't you?"

"Why not?"

They both laughed until tears rolled down their cheeks.

"Are we horrible?" Marianne asked, taking out a handkerchief to dab away the moisture.

"He deserves it."

"He does," Marianne agreed, getting to her feet. "I had better be off. I just wanted to deliver your invitation and Blade's. Do you think she will come?" ·

"Who knows with that one?"

"I took it by her address, but she no longer lives there."

"That's strange. I didn't know she'd moved. Do you want to leave it with me, and I will give it to her tonight?"

"If you don't mind?"

"Not at all." Cecile smirked. "Indeed, this way I can browbeat her into coming."

"Let me know if you need help with that."

Cecile nodded, her mind already racing ahead to the gown she would need to buy for her first *ton* event.

As things turned out, Cecile didn't see Blade until early Sunday morning, when Cecile was, yet again, in her office paying bills.

The first thing Cecile did when the other woman entered was hand her the invitation to the ball.

Blade looked at it as if she'd never seen a piece of parchment in her life. "For me?"

"Yes, for you."

Blade turned the expensive envelope over and over in her hands. She glanced up. "Are you sure?"

"Your name is on it. Marianne hand delivered it for you. It is her first big *ton* party."

Blade nodded, both she and Angus staring at the invitation.

"Don't let that bird eat it," Cecile said, hoping to tease the quiet woman out of her obvious state of shock.

"No, Angus isn't fond of paper," she mumbled, her forehead furrowed. "But . . . why?"

Cecile felt a pang in her chest at Blade's utter confusion. As if she'd never been the recipient of an overture of friendship before.

"Because she likes you, Jo. And I'm sure she is grateful for all the help you gave her in France last year." She chuckled. "I know *I'm* grateful to you for saving us."

"I was only doing my job—what I was paid to do."

"Whatever Marianne's reasons, she told me she'd appreciate your being there. It is the first event she will hostess as the Duchess of Staunton. I daresay she wants her friends around her."

"*Friends*," Angus echoed, rubbing his head against his mistress's cheek.

It was something he did often, but the fact that he did it just then—when Blade was visibly unsettled—made Cecile wonder just how much the bird understood.

"I don't know how to dance," Blade finally said.

Cecile felt a smile tug at her lips. "It just so happens I have one of the best dancers in Britain living under my roof and working for me."

"Guy?"

"Who else?"

"You think he is going to the ball, even after . . . everything?" Blade asked.

"Actually, I haven't asked him—I've been so busy training Helen that I seem to have no time. But I can't imagine why not."

"He's been performing for weeks; don't you think it will be embarrassing for him to go back to all the people who used to know him as a duke?"

"I don't know. But even if he doesn't go, he can still teach us to dance."

A slow smile crept across Blade's face, and it grew and grew, until it was a grin. "Us?"

Cecile again tried to shrug off the comment.

"You don't know how, either?" Blade persisted.

"Where would I have learned to dance?"

"Do you think there is enough time to learn?"

"Two weeks? I should think so," Cecile said, smirking as she imagined telling Guy about his newest duties.

Chapter 21

Guy was sitting in the kitchen, swallowing cup after cup of coffee and trying to wake up while listening to Cat's constant stream of chatter. He'd stayed up far too late with Elliot the night before, the two of them going over the contract between Curtis Blanchard and Cecile, looking for irregularities.

Unfortunately, they'd found nothing—at least nothing glaring.

"Helen is taking me to the Tower to learn about the Royal Mint," Cat said, bouncing up and down in her chair.

Guy smiled, amused by her enthusiasm. "That sounds nice."

"Could you go with us?"

Before he could answer, the kitchen door opened and Cecile swept into the room.

She paused in front of Guy. "You are looking rough this morning."

"How kind of you to notice—and then point it out."

Cecile chuckled and poured herself a cup of coffee.

"Can you go with Helen and me to the Mint, Guy?" Cat asked.

"Er . . ." He looked from Cat to her governess.

Helen shrugged, making it clear it hadn't been her idea.

"Well, I'm not sure what I have to—"

"He will go with you," Cecile said.

"I will?"

"Yes," she said firmly.

"Will you come, too, Cecile?" Cat asked, giving Cecile the lethal combination of imploring blue eyes and a trembling lower lip.

"Yes, Cecile, *please* go with us?" Guy chimed in, attempting to ape Cat's pleading expression. Judging by Cecile's disgusted look, he wasn't nearly so adorable.

"Will it disrupt your teaching plans if we go with you, Helen?" Cecile asked

"Not at all. The more the merrier," Helen said in her dry way, her eyes twinkling at Guy; obviously she'd guessed that a trip to the Mint was not high on his list of things to do on a Monday. Or any day, for that matter.

"*Pleeeeeese*, Cecile," Cat begged.

"Fine, fine. I will go, too," Cecile said.

Guy winced at Cat's high-pitched squeal. "Huzzah!"

Helen chuckled. "We were planning to leave after elevenses, if that is all right?"

"We'll be ready and waiting," Cecile said.

Helen and Cat left the room and Guy glanced at his watch. "I should have enough time to run the laundry over to Mrs. Bascom before we go on our little jaunt." He threw back the last of his coffee and was pushing to his feet when Cecile's voice stopped him.

"Are you going to this ball of Marianne's?"

"Yes, I'm going," Guy said. He frowned. "Why? Shouldn't I be going?"

"I was just wondering. No need to get excitable."

Guy snorted. That was rich coming from the Queen of Excitable.

"Why would you think I wouldn't go to my best friend's first ball as a married man?" he couldn't help asking.

"It was Blade who thought you'd be too ashamed."

"Lord. I didn't suppose she thought so little of me."

"She doesn't think little of you. Most people wouldn't want to consort with their former friends after they lost their status, wealth, property, and were rejected by their betrothed and forced to work in a circus."

"*Thank* you for laying out my tragic downward trajectory so articulately."

"Don't pout, Guy. It does not become you."

Guy just stared. Which was why he happened to be looking when a strange expression crossed her face—one he'd not seen on her before: doubt.

Even on their journey through a war-ravaged country and after she'd been forced to fatally shoot a man, she had not looked so doubtful.

"I've been invited to the ball. And so has Blade."

"Yes, I assumed you had."

"You don't think it odd that we were invited?"

"It is Marianne's party. Why wouldn't she invite her closest friends?"

"I thought you might think it was inappropriate."

Guy shrugged.

"What does that mean?"

"Who cares if it's inappropriate."

Her questioning look turned into a scowl.

"Not that I'm saying it *is* inappropriate," he soothed. "I'm not exactly on the *haut ton* list either, you may have noticed."

She looked intrigued. "Is there such a thing?"

"I'm teasing," he said gently.

"Oh."

He could see that her ignorance of *ton* matters was a sore point.

"Can I claim two dances—preferably the supper waltz?" he asked.

Impossibly, her cheeks darkened. Uncertainty *and* embarrassment all in one day? What was the world coming to?

"That was actually what I wanted to talk to you about—er, dancing."

They'd not even had their first lesson and Cecile was already sorry she'd entrusted the task of teaching them to dance to Guy, who was behaving like a dance master tyrant and enjoying himself far too much.

"Are you paying attention?" Guy demanded, clapping his hands loudly.

"Yes."

"Yes."

Both Cecile and Blade spoke at the same time and rolled their eyes.

"I saw that," Guy said. "Such disrespect will be punished by time after class."

"Can't we just learn the steps?" Cecile said, ashamed by how plaintive she sounded.

His eyebrows crashed down. "Of course, you can't just *learn the steps*. This first part is critical. Now shush and allow Helen, Cat, and me to demonstrate the proper way to respond to a gentleman's request for an introduction and invitation to dance."

Cecile decided to ignore the fact that he had just *shushed* her. If she argued with him, they'd never learn to dance.

"I will play the fresh-from-the-schoolroom debutante, Lady Giggleandblush," Guy said, fluttering his eyelashes and assuming a look so silly that Cecile couldn't help smiling.

"Helen will play the Dowager Lady StiffUpper-Lipington, Lady Giggleandblush's chaperone, and Cat will play the adoring swain, the Duke of Fumblefoot."

Blade choked, snorted, and then doubled over, laughing so hard there were tears on her cheeks.

The rest of them turned to stare at her rare loss of composure.

"What?" she said when she realized they were all looking at her in surprise.

"I'm pleased that *some* of you at least appreciate my theatrical efforts," Guy said. "Let us now begin." He nodded at Helen.

The incognita heiress was almost as quiet as Blade, so Cecile wasn't the only one to goggle when she whipped out a gaudy-looking lorgnette, threw her shoulders back and tilted her chin, somehow managing to look down her nose at Guy even though he was almost a foot taller.

"My dear Lady Giggleandblush, His Grace of Fumblefoot has begged the honor of being introduced to you."

Cat looked from one of the adults to the other, and then dropped an impressive court bow. "It is such an honor, Lady Giggleandblush—"

Cat had to take a moment to do some giggling of her own but was quick to recover.

"May I request the honor of the next set?"

True to his name, Guy let out a horrific whinny, sounding like a mare that had just come into season. "Oh, my goodness!" he shrieked, and then unfurled a fan that seemed to have appeared from nowhere. "Why, I would be so honored, Your Grace. Hmmm, now let me see—" Guy consulted a piece of parchment he'd tied to his wrist for the occasion. "No, not that one . . . Hmm, no, not then. I can't do that one—"

Helen rapped him on the shoulder with her quizzing glass.

"Oooooh, yes, of course I shall be delighted to reserve the third set for you, Your Grace."

Cat bowed and then all three of the actors turned to their tiny audience and bowed again.

Blade and Cecile clapped.

"There now, you see how it is done?" Guy said. "It is important to remember that you *never* turn down a request to dance for a set and then give that same set to another gentleman, later. That is a terrible faux pas."

"Fox paws?" Cat repeated, looking transfixed by this unexpected turn of events.

"Mr. Darlington is making a jest by purposely mispronouncing the phrase, Cat," Helen explained.

"I wouldn't wager on it being purposeful," Cecile said under her breath, causing Blade to snort.

"It is actually pronounced *foe pah* and it means you would be doing something not acceptable, and it would be considered rude," Helen clarified.

"*Very* rude," Guy added. "And the poor gentleman you rejected would likely go home and cry himself to sleep."

"How would you know?" Cecile couldn't help retorting.

"Oh, I've had my heart crushed under the slippers of your cruel sex on more than one occasion," he assured her.

Cecile made a mental note to question him about that improbable claim at a more convenient time.

"As there are only two weeks remaining before the ball, we shall focus on learning the most popular and often used figures of country dances and my favorite . . . the waltz." His brown eyes heated like caramelized sugar as he stared at Cecile, the look probably illegal in some countries.

Cecile swallowed.

He grinned and strode over to the piano, taking two slim pamphlets from the top of it. "When I learned I was to be your dancing master, I took the trouble to lay hands on two copies of this lovely little book."

Blade and Cecile exchanged a worried look and then each took a copy.

Thomas Wilson's *An Analysis of Country Dancing.*

"You must study and memorize those entire booklets. There will be an extensive, five-hour examination the night before the ball."

Cecile's jaw sagged.

Guy chuckled. "Lord, you should see your faces! I'm only teasing you."

Blade gave her a look that told Cecile *exactly* what the other woman was thinking: Guy's next evening on stage would be extra-humiliating.

"Once you've familiarized yourselves with the figures in your booklets you'll be able to use *these.*"

Once again, he went to the piano; this time he picked up two fans. He unfurled one and Cecile saw it was covered with tiny writing.

"These will help you cheat when you are at the ball. You'll notice there are names of dances with brief lists of the figures used. Of course, whoever is leading a particular dance can always dictate their own figures, but then they have to demonstrate them first, so you just have to follow."

Cecile already felt better looking at the fan.

"Good?" he asked, his gaze on Cecile when he asked the question. She nodded. "These are a very clever idea. Thank you, Guy."

He looked genuinely pleased. "You are most welcome."

"But . . . there are so *many* different steps," Blade said, her pale gaze riveted to the writing on the fan.

"You will learn them in no time," he assured her. "Helen has graciously agreed to play the piano, and the four of us will take our positions in the line."

He clapped his hands. "No dawdling, now! Let us learn how to dance!"

Chapter 22

Cecile was surprised when Blade showed up for their agreed upon shopping trip to Bond Street.

"What?" the other woman said when Cecile stared at her rather ugly mustard-yellow day dress and the huge black bird perched on her shoulder.

"That is the nicest clothing you have?"

"Unless you count my costume." She gave Cecile a sarcastic smile. "Should I change into that?"

"Very droll."

"Well, I'm sorry you don't care for my clothing, but it is what I have."

Cecile realized that she'd finally said something that had pierced the other woman's seemingly impenetrable armor.

She laid a hand on Blade's shoulder—the one without a bird standing on it. "I didn't mean to be insulting."

"I know you didn't." She heaved a sigh. "I'm afraid frivolous clothing has never been a priority."

Cecile wanted to tell her that a decent walking or carriage costume was not frivolous, but then she had no idea of the woman's financial situation. Oh, she knew how much Blade earned, of course, but she didn't know how great her expenses were.

"Are you reluctant to go shopping because of money, Josephine?"

Blade looked startled, either by the question or the sound of her full name. "No. It's not that. I have money to buy a ball gown." She gave Cecile an uncharacteristically shy look. "I don't wish to look like this"—she held out her arms to display her out-of-fashion gown, gray cloak, and practical black ankle boots—"but I've never had any reason to dress otherwise."

"When you say clothing—"

"I mean more than just a ball gown—some other clothes, too."

Was that eagerness in Blade's opal eyes?

"You will be a delight to dress," Cecile assured her. She glanced at Angus. "Er, I'm not so sure—"

"Don't worry; Angus won't want to go into the shops with us."

Cecile glanced at the bird—who gave her a cool, scathing look—and she dropped the issue.

Soon the three of them were rolling along in a hackney, headed toward Bond Street.

Cecile took out her notebook and tiny pencil. "It will be best to make a list. What do you wish to buy?"

"Oh. Well." Blade's eyes flickered over Cecile's emerald-green ensemble, which was trimmed with chocolate-brown suede and sported large brass buttons on the mannish-looking spencer. "Something like what you're wearing. And I suppose a few other dresses." She shrugged. "I don't know all the names for things. Whatever you suggest."

Cecile grinned.

Blade suddenly looked apprehensive. "But not *too* much. I don't wish to be bogged down with a great deal of clothing when I move."

"You're moving?"

"Oh, not now. But when I do."

"Why are you moving?"

"I always move," she said simply.

"But . . . why?"

Blade opened her mouth and then closed it and stared out the window.

Cecile sighed. Would this reserved woman ever confide in her? Or was she simply banging her head—

"I've always moved a lot—ever since I can remember." Blade's voice was low, her words leaving a slight fog on the window.

"Why have you moved so much?"

Blade's slim shoulders shrugged, and Angus roused himself, looking annoyed by the disruption to his nap.

"Do you have family, Jo?"

"No."

Cecile didn't bother to point out that Blade had, last year, claimed to need time away from the Fayre to go and visit a sick cousin.

"There was only my uncle Mungo, but he died."

"Mungo? That's an interesting name."

"He was named after the patron saint of Glasgow."

"Ah, you are Scottish. And he was the one who raised you?"

"Yes. My mother died when I was a baby so I only had my father," Cecile said, but then scowled and added, "Well, and I have a cousin here in London, but I don't count him. My father and I moved almost constantly once the Revolution broke out."

"Yes, so did we."

Cecile would have loved to pry, but the connection between them was tenuous and she knew she could be . . . intrusive, so she held her tongue.

"We spent time in France, the Prussian states, all over the Continent, really," Blade volunteered.

"Your uncle took you there during the War?"

"Oh yes. It was safer with him than anywhere else."

Safe from what?

But Blade turned around again, her shoulders, usually so straight and proud, oddly slumped.

Her message was clear: The conversation was over.

Guy paced in the book room, wishing he'd simply gone on to Sin and Marianne's ball and let the women show up on their own.

He knew that was a boorish and ungentlemanly thought, but he was so bloody wound up waiting for them, he was about to—

"Guy?"

His head whipped around. "What?" he asked Helen, who was sitting on the settee beside a yawning, sleepy-eyed Cat, who'd been allowed to stay up late so she could see everyone in their finery.

"You're walking a hole in the carpet," Helen teased, looking up at him with a glint of humor in her gray eyes.

He scowled and then dropped into a chair, picking up the ancient marquetry box that he'd set on the side table an excruciating half hour earlier. It was his bloody fault for being ready so early, but he'd been too damned keyed up to do anything else.

"Do you think—"

"I think she'll love it," Helena said softly.

"But is it too much?" Guy wanted to chew his tongue out for asking such a stupid question. He'd been giving women jewelry since he'd had his first lover at the age of seventeen. He was thirty-three years old and behaving like an idiot.

"I think it is perfect," Cat piped up, looking up from the book she'd been reading.

"Thank you, sweetheart," Guy said, smiling at her.

He inhaled deeply, held it, and then exhaled; tonight was the night he was going to tell her everything. He was done hiding in the shadows. If she didn't want him? Well, he'd hang about until the end rather than run off like a rejected boy. There was Cat to consider, after all. Because even if Cecile didn't want him, he didn't want to abandon the little girl. Not that he could consider taking her with him; she was far better off in London than in some backwater in America. She could come and see him when she was older. If she still remembered him.

An almost suffocating wave of self-pity rose up in his throat and Guy shook himself.

What was he doing admitting defeat before he'd even engaged in battle? He knew Cecile felt *something* for him. The only question was whether it was enough for her to overlook their past and trust him with her future.

★ ★ ★

"You look just like an angel," Cecile said, not exaggerating even a little as she stared at Blade.

"That she does, Miss Tremblay, that she does," Lorna Biggles said, grinning.

Lorna worked for Cordelia Black's harlequinade players and did the more complicated face paint the troupe required. She also knew a great deal about dressing hair and had been cutting Cecile's ever since she'd joined the Fayre.

"You did a lovely job on her hair," Cecile added.

"There was certainly plenty to work with. I've never seen such a beautiful color. Leastways not on a grown person," Lorna admitted.

"You two are making me feel self-conscious," Blade said in her slightly froggy voice. Her pale eyes—which Lorna had subtly and skillfully made to look even bigger and more luminous—flickered over Cecile, and she smiled. "You look like a goddess come to earth."

Blade seemed surprised by her own comment and her cheeks turned a delicate pink, which made her look even lovelier.

"Thank you," Cecile said, turning to have one last look in the mirror. She *did* look like a goddess come to earth. Her reflection smirked as she imagined Guy's reaction.

Her gown was a lustrous peacock-blue silk net over an emerald-green underdress, and the tissue-thin fabric flowed like water around her when she moved. The current high-waisted style was good for her figure, which had always been an hourglass but had become fuller as she'd aged.

Cecile was no spring pullet, as the saying went, but she was satisfied with what she saw in the mirror: a woman past her first bloom of youth but who was still beautiful. Her hair was still the same dark brown it had been when she was a girl. And if there were some lines around her eyes, well, she had earned them honestly.

Lorna had dressed her hair simply, the only adornment some small brilliants in blues and greens.

Around her throat she wore an emerald pendant that she'd taken from the cask of paste jewels Guy had found in one of the box rooms.

There had been several lovely pieces she'd kept for herself; the rest she'd given Cat to play with.

Her father had needed to sell anything of value to afford their passage, and even the few simple jewels she'd had of her mother's had been lost on her crossing.

Lovers had tried to give her expensive baubles in the past, but such gifts had always smacked too much of payment for her to accept.

And so here you are without anything nice, going to your first ton *ball wearing a theatrical prop.*

Cecile wasn't bothered by the thought. No, all she felt was excitement.

She turned to find Blade staring at her own reflection in the mirror above the fireplace. Their eyes met and the other woman smiled, her expression revealing her pleasure at what she saw. And no wonder. She looked like a young girl in the delicate silver-spangled muslin, the cut and fit simple in the extreme. At her throat she wore a truly exquisite set of pearls, complete with earbobs. As ever, Cecile burned with curiosity to know where she'd come by such expensive jewels, but she suppressed her questions.

Lorna had cut a great deal off Blade's hair. As beautiful as the pale corn silk color was, it had overwhelmed her fine features. With so much of the length and weight gone, it showed a natural propensity to curl. She really did look like an angel.

Lorna set a gorgeous green, blue, and gold wrap on Cecile's shoulders. "You ladies will be the belles of the ball," she said, her eyes sparkling even though she wasn't going with them.

They fetched their reticules and special fans, then went down to the book room, where they'd promised to model their finery for Cat and Helen.

When they walked into the room, Cecile didn't see Guy at first because he was sitting in the high wing-back chair facing Helen and Cat, who were looking toward the door.

Cat's eyes grew flatteringly round. "Oh," was all she was able to manage.

"You both look so beautiful," Helen said, her normally reserved face breaking into a big smile, her eyes glowing with admiration.

Guy rose from his chair, shoulders impossibly broad in his exquisitely fitted evening blacks.

And there he was, the Darling of the *Ton*, standing in Cecile's humble book room.

The phrase *he looked like a god* was something she'd read dozens of times over the years. But what else could you say about the physical embodiment of masculine perfection?

His full lips parted and his eyes moved over her in a way that was so intimate and caressing she actually blushed.

He opened his mouth, but then shut it again and swallowed, his big hands squeezing something he was holding.

The silence stretched and Guy showed no sign of breaking either it or his stare.

"Are you ready?" Cecile finally asked, jolting him from his fugue.

His face darkened as he realized his lapse and quickly turned to Blade. "Lord. You look like an angel."

Blade gave a low chuckle. "That seems to be the consensus."

Guy's eyes moved to the pearls at Blade's throat. "That is quite an impressive set of pearls."

Blade's hand moved to the necklace, and she stroked the glowing gems absently, as if she'd forgotten about them. "Thank you."

Guy looked around. "Where's Angus?" He pulled a face. "Oh no! Don't tell me that he didn't get his invitation?"

Cat giggled and even Blade smiled at his teasing.

"A ballroom wouldn't be a good place for him."

Guy winced. "Indeed, no—all those jewels to tempt him. Speaking of which—" He turned to Cecile, his expression one she'd never seen before—tentative. "This is for you." He held out a lovely old marquetry box.

"What is it?" she asked, not reaching for it.

His smile was strained. "You need to open it to find out."

"But why—"

Blade nudged her in the ribs, hard.

Cecile reached for the box. "Thank you."

He nodded and she looked down, almost afraid to open it.

"Oh, my goodness," Blade whispered when Cecile lifted the lid.

Cecile wished she had even that many words. It was a gold and diamond necklace—and there was no denying the stones were real, not paste—along with earbobs and a bracelet.

"My grandmother said there had once been a girdle and tiara, but they were broken up before her time," Guy said when Cecile could only stare.

She wrenched her eyes away from the glittering gift. "I can't—"

"Don't," he said, the single word heavy with suppressed emotion. "Please. It is a gift—contingent on nothing. It is a sign of my regard for you."

Cecile wanted to argue—it was simply too much—but she could see by the guarded look in his eyes that her rejection would be one too many after the long line of refusals these past weeks and months.

She swallowed down her automatic response and said, "Thank you. It is exquisite. Will you put it on—the necklace?"

Cecile's heart raced at how happy he looked. He had made himself vulnerable to her—that was obvious even to a woman who could be as obtuse as Cecile.

It was time to stop pretending that she didn't return his feelings.

"Are you both warm enough?" Guy asked after settling them into the coach Sin had insisted on sending for them.

They both nodded, looking around at the luxurious leather interior of the spacious carriage with wide eyes.

Guy settled into the back-facing seat, for once not needing to keep his long legs bunched up under his chin. Sin, who was as tall as Guy, had ordered the town coach custom-built to his dimensions, something Guy had never been wealthy enough to do.

There had been a time in his life when such a thought would have given him a pang. Now he realized it just wasn't that important any longer. He could rent a hackney to take Cecile somewhere if need be. But if he had enough money to afford a coach like this, the woman sitting inside it wouldn't be Cecile.

It took you long enough to accept that.

Guy couldn't disagree.

"Tell us what to expect when we arrive," Blade said, a nervous quaver in her low voice.

He glanced at Cecile, who just nodded. Given all the society papers she'd read over the years, Guy suspected that she probably had more experience describing a ball than he did since he usually arrived late, slipping in to avoid being trapped by the hostess and forced to dance with all the fresh-from-the-schoolroom chits.

"There will be a line of carriages—a very long one as this is the first ball Sin and Marianne have given. Indeed, I doubt there has been a ball at Staunton House since Sin's last wife died."

"He was married before?" Cecile asked.

He glanced at Blade, but of course she knew everything, so she didn't seem surprised.

"Yes, but not for very long. His wife and son died in childbed."

Pain flashed across her face—gut-wrenching and breath-stopping in its intensity—but it was gone in a flash.

A quick look at Blade—who wasn't fast enough to hide her pity—confirmed Guy's suspicion.

Guy wanted to stop the luxurious coach and take Cecile back home, where he could comfort and protect her against—well, he didn't know *what*, did he?

Perhaps if things went as he hoped tonight then she might confide in him.

And if she never did . . .

He shoved that thought aside. He'd worry about that if and when it happened.

Guy cleared his throat and said, "After we've waited in the interminable carriage line we'll join a receiving line. Sin will look as if he is actually enjoying himself and Marianne will appear calm and not as if her heart is beating out of her chest."

The two women smiled.

"I saw her two days ago," Cecile said. "She was most certainly not *calm*."

"She probably won't be calm again until a few days from now, when she discovers what a success the ball was."

"Do you think it will be?" Cecile asked.

"Sin didn't want to tell Marianne until tonight, but Prinny will pop in, ensuring the event is proclaimed one of the finest of the Season."

Cecile's eyes threatened to roll out of her head at this information. "How wonderful," she murmured.

Guy didn't disabuse her; she'd see soon enough what a florid, corpulent, self-indulgent old gasbag he was.

Personally, Guy dreaded seeing the Regent. His father had been a great friend of the Prince of Wales, the two of them bringing out the worst in each other. What made the situation even more complicated was that Guy's grandfather had been close friends with the king. Since his grandfather had never been one to mince words, he'd once, over port and cigarillos at Fairhurst, pinned the Prince's ears back on the subject of filial responsibility. Prinny had cut his stay short after that dressing down and had never visited the ducal seat again.

Guy realized he'd been gathering wool and shook himself, looking from Cecile to Blade. "I'd like to claim my two sets with you both now, before what will surely be an eager rush. Cecile, may I have the first waltz and the supper dance?"

"You may," she said.

He turned to Blade. "How about the first set and the after-supper dance?"

Blade's lips curved into a faint smile. "You may."

Guy and Cecile had discussed the matter of Blade and Elliot only yesterday. It had been Cecile's idea that Guy should ask Blade for the first dance.

"But Elliot will be there; perhaps he'd like to ask her for the first dance," Guy had pointed out.

"No, this will be better. It will give him something to think about."

Guy had laughed at that. "If you think I can make Elliot jealous, think again. The man is as unflappable as they come. Besides, I haven't stayed friends with him for so long by behaving like a cow-handed thruster."

"I take it that is some sort of hunting cant?" she had asked, cocking a glossy black eyebrow. "If Elliot *is* interested in her, then he needs to show it."

It just so happened that Guy agreed with her sentiment. If *he* had to suffer the slings and arrows of love, he wanted his friend to suffer, too.

"So, here we are," Guy said as they approached the square. He pointed out the window. "It's just ahead—four houses away."

"People won't just get out and walk?" Blade asked, her eyes wide as she took in the line they'd joined.

Guy gasped. "For shame, Miss Brown! You would ruin your dancing slippers."

Blade glanced down at her feet as if she couldn't recall what she was wearing.

"Are they comfortable?" he asked.

"Not as comfortable as my boots."

Guy laughed. "I couldn't agree more."

Cecile knew she was staring around the massive foyer and grand staircase like a yokel, but how could she not?

It had been many years since she'd lived at the Duc de La Fontaine's country estate, and even then, she'd not gone into any part of the house other than the servant areas.

"I'm so glad you could come," Sin said, looking every inch the duke he was, his pale blond hair gleaming, his green eyes like peridots in his handsome face.

"Thank you, Your Grace. It is a pleasure to see you again," Cecile said, offering her hand in greeting.

The people surrounding them were deadly silent and Cecile knew they were all waiting to hear what was exchanged. Not just because of Guy—who had certainly caused a flurry of chatter when he'd entered the house—but also because a goodly number of the men would recognize her.

Blade was more fortunate; thanks to the mask she wore for all her performances, nobody would suspect that she was the knife expert at Farnham's Fayre.

Marianne, who stood beside Sin, looked every bit as grand as her magnificent husband in a flattering gown of gold silk. The gems around her neck were reminiscent of some of the ones Cecile had seen at the Tower.

She had to admit that as grand as the other woman's jewelry was, she preferred her daintier filigreed necklace.

Marianne squeezed her hands so hard it hurt. "I'm so pleased you could come," she said, taking one of Blade's hands, too. "Both of you." She leaned close to Cecile, as if to inspect her necklace and said, "My, what a lovely setting that is! So beautiful and unusual." Before Cecile could respond, Marianne whispered, "We shall save places for you at our supper table." She pulled back and smiled, her mask firmly in place. "I do hope you enjoy yourselves."

"Well, that was that," Guy murmured once they'd stepped away from the receiving line. He smiled and offered Cecile and Blade an arm. "Shall we, ladies?"

"I don't think that will be necessary," a low voice said from off to their right.

Guy grinned at his friend. "Ah, Elliot, punctual as usual, I see. Perhaps you might escort Miss Tremblay as well. Miss Brown has promised her first set to me."

Elliot gave his friend an unreadable look before turning to Cecile. "Would you honor me with a dance?"

"It would be my pleasure."

As Elliot escorted her up the stairs to the ballroom, he leaned close. "What is Guy up to this evening?"

"Is he up to something?"

"His eyes had a certain gleam in them when they landed on me."

"Well, I'm glad he is fixated on *you* this evening rather than me." She leaned a bit closer and asked softly, "Is it my imagination, or are people staring?"

"No, it's not your imagination; they're staring."

"Do you think they know who I am?"

"Perhaps a few of them, but it is more likely that most of them are staring because you and Josephine are both exceedingly beautiful women. And of course, everyone stares at Guy."

Cecile laughed, her gaze darting around the grand ballroom as she tried to take in everything. "I am new at this."

"Balls?"

"Dancing."

"Ah. Do you wish to sit this one out?"

"Not at all. Guy taught us a good many figures."

He looked amused. "Well, you couldn't have had a better teacher." He guided her toward the far side of the ballroom. "It will be less of a crush away from the entrance," he explained. "This first set should be an easy one for you—Drops of Brandy, it is called. Do you need—"

Cecile unfurled her fan and quickly found the dance in question. Elliot laughed. "Good thinking."

"It was Guy's idea."

Cecile couldn't help noticing that Elliot's gaze lingered on Blade as she and Guy took their positions. She leaned close to him and said, "He asked her for the first dance because he didn't want her to feel left out. He knew I'd enjoy myself whether anyone asked me or not. But Blade . . . well, ballroom dancing is not something she ever imagined for herself."

"I'm stunned you persuaded her to come." Elliot swallowed, his expression positively ravenous as he stared at Blade. "She looks…"

"Yes?" Cecile prodded, amused by this unprecedented emotional display from such a reserved man.

Elliot wrenched his gaze away from Blade with obvious effort and his sharp cheekbones stained with red when he realized he was staring at another woman while ignoring his own dance partner. "Er, you look quite ravishing this evening, too."

Cecile laughed and tapped him on the arm with her fan. "Poor Elliot."

He gave her a sheepish look. "That obvious, am I?"

"I think it's charming." Cecile couldn't help wondering if Blade knew just how taken with her Elliot was.

"We'd best take our positions," Elliot murmured.

Cecile quickly discovered that dancing in a ballroom with a full orchestra playing and a hundred other people chattering was far more challenging than dancing with three other people at home. She found it extremely difficult to talk, concentrate, *and* dance, so she was relieved that Elliot was too busy sneaking glances at Blade to require much conversation.

By the time she was comfortable with the formation and steps, and just beginning to enjoy herself, the dance was almost over.

"Well done," Elliot said as he led her off the floor.

Cecile laughed. "I would say *adequately* done is more accurate."

It was easy to spot Guy in the crowded room because he was taller than most of the other men.

"How was it?" Guy asked as they approached. "Did Elliot knock you over or tear your frock?"

"He dances exquisitely," Cecile assured him.

For his part, Elliot was so busy gazing at Blade that he didn't even hear his friend's teasing.

Cecile and Guy exchanged an amused look as Elliot and Blade stared silently at each other.

A handsome blond man appeared at Guy's elbow, his eyes admiring as he looked at Cecile. She couldn't recall the newcomer's name, but she'd seen him at the Fayre many times, always in the company of several other loud, ill-behaved aristocrats. "I say, Fairh—er, that is, Darlington—could you introduce me to your lady friend?"

Guy's good humor evaporated like a drop of hot water on red-hot steel. "No, Lorimer, I will not introduce you. Go back and frolic with all the other young pups."

Cecile almost felt sorry for the younger man, whose face turned an alarming shade of red before he beat a hasty retreat, scurrying away like a rodent.

Guy glared after him, his expression thunderous.

Cecile knew it was a breach of etiquette to ask for an introduction in such a way. Clearly Lorimer hadn't thought a mere circus worker merited much courtesy.

"Good show," Elliot commended his friend. "Best to nip that sort of behavior in the bud," he added, looking rather fierce himself. He turned his intense, dark blue gaze on Blade. "May I have the next set and the supper set if you've not already thrown it away on this rogue?" He jerked his chin toward Guy.

Blade gave him a surprisingly arch look. "You may."

"And may I also say that you look quite stunning this evening, Miss Brown?"

Blade's cheeks flushed, but her expression remained cool. "I believe you just did, Mr. Wingate."

Guy threw his head back and laughed.

Chapter 23

Guy knew it was petty of him to want to keep all Cecile's dances to himself, but he could accept that he was petty where she was concerned.

However, what he wanted was not what he would get.

Marianne made a constant stream of introductions to both women after she left her position in the receiving line. By the time the supper waltz came around, Guy was bloody tired of seeing every bloke in the *ton* lining up to have a dance with Cecile. He was grateful to Sin and Marianne for saving them places at their supper table.

"I don't suppose you know where Elliot and Blade have disappeared to?" Sin whispered to Guy as Marianne and Cecile chatted happily with Sin's aunt Julia.

Guy eyed the very conspicuous two empty chairs at their table—prime real estate—and gave a slight shake of his head. "It's not like Elliot to be so obvious," he admitted. "You might as well give the seats away."

"Not just yet. They may show up," Sin said.

But neither Elliot nor Blade made an appearance at supper.

"Can you make sure nothing has gone amiss with them?" Sin asked as their table broke up.

"I'll keep an eye out for both of them if you can convince your wife to quit bringing me giggling dance partners," Guy retorted.

Sin laughed. "I'll see what I can do. Right now, however, I'm engaged to dance the next set with Cecile," he said, glancing around. "Where did she disappear to so quickly?"

"I don't know, but you'd better not keep her waiting," Guy warned, amused when Sin went hurrying off.

Guy had no dances with Cecile to look forward to after supper, so the evening loomed before him. Given the current state of his reputation, he'd hoped that he'd not be called upon to dance with many debutantes. Unfortunately, it appeared that a goodly number of matchmaking mamas still considered him eligible husband material, if only for his august connections, so he'd been trapped into more sets than he would have liked.

It was during one of those unwanted dances that Nathan Whitfield saw an opportunity to claim a dance with Cecile. A waltz, no less.

Guy wasn't engaged for the set so he was at liberty to keep his eye on the other man.

He was glaring at Whitfield, tapping his toe with impatience, and waiting for the bloody dance to end when Elliot appeared beside him.

"Where have *you* been?" Guy demanded.

Elliot cocked an eyebrow at him. "I wasn't aware that I was missing."

"You know bloody well that you can't disappear right at supper—coincidentally at the same time as Blade—and think your absence wouldn't be noted. Especially not when Sin and Marianne held seats for you both at their table."

Elliot snorted. "It warms my heart to know you pay such close attention to my activities, Guy."

"I brought Blade here, Elliot. It's my duty to make sure that—"

"She is her own mistress," Elliot said, no longer amused. "And—not that it's any of your affair—we weren't doing anything inappropriate; we've been in the cardroom for most of that time."

"You played cards during supper?" Guy persisted, not put off by the edge in the other man's voice.

Elliot ignored his question. "Jo's tired so I'm taking her home. In fact, I was just looking for Cecile so I could tell her."

Guy felt a stab of envy at his friend's words. Leaving early sounded like a wonderful idea but he suspected Cecile wouldn't want to leave her first ever *ton* event before dawn.

"You can go and I'll tell Cecile that you took Blade home," he said.

Elliot stepped closer. "I was going to tell you this tomorrow, but since we have a moment . . ."

"Yes?"

"I was thinking some more about Cecile's contract with Blanchard."

"Oh?"

Elliot cleared his throat and then said, "Don't be angry, but Jo told me the rest of what she discovered."

"You mean the details she has *refused* to tell me?" Guy snorted. "Why would that make me angry?"

Elliot at least had the decency to look embarrassed. "I'm sorry, but it's her investigation and . . . well, I happen to agree with Jo: You should be asking Cecile about her past."

"Don't worry, I plan to. So, what idea did you have about the contract?"

"Thanks to what Jo told me, I think the contract could be void due to duress. It wouldn't be an easy process to prove this—and it would likely become ugly—but there are hundreds of thousands of pounds at stake, Guy. While Guthrie's stopped using the part Cecile designed a few years ago that doesn't diminish the fact that the company made a fortune off those government contracts. She deserves her share of all those profits."

Guy nodded, his expression grim. "Come to the house tomorrow; you can explain the legal aspects to her better than I can."

Elliot's eyes widened. "Tomorrow? You want *me* to tell her about—"

"No, I am going to tell her everything tonight. But I don't doubt that she will have questions."

The dance ended and Guy noticed that Cecile and Whitfield were engaged in a discussion—not exactly heated, but other dancers were staring at them.

"I need to go," he murmured to Elliot, not waiting for his response before following the couple through a set of French doors out onto the terrace. Because the weather was unusually chilly, there were no others around and Whitfield and Cecile had the terrace to themselves.

As Guy got closer to the pair it was clear they were arguing.

He smiled tightly at Cecile when the two broke off and turned to him. "Ah, Cecile—there you are. Marianne was looking for you, my dear."

Her expression went from irritated at Guy's interruption to concerned. "Oh, is something wrong?"

"She didn't say, but I shouldn't think it's anything dire, although she did ask that you make haste."

Cecile turned to Whitfield and said, "I'm sorry, but I must—"

"Of course, you must go." He snagged her hand and kissed the back of it, his eyes on Guy. "We can finish this discussion later, at our leisure."

Cecile cut him an odd look but didn't linger.

Once she'd gone out of earshot the baron turned to Guy, a smirk on his handsome face. "Here you are, Darlington. Again. Interrupting and pulling Cecile away for one silly reason or another. Again."

"She didn't look too sad to leave you."

"No, but then she knows I am not an inconstant bounder who will run off and get betrothed to another woman while I am out of her sight."

Guy would have liked to know how Whitfield had learned about that. Indeed, he would have enjoyed beating an answer or two out of him. But now was neither the time nor place.

"She did not appear to be pleased with whatever you were saying to her, Whitfield; that much was evident to everyone in the ballroom."

Whitfield returned his glare, his face hard and determined. "Not that it's any of your affair, but I was offering to make her my wife."

That gave Guy pause.

He eyed the younger man with grudging respect. "I can't say that I wish you any luck, Whitfield. But you've certainly risen dramatically in my estimation. May the best man win." Guy turned and made haste toward the retiring room; he needed to find Cecile before *she* found Marianne and asked—

"Looking for me?" The familiar voice came from inside a small alcove as he passed by.

Guy stopped and met Cecile's mocking gaze. "Er, I wanted to—"

"I know that Marianne did not need me."

"And yet you left Whitfield, anyhow?"

"I wanted to get away from Nathan but was not sure how to do so without drawing attention. You just gave me a good excuse."

Guy smiled.

"Not that you should be proud of yourself for all the fibbing you do."

"No, ma'am, absolutely not."

She snorted and shifted, a pained expression flickering across her face.

"What is it?"

"My feet hurt."

She sounded so angry that Guy chuckled. "That isn't so unusual. Do you want to find somewhere to sit for a while?"

"What time is it?"

"Just after two."

"There are still several hours to go, aren't there?"

"Yes, I'm sure the revelry won't stop until five or maybe six. But—"

"But?" she prodded.

"We don't *have* to stay to the end."

"What do you want to do?"

"Whatever you want to do."

"I should ask Blade." She pulled a face. "If I can actually find her, that is."

"Oh, I forgot—she left with Elliot."

"Why didn't they come to supper?"

"If Elliot is to be believed, the two of them were playing cards. I pity whoever sat across the table from Elliot—you can never tell what he's thinking and he's got the devil's own luck."

"I've played cribbage with Blade, and she never loses."

"I suppose we should be grateful there aren't aristocratic men with pitchforks and torches looking for the two of them."

She laughed and met his gaze. "Let's go home."

Guy grinned. "Sweeter words I've never heard."

"I don't want to wait for Sin's carriage to be brought around," Guy said. "I'll go and hail a hackney and then come back for you."

"I can go with you."

"But your feet?"

"I'll be fine," Cecile promised.

"Let us sneak through the refreshment room. We can slip out a side door and perhaps avoid any notice."

Cecile gave him a look of mock surprise. "The Darling leaving without attracting notice? Unheard of!"

"Ha, ha, very droll."

Another set had just begun, so the refreshment room only held a few stragglers, all young bucks.

Guy scowled at them, and they scattered. "Good," he muttered, "now there are no witnesses to our heinous crime of early departure. Let's make haste before somebody comes looking for us."

He led her first to the cloak room and then out through the surprisingly empty foyer.

"So," he said, once they were out in front of the houses that bordered the square. "How was your first ball—other than the sore feet?"

"It was lovely." Cecile hesitated and then asked, "How was it for you, Guy? Truly?"

"It was strange and a little awkward." He cut her a quick, not entirely happy smile, "The one thing I can say for losing my estate and title is that it's easy to see who my real friends are."

"Were people rude?"

"Rude? No, just . . . dismissive. I expected most of them to be that way—a few were downright unpleasant—but there were some mates from school who . . . well, let's just say they obviously wanted to be friends with a duke, not with Guy Darlington." He escorted her to the hackney at the head of the queue, flipped down the steps, and handed her in.

Once they were settled inside the old but clean carriage, he sighed. "I'm glad it's over. I'm not sure how I managed to do that night after night, to be honest."

"You prefer having knives thrown at you and cleaning out the night-soil closet?"

He chuckled. "Well, perhaps not the night-soil closet, but I don't mind being in either of your routines. After the first few weeks, I scarcely noticed all the raucous taunting by my former contemporaries." The smile slid from his face, and he leaned across the carriage and held out his hand. After a second's hesitation she set hers in his. "It is no exaggeration to say that I enjoy living in the same house as you and working with you more than anything else I've ever done."

Cecile's eyes stung and she was terrified that she would start weeping. The tears had been building all night. She'd realized somewhere in the middle of the waltz with Nathan—who'd apologized about his letter and then commenced importuning her—that she just wanted to be home with Guy. She wanted to quit tormenting them both and take him to her bed. She wanted to forget about the past and seize the future.

"You're looking at me strangely," he said. "I'm not teasing you, Cecile. I—"

Cecile leaned toward him and covered his gorgeous lips with her mouth.

Chapter 24

Guy pulled Cecile onto his lap and cradled her in his arms; how could a woman feel so comfortable and familiar in his embrace while, at the very same time, still be the most mysterious, exciting person he'd ever met?

It was Cecile, finally, who pulled away to gasp for breath.

Guy heaved a sigh of contentment. "I thought I was going to have to do something truly desperate to get you to kiss me again."

"Oh, like what?"

"I was considering serenading you beneath your window."

She laughed. "Can you sing?"

"No, that's why it would be truly desperate." Guy gazed down into her heavy-lidded eyes as they bounced along in the old hackney, the light from the streetlamps flickering over her. "God, you look beautiful tonight, Cecile. That gown is superb on you. But I have to admit I can't wait to get you out of it." He gave her another lingering kiss but then pulled back as a thought struck him. "I don't want an affair with you this time, Cecile. I want more."

She groaned. "Guy, this is not—"

"I love you. I loved you last year but was too foolish to recognize it. I'll never be able to erase what I did and said to you back then, nor can I deny that I would have probably married a different woman to save the dukedom. It was the duty I was raised for, Cecile. I simply didn't believe I would ever have the choice to marry who I—"

"I won't get married, Guy—not to anyone—but I will be your lover for as long as you want me."

Guy inhaled deeply, held his breath for a count of five, and then exhaled and asked, "Why, Cecile?"

Even in the dimness he could see she was choosing her words carefully.

"I should have said I won't marry you *now*."

"You mean you might change your mind?"

"I might. But I might not." She chewed her lip in an uncharacteristically indecisive way. "I don't know."

Honestly, Guy was just relieved that she'd not rejected him outright. If she allowed him to stay with her then he could convince her over time; he felt confident of that.

He kissed the tip of her nose. "You don't need to decide now. We're in no rush and can take all the time we need."

Cecile felt like an ogre for stepping on his joy, but she couldn't in good conscience agree to marry him. At least not right now. And maybe never. Putting her life in a man's hands—giving over control of not just everything she owned, but her person, too, would be a huge step, maybe too huge.

Still, it was something she could think about. As he'd said, there was no rush.

The house was as quiet as a tomb when they unlocked the door a short time later.

"Come to my room?" she asked when they reached the top of the stairs.

To her surprise, he hesitated.

"You don't want to?"

"Oh, I do—you have no idea how much I want to get you into bed, Cecile. But there are a few things I need to tell you first."

Something unpleasant twisted in her belly. "You want to speak to me *now*?"

"If that would be acceptable to you?"

Cecile found it more than a little worrisome that Guy would turn down an offer to take her to bed after nagging her for weeks on end, but she kept her concern to herself.

Instead, she said, "Of course we can have a talk. Come up to my chambers."

The moment they reached her sitting room Cecile tossed aside her reticule, toed off her slippers with a groan of pleasure, and flung herself onto her favorite chair. "Ah, that feels so good."

When Guy didn't respond she looked up.

He was staring at her with a look of savage hunger that restored her faith in his affection but made her worry even more about what he needed to tell her.

"I'll pour us something to drink. Is whiskey good?" he asked her.

"You read my mind," she said.

Once they both had glasses and were comfortably seated, Cecile said, "I'm listening."

Guy turned the glass around and around in his hands, his expression more pensive than she'd ever seen it.

"There's no other way to say it except I hired Blade to look into your past. Specifically, I wanted to know what happened that left you unable to pursue gunsmithing in England."

It took her a long moment to grasp his meaning. It wasn't as if the words themselves were difficult to understand, but they were utterly unexpected.

"But . . . why?" she finally asked.

"I just—well, something about your story didn't sound right."

"You thought I *lied* to you?"

"No, no," he said quickly. "Of course, I didn't. It is only that you seemed so *angry* both times you mentioned your cousin. Especially about the fact that you weren't allowed to ply your trade in this country." He shrugged. "I thought perhaps your cousin had taken advantage of you. After all, you were barely a child when you arrived, and not much older when you sold the rights to your designs to him. And then he stopped producing guns barely a year later. It just didn't make—"

"No, not a year. He closed the company after almost ten years."

Guy looked at her strangely. "No, Blanchard hasn't made guns in ages—not since I was a schoolboy, at any rate."

"You must be wrong," she insisted. "He paid me my share of the profits for nine years—until he closed the shop."

"He might have paid you for nine years, Cecile, but the money wasn't connected to Blanchard's or its profits."

Cecile could only stare.

"But that's not the important issue."

She gave a scandalized snort. "It's important to *me*."

"Er, well, that's just because I'm guessing you don't know the whole story."

"What whole story?"

He grimaced. "I'm getting all turned around with my explanation. I wanted to first tell you about—"

"Just tell me everything you know, Guy."

Guy took a deep breath and said, "Let me start over and explain things the right way."

"Please do."

"The contract you signed gave Blanchard the rights to all your father's designs as well as your own?"

"My father's, yes. But I had nothing significant of my own. Just a few sketches and ideas."

"One of those was a percussion cap, was it not?"

"Yes, I had several different designs. My father had worked on something not long before he died, but Curtis said his idea had already been duplicated by an English gunsmith—Manton, I believe."

"Yes, that is all true about your father's invention, but one of *your* ideas was quite valuable and Blanchard sold the patent for an immense amount of money to Guthrie's."

Cecile's lips parted in shock. "Surely you're mistaken?"

"No, it's true. Guthrie's used your design in the guns they manufactured for the army. They had several large and lucrative contracts."

A myriad of emotions flickered across her face.

"Cecile?"

She shook her head, her expression one of disbelief. "I can hardly believe this. What else did you discover?"

"Well, apparently there is more, but that is all Blade would tell me. She said she'd look into your cousin and any dealings you had with him, but she drew the line at sharing any details that she deemed too personal." When she didn't say anything, he grimaced and asked, "Are you angry with me? Blade said you would be, even with the scope of the investigation limited."

"I'm not angry with you," she said. "But I don't see that your investigation changes anything. After all, I *did* sign a contract with him."

"Why did you sign over your family's designs to him, Cecile? It doesn't seem like something you would have done."

"I was young and foolish and I *had* to sign everything over— there was no other way."

"I don't understand."

Cecile gave him an almost agonized look. "It is a shameful story, Guy—one I've never told another person."

He took her hand in both of his. "I don't wish to force confidences, Cecile. But I feel that I should tell you that if Blanchard *made* you agree to this contract using any sort of threat, it could be the contract is not enforceable due to duress. It is possible you might get back the designs you sold. As for the patented idea, you may be entitled to compensation."

Her eyes widened and she looked momentarily hopeful. But a second later that expression turned to near despair.

"To do so I would need to give evidence of what happened?"

"Yes."

She shook her head. "I could never do that. Never."

"You don't have to do anything you don't wish, Cecile. I just wanted you to know your rights," Guy said, hoping he was able to conceal his disappointment. Not just that she didn't trust him enough to confide in him, but that Blanchard would get away with stealing tens of thousands of pounds.

"I don't want to confess any of this to a judge or strangers," she said. "I understand."

Cecile sighed, her expression one of shame and pain. "However, much as I hate to even *think* of any of this again, I *do* want you to know what happened all those years ago."

Chapter 25

If you tell him this, he will know the very worst about you, Cecile. He will never look at you the same way again.

She knew that was true, but she owed Guy the truth. Until he knew, he wouldn't be satisfied to remain her lover; he'd want marriage. Once she told him what she'd done, he'd probably abandon her altogether.

"Cecile."

She looked up from her miserable thoughts.

"You don't have to tell me anything. I will stand by you whatever you decide to do." He gave a humorless laugh. "I have to admit it sticks in my craw to let Blanchard get away with stealing from you, but that is your decision to make. I just—well, I just wanted to do something for you. Perhaps finding out what really happened wasn't the best—"

"What you've told me is a gift, Guy."

He didn't look convinced.

"You already know that Curtis was the only family I had left. We aren't really cousins—well, distantly—but my father had kept in communication with him and his father, so the family bond seemed closer than it actually is. He is twelve years my senior and when I first met him, I was in awe of my handsome, dashing older cousin. I had nobody, and he immediately took me in."

Cecile couldn't look at him while she confessed this next part.

"He brought me into his house, bought me lovely clothing, and treated me like a daughter. He was married and his wife, Martha, was . . . well, she was not welcoming. At the time it seemed unfair, but given what happened later"—she shrugged—"Martha was justified in hating me. At first, she was only stiff and reserved, but once I started to go into the workshop with Curtis, she was openly hostile and it became increasingly unpleasant to live in the same house with her, but I had nowhere else to go. By the time I was sixteen, Martha had suffered two miscarriages. After the second she was very ill and her doctor advised my cousin to put her in a sanitorium in Bath, where she could take the waters." Cecile raised her glass to her mouth only to learn it was empty.

"Here, let me." Guy took both their glasses and left to refill them.

Cecile used that moment of privacy to gather her courage and gird herself for what she was about to admit; it was not a pretty story.

"Thank you," she said, taking the glass and drinking deeply before continuing. "Martha was gone for a long time—two years—and during that time Curtis and I became lovers."

She wrenched her gaze away from the amber liquid and looked up to find Guy watching and waiting. His expression was . . . well, it was much as it ever was.

"Are you not disgusted?" she blurted.

He laughed. When Cecile jolted, he said, "Oh, love. I am not laughing at you—I'm laughing at your question. Do you truly believe that I would revile you for doing no more than I've done?"

"But you are a man, and—"

"I do not hold you to a different standard, Cecile," he said. "And I certainly would not pass judgment on a woman who was . . . what—seventeen, eighteen?"

"Eighteen."

"If anyone should be blamed, it is Blanchard, as he was the one who took a vow before man and God to be faithful to his wife."

His words eased her mortification, but she knew that what she'd done was wrong and would always feel shame at her behavior.

"Curtis told me he loved me and his marriage had been a business arrangement, devoid of affection. Martha's father owned a small smithy, and the two enterprises had become one upon their union. He said she despised him and loathed his touch." Cecile heaved a sigh. "I know you will believe me a fool, but he promised me that he would petition for a divorce, that the expense and public shame would be bearable if we could be together."

"Let me guess," Guy said, his expression icy with restrained anger. "He wanted to wait until she was better?"

"Yes. And how could I disagree? So we said we'd wait until she was well enough to come home."

The situation had been unbearable, and Cecile had been horribly ashamed when Martha finally returned, weak and sickly.

"I told Curtis I could not be with him while his wife was in the house." She gave a bitter laugh. "I know that it was too little, too late, but I simply could not bring myself to continue with him until I received evidence that he was going through with what he said. I will admit that by that point my feelings for him had begun to pall somewhat. Unfortunately"—Cecile looked up and met Guy's concerned gaze—"I discovered I was with child and therefore my options had narrowed to very few."

"Oh God, Cecile," he muttered.

She squeezed his fingers hard, more grateful than he would ever know for his touch and his lack of condemnation.

"When I told Curtis, he had a surprise for me."

"His wife was pregnant, too," Guy guessed.

"Yes."

Guy brought her hand to his lips and kissed her palm before pressing it against his cheek.

The gesture reassured her more than words could ever have done. He wasn't disgusted with her; he was sorry for the pain she'd brought upon herself. How could she ever have believed that Guy would be cruel or cold to her?

"I am so very sorry, Cecile. You must have been devastated and so frightened."

"And so very stupid." She gave a helpless laugh. "I might have still been stupidly waiting for him to marry me if it hadn't been for

Martha. First, she told me I was not the only woman he'd promised to marry. Second, she told me he would never divorce her because of the way her money was tied up; he would forfeit that money if they were to divorce."

She drained the rest of her glass, her hand shaking as she set it down. "It was the third thing she told me that made me sign over the plans and give them what they demanded."

Cecile took a moment to steady her breathing, stunned by how it all came flooding back to her—the terror, the helplessness.

"Because I was not of age, Curtis, as my nearest male relative would have me confined to an asylum if I did not agree to their terms. Martha told me it would be easy to convince a magistrate that I was not stable or fit to be a mother. It would be my word—the word of an émigré who spoke broken English and had no visible means of support—against Curtis and Martha's, both pillars of their community. I would be accused of getting pregnant by some unknown man who then abandoned me. She said they would take away my baby when it was born, and I would never see it again."

"Oh God, Cecile."

She dragged the back of her hand over her eyes, furious to discover she'd been crying.

A snow-white handkerchief appeared in front of her blurry gaze, and she smiled. "Thank you."

Once she'd dried her eyes and collected herself, she went on. "It was Martha who dictated the terms. I was to sign over everything in exchange for quarterly payments. The payments were contingent on my going to America and remaining there, where I could cause them no embarrassment." She shrugged. "It was my only real choice. And so I signed."

Guy held her hand tightly, the sympathy in his beautiful brown gaze almost making her fall apart.

Cecile covered her eyes with her free hand and pinched the bridge of her nose until it ached, the pain driving away the tears.

"I lived in Boston as Mrs. Tremblay, a war widow who'd left England to have her child and start a new life. But—but the baby came early, too early to survive." She squeezed her temples in a vise-like grip, but even that wouldn't stop the tears.

Guy came to sit on the settee beside her, his arm around her shoulders, his big body pressed alongside hers.

He took his crumpled handkerchief from where it had fallen and dried her cheeks. "You've had a terrible time of it, haven't you?" He kissed her hair, the feel of his soft lips against her scalp quite possibly the most comforting touch Cecile had ever experienced.

It was that simple touch that broke the iron control she'd struggled so hard to maintain.

Cecile sobbed—releasing the tears she'd been too afraid to cry all those years ago—and Guy held her and murmured soothing nothings until she'd cried herself out.

Finally, exhausted, she sat back and risked a look at him from beneath her damp lashes. "I'm a mess."

He curled a finger beneath her chin and tilted her face up. "No, you are one of the fortunate human beings who looks even lovelier when they weep. But no matter how lovely you are, I don't want to see you sad, darling. Is your past with Blanchard—the baby—the reason you refuse to marry me?"

"That is most of it."

"What is the rest?"

"I saw how it was tonight, Guy. You may no longer be the Duke of Fairhurst, but the beau monde still sees you as one of their own; if you want to go back, they will welcome you with open arms. But if you are married to me? Well, I will *never* fit into your world."

"You seemed to do just fine this evening, sweetheart. I was lucky to get two dances with you."

"That was an unusual event—and I was a novelty. Besides, that was Marianne and Sin. Who else would invite you and your circus performer wife to their house? And the truth is that I will continue to operate this business because it is how I make a living; I *am* a circus performer."

"You don't think you could be a farmer's wife?" he asked with such hope in his eyes that she hated to disappoint him, but . . .

"I want to be with you," she said, charmed by the flush her words evoked. "But I do not wish to return to America, Guy. As for marriage . . . well, perhaps in time. But—" She broke off, not wanting to confess her fears.

"But you are—justifiably—leery of giving yourself and everything you've worked for over to a man," he said. "I understand. I really do. The solution is that we shall stay here and go on as we have been."

"You could be happy with this life?"

He pulled her close and obliterated her wits with a lingering, thorough kiss, leaving her breathless when he pulled away.

"I already *am* happy with this life. You may not believe it, but I enjoy the work I do for you. My mother and no doubt the rest of my family want me to do something else, but the truth is, darling, none of those other jobs would suit me. So, yes, to answer your question. I could be happy with this life as long as you are in it. And I have to admit I've become quite attached to a certain little waif."

Cecile gave a watery chuckle. "Yes, Cat would be devastated if you were to move all the way to America."

"Then let's say I'll stay, shall we?"

She nodded.

"There is one thing I am still wondering about."

She felt the usual stab of fear that struck her whenever somebody wanted to ask her a personal question, but then remembered she'd already told him the worst.

"You can ask me anything," she said.

"Your name. My understanding is that your real name is Manon Cecile Blanchet. Why do you use Cecile Tremblay?"

"Oh, that. I've always preferred to go by Cecile. As for Tremblay, I just chose to use that name so my cousin wouldn't complain that I was soiling the Blanchet name—and him by extension—by working in a circus. Tremblay was my mother's name, so it was an easy choice."

"So your father named you Manon hoping you would follow in his footsteps?"

"Yes." She smiled. "When I was younger, I *hated* the name Manon and insisted on being called Cecile. But now I rather like it."

"Which do you prefer I call you?"

"Cecile." Her lips twitched. "Or darling."

He laughed.

Cecile bit back a yawn, but not very successfully.

"Let's put you in bed, darling. You're simply not up to dancing until dawn, are you?" he teased.

"No, it is much harder than I expected."

"A person needs to work up to it."

"I still want you to come to my bed tonight," she said, her face heating at her shamelessness. "I might not be very entertaining, however."

"Sweetheart, I can be entertaining enough for the both of us."

As it turned out, by the time Guy ran down to the kitchen and heated some water, made a pot of tea, and then headed back up to Cecile's chambers, she was fast asleep—still fully dressed—while sprawled out on her bed.

Guy was tempted to just remove her slippers and jewels and cover her with a blanket, but he knew she'd have a miserable sleep wearing all her clothing.

"Darling?" he murmured.

"Hmmm?" Her eyelids lifted only to slits.

"I'm going to help you get undressed, Cecile."

She yawned and said, "You are very useful."

Guy laughed. "Well, a man should have some skills."

She smiled and her eyes drifted closed again.

"Just stay awake a bit longer, darling."

She made it until she was down to her chemise before he heard deep, measured breathing.

Guy rolled down her stockings and then tucked her beneath the blankets.

He chewed his lip as he considered her hair. There were pretty brilliants sparkling in among the near-black tresses. With excruciating care, he teased the pins from her hair. It would be a tangled mess when she woke, but it was better than getting jabbed in the head.

He blew out the candle but when he turned away, she caught his wrist.

"You're staying?"

"You can rely on that."

Once he'd undressed, locked the door, and snuffed the last candles, he slid in between the cool sheets and stretched out on his back, all too aware of the woman beside him as he stared into the darkness.

Guy was as hard as a poker and he wanted Cecile worse than he'd ever wanted anyone in his life.

Still, he'd rather lie beside her in a state of heightened—and frustrating—arousal than make love with any other woman.

Yes, he was truly smitten.

And he'd never been happier.

Cecile couldn't believe that she'd finally got the Darling into her bed, and then she'd fallen asleep.

But she was awake now—more than just awake.

She'd been having a dream about Curtis of all people. What Guy had told her had both shocked her and yet, strangely, not really surprised her. Oh, *how* Curtis had stolen from her had surprised her, but not that he *had*.

Curtis was the sort of man who got through life on his charm and appearance. He was an extremely handsome man—although nowhere near as attractive as Guy. And when she said *attractive*, she meant Guy's entire person, not just his face and body, but the man inside.

Guy had been a shameless rake for years, but to the people he loved, he was true blue, the sort of man who'd rescue a grimy urchin and her dog. And not once had he complained about losing his status, home, and security to his cousin.

And Cecile loved him.

It had been hard to admit that, even to herself, because the last time she'd loved somebody she'd been so very, very wrong in her choice. But what was the alternative to admitting how she felt about Guy?

Denying her feelings because she was afraid of being wrong? Living the rest of her life alone because she was too scared to take a chance?

She *loved* having Guy working at the Fayre. And she loved living with him.

The past was the past. It was the future that concerned her now—hers, Guy's, and Cat's.

Cecile turned toward his big warm body and molded herself along his side, shamelessly groaning at the exquisite feel of six feet of hot, hard male.

She lightly brought her knee over his thighs and then skimmed his pelvis, gently stroking the hardest part of him.

He woke with a low, sleepy chuckle. "I'd better not wake up if this is a dream."

"This is no dream," she whispered.

He made a growling sound and slid a hand around her knee, pulling her leg tighter against his scalding hot length.

"You feel like heaven, Cecile." His hips pulsed, stroking the sensitive skin of her inner thigh and leaving streaks of moisture. "I've been hard for you for so long."

Cecile shuddered at the raw desire in his voice and slid her leg to his other side, bringing herself astride him.

"Ooooh, my favorite," he said, his voice a purr.

"You like me on top because you're lazy."

"For your information, I like you on top because I can use both my hands *and* I can see almost all of you. And I'm lazy."

Cecile laughed.

Guy caressed his hot palms from her knees, up her thighs, one dipping low and pushing into her private curls while the other cupped a breast, supporting its weight while he tweaked and teased her beaded nipple, each pinch sending jagged bolts of pleasure to her sex.

Cecile did some growling herself when he parted her lower lips and teased her engorged bud.

"So wet for me," he praised, and then pushed a finger inside her, lazily pumping her while tormenting first one nipple and then the other.

Cecile bucked her hips, desperate for more, deeper, harder.

"You want more?" he teased, his slitted eyes wicked and smug.

"Guy," she bit out, the word both a warning and a plea.

He laughed and released her nipple with a sharp pinch.

Cecile whimpered at the loss of him.

"Don't be greedy," he murmured. "I need my other hand, but you've got two that are doing nothing. Play with yourself for me, darling."

Cecile used both hands to pick up where he'd left off, pinching the aching buds far harder than he'd done, the line between pleasure and pain blurring.

"Bloody hell, that's lovely," he rasped, easing a second finger in beside the first. "So is this." He used his newly liberated fingers to spread her lower lips and expose her to his hungry gaze. "Such a pretty little thing."

Cecile moaned when he circled her sensitive nub, one hand teasing her with light caresses while the other worked her with increasingly powerful strokes.

She gloried in the sensation of being filled and stretched, grinding hard against his hand as she gorged on his muscular torso and the way his biceps bulged as he pleasured her.

"Yes, that's my good girl," he said, meeting her thrust for thrust. "Use me hard and make yourself come."

His words were like the sharp prod of a whip and Cecile dropped her hands to the bed, bracing them beside his shoulders, taking his fingers deeper and harder, hurtling toward the brink of bliss all too quickly. Wave after wave of pleasure rolled through her body and she lost herself to sensation as Guy covered her face with butterfly kisses and whispered sweet nonsense in her ear. He soothed and caressed her back from her little death, his hips barely pulsing beneath her, his hard shaft rubbing against her lower belly.

"Put me inside," he murmured.

Cecile reached between their damp bodies, closed her fingers around him, and grazed his sensitive crown with her thumbnail.

"Cecile!" he half shouted, half-groaned, his hips lifting her off the bed.

She laughed and struggled up onto her knees, using only one hand since the other was busy teasing.

"Witch," he muttered, stilling while she positioned him at her opening.

"Now?" she asked.

"Please."

Cecile wanted to make him beg, but she needed him too badly. "As you wish," she said, slowly taking him inside her body, inch by delicious inch.

"God, yes!" He forced the words out through clenched jaws, holding her steady while his hips pumped into her with powerful, snapping thrusts, filling her completely with each savage stroke.

"You feel so good," she murmured. "So big and hard."

He gave a helpless-sounding laugh. "You're trying to kill me."

She laughed, riding him harder.

"Not . . . going . . . to . . . last."

Cecile clenched her inner muscles, squeezing with all her might.

A groan tore from his chest and he exploded in a flurry of savage thrusts before hilting himself deep, his body arching all the way off the bed, his shaft thickening and jerking with each jet of seed

"Love you so much," he murmured groggily, his arms sliding around her waist and pulling her down, until they were chest-to-chest.

Cecile opened her mouth to tell him she felt the same, that she didn't want to ever be without him again, but the words wouldn't come.

Coward.

She *was* a coward, and it disgusted her.

Just say it.

She swallowed, shifted slightly, and said, "I—I love you, too."

For a moment there was no answer.

And then, the softest of snores.

Chapter 26

Cecile didn't wake until eleven o'clock the following morning. It was the first time she'd slept past eight o'clock in years.

The bed was empty, and she'd never even heard Guy get up and leave.

It was just as well he was gone because she'd woken up with a plan forming in her head.

By the time she'd washed, dressed, and eaten a very late, solitary breakfast in the kitchen, most of the pieces had fallen into place.

She smiled grimly and poured herself a third cup of coffee while she considered her next move.

"Where is Guy—do you know?" Cecile asked Cook when the older woman came bustling in a few minutes later.

"He took the wagon to fetch all the replacement fly lines."

"That's quite a long drive, isn't it?"

"Yes, but he said that he'd be back in plenty of time for dinner."

Good. Things could hardly have worked out any better. That meant he'd be gone for most of the day, which was just as well.

Otherwise, he would have had questions for her when she left the house wearing her pistols.

★   ★   ★

The first thing on Cecile's list of errands was a visit to Mr. Jordan, her man of business, to request that he determine exactly how much was needed to pay off her three silent partners.

If Mr. Jordan wondered why she was wearing such a heavy cloak on a fine spring day, or why she refused to remove it in his stuffy office, he didn't mention it.

He did raise his eyebrows when she told him to prepare a contract of sale for the circus and have it delivered to her house.

Her next visit was not nearly so harmonious.

It had been many years since she'd last seen either her cousin or his wife. When she'd lived with Curtis and Martha, their house had been far from the fashionable part of town and closer to the gunsmithing shop. But a quick look in her London directory showed Cecile that her only surviving relatives had shot up in the world. That shouldn't have surprised her if what Guy had said about Curtis's newfound wealth was true.

And yet she'd not understood just how much money Curtis must have made.

Indeed, their rise, geographically at least, had been meteoric, and their new house was just off Orchard Street on Portman Square, a property that was near enough to Mayfair to be within shouting distance, where the newly wealthy rubbed shoulders with bankers and Harley Street physicians.

The house in question was an attractive four-story, fronted with Portland stone.

Cecile had the driver wait for her as she suspected her visit might be of extremely short duration, depending on who was at home at the unfashionable hour of five o'clock.

A liveried domestic answered the door and bade her wait in the foyer while he inquired if anyone was at home.

Cecile amused herself by examining the showy, tasteless objets d'art in the vestibule while she awaited the verdict.

Perhaps a quarter of an hour later, she was contemplating returning another day when the footman returned.

"Mrs. Blanchard will see you now, Miss Tremblay."

She followed him up the curved staircase to the second floor, where he ushered her into a surprisingly elegant sitting room in shades of gold and yellow.

Martha did not stand when Cecile entered, nor did she look especially surprised to see her.

"Wait outside the door. Miss Tremblay will not be long," she told the servant, her chilly blue gaze on Cecile.

Cecile sat without being offered, pleased by the pinched look her forward behavior earned her.

"You don't look surprised. How did you know it was me?" Cecile asked.

"We have known of your return for several years."

"Let me guess—Curtis saw me perform?"

Martha ignored the question, but the hard glint in her eyes told Cecile she'd guessed correctly.

"Why are you here, Cecile? What do you want?"

"I want to speak to Curtis."

"Mr. Blanchard is not at home right now."

"When will he *be* home?"

"I really couldn't say."

Curtis had always come and gone with no regard for his wife. Cecile had suspected even back then that he'd kept lovers—probably at the same time he was bedding her.

"Does he have a place of work?"

Martha sneered. "We are no longer connected with trade."

"Does he have a club?"

"He is a member of White's, not that you could visit him there."

"Thank you, Martha." She stood and strode toward the door.

"Surely you are not going to track him down at his club?" Martha called after her.

Cecile didn't bother answering.

Twenty minutes later she was caught up in a snarl of vehicles on St. James's Street and the carriage had slowed to a crawl.

Cecile slid open the divider and said to the driver, "Just let me off here."

"Here?" He eyed her up and down and she knew what he was thinking—that she looked like a woman of quality and such women did *not* parade up and down what was generally considered the domain of male aristocrats.

"Yes, I will walk. I want you to wait for me outside White's."

"Er, White's?"

"Yes, White's. I shan't be long." Unless they decided to seize her and summon the constabulary.

As Cecile strode down the street, she couldn't help noticing that she was the only female pedestrian. Her pulse was pounding at the base of her throat and her skin prickled with sweat and awareness as she approached the entrance to that hallowed bastion of masculine privilege.

The five short steps felt like a hundred, and the sensation of being watched made her look to her left, where she encountered the infamous bow window.

Male faces with wide eyes were pressed up against the glass. None of them was Curtis, of course—he was not esteemed enough to merit such a prime seat.

The door opened before she could reach the top step and a startled servant stood in the middle of the doorway, as if barricading it from invasion.

"Madam? What are—"

"I am looking for Mr. Curtis Blanchard. I am told he is here today."

The man's jaw sagged comically.

"Well?" she prodded when he continued to gawk.

"Y-yes, he is here, but you cannot think to—"

Cecile pushed her cloak to the side, a motion that drew the porter's attention to her gun belt.

"Good God!" he yelped, stumbling backward, so that he was no longer blocking the doorway.

Cecile took that as an invitation.

She set her right hand lightly on the pistol butt that jutted from the holster on that side. "Be a good fellow and lead me to Mr. Blanchard."

The lackey spun on his heel and charged toward a staircase.

Word spread quickly that a woman had entered the sanctity of the club and men flocked in doorways like ravenous gulls hovering around a fishing boat as she followed the servant up the stairs toward a set of double doors.

"There he is." The man pointed to a table in the corner, where Curtis sat alone, enjoying a newspaper and a glass of something amber.

Voices erupted around her but Cecile ignored them as she strode across the room.

Curtis glanced up, looked back at his newspaper, then whipped his head up again, his eyes widening with shock and horror. He shot to his feet. "Good God! What is the meaning of this, Cecile?"

She grinned and he recoiled so violently that he collided with the chair he'd just vacated, his limbs tangling with the chair legs in a way that would have been comical if her entire body hadn't been shaking with almost two decades' worth of anger and shame.

"I'm so glad you asked me that, Curtis," she said as she removed the gauntlet from her right hand, tugging it off slowly, finger by finger.

She'd found the gloves in a trunk full of costumes and had chosen them specifically because they spoke of an earlier age, the smooth black kid leather joined to heavy black cuffs that were studded with silver nailheads.

A tentative voice came from behind her, and a hand landed on her shoulder. "Er, madam, you can't be in—"

Cecile spun around, causing the room to erupt in gasps when the crowd saw her pistols.

"Unhand me," she hissed, driving the servant back so quickly, he stumbled into a table full of stout, elderly men.

"Leave her be." The quiet but firm voice came from the knot of men who'd gathered in the doorway.

Cecile met Elliot's gaze as he came toward her and then stopped in the middle of the crowded room and stood with arms akimbo. "Let her speak her piece," he said, his commanding tone cutting through the muttering.

Cecile turned back to Curtis, who'd collected himself enough to begin talking.

"You're making a terrible mistake, Cecile. You must come with me and—"

Cecile held her glove by the soft kid and struck him across the face with all the force she could muster.

A gasp erupted around her as Curtis staggered back, his hand going to his cheek, which bore three red streaks and a cut on the corner of his mouth.

"I challenge you to a duel with pistols tomorrow at dawn."

You could have heard a pin drop.

Curtis gave a weak laugh, his stunned gaze darting around the room, which was filled with the most powerful men in Britain.

"Duel?" he squawked, his voice breaking on the word. "What in the world are you talking about?"

"Do you really want me to lay out my grievance in public, Curtis?"

He held up his hands. "No!" he gasped. "But, er—you don't understand."

"What don't I understand?"

"You don't get to choose the weapon—that is—according to etiquette you're the challenger and you can't—"

"I don't follow your stupid rules," Cecile retorted. "Meet me at dawn with your pistols or be known to every man in this room for the gutless, puling coward you really are."

Curtis's jaw sagged, but no words came out of his mouth.

"I'll stand as second for Miss Tremblay," Elliot said, his voice loud enough to reach every ear in the room and the corridor beyond. He smiled grimly and offered his arm to Cecile.

"Thank you." She set her hand on his sleeve, pleased to see she wasn't shaking.

"Stand aside!" Elliot barked, guiding her through what seemed to be a wall of men.

Later, Cecile would have no memory of how she got from the club to a hackney to Newcastle Street.

Guy shoved his hands into his hair and pulled hard enough to make his scalp ache. "You did *what?*"

Before Cecile could answer him, Guy turned on Elliot.

"And you were there and allowed this to happen?"

"It was not for him to allow or disallow!" Cecile snapped, finally coming out of the fugue she'd been in since Elliot had led her into the book room.

"You are going to fight a duel, Cecile? Have you lost your mind?" Guy demanded, uncowed by her anger.

"You were the one who said it would be a shame for Curtis to get away with what he'd done."

He made a strangled choking sound as he tried to come up with a response to her ridiculous statement.

"Besides," she said, "he won't meet me. He knows I am a better shot. And he won't ask for swords or some other weapon because it will make him look like a coward to all of London."

"She's right," Elliot said.

Guy flung up his hands. "So you think—what, exactly? That he will apologize? What good will that do?"

Cecile stood suddenly and strode out into the corridor.

Guy and Elliot exchanged confused looks.

When Cecile returned a moment later, she handed a thick bundle of parchment to Elliot.

Guy watched as his friend skimmed over the document.

When Elliot looked up, he was smiling appreciatively. "Very good, Cecile." He cocked his head. "Or do you prefer Manon?"

"Call me Cecile." She jerked her chin at Guy. "Explain it to your friend."

Elliot turned to Guy. "If Blanchard wants to get out of being shot, he's going to have to pay her enough to buy out Cecile's partners in the circus as well as paying an additional ten thousand pounds. He also needs to return the rights to every single one of the designs she reproduced for him and grant her exclusive use of the Blanchet name."

Guy did some quick mental calculations based on how much the Fayre property might be worth and then added ten thousand onto that figure. "That's a nice sum of money, but not nearly what he owes you, Cecile."

"I know. But this is what I want. The business will be mine and I will have enough to make the repairs we need and also to purchase the stables rather than continue to rent." She smiled at Guy in a way that turned his brain to mush. "You will need somewhere to keep your horses."

Guy suspected he had a stupid, fatuous expression on his face, but he didn't care.

Elliot handed Cecile the contract. "This is far less than you are legally owed, but that sort of case would drag on for years. Not only that, but you would be forced to give exhaustive testimony to prove your claim. This makes sense in several ways."

"What makes you think Blanchard will agree to it?" Guy asked Cecile.

"Because it isn't enough money to break him—not if he made as much money as you say he did—and because he has no choice if he wants to save face. If he shows up tomorrow morning, I *will* shoot him, and he knows me well enough to believe that. Trust me, Guy; he will agree to my demand."

"He will," Elliot said.

Guy heaved a sigh and shook his head. "I hope to God you are both correct."

Chapter 27

Less than eight hours later, after Cecile's performance that night—to which she'd authorized her theater manager to sell standing room only tickets—Curtis Blanchard signed off on the contract Cecile presented to him.

Cecile had been tempted to allow matters to go through her solicitor, which was what Elliot and Guy urged her to do, but she decided she needed to look Curtis full in the face one last time.

Guy wasn't happy about the idea of an in-person meeting, but he did not try to dissuade her.

He did, however, have one rather strange request to make of her.

"What?" Cecile had goggled at him when he told her what he wanted.

"Please just let him come, Cecile."

"Why in the world would I want Sin to be here for this, Guy?"

"Because Curtis Blanchard is the sort of man who rolls over for authority like a dog for its master. And there is nobody who embodies power so well as the Duke of Staunton. If Blanchard has any tricks up his sleeve, Sin's presence here will put paid to them."

And so, at just a few minutes after midnight, Cecile, Guy, Elliot, and the Duke of Staunton were waiting for Curtis in the book room when the maid showed him in.

Objectively, Cecile knew her cousin was a handsome man. But

knowing what she did about him, she thought he looked no better than a rodent dressed up in expensive clothing.

His eyes bounced around the room and went round at the sight of the duke. "Er, Y-Your Grace," he stammered, not even bothering to greet Cecile in her own home.

Sin's expression—which was already cold—turned positively frosty at the other man's social faux pas.

Curtis flushed under his scathing stare. "Oh, I beg your pardon, Cecile."

"That's Miss Tremblay to you, Blanchard," Guy said, pushing off from the wall near the fireplace and strolling over to Curtis. While he didn't exactly tower over the other man, he was far broader and fitter and was oozing so much menace that it lowered the already frigid temperature in the room by a few degrees.

"Y-yes, of course, I meant to say Miss Tremblay."

"You've come to apologize," Guy said.

Cecile jolted at his words, which had not been part of the plan.

Curtis frowned. "Er, there was no mention of an apolo—"

"I think an apology is merited." Guy stepped closer to Curtis, his hands fisted at his sides.

"I think that is an excellent idea," Sin said mildly, his green eyes glinting with malice as he looked down his aristocratic nose at Curtis.

"That makes three of us," Elliot piped up. "Cecile?"

The urge to throw back her head and laugh in exultation was strong, but she decided to keep that for later.

"Yes, I think I would like an apology."

Curtis snorted "Fine. But if you think I'm going to admit to being culpable to anything legally actionable *and* sign this extortionate agreement of yours, you're sorely mistaken."

Guy turned to Elliot. "That didn't sound like an apology to me."

"No, me either," Elliot said.

"It most certainly did *not*," Sin agreed.

Curtis made a noise of frustrated rage and turned to Cecile. "I'm sorry about everything that happened."

Guy cleared his throat.

Curtis heaved a sigh. "I'm sorry about everything I did to you."

As apologies went, it was pathetic, and his hostile expression belied the truth of his words.

Guy turned to her. "Is that good enough? Or would you like him on his knees?" Elliot and Sin stepped closer to Curtis at Guy's words.

Cecile couldn't hold back her smile. "That is tempting, but the less time I have to look at him, the better."

"You've got a good point," Guy said. The other two men nodded.

"If it's any consolation to you," Curtis spat, "you've all but destroyed my standing and reputation at my club with this afternoon's stunt. I shall probably be asked to leave."

Cecile shrugged and said, "That is actually of some consolation. Of course, if you don't wish to go through with our agreement, we can always meet tomorrow morning." She glanced at Elliot. "It's not too late, is it?"

"Not too late at all," Elliot said. "All Blanchard needs to do is give me the name of his second and the two of you can be standing at fifty paces in a matter of hours."

Curtis scowled. "I said I'd sign the agreement—now where the devil is it?"

Elliot smirked and even the duke cracked a faint smile.

Guy pointed to the desk, where the agreement was laid out. "Now sign and then get the hell out."

Elliot offered Cecile his arm. "Shall we leave them to it?"

Cecile nodded, smiled, and set her hand on his sleeve.

They'd agreed earlier that she didn't need to stay and witness the formalities, that Guy and Sin would make sure Curtis did everything he was supposed to do.

Cecile was almost at the door when Curtis's voice stopped her. "Cecile."

She stopped but didn't look back. "What?"

"I really did love you, you know."

Cecile left without a word.

★ ★ ★

Cecile was lounging in the bath she'd found waiting for her, when the door to her chambers opened and Guy strolled in.

He grinned when he saw her. "Ah, I was hoping you'd still be reclining in your half shell."

She snorted at the reference. "Thank you for thinking of this."

"I thought you might need a soak after the day you had." His eyes moved over her in a way that made every nerve in her body snap to attention.

"Did everything go as planned?"

"Mmm-hmm," he murmured, shrugging out of his coat and tossing it onto a nearby chair and then rolling up his sleeves.

"What do you think you are doing?" she asked, lifting a foot out of the water to wash it.

"I thought you might need some help."

"I've been bathing myself for a very long time."

"Well, yes, so that's why you should allow me to take over. You find it a chore and I will get a great deal of pleasure out of it."

Cecile chuckled.

"Besides, I earned a reward tonight."

"Oh, how so?"

"Because I didn't knock Blanchard's head right off his body." He knelt down beside the tub and leaned against the edge.

"You were very well-behaved."

Cecile hissed in a breath as he slid a large hand over one of her breasts, teasing the already tightened nipple to a peak.

"God, you're lovely, Cecile," he murmured, and then lowered his mouth to her sudsy breast.

"There's soap all over—ah," she groaned when his lips latched on to her.

"Harder," she ordered, gasping when he complied.

Cecile slid a hand between her thighs only to have it shoved out of the way.

"Mine," he mumbled, switching his mouth to her other breast while his sinfully skilled fingers parted her lower lips and caressed the sensitive nub of flesh.

Cecile laid her head back and let her knees fall open.

He chuckled, his lips curving against the slick skin of her breast. "Such a good girl," he praised, soap bubbles clinging to his mouth and chin.

"Good girls deserve a reward," she pointed out in a breathy voice.

"Yes, they do." He penetrated her with two fingers and she shivered at the sudden stretch.

His eyes were hard and hungry as he pumped her. "Good?"

"Harder, more."

He immediately obeyed, his thrusting just on the edge of pleasure and pain, water sloshing over the rim of the tub as she bucked up to meet him.

Cecile's orgasm was sudden and shattering. She was vaguely aware that she'd shouted out his name, but not until she felt goose pimples forming on her skin did she realize he'd lifted her out of the tub.

"What?" she asked in a muzzy voice, the room moving around her as he strode across to her bed. She blinked blearily up at him as he tossed her down and then shoved her legs wide.

"But I didn't rinse off the—"

"Hush," he ordered, dropping to his haunches and claiming her with his mouth.

Cecile spread even wider for his lips and tongue, grinding against him like a shameless harlot.

She lost track of how many times he brought her to climax.

Not until she grabbed his hair and yanked him away did he stop.

"Too sensitive, sweetheart?" he asked in a raspy voice, staring up at her through eyes that were black with lust.

"Want you inside me, Gaius."

He grinned. "You actually make my ridiculous name sound good, darling." He prowled up the bed on his hands and knees.

She glanced down at the feel of cool leather on her hot thighs and saw that—in addition to his shirt and waistcoat—he still wore his butter-soft old buckskins and stockings. "You're still clothed," she said somewhat foolishly.

He glanced down, as if he didn't believe her. "Good Lord; so I am! I haven't been so excited since my first time, sweetheart." He began to get up, as if he were going to undress.

"No. I want you this way," she smirked up at him. "It feels wicked to be naked while you are fully clothed."

"I love the way your mind works." He rose up high on his knees, his hand going to the obscene bulge in his placket.

"Is that for me?" she asked.

"I've been saving it for you."

"Indeed?"

He nodded, flicking open the catches and buttons with exquisite slowness. "There is no other woman like you, Cecile." He opened the last button and his thick rod sprang free.

She admired his proportions. "You are rather singular, yourself, Mr. Darlington. I want to watch you stroke yourself."

He clucked his tongue. "My, my, what a dirty thing you are." He fisted his thick shaft and winked at her. "I heartily approve."

Cecile laughed at his foolishness. One of the things she loved most about Guy was how much he made her laugh, even in the midst of passion; she'd never laughed with a lover before him.

"Is this what you wanted?" he asked, stroking himself from thick root to tip.

"Don't stop," she ordered when he reached for her.

"I have two hands, darling." Not pausing his mesmerizing stroking, he reached between her thighs and teased the entrance to her body.

Cecile arched against his hand, her body begging to take him deeper.

His dark eyes glittered down at her while he worked them both, the veins in his forearms popping beneath skin that was sheened with sweat. "I'm getting too close," he warned. "I want to be inside you." Moving with swift, sure grace he lowered his body over her, positioned himself at her entrance, and drove into her.

She cried out at the intense pleasure of their joining and wrapped her arms around his neck, gazing up into his whisky-brown eyes.

"Hello, darling," he murmured, holding her pinned and stretched and full. "Did I tell you in the last few hours how much I love you?" He nuzzled her jaw and throat while he flexed his shaft inside her.

His question sent a frisson of fear spearing through the cloud of lust.

Tell him you love him. Say something!

But she couldn't say the words . . .

"Mmmm," she purred, tilting her pelvis to take him deeper.

If he was disappointed in her response, he didn't show it. Instead, he began to rock his hips, grinding against her swollen peak and quickly working her toward yet another climax.

"God, yes," he groaned, stilling as she convulsed around his shaft, her orgasm so much more rewarding when he was inside her.

The last waves of pleasure hadn't quite dissipated when his hips began to move and he whispered in her ear, "Come once more for me, Cecile."

She tried to protest, but her body was already moving to meet his thrusts.

"So greedy," he praised, holding up his weight on one elbow and reaching between them while his hips drummed.

Something was different about this climax—it was much, much more intense and the sensation seemed to reach even the tips of her toes and fingers, wrapping her in a thick fog of bliss.

Cecile was only half aware when Guy reached his own crisis, calling out her name as he flooded her with warmth.

"I love you, Cecile," was the last thing she heard before she sank into unconsciousness.

Chapter 28

"Cecile!"

Cecile jolted upright and blinked, her heart pounding.

Rap, rap, rap. "Cecile, you need to wake up. You've got visitors. Important visitors."

Even through the door and muzzy with sleep, she could hear the tension in Guy's voice.

"Come in," she called in a groggy voice.

The door opened a crack and Guy poked his head inside. For once, he wasn't smiling.

"What is it?"

"You have two guests waiting for you down in the book room."

"Who are they?"

He stared at her for a long moment. "One is a French solicitor named Jean Dumas and the other is the Duc de La Fontaine, who claims to be your cousin by marriage." He paused and then said, "*Your* marriage."

Cecile's lips parted, but no words came out.

"Cecile?" he asked, a definite edge to his voice. "Is there something you haven't told me?"

"You probably won't believe me, but I didn't mean to withhold anything from you." She winced. "I just . . . forgot."

"You forgot you were married," he said flatly.

Cecile floundered for words.

"How long shall I tell them you'll be?" he asked, his expression grim.

"Thirty minutes. And send Mary up, please."

He shut the door without another word.

Oh. God. Why was this happening now, of all times?

Cecile found Guy waiting for her outside the book room when she came down the stairs a bit more than half an hour later. She was wearing one of her nicest day dresses, a dusty rose color that flattered her.

"You look lovely," he said quietly, his normal ebullience nowhere in evidence. "I've had Cook prepare a tea tray, just ring when you want it. Are you ready?"

She nodded.

He turned toward the door and she caught his wrist. "Guy."

"Yes?" he asked her, his even tone at odds with the hurt in his brown eyes.

"I want you to come in there with me."

His eyebrows shot up. "Are you—"

Cecile pulled him close and kissed him hard, not releasing him until she felt some of the tension leak out of his body. When she pulled away, he looked more like his normal self.

"I wasn't keeping this from you on purpose, Guy. It was not a love match, I assure you. The old duke was dying in La Force Prison and my father brought me to him. I was fourteen and he was probably in his seventies. It was a marriage in name only, so that I would inherit his personal property—he feared the dukedom would not survive the Revolution. I had a copy of the wedding lines and his will, but everything was lost during the crossing. I didn't tell anyone—it wasn't just you. I just didn't think anyone would believe me."

"I would never think you a liar."

"I know that . . . now." She snorted softly. "I'm afraid it really did slip my mind given all the other excitement of the past few days. And before that"—she shrugged—"I haven't thought about that part of my life in years."

It was obvious he was brimming with questions, but he merely nodded.

"Come inside with me," she begged.

Again he nodded and then opened the door.

Cecile strode into the book room with her head held high, her heart pounding so loudly she wondered if those around her could hear it.

Two men shot to their feet, one stick-thin and perhaps in his fifties, the other an astonishingly attractive man Cecile's age.

"I understand you wish to speak to me."

It was the older man who answered. "You *are* Manon Blanchet?"

"That is my name."

The younger man took a step toward her, a curious but not unkind look on his face as he held out his hands. "We have been looking for you for some time, Your Grace."

Cecile started at the unexpected form of address. "You may call me Miss Tremblay."

He looked as if he wanted to argue, but instead said, "Do you have some time to talk with us?"

"Yes, of course. Please sit."

The men looked at Guy and back at Cecile.

"Mr. Darlington may hear whatever it is you have to say. He is aware that I was married to the duke."

The men exchanged yet another look, but then nodded.

Guy murmured, "Perhaps now would be a good time to ring for tea."

"Now that matters in France are beginning to settle, people like your cousin"—Mr. Dumas gestured to the Duc de La Fontaine—"have started to petition His Majesty for the return of their family properties. That is a process fraught with numerous difficulties, not the least of which is the fact there is a new group of individuals claiming rights to many of those same estates."

"You mean the people Bonaparte ennobled?" Cecile asked.

Dumas nodded. "I did not have the honor to know your deceased husband, Your Grace, but my firm has handled the affairs of the de La Fontaines for over one hundred years. Indeed, we were so intertwined with our clients that we, too, were driven into exile for almost a decade."

Guy couldn't help thinking the man sounded rather proud of that fact.

"The priest who conducted your wedding ceremony also went into hiding. I learned from his successor that he was killed only days after he performed your marriage, and the papers were never filed in the church until almost four years later, when the deceased priest's family finally received his personal effects. The duke's death was known to his cousin—er, the present duke's father—who was living in Brussels, where he'd moved his family for their safety." He turned to the duke and nodded.

"My father died before he could ever visit the family estate," the duke said. "Indeed, I myself did not have a chance to go to Château de La Fontaine until late last year, after Bonaparte was finally routed." He cocked his head at Cecile. "I understand you lived there when you were a child?"

"It was my only real home in France," she admitted. "When the duke went to Paris, my father occasionally accompanied him, but for the most part we lived on the estate, where there was a small shop where my father and several other gunsmiths plied their craft."

"I'm afraid you would find the château much changed; the years have not been kind to Fontaine." The duke's mouth tightened and his dark blue eyes sparked. "The property was passed around from faction to faction for at least ten years, a prize to be awarded and jerked away depending on the whims of whomever was in power. For the last eleven years it was held by the Comte d'Allard."

"Wasn't he one of Bonaparte's generals?" Guy asked.

The duke cut him a quick look. "Indeed, he was. He was among a handful who were executed last year after the king returned to Paris."

Ah, so the property was once again ownerless.

"My petition was recently approved," the duke continued, "which means the house and some portion of the surrounding area have been returned to my family." He turned to Dumas and gave a slight nod.

The older man cleared his throat. "Which brings me to your portion of the ducal estate, Your Grace."

Cecile blinked. "My portion? But I would have thought all this passed to the heir since there is one?"

"Everything that went with the dukedom passed to the current holder of the title. But a great deal of the duke's property was personal."

"Please explain what this means to me?"

"The duke inherited the house and title. Everything else, including four estates—two in France, one in New Orleans, and one here in England—as well as numerous and substantial bank accounts in several nations, belongs to you, Your Grace."

The room was utterly silent for a long moment.

It was the duke who spoke first. "You are probably wondering why I have accompanied Monsieur Dumas."

Guy had a pretty fair notion why the man was there.

"I will not dress up my words." He gave a charming laugh. "I think that is the phrase for plain speaking?"

Cecile, clearly rattled, merely nodded.

"Part of what you inherited was the land that has always supported the dukedom. Without it—well, suffice it to say that without it, Fontaine cannot prosper."

Guy frowned. "That is unfortunate, but surely you don't blame Miss Tremblay for her former husband's disposal of his property."

The duke gave him a look of annoyance, his sharp blue gaze flickering to Cecile.

"Please answer any of Mr. Darlington's questions as if they came from me," she said softly.

De La Fontaine's lips twisted into a brief, sour expression, but he nodded. "No, not that she is to blame. However, there are legalities that must be observed for a marriage to be considered valid."

"What are you saying?" Cecile asked.

The duke's pale skin flushed, and he glanced at Monsieur Dumas. The older man looked less than eager to speak.

Guy cleared his throat and six eyes turned to him. "What he's saying is that the family could challenge the marriage's validity by insisting it is a white marriage, meaning the union has not been consummated."

Cecile looked from Guy to the other men. "Is this what you will do?" She sounded curious rather than angry, which was what Guy was starting to feel.

"His Grace has made no decision as of yet," Dumas said hastily.

"It is my understanding that you have never remarried," the duke said.

Guy opened his mouth to demand what the hell business it was of his, but this time it was Cecile who beat him to it.

"I have not. But what has that to do with anything?"

"I am a widower with two daughters and no heir—"

"Bloody hell!" Guy got to his feet and took a step toward the other man.

The duke did not hesitate to rise to the occasion. While he was a few inches shorter than Guy, he stood his ground.

"Guy, please," Cecile said.

When he refused to turn away from the duke, who was glaring right back at him, Cecile came to stand beside him and set a hand on his cheek to turn him away from the other man.

Guy met her pleading gaze and felt like a fool.

He huffed out a sigh and stepped back, dipping his chin to her.

"Perhaps it might be best if Her Grace and His Grace were given a few moments to speak to each other. Alone," Dumas added.

Guy was about to say *over my dead body*, when he saw that Cecile was nodding.

He knew he was gawking but couldn't shut his mouth.

"Please," she murmured. "Just for a few minutes."

He felt breathless, as if he'd been kicked in the stomach by a mule.

Guy glanced at the duke and clenched his jaw at the smug look on the Frenchman's face.

"Please," Cecile said again, the word so soft it was barely audible.

Guy nodded. "As you wish."

Once Guy and Mr. Dumas left the book room, the duke's expression softened. "I'm terribly sorry to have upset you, my dear. Won't you sit?"

Cecile sat and the duke took the chair beside her, the one Guy had just vacated. "I did not understand that you and Mr. Darlington were, er, betrothed."

"We are not betrothed," she was forced to admit, wishing for a moment that they were because it would probably make this conversation shorter, if not easier.

She shook off thoughts of Guy's pained look and forced herself to concentrate. "I take it you were about to suggest a union between the two of us?"

"I only thought to do so when I believed you were at liberty. But if your affections are otherwise engaged, I would never suggest such a thing."

"If I do not marry you, then you will challenge the validity of the marriage?"

He opened his mouth and then hesitated, sighing. "I do not wish to commence our association in an adversarial way."

"And yet you have."

"I assure you that my family and I are by no means committed to such a path."

"Your family?"

"Yes, I have three younger brothers, five sisters, many nieces, nephews, aunts, uncles, and my mother."

"That is a large family," Cecile said. And they would all suffer at losing the duke's fortune to her, a stranger.

"It was even larger, but three of my brothers died fighting against the Usurper. Like you and your father, we were forced to flee and leave everything. These past twenty years have been . . . well, I'm sure you know."

Cecile *did* know.

"May I make a suggestion?" he asked.

She nodded.

"Before you make any decision at all, why not come and visit Château de La Fontaine and meet my family, which is your family, too. Not only are there all of us, but there are several of your own blood relatives who were most eager to meet you upon learning you were alive and well."

She frowned. "But . . . I don't have any family. Just one cousin here."

"Perhaps that is true on your father's side, but your mother— Vivienne Tremblay—has a large family."

"How do you know about them?"

"Even before returning to Fontaine, I have helped Dumas search for you." He gave her a slightly embarrassed look. "You see, the old duke's estate was in a state of limbo until you could either be located or . . ."

"Declared dead," she supplied.

He nodded. "In the course of our investigations I met your mother's family, hoping they would have some word of you. But apparently the estrangement between your father and mother predates—"

"Estrangement? What estrangement? My mother is dead."

The duke frowned and then leaned toward her and took her hand. "But no, my dear, your mother is very much alive—as is your younger sister, Sandrine."

Chapter 29

Guy didn't return home until almost two o'clock in the morning.

He'd walked for miles and miles struggling to come to terms with the cauldron of emotions inside him, telling himself to consider what was best for Cecile rather than what *he* wanted.

Yes, he wanted her. But she'd not once told him that she wanted to marry him or loved him or even that she had missed him. Indeed, she'd been most emphatic in her refusal to marry him.

It had been all Guy, pressing his suit from the moment he'd re-entered her life.

Cecile had given him a job, a place to live, and had—probably without realizing it—helped him gather the tattered remnants of his dignity.

Guy knew most people would think performing in front of his erstwhile friends was yet another indignity, but, strangely, it hadn't left him feeling ashamed.

The truth was that he'd been tested by life and had proven he could do what was necessary to feed and house himself. His sisters and mother were not materially worse off, thanks to his sale of Darlington Park, so he'd taken care of all his responsibilities.

He loved Cecile and had done, he now knew, almost from the beginning. But he could not force her to love him. She had to *choose* him.

And now . . .

Well, he had to laugh out loud at the irony that it was now *she* who had a family and a title with responsibilities.

Cecile was a duchess.

And he could not deny that he had refused to marry her when he'd been in a similar situation. How could he expect her to do otherwise? In fact, his present circumstances were considerably *worse* than hers had been. She'd at least been gainfully employed with a valuable skill. He was a man whose only possession was a farm on the edge of civilization—and he had no idea how one grew anything.

Guy owed her the same courtesy she'd given him over a year ago—that of leaving when their affair had run its natural course, which was apparently two days.

Thinking of her married to the handsome Frenchman he'd met earlier was like swallowing a pint of broken glass.

Was that how Cecile had felt when he'd become betrothed to Helen? As she wasn't in love with him, he could only hope he'd not caused her that much pain.

He would be a hypocrite if he begged her to stay and marry him—or even begged her to go on as they'd planned, as lovers. She was a wealthy duchess. Whether she realized it yet or not, her life with the Fayre was already a thing of the past.

The house was dark and silent when he unlocked the door. Good. The last thing he wanted was to talk to—

"Guy?"

He yelped and spun around to peer into the book room; the door was open but no candles were burning.

"Good God, Cecile. You scared me half to death. What are you doing in the dark?"

"I was waiting for you."

"Well, here I am." He squinted into the gloom and could just make out the shape of her. "Is something wrong?"

"I'm sorry I asked you to leave today."

Her voice sounded so small and sad and . . . un-Cecile-like that guilt at his disappearance flooded him.

"You needn't be sorry, darling. Your inheritance is none of my concern and I wasn't behaving very well, in any case."

He heard her moving before he saw her coming toward him, the light from the lantern outside the door fracturing in the leaded glass sidelight and illuminating her face, which looked drawn and haggard.

"What's wrong, love? You look like you've seen a ghost."

She gave a watery chuckle. "In a sense I have. My mother is alive—and I have a sister."

"What?"

She nodded.

"I thought you didn't have any siblings."

"So did I." Her eyes looked glassy even in the gloom. "I learned today that my parents were estranged because my mother did not want my father teaching me his craft. They separated and each of them kept a child. Can you imagine doing that? Splitting up your family as if they were nothing more than a litter of kittens?" Guy reached for her, and she immediately fell into his arms. "I have an entire family I never even knew existed," she mumbled into his shoulder. "Not just a mother and a sister, but aunts, uncles, and scores of cousins."

He stroked her hair, unable to come up with the right words.

"And then there is Gaston's family."

"Gaston? Who is—oh, the duke." Guy ground his teeth at the thought of her being on a first-name basis with the smug, far-too-handsome Frenchman.

Behave yourself! he mentally chided.

"What about him, darling?"

"His family is enormous, and they've been hiding for decades. Now they are finally able to return home, only to discover they've been cheated out of their inheritance thanks to the duke's will."

"It was the duke's decision, and it was his property to dispose of however he pleased. He didn't cheat them and neither did you."

"I know that is true. But I can't help thinking he would not have left his fortune to me if he'd had even a small hope of his family ever returning—or having anything to return *to*. Without that land there is nothing to support the château, Guy. Gaston would have to sell it, and his family would be left with nowhere to live yet again."

He put her away from him just far enough to see her face. "What are you trying to say, Cecile?"

She shook her head and sniffed, pulling a handkerchief from her sleeve and dabbing at her nose. "I don't know. This is just so much to take in."

"You don't have to decide everything tonight. There's plenty of—"

"No, there isn't plenty of time. Gaston received his rights back to the property, but it is horribly encumbered and—don't ask me to explain it all, but Monsieur Dumas says the creditors have begun some sort of legal proceeding and will take the château before the end of the summer."

"Well, that's a shame, but—"

"You don't understand, Guy—my mother and all that side of the family still live on the duke's property, they have been there all this time and I never even knew about them. You see, they lived far away from the château itself on one of the duke's tenant farms. But if these creditors take over, they will have to leave their home."

Guy had a sick feeling in his stomach. "What are you thinking, Cecile?"

"Gaston's family will have to challenge the marriage in order to get the money necessary to fight the proceedings, but that will take years and the château will be lost in the meantime. I can't allow that to happen if there is any way I can stop it."

He didn't speak. What in the world could he say that wouldn't betray his feelings—his selfish desire?

"It sounds like you are planning to go to France."

"I know you don't think—"

"I think you should go."

She blinked. "You do?"

"Absolutely."

She stared at him.

"You can take Cat and Helen with you. As for the Fayre, Beryl and Wilfred will do fine managing the theater." He forced a chuckle. "You can't go back on stage after this recent discovery."

She stared. "And you?"

"You know I have the property in America—I told you I'd be here for six months. I'll stay if you think I'm needed." He cleared his throat. "I didn't want to mention it, but I received a letter from the man who's been leasing the farm and he asked if I would be amenable to letting him out of the agreement early. He's ill and apparently his—"

"You're leaving?" she asked, cutting off his babbling.

"Well, yes, darling, that was always the plan, wasn't it? So," he said briskly, "when are you planning to go?"

She blinked, as if struggling to focus.

Guy almost gave in to his selfish desires then—he almost dropped to his knees and begged her to stay.

But then he remembered who she was now and that he had nothing to offer her.

He swallowed down his misery and said, "I imagine you'll be wanting to go soon?"

She nodded slowly, as if she were coming out of a trance. "I—well, Mr. Dumas and Gaston were going to leave two days hence, but if I am to go with them, they will wait until next week."

"Ah, yes, it makes perfect sense to travel with them. They'll take excellent care of you. And we'll take care of everything here, so you don't have a thing to worry about."

"Oh. Well, that won't be necessary. I've already told Beryl we'll take our seasonal break a month early this year—starting tomorrow."

"Jolly good thinking," Guy said, unable to get the dreadful smile off his face. Suddenly, he couldn't look at her stunned expression even a second longer. "Well, then. It sounds as if you've got it all sorted. I daresay you'll be terribly busy with preparations for your trip, so if I don't see you before you leave, then I do wish you the best of luck with everything." Guy paused, waiting for her to say something. Anything.

But she merely stared at him, her gaze blank.

"All right, then. Good night, Cecile."

"Good night, Guy."

When he got to the top of the stairs he didn't look back. And it was the hardest thing he'd ever done.

Chapter 30

Guy closed the lid on his trunk and was buckling up the straps when the door banged open. Cat flew across the room and flung her small body on him. "Where are you going? You can't be leaving! I won't let you!"

He looked up and met Helen's worried gaze. She was standing in the doorway, the little dog beside her. Even George, who was sitting quietly rather than capering around his mistress, appeared to have a furrow or two on his dog brow.

Guy stood, lifting Cat's clinging, shaking body with him.

"Here then," he murmured. "What's all this?"

"You're *leaving* us. You don't even care about us. You're going away, and I'll never see you again."

At least that's what he thought she said. He cut a look at Helen and mouthed *Give me a few minutes.*

Helen shut the door and he sat down on the bed, gathering his scattered wits and staring at the dog—who was shooting him accusatory looks.

He decided to let her get the worst of it out, waiting until her sobbing turned to crying and finally sniffling before prying her arms from around him and tilting up her face.

"Sit back now—let's see the damage," he said, using his handkerchief to wipe away her tears.

Her blue eyes were anguished as she glared up at him. "Why?" she demanded.

Guy cleaned up her cheeks and dabbed at her nose clumsily before she snatched the handkerchief from his hand.

"*Why?*" she repeated.

"I have a property that needs my attention—it is an adult responsibility," he added lamely, deserving her scathing look. "You'll see me again, Cat. Perhaps in a year or two, when you're tired of being a princess who lives in a castle in France, Cecile might send you to me for a visit. You can see how commoners live then—I'll harness you up to a plow, make you gather eggs from beneath terrifyingly huge American hens, and force you to harvest cranberries from a bog."

But she didn't laugh; she just stared, her accusatory gaze making him feel like the world's biggest villain.

"But why are you leaving?"

He sighed. "Because I must make my way in life, Cat. Working at the Fayre was just—well, it was just a stop in the road for me."

"But why can't you come with us to France? It's a castle, Guy!" A smile flickered across her face at the wonderful thought, but it was quickly gone when she recalled she was supposed to be angry with him. "The duke said there are lots of rooms. You can have one of them. Me and George—"

Guy cleared his throat.

"I mean George and I will have a room. You won't have to share with anyone." She glanced around his cupboard of a bedroom. "You will have a bigger room with a bed that fits you—so your feet don't hang off." A single tear slid down her cheek when he didn't answer, and it was far more painful than all that weeping. "Won't you miss me if you go away?" she asked in the most pitiful voice imaginable.

Guy's eyes burned and he tilted his head back to keep from blubbering like an eight-year-old. When he could look down again, she was still staring and waiting.

His relentless Cat.

"Cecile has a different life ahead of her, Cat—and I think you know that. It isn't the life of a circus worker. She's a *duchess* now. You know what that means." He could see by her angry look that somebody had explained it to her. "She has responsibilities and isn't just free to live wherever she wishes and do whatever she wants. As for me? Well, I'm a poor farmer—and I'm bloo—er, I'm very fortunate to have even that."

He couldn't explain to her about Gaston de La Fontaine and what marriage to him would mean to Cecile because she was simply too young to understand.

He also couldn't speak of that because it made him violent and want to smash things.

"But I don't want to go to live in a castle without you."

"You'll have Cecile and Helen and George."

But she was inconsolable, and all Guy could do was hold her until she'd cried herself to exhaustion.

He kissed her forehead. "I'm sorry, Kitty-Cat," he whispered. "I love you both and I hate to leave you, but it's for the best."

And it was. Even if it killed him.

George gave him a woeful look as Guy balanced Cat in his arms to open the door. After taking her to her room and tucking her into her bed, he went to find Helen.

She was in the kitchen with Blade, the two of them sipping tea. The atmosphere in the room felt . . . odd, like the undisturbed air in an ancient crypt, as if it had been a long, long time since any words had been spoken.

Guy couldn't help smiling. All they needed to make it feel even *quieter* was Elliot's presence.

"She cried herself to sleep," Guy said to Helen. "I put her in her bed."

Helen nodded while Blade and her bird just stared.

Guy waited for one of them to speak but neither seemed inclined, so he said, "I'm going to spend a few days with my mother and sisters before my ship departs. I was going to stop by here on my way out to say goodbye, but I think it just upsets Cat too much."

"So, you're going to leave without saying goodbye?" Helen demanded, her expression uncharacteristically . . . stern.

"Erm—"

"Men like to leave without saying goodbye," Blade said.

The two women exchanged a speaking look.

Guy frowned. "Now wait just a moment. I'm not avoiding her for my own sake. I'm—"

"He's avoiding Cat for *her* sake," Helen explained to Blade.

"Of course, he's doing it for Cat's sake," Blade agreed.

Both women turned to face Guy. "Otherwise that would make him a coward."

"*Coward*," Angus echoed.

Guy pointed at the bird. "Now you just stay out of this. Besides, what ever happened to standing up for your sex?"

Angus ignored him.

The two women stared.

Guy flung up his hands. "Fine. I'll come by before I leave."

He waited for a response—any response—but received none.

"I heard Cecile leave early this morning with Dumas and de La Fontaine." Guy couldn't help sneering a bit when he said the name. "Do you know when she'll be back?"

"He wants to make sure he's not here when she gets back," Blade said to Helen. Both women nodded.

Guy scowled. "Stop talking about me as if I'm not standing right in front of you."

"Cecile didn't say when she'd return when she left this morning," Helen said.

"Probably having too good a time with *le duc*, was she?"

Damnation! Why did he say that? He wanted to chew out his own tongue.

Especially when both females smirked.

"Well," he said, gesturing to the still steaming pot on the table and the plate of butter biscuits. "Thank you for the kind offer of tea, but I really can't join you," he said sarcastically.

Blade looked untouched, but Helen had the grace to blush at her inhospitable behavior.

"I'll be off. But don't worry," he added when Helen opened her mouth, "I'll stop by to say goodbye to Cat." He turned to Blade. "If I don't have the pleasure of seeing you again before I go, I'd ask that you have mercy on poor Elliot."

The fiery blush that flooded Blade's pale cheeks was both fetching and rewarding.

She opened her mouth, but Angus beat her to it. *"Poor Elliot."*

Guy laughed and left while the leaving was good.

As he walked out the front door, he felt a sadness that made it hard to move his feet. He'd only lived there for a few months, but he had to admit they were some of the happiest months of his life.

The urge to stay—to turn around and head back up to his tiny cupboard and unpack his bag—was strong.

But it wasn't the house that had made it a home. It was the woman who owned it. And she wouldn't be living there again, either.

"If he wants to go, let him!" Cecile retorted, pleased when her voice came out angry rather than hurt.

The truth was that she'd been furious to come back home yesterday to the discovery that Guy had slinked out of the house while she'd been away.

"Good riddance!" she added.

For a man who claimed to love her, he certainly hadn't let any moss grow between their last conversation and his departure.

But why did that surprise her? Why did she ever believe anything a man said?

Helen's soft voice broke into her fuming. "I think, perhaps, that he believes he is not, er, good enough for you now, Cecile."

"He isn't."

The other woman gave a startled laugh.

"He's an idiot if he thinks any of this changes the way I will think and behave," Cecile added.

"But he is your idiot," Helen pointed out.

It was Cecile's turn to laugh—but bitterly. "Not any longer."

In his way, he was no better than Curtis—just another man who threw around the word *love* to ensnare and fool a woman. It was horrifying how close she had come to reciprocating.

Helen sighed.

"What?" Cecile demanded.

"You didn't hear the way Guy talked about you when the two of us were betrothed and we both thought we would be stuck together for the rest of our lives."

Cecile wanted to ask for specifics, but she still had a little pride left.

And will pride keep you warm?

You shut up! She snapped in the privacy of her own mind.

She glared at Helen. "I was more appealing to him when he *didn't* have me. That is not so surprising with men like him—it is the thrill of the chase they like."

"I just don't believe that," Helen murmured.

"Yes, well you didn't hear him the other night when he urged me to go—insisting that I had my own life. He knows what Gaston wants of me, and yet he practically thrust me into his arms. So while it is nice that he said good things about me many months ago, it bothers me that he is so easy about giving me up *now*."

"I don't think he is easy about it. I just think he is—well, ashamed of his situation."

"*What?* He is the Darling! How can he be ashamed?"

"He is a poor man, Cecile—you are now an incredibly wealthy woman. He is a man who has been publicly knocked from his pedestal. You are a duchess. Try to think about things from his point of view."

Cecile knew the other woman was making sense, but she was

too angry to care anymore. And too hurt. "What would you have me do, Helen? Go to him on bended knee and beg him to stay?"

Helen gave a faint smile. "Perhaps there is a middle road."

"If there is one, I've not been able to think of it." And she didn't want to admit just how much of last night she'd spent *trying* to come up with a reason to make him stay *and* save her pride.

Now coming up with a reason no longer mattered.

Because he was already gone.

"Cecile?"

At the sound of Helen's voice, Cecile looked up from the book she had not been reading. "Yes?" she asked dully.

"Guy has come to say goodbye to Cat but I can't find her anywhere." Helen's brow was furrowed with concern.

"Have you checked the laundry cupboard? That's where I found her last night."

The first time Cat had disappeared, it had driven Cecile and everyone else frantic looking for her; they'd not found the child for almost five hours. When they'd finally thought to look in Guy's clothes cupboard, they'd found her sound asleep.

"She's not there. Nor is she in Guy's cupboard," Helen added before Cecile could ask.

"What about up in—"

"She's not up in the gods or under the stage, either. She's not in any of her favorite haunts." Helen heaved a sigh. "I went to look for the key to the counting room, but it wasn't there. When I knocked on the door to the room, she didn't answer. Still, she might be in there."

"It's more likely that Angus took the key again."

"I don't know," Helen fretted. "She likes to go in there—she asks for it as a reward when she's done well on her schoolwork."

Cecile closed her book and set it aside. "I'll fetch the extra key and go check."

When Cecile descended the stairs a few minutes later, she saw a familiar set of shoulders blocking most of the hallway.

"What are *you* doing here?" Cecile snapped, although Helen had already told her that he would be stopping by. "Don't you have a boat to catch?"

Guy turned and Cecile felt the same jolt of emotion she always felt upon seeing him.

Was he thinner? Or was it the clothing he was wearing—not his work clothes, but the Darling clothing.

And good God did he look delicious in his dark green clawhammer coat, fawn pantaloons, and glossy Hessians.

"They prefer that you call them *ships*," he said, smirking down at her.

"Hmmph." She slid the key into the lock and turned it, but the tumbler didn't click. She turned to Guy and Helen. "I thought you said it was locked?"

Helen raised her eyebrows. "I'm sorry, I thought it was."

Cecile opened the door and frowned at the candle burning in the wall sconce. "Cat? *Cat*, are you hiding in here?" she asked louder.

There was no answer, but there were two bottles of wine on the heavy counting desk, along with a loaf of bread, a wax-wrapped cheese, and a bowl of grapes.

"What is all this?"

"It looks like somebody was planning a picnic," Guy said, looking over her shoulder.

"What's that over in the far corner?" Helen asked from the doorway, pointing at something on the other side of the room.

Cecile took a few steps toward what she was pointing at. "There used to be a chair there," she murmured, squinting through the gloom at what appeared to be a chaise longue.

"That's new," Guy said from right behind her.

"I didn't put it in—"

The sound of the door clicking shut behind them cut off her words and Cecile turned and bumped into Guy in the confined space. The distinctive sound of the tumbler turning in the lock filled the room and Cecile pushed past Guy, grabbed the door handle, and tried to turn it. "It's locked," she said stupidly. She turned to Guy when he didn't answer. "What is that you are looking at?"

Guy held a piece of paper up to the wall sconce and they both leaned close to read it.

Their names were written in a very familiar childish scrawl.

Dear Guy and Cecile:
Because you have been behaving childishly, we have locked
you in a room to think about your actions and—

Guy hooted but Cecile ignored him and kept on reading.

—and consider the error of your ways. You both love each
other and yet you are behaving like spoiled, willful children. There
is food and wine and even some blankets if you get cold. With
nowhere to go, you can sit and discuss your problems like adults.
Sincerely,
Cat and George

Guy laughed. "Well, how do you like that?" he demanded, more than a little admiration in his voice.

Cecile glared at him. "Did you put her up to this?"

He scowled. "*What?* Of course I didn't! How do I know that *you* didn't put her up to it?"

"Why would I scheme to keep you here?"

"Oh, darling—don't try to pretend you don't want me."

"You are *delusional!*" she retorted. "If you weren't already running off like a coward, I'd kick you down the steps."

"A coward?" He gave an intensely annoying chuckle. "I'm leaving for your own good, sweetheart."

"*My* good?"

"That's right; you'd never be able to resist me and do the proper thing if I stayed."

"*What* proper thing?"

"You're a duchess now. The same way you had responsibilities as the owner of the Fayre, you now have responsibilities to the people who rely on you. If I stayed, you'd never do what you're doing."

"And just what do you think I'm doing?"

"It's obvious."

"Indulge me."

He sighed. "You're going to France to assume your responsibilities."

"I still don't know what you mean."

His mocking smirk faded away. "Don't make me say it, Cecile."

She planted her hands on her hips. "I think I'm going to make you say it, Guy."

"You're going to France to marry the duke."

She laughed.

He glared. "Just what is so amusing?"

"That you would assume I would behave as stupidly as you did last year."

"*Stupidly?*" he repeated, his loud voice filling the small room. "I was doing the honorable thing."

"Just as you are doing the honorable thing by going to Massachusetts?"

"As a matter of fact, yes."

She smirked at him. "And I was allowing you to get that out of your system."

"*Allowing* me?" he thundered.

"Yes, allowing you. For your information, after I tidied up my affairs in France, Cat, Helen, and I were going to get on a *boat* and come visit you at your cranberry bog."

Joy threatened to spin out of control inside Guy like a Catherine wheel, and his brain scrambled for a response to her shocking announcement.

"Oh, you were, were you?" was all he could manage.

She closed the distance between them and slid her arms around his neck. "Yes, I was. And when I got there, I was going to drag you to the nearest vicar, although they call them by many different names in America, and force you to marry me." She pulled his head down and claimed his mouth.

Guy groaned and slid his hands beneath her lush bottom, lifting her off her feet.

She laughed and he caught the magical sound in his mouth, kissing her breathless before releasing her lips.

"You really were going to come after me?" he asked when he could pull himself away.

"I really was."

"Why not just ask me to wait for you?"

"Why not just tell me you'd wait for me?" she countered.

"I was trying to do the right thing, darling."

"You mean like you did last year—leaving me to go and marry a stranger for the good of your dukedom and then regretting it every day of your life?"

"When you put it that way, it doesn't sound like such a fine idea, does it?"

"No, it doesn't."

"I could hardly encourage you to throw wisdom to the winds and follow your heart without looking like the world's worst hypocrite, could I?"

She cupped his face in both hands. "Fortunately, I didn't need your encouragement. You see, I learn from the mistakes of others because I am much smarter than you."

He threw back his head and laughed. "That you are, darling, that you are." He gave her a ruthless kissing, leaving her breathless.

"If you're not marrying de La Fontaine then what *are* you planning for your visit to France?"

"I'm not sure, yet. Why don't you come along with me?"

"You'd want me there?"

She grabbed his face and held him steady. "There was one thing I wouldn't have liked to have left without telling you, Guy."

"Oh?"

"I love you."

Guy heaved a huge sigh of contentment. "Oh, darling. You have no idea how badly I wanted to hear that."

"Oh, I have some idea," she demurred. "Don't you have something to say to me?"

"You already know I love you."

"And yet you would have let me go."

"I thought it was a noble sacrifice. But I was just being a fool, wasn't I?"

"Yes. But you are my fool—a big, handsome, gorgeous fool."

He grinned, well-pleased with the epithet. But then something occurred to him.

"What is it?" she asked, nibbling on his neck.

"I know the Fayre is closed for performances and that you've given the employees a holiday, but there are still lots of things that need doing. I could always stay to make sure it all runs smoothly."

"Actually, I have a bit of a secret for you."

He groaned. "Not another one."

"This isn't a bad one. Helen wants to purchase the Fayre."

"Helen! But I thought she was penniless."

"Apparently, she has some money from her mother. It's not a fortune and she will either need to take partners or make payments."

"Do you think she's thought this through, Cecile? Does she really wish to spend her life as a sharpshooter?"

"I don't know if she will ever become good enough for that, but she has an aptitude for organization and is a positive wizard when it comes to keeping a ledger."

Guy knew the younger woman had taken on some of the Fayre's crushing paperwork.

"Leaving her gilded cage to come work in a circus seems the act of a reckless person," Cecile said, "but I don't think she made the decision impulsively."

"I don't either," Guy conceded. "I think this is a good decision for her."

"So do I. She took a stand against her draconian father and came here with a broken, or at least bruised, heart, but I think she no longer regrets the loss of her fickle beau as much as she did even a few weeks ago."

He snorted softly.

"What is it?" she asked.

"Life is indeed stranger than fiction, isn't it? England's erstwhile wealthiest heiress now managing a circus for an excessively wealthy duchess."

"It's no stranger than the Darling of the *ton* marrying a female circus performer."

"Touché."

She winced.

Guy laughed. "Oh, come now, my accent cannot be so dreadful with just one word."

"Oh, yes it can. But your kissing . . . well, that is sublime."

"I'll have you know that this level of kissing requires lots and lots of practice." Guy slid his hands beneath her fine bottom again and lifted her to his lips.

All too soon, she squirmed. "Put me down. I know I am heavy."

"A mere feather." But he set her bottom on the desk where he'd found the note. "So, what do you think we should do?"

She glanced around the room. "Blankets, food, drink, and blissful privacy? What do you thin—"

Cecile didn't finish that sentence, or any other, for a long, long time.

Several blissful hours later . . .

"Do you think she has hurt him?" Cat asked, her brow furrowed with anxiety.

Helen smiled at the little girl. "I doubt it."

"Or at least not much," Jo was unable to resist adding, smirking at the other woman when Helen gave her a chiding look.

Angus gently nipped her ear, and she lifted her hand to rub the back of his neck. Jo knew from experience that if she didn't heed his demand, his nips would get progressively less gentle.

"How long have they been in there?" Jo asked.

"Almost five hours," Helen said. "Do you think we should let them out?"

"Yes, should we?" Cat asked.

Jo shrugged. "What's the rush?"

They both goggled at that.

"I'm not jesting," Jo said. "If they're quiet and haven't demanded to be let out, you might want to just leave them in there."

Cat still looked anxious, but Helen's cheeks turned a bright pink.

"Er, I expect Blade is correct, Cat. Let's go have a cup of tea and come back in a half hour."

"I should think an hour would be better," Jo advised, thinking back to the trip through France when Cecile and Guy had often not come out of the caravan they'd shared for days on end.

"*Priests of the raven*," Angus muttered.

"What did he say?" Cat demanded, looking at Angus with a worshipful expression that was bound to go to the raven's head.

"It's his favorite part of a poem. For obvious reasons," she added.

"Angus knows poetry?" Cat asked, forgetting all about her two favorite people locked in the counting room.

"He only remembers the parts he likes. Isn't that true, Angus? Do you like Byron?" she asked him.

He stopped his purring long enough to say, "*Raven tress.*"

Helen laughed, delighted. "That's from 'She Walks in Beauty.' Do you read them to him?"

"No, I don't care for poetry; he reads them himself."

Both Helen and Cat gaped at her.

Jo snorted; people really would believe anything.

Helen clucked her tongue. "Shame on you, you fibber. I can't believe I believed you."

"Neither can I."

"May we read the poem, Helen?" Cat asked her governess.

"Er, well, perhaps not yet," she demurred, ushering the little girl toward the kitchen. "You'll stay for tea, won't you?" she asked Jo over her shoulder.

"Yes, I actually needed to talk to you." Jo waited until Cat had skipped ahead with her dog to say, "I understand you'll be taking over from Cecile?"

"How did you know that? We only just spoke of it a few days ago."

Jo ignored the question. "I wanted to let you know that I have some money saved up."

"You mean you'd want to invest?"

"Yes, if you need somebody." Jo didn't tell the other woman that the Fayre was the closest thing to a home she'd ever had.

Helen smiled at her. "I'd much rather take you as a partner than some unknown—although Cecile said at least one of the men that she recently bought out might be interested. Her man of business is to pay a visit in two days. Once Cecile comes out of the counting room, we can speak to her about it, of course."

Jo nodded.

Helen leaned closer and whispered, "Do you think we did the right thing locking them in there?"

"I think that if it hadn't been the right thing, we'd be able to hear Cecile all the way down in the kitchen."

Both women laughed.

"If they bridged their differences—which I hope they have—then I wonder how that will change things," Helen mused.

Jo recalled what she knew about Guy but couldn't yet prove and smiled. "Oh, I daresay things will change a great deal over the next few weeks. For both of them."

Epilogue

Château de La Fontaine
Three weeks later

Cecile waved as the duke's ancient coach rumbled off, bearing her mother and sister back to the home they'd shared ever since her sister's husband had died in the War.

While Cecile had enjoyed their two-week visit, she had not grown close to either her mother or sister and doubted she ever would.

Perhaps it was petty of her, but the fact that her mother had willingly given her up when she'd separated from her father was something Cecile would never forget.

She turned away when the carriage disappeared from view, shaking away her conflicting emotions and smiling at Dupuy, the butler. "Do you know where my husband is?"

"Pierre just brought the morning mail up to your chambers, Your Grace."

She nodded her thanks and crossed the grand foyer toward the sweeping staircase, her mind still on her female relations as she made the considerable trek to the ducal chambers.

Cecile had tried to convince her cousin that they did not need to stay in the duke and duchess's rooms, but Gaston had been adamant.

"I have no wife—as yet—and have never moved my possessions

into those rooms. I would be honored if you used them during your visit."

And so Cecile had accepted his gracious offer as this would probably be the only time she came to stay at the de La Fontaine estate.

Although she'd reached an accord with the duke and his family, relations between them were stiff and likely always would be. Even though Cecile had given half her inheritance to the new duke to avoid protracted legal proceedings, Gaston's mother and uncles were still not pleased.

Guy had been furious at the family's demands and had accused them—thankfully only to Cecile—of behaving much like Curtis, using coercion to get her to do their bidding.

While they'd certainly used the threat of legal action to compel her, Cecile knew she had done the right thing.

The old duke could not have known that there would be anything left of his family when he'd written his will. If he had, she believed that he would have wished his heir to have at least half.

Besides, even half of the bequest left her an incredibly wealthy woman.

The duke had possessed a great deal of personal wealth which—with nobody to draw on the capital—had been steadily earning a profit over the prior two decades.

Even after giving Gaston half and settling her mother and sister in a house of their own, there was still more money than she would ever need.

Indeed, Cecile felt guilty that she'd received a windfall that she'd done nothing to earn.

Marianne, who'd found herself in a similar situation upon marrying the Duke of Staunton, had known exactly how Cecile felt even before she'd confessed her thoughts.

"You'll become accustomed to it," Marianne had whispered as they'd sat in an exclusive dress shop and watched while models paraded gorgeous clothing for the Duchess de La Fontaine's viewing pleasure.

They'd been shopping for Cecile's wedding trousseau—the first time in her life she'd been able to buy whatever she wanted without worrying about the cost—and the experience had left her feeling uncomfortable rather than happy.

Cecile had given a disbelieving laugh at her friend's words. "I now know why you were so adamant about just *giving* me the Fayre and the house," she'd admitted.

"I was furious with you when you insisted on purchasing it from me," Marianne had reminded her.

"Yes, I feel the same way about Helen and Blade."

Cecile had tried to split the property between the two women and leave them equal partners. They'd reacted the very same way Cecile had done with Marianne.

And so she'd sold them the business, feeling like a greedy toad about the payments they'd be making to her for years.

"They are proud women, Cecile," Guy had pointed out when they'd discussed the matter the night before their wedding.

They'd been lying in bed—Cecile's, not Guy's narrow cot—both unable to sleep.

"Yes," she'd admitted, "they are foolishly proud."

"Not to mention stubborn, rather like another woman I know, who won't admit that she's been dreaming of a St. George's wedding."

It had amused Cecile that Guy believed she'd wanted a grand society wedding.

"Don't you wish to read about yourself in the gossip columns the next day?" he'd teased.

"I suspect that experience is far less entertaining when it is one's own business one is forced to read about."

He'd laughed. "You can take my word that it is *much* less entertaining when one is the subject under scrutiny. Especially if one's mother reads those same papers," he'd muttered beneath his breath. "Oh, go ahead and laugh, madam. Unfortunately, you'll discover exactly what I mean once the invitations begin pouring in."

"Nobody will invite me to anything."

But Guy hadn't been the only one to assure her she was wrong about that.

"Everyone will want to have you at their dinner or party," Marianne had said when Cecile had expressed her thoughts on the subject. "You can take my word on that. By next Season I will be an old hand at navigating the dangerous shoals, and Aunt Julia and I shall be thrilled to help you."

Cecile still wasn't sure just how much of the Season she'd want to *navigate*, but it was there waiting for her once she made her decision.

She was huffing and puffing by the time she reached the double doors that opened to the duke's private study, where a familiar curly brown head was bent over something on the desk.

"Guy?"

He didn't even move.

"*Guy*," she repeated, louder.

He jolted and wrenched his gaze from the letter on the desk with visible effort, blinking at her. "Oh. I didn't hear you come in."

"I know you didn't." She gestured to the piece of paper. "What is that?"

"This? Well, er . . ." He looked back at the paper and again seemed transfixed.

"Guy?"

"Yes, er, it's a letter from Elliot," he said when she came to stand beside him. "You should read it."

He shoved it into her hand and then stood and went to the collection of bottles on the mirror-encrusted trolley.

Everything in the duke and duchess's chambers was very Versailles in style and was either gilded, mirrored, or encrusted with semiprecious stones. It was a trifle overdone to her way of thinking, but there was no denying that it was the most luxurious place she had ever stayed.

"It is only eleven thirty, Guy," she protested as he poured himself a hefty portion of brandy.

"Mmm-hmm." He tilted his head, threw back the contents of

the glass, and then poured another. "Read the letter, my dear. I'll pour you one, too."

Cecile looked down at the page of writing, and the first line leaped off the page: *Your Grace.* Her head whipped up and she found him staring at her.

He nodded even though she'd not spoken. "Read it out loud," he ordered, striding to the chair across from the desk—gold leaf and royal-purple brocade—and dropping gracelessly into it.

Your Grace,

Yes, you read that correctly and no, I've not been on the tipple. I know you didn't wish me to look into your cousin's claim on the dukedom, but Sin and I decided it would be remiss to allow things to go ahead without any verification of his identity.

Cecile looked up. "You didn't want to look into your cousin's background?"

He shrugged but refused to meet her gaze.

She gasped as she realized what he'd done. "Guy! You suspected that he was lying, didn't you?"

Again he shrugged, a deep red shade creeping up the muscular column of his throat until even the tips of his ears were pink.

He didn't look for the truth because he wanted to be with me—he didn't want to be forced to choose between his responsibilities and me.

He loves me enough to give up everything.

"What?" he demanded rudely as she stared at him.

Cecile just shook her head, too choked up to trust herself to speak.

So, with that confession out of the way, let me just tell you a story. It is about a boy named Etienne Boulanger who was the son of a working woman and one of her long-term clients—Henry Darlington—an Englishman who often crowed that he would one day be a duke.

Etienne grew up hearing fascinating, drunken tales of the

luxury that awaited his dear papa. He heard about a life that would never include an illegitimate son.

Yes, Etienne is your blood cousin, but without the benefit of marriage.

Interestingly, you really did have a legitimate male cousin named Barrymore Edward Darlington, but he died at the age of only ten days.

The unfortunate Barrymore was a mere five weeks older than his illegitimate half brother Etienne, and the two were actually born on the same estate where your uncle lived with his wife— albeit Etienne was born in a tiny cottage where Lord Henry kept his mistress until he lost the entire property.

While your aunt died in childbed, Etienne's mother survived and is still living on Réunion island along with three other children, none of which share the same father.

The gentleman I sent to Réunion (a former government operative who is well accustomed to dealing with matters of the utmost delicacy) was able to assemble the requisite affidavits and paperwork necessary to overturn your cousin's claim.

Etienne's mother must have written to warn her son that his masquerade was nearing an end. So, I regret to tell you that "Barry" and his small cadre of associates fled England two days ago. They left on a ship bound ultimately for Calcutta. I've sent letters to the authorities in several possible ports of disembarkation, but there are simply too many places for him to slip through the cracks, so I would not hold out any hope of ever seeing or hearing from him again.

I thought you might wish to lay hands on him given the unfortunate fact that he has, I'm afraid, stripped at least part of Fairhurst Hall and most of the London house of valuables and family heirlooms.

In any event, this information has been conveyed to your family solicitors—who allowed this plundering to go on with their knowledge, and during their watch. I imagine they are, even as I write this letter, on a packet to France to beg you for leniency.

So, congratulations on your elevation in status, Your Grace.
All is well here. Helen has engaged a new duo for the
Fayre—a rather spectacular rope-dancing act called The Siren
Sisters—that has been drawing quite a crowd.
I look forward to seeing you when you return.
Yours respectfully,
Elliot

Cecile looked up to find Guy had moved closer to the desk and was sliding a glass toward her.

"Thank you," she said. Although she didn't swallow it in one gulp, she did take a large drink.

"So," he said.

"So."

"You are a duchess twice over it would seem."

Cecile laughed. "How does that work, I wonder?"

"Lord only knows. We'll likely need to get one of the royal heralds involved to sort out this mess."

She put down her glass, stood, and stepped into his already open arms.

"My duchess," he murmured.

"My duke." She snuggled up closer to him, not caring how badly she was wrinkling his cravat. "I'm sorry that your fake cousin sacked Fairhurst House," she said, kissing him gently. "If your solicitors knew and did nothing then they will owe you a great deal of money, won't they?"

"Yes, it could go quite badly for them."

"What are you going to do?"

He seemed to shake himself from his fugue, and when he looked down at her, his eyes were once again warm. "I'm not going to *strain at a gnat and swallow a camel.*"

"*What?*"

He chuckled. "It means I'm going to count my blessings, darling. While it's unfortunate that Barry—or Etienne, rather—managed to steal some family heirlooms, I still owe him mightily for giving me a second chance with you. I think I'll thank him by letting him disappear into the sunset. What?" he asked when she stared. "Why are you looking at me like that?"

"I'm just thinking about how much I love you."

"Oh, sweetheart." He cupped her face with both hands and kissed her as if she were the most delicate, precious object on earth.

Cecile didn't think she'd ever tire of watching the effect of those words on her husband. Even though she woke up beside him every day and wore his ring on her finger, she still couldn't believe he was hers.

His glassy-eyed look shifted subtly into a more earthy, wicked expression. "Is your mother gone?" he asked in between kisses.

"Yes, I saw her and my sister off before coming up here."

"And your cousin is in Paris for the next few days?"

"Yes. Why?"

"Well, Cat told me about a room where the two of us might lock ourselves in and enjoy a bit of privacy."

Cecile chuckled. "Yes, she told me about that room, too—unfortunately I think it is in the dungeon."

"What?" he asked in mock surprise. "Are you saying you don't wish to be locked in the dungeon with me?"

"I'd choose being locked in a dungeon with you over being crowned queen of England."

His jaw sagged at her passionate, if bizarre, declaration.

Cecile thrust her fingers into his silky hair and yanked him down for a thorough kissing.

"Goodness," he murmured, when she released him several moments later, his eyelids heavy and lips slick and red. "What in the world did I do to deserve that?"

"I never said *thank you* for coming back to me, Guy—and then persevering—even though I was so—"

"Cruel? Beastly?"

She laughed. "Probably."

"So," he said, cocking an eyebrow suggestively. "What about that trip down to the dungeon?"

"Hmmm. Well, I think if you walk across the room and lock the door, we can avoid the dungeon entirely."

He grinned down at her. "Ah . . . beautiful *and* clever! I love the way you think, darling. What did I ever do to deserve you?" He kissed her and then turned and strode toward the door, an adorable, eager spring in his step.

No, Cecile thought, unable to pull her hungry gaze off her gorgeous husband. *How did I ever get so lucky?*

Their path toward love might have been rocky, with several strange diversions, but the destination had most certainly been worth the journey.

He returned to her and held out his hand. "Coming with me?"

"Always, my love." Cecile took his hand and followed him into their chambers. The best part of their journey—the part they would spend together—was only just beginning.

Author's Note

I know your burning question is, "Was there really a Dueling Duchess?"

Well, I'm sorry to say there wasn't.

However, there are accounts of women dueling, using both swords and pistols. As usual, the information is sparse, unsubstantiated, and (probably) greatly exaggerated.

The infamous duel (with rapiers) between Princess Pauline von Metternich and Countess Anastasia von Kielmannsegg—allegedly over a floral arrangement—is among the most referenced when it comes to female aristocrats who decide to settle their differences on the field of honor. Some versions of the story claimed that the duelists stripped to the waist—a detail that sounds more like the product of some male journalist's imagination than reality.

Other famous female duelists include Mexico City socialites Marta Duran and Juana Luna—who also chose to settle their differences with swords and the French Comtesse De Polignac and the Marquis De Nesle who chose pistols—both of the above duels allegedly occurred over men rather than flowers.

More interesting, at least to me, are the scattered journal and diary references to female camp followers who picked up the weapons of their fallen male companions and marched into battle. Thousands of women followed the armies that fought throughout Europe during the Napoleonic Wars. It's easy to imagine the fear and terror these women must have felt when they found themselves alone and unprotected in a foreign country, oftentimes with children. Arming oneself in such a situation would have made sense given the lawlessness that pervaded the continent for decades.

Please read on for an excerpt from *The Cutthroat Countess,* coming soon!

Prologue

France
1816
A year and a half ago

Elliot lost count of the number of times the three men hit him.

Whenever he slipped into unconsciousness one of them threw a bucket of freezing water on him and shook him until he awakened.

And then they started hitting him all over again and asking the same question:

À qui rapportez-vous?

Who do you report to?

Elliot always gave one of three answers, all in impeccably accented French:

I don't know what you mean.

I report to nobody.

You must have mistaken me for somebody else.

That had been going on for days. Today, for some reason, the men seemed angrier.

"We are running out of patience, you English bastard!" A fist connected with Elliot's jaw and slammed his head back, turning everything gray and hazy.

Rough hands shook his shoulders until his teeth rattled. "Wake up, you!"

Elliot couldn't force his eyelids up; they felt as though they'd been weighted down with lead.

A voice pushed through the thick fog, "Should I hit him again?"

"Too much more and he won't talk at all," a different voice said, the words followed by loud, raucous laughter and yet another jaw-cracking fist.

White, agonizing explosions blossomed inside his skull.

And then darkness...

"Smithy?"

The voice—low, calm, and feminine—insinuated itself through the fog of pain. It sounded . . . familiar.

"*Smithy.* You need to wake up."

Elliot could only force one eye to open.

The sight that met his gaze was a filthy face fringed with ragged strands of gray hair. A stranger's face.

He squinted and then gasped at the pain the action caused, his head throbbing and eye watering as he stared and stared.

Jo.

Only the eyes gave her away because that was something she couldn't hide: pale, opalescent eyes that he'd know anywhere.

"Why, if it isn't Josephine Brown," Elliot teased, or at least tried to. But his voice came out a cracked wheeze and the words were slurred.

"Can you walk?" Jo asked, her face and voice expressionless.

Elliot gave a rusty laugh. "I'll bloody well walk out of here."

Jo—or Blade as she was known by just about everyone at the circus where they both worked—helped Elliot into a sitting position and then hooked his arm over her shoulder. "On three we're going to stand," she murmured. "One . . . two . . . three."

They pushed up together, although Elliot had to admit it was more Jo's effort than his own that actually got him to his feet

His head felt like a bowl full of liquid that had been set spinning, sloshing and pitching so badly he was surprised nothing leaked out his ears.

"Can you stay upright?" she whispered.

Barely.

"Yes, I'm good," he lied.

She shifted her shoulder beneath his. "Ready?"

No.

"Yes," he lied again. "But you'll have to guide me as I seem to have some trouble seeing."

Rather than answer, she took a step.

Elliot's stomach joined his head, both pitching and sloshing, but in different directions. It reminded him of his unpleasant journey across the Channel on the way to France—a memory he could easily do without.

The first step was the worst, but the next one wasn't much better. After ten steps he was shivering, rivulets of sweat were running down his skin, and he was shaking so badly it was almost impossible to control his legs. He staggered against her, almost knocking her off her feet.

Shame joined nausea as she struggled to keep them both standing and moving. "I'm sorry," he muttered. "You should just leave me, Jo. I'll only slow you down."

She didn't answer or even acknowledge that she'd heard him. Instead, she kept walking, her slim, strong body bearing more of his weight with each step.

Just five more steps, he ordered his body.

After four more steps they paused so she could open a door. Elliot noticed the worn bottom of boots first, and then the man they were connected to—it was one of his captors, the one who'd smiled while beating him. He wasn't smiling now—at least not his mouth. Instead, he looked surprised, eyes wide and unseeing, the slash across his throat a red grin.

Jo guided him over the man's body, saying only, "Lift your feet a bit here."

He obeyed, eager to put the corpse behind them. He'd hated his tormentor, but couldn't bring himself to rejoice at the sight of his mutilated body.

"Almost there," Jo murmured beside him.

Elliot ordered his limbs to cooperate, to help her, but the next time he tried to pick up his foot, his opposite knee buckled.

Jo gave a muffled grunt and sagged under his weight, but she didn't fall. "Just a little bit more, Elliot."

He blinked at the sound of his Christian name on her tongue. How did she know it? He'd told everyone at the circus where they'd met to call him *Smithy*.

Elliot was so intrigued by the mystery that he took a few steps without even realizing he was moving.

"Fifteen more steps until the door," she said. "You can do it. Just fifteen."

Elliot closed his eyes and counted in his head. *One, two, three, four—*

Somewhere between five and nine he must have lost consciousness and her voice jolted him awake. "You have to hold on to me, Elliot. Only four more."

One, two, three, four.

He forced his eyes open when he noticed they were still walking. "That's four. Why are we—?"

"I lied," Jo said. "Keep going, you can do it."

He kept walking, but he was no longer lifting his feet.

"Take his other arm," Jo said.

Elliot's eyelids lifted slightly at her low but sharp command. "I don't know what you—"

A hand—far bigger than Jo's—took his upper arm and a second set of shoulders slid beneath, somebody taller and far broader than Jo.

Elliot was just conscious enough to feel mortified that he'd not even heard someone approach.

"We've got steps now, Elliot, so you'll need to lift your feet."

Steps?

Elliot blinked rapidly, struggling to keep the darkness at bay, and lifted one foot; this time both his legs gave out.

A male voice cursed in French and said, "Let him go and I'll carry him, Blade."

Burly arms shifted and positioned Elliot's body as if he were a child and he gave a hoarse yelp when his feet abruptly left the floor. Up suddenly became down and an arm clamped around his thighs, a hard shoulder pressed against his midriff. This time when the blackness came for him, he welcomed it.

Josephine Brown—or at least that was the name she'd been using for the last eight months—stared down at the Honorable Elliot Wingate, foreign and unnerving emotions churning inside her as she studied his handsome but badly abused face.

Jo had already deviated from her very well-paid job by pausing to rescue him. Instead of staring at his sleeping face Jo should be hundreds of miles away.

Leave him, hen, Mungo's voice hectored. *Ye've already done more than enough for him. Ye cannae allow anythin' to get between you and your mission.*

Jo couldn't argue that Elliot had interfered with her current *mission*—as Mungo had always liked to call their services, but it hadn't sat right with her to leave him in the hands of his brutal captors.

It had been foolish, reckless, and dangerous to steal Elliot away from the Red Shirts—a vigilante militia that flourished in the war-torn French countryside and preyed off terrified provincials.

While the men who'd been torturing and questioning Elliot were not part of the army, the French government often paid coin for the information the Red Shirts came across.

Regardless of what Elliot was actually doing in France the capture of a British Home Office agent would likely fetch a handsome price. Elliot's future would have been beyond bleak—and probably very brief—if Jo and her small cadre of ruffians hadn't liberated him. Not that it had taken much skill or stealth thanks to the fact that the Red Shirts were too fond of spirits and women of easy virtue to set more than one guard over the cell where Elliot had been held.

They'd been working on Elliot for five days and he'd not broken yet, a fact which had impressed Jo as much as it horrified her. But she knew far too much about torture and how effective it was; Elliot would have eventually given the men all the information they wanted, no matter how good an agent he was.

And once the Red Shirts had established his identity it would have been one short step to linking Elliot to Farnham's Fantastical Female Fayre and the woman Jo was supposed to be protecting: Marianne Simpson.

So, in actuality, Jo could claim that by rescuing Elliot she had taken care of a small problem before it could blossom into a much larger one that threatened her mission.

Ye ken that yer interest in the man cannae come to anything, lass, Mungo persisted, just as he would have persisted if he'd still been alive. Not that Jo had been idiotic enough to develop such an interest—fine, an *obsession*—in anyone in all the years she'd been with Mungo.

He had made sure they'd never lived in any one place long enough.

We must keep moving.

It was Mungo's mantra and the two of them had lived by it for most of Jo's twenty-five years. Or at least as long as she could remember.

She was still living by it, even though Mungo was now gone.

He'd been gone almost six months and the pain of loss was still as sharp as the edge of any of the seven knives currently secreted all over her person.

Elliot groaned and shifted on the bed, his eyes fluttering open. His gaze flickered around the room, his forehead furrowing as he obviously struggled to recall where he was.

Finally, his eyes settled on Jo. The tension seemed to drain from his body and his face—taut only seconds before—softened slightly; although features that were as sharp and angular as Elliot Wingate's could never look soft.

"I thought I dreamed you," he said in a raspy voice.

Jo's heart sped at his words. And then her face heated when she realized he didn't mean them the way they sounded—not that he'd *dreamed* of *her*. But that he'd dreamed his escape.

"How long?" he asked when she remained silent.

"Three days."

His eyes widened and he winced. Although the black eye had lost a great deal of its prior swelling Jo knew it must hurt.

"Where are we?"

"Not far from Charleville."

The tension returned in an instant. "The men who had me were based—"

"They won't find you because we've taken care of it," she assured him quietly. "I sent three of my people out to lead them on a wild goose chase. We're safe here for the moment."

He sighed. "Thank you."

Jo nodded, using the tail of her shirt to wipe the oil from the blade she'd been sharpening.

Elliot's gaze dropped to the knife, the flicker of emotion in them so quick and subtle that she almost didn't catch it: he was recalling the body of the Red Shirt she'd dispatched when she'd rescued him.

He was remembering that she'd committed murder to free him.

"He's not dead because of you."

He looked away from the knife and met her eyes.

"I could have knocked him out, but I didn't."

He inhaled deeply, as if he'd need a lot of air for what he had to say.

There was a tapping at the room's tiny window and they both turned.

Her raven, Angus, was standing on the sill. Jo lifted the sash and he hopped inside.

"There's a good fellow," she crooned, taking a lump of sugar from her pocket and offering it to him.

Angus made a soft *quork quork* and fluffed his feathers—his polite way of demanding petting—while delicately taking the treat from her fingers with his beak.

Jo scratched his neck beneath the feathers and turned back to Elliot, waiting for whatever he'd been working himself up to say— judgment, condemnation?

But the tension had leaked out of him and he was merely watching her and Angus with interest.

It worried her how glad she was that he'd decided to let the matter be. "Marianne and the others are only about four or five days ahead of us," she said.

"How do you know that?"

"Angus just told me."

Elliot snorted softly.

Jo dug around in her boiled leather satchel and removed an apple, a heel of bread, and a chunk of dried ham. When she placed the food on the rickety table Angus wasted no time helping himself to the meal.

Jo turned back to Elliot. "Angus left early this morning and it's now almost nightfall. He follows the roads and I can make a fairly close guess based on how long he was gone and how hungry he is. It's not precise, but the time of his return tells me where they are within a day."

"What does his appetite have to do with measuring the distance?"

"He's hungry so that means he didn't stop to feed anywhere. Sometimes it can take him hours to find something to eat. Again, it's not an exact science."

"It's Marianne you are protecting, isn't it?"

Jo didn't bother asking how he knew that. Elliot Wingate was one of His Majesty's spies; it was his job to know such things.

"I'm not doing such a grand job protecting her," she pointed out wryly.

"You've fallen behind because you helped me," he said.

Jo shrugged. "I had some other matters to see to that took me out of the way." Not as much out of the way as rescuing Elliot, but there was no point in making him feel guilty.

"I should get up and—" He pushed back the covers and then yanked them up again. "Er, or perhaps not. It appears that I'm naked."

"Your clothes stank and weren't worth saving." Jo could see

by his expression that he took her meaning. Naturally his cheeks darkened, although—in her opinion—there was no shame in soiling oneself when one had undergone days of excruciating torture.

"Who undressed me?" he asked, twin bright spots of color on his high cheekbones, standing out on his pale skin even though there were so many bruises and cuts.

"I did." She turned away to give him a moment to collect his shattered pride. She dug another apple from her bag and slipped a knife from her boot, quickly peeling, coring, and quartering the apple before re-sheathing her knife.

When she turned around he looked flushed, but no longer discomposed.

She offered him the peeled fruit.

"Thank you," he said, taking one piece.

"I peeled it for you; take it all."

Jo wiped her hands on her skirt and gestured to his left hand. "Can you manage a sandwich if I make one?"

He stared silently at the two smallest fingers, which Jo and Gaston had splinted while he'd been unconscious. He'd screamed during the horrible procedure but, thankfully, he hadn't woken up.

"I suppose you did this, too?"

She nodded.

"Thank you again," he murmured, flexing his three free digits and only wincing slightly. "Yes, I can hold food."

Jo unwrapped the meat, bread, and cheese and busied herself making a sandwich rather than looking at the object of her fascination.

"I must be holding you back," he said.

Jo shrugged.

"I know you're following Marianne and the three wagons that are traveling with her," he continued, "but I don't know *why*."

Jo smirked faintly at his pained admission. For a man whose duty it was to gather information such an admission must rankle.

He snorted softly. "You aren't going to tell me."

It wasn't a question, so she didn't answer. Instead, she gave Angus a chunk of cheese before wrapping it back up.

Once she'd poured a glass of buttermilk from an earthenware jug she turned and carried both it and the sandwich to Elliot.

"I hope you like buttermilk," she said.

"I do, although I've not had any since I was a boy." He took the sandwich. "Thank you. I seem to be saying that a great deal."

Jo ignored his thanks. "I'm leaving tomorrow morning. I'll pay for the room for the next week and give you enough money to make your way back home."

He lowered the sandwich without taking a bite. "I'll be going with you."

Rather than argue Jo just allowed her eyes to roam down his prone body and then back up. By the time she reached his face, it was flaming and his lips were compressed in a thin line.

"You needn't worry that I can't keep up," he assured her.

"I'm not worried. I just don't want you with us." That was both a lie and the truth; Jo wanted him to come with her, but it wasn't something that she *should* want.

His jaw dropped and then he laughed softly. "Don't sugarcoat it for me," he said wryly. "You might not want me along but you can either take me with you or I can trail behind you. We're heading in the same direction with the same goal in mind."

Jo doubted that but didn't argue. Instead, she said, "Fine."

Once again, he appeared nonplussed, this time by her easy acquiescence.

"Unfortunately, I'll need to borrow money from you. The Red Shirts took everything I had on me—including my horse, obviously. But I've got more money stashed in our caravan."

He meant the caravan that he and two of his friends—both aristocrats—had been using while pretending to be workers in Farnham's Fantastical Female Fayre.

Elliot had managed to blend in as an employee, but his friends—the Duke of Staunton and the Marquess of Carlisle—had been as inconspicuous as tropical parrots among a flock of pigeons.

Jo knew the men had come to France to rescue the duke's brother. She also knew that Elliot was probably acting without the approval of the Home Office.

Angus hopped up onto the chairback and then flew the short distance across the room to Elliot's bed, landing on the blankets near his hip.

Elliot made a surprised sound but otherwise didn't move.

It was Jo's turn to be startled; Angus rarely showed any interest in people.

"He must want some of your sandwich," she said.

But when Elliot broke off a piece and handed it to the bird, Angus ignored the food. Instead, he fluffed up his feathers.

Jo's lips parted in disbelief.

Elliot cut her a glance. "What should I do?"

"I think he wants you to pet him," Jo was forced to admit, more than a little bit jealous.

Elliot lifted one eyebrow in surprise but then tentatively reached for the bird, his cut and swollen lips curving into a smile when Angus purred just like a cat, a noise he'd learned to mimic from the two mousers who lived in the London theater that housed the all-female circus.

Angus and Jo had been together almost eight years and not once had Angus showed any interest in anyone else. Not even Mungo, whom he'd tolerated, but never begged for affection.

Jo narrowed her eyes at her bird, but Angus refused to meet her gaze.

Just why was her normally reserved raven suddenly showing affection to the very same man Jo was trying—and failing miserably—to resist.

Visit our website at
KensingtonBooks.com
to sign up for our newsletters, read
more from your favorite authors, see
books by series, view reading group
guides, and more!

Become a Part of Our
Between the Chapters Book Club
Community and Join the Conversation

Betweenthechapters.net